The Heliotropians

Eileen Kramer

Illustrations by Eileen Kramer
Typesetting by Carolyn Kuhns
Book designed by Terry L. Bare
Author photo by Ellen Brody
Cover photo by Josh Vaughan
Editorial Assistance by Trudy Laurenson

Order this book online at www.trafford.com
or email orders@trafford.com

Most Trafford titles are also available at major online book retailers.

Printed in the United States of America.

ISBN: 978-1-4269-1882-7 (sc)
ISBN: 978-1-4269-1888-9 (hc)

Library of Congress Control Number: 2009938920

Trafford rev. 07/17/2012

 www.trafford.com

North America & international
toll-free: 1 888 232 4444 (USA & Canada)
phone: 250 383 6864 ♦ fax: 812 355 4082

To the board members, dancers, and technicians of Trillium Performing Arts Collective who welcomed me in the dance studio when I came to Lewisburg and gave me the support I needed to create my dance works and thanks to Trudy Laurenson, one of our beloved board members who gave me support during the editing of the book.

Thanks to all the "Old Earth" people in Paris
who inspired me, thanks to Picasso for his magical garden
in the South of France, thanks to Percival Savage for letting
me wear the Schiaparelli gown and thanks a million
to Belinda Anderson in Lewisburg for her easy,
graceful style of teaching.
Also to Greenbrier Printing for the help they have
accorded me in helping prepare my books for
the publishers.

Chapter 1

The Mystery House of Heliotrope

When Marius was a child, he walked up the long winding path to the top of the hill, intent upon seeing for himself the Mystery House of Heliotrope. It stood on a cliff top overlooking the Sea-of-Silver Beach.

At the top of the hill he unexpectedly came upon a very high garden wall. But he saw no gate anywhere! Nor did it have rough stones or footholds, and so there was no way to climb over it. He sat down and waited, gazing patiently at the wall. Before long the wall allowed him to see the hiding place of the missing gate. Through it he entered the garden and was delighted by what he saw.

He didn't linger there, but opened one of the many doors to the house and fearlessly entered into its mysteries. As he moved about inside, spaces opened before him and closed behind him. Misty forms led him into other dimensions that no child of this planet could ever describe. Sparkling fragments of time and space accompanied him up wide curving staircases, leading him to think that he had uncovered vast secrets. But he hadn't really, since the two biggest mysteries had not yet revealed themselves.

That evening when he told his parents what had happened, they smiled knowingly, and said they had no reservation about him spending more time at the Mystery House. So he continued his explorations of the ancient structure. He was never harmed by the magical things that happened. As time went by he began to imagine that a special relationship existed between the house and himself.

One day shortly after his twenty-fourth birthday, Marius went to sit in the garden and enjoy his thoughts. For several months he had been experimenting with light power, convinced that it was possible to build something larger than the paintings and sculptured forms he was known for. Inspired by what happened in Heliotrope during the Festival of Light, he envisioned a radiant city made of light, alive with beautiful people. This festival took place every four years and included the Rites of Love and Passion that enriched the lives of the people, although its main purpose was to give thanks to the Light. Centuries ago when ice suddenly covered the surface of Earth, the Light had appeared. With its mysterious power it saved the people, the town and the hills above it. The centuries passed but the ice never melted. On the frozen planet with no neighbors, friends or enemies, they lived in peace with very little excitement and with only mild emotions of love. To compensate for this, they revived ancient festivals which became important to them. They lived on in awe and gratitude for what they believed the magical Light had done for them.

Over time the Heliotropians had developed remarkable powers. They were simple people not at all ambitious, but once in a while a clever child was born who grew to be a genius. The parents of Marius believed that he had been such a child. As for Marius, he had no opinion about it. He simply enjoyed being himself.

Seated on the marble garden seat, Marius relinquished for the moment, his dream of a radiant city. Turning his head he gazed at the house. There it was, a mass of stone, steel, wood, bricks, towers and a dome. Nothing to get excited about. The next minute it was a blaze of glorious rosey light. In his excitement, Marius almost fell over the edge of the cliff to the sandy beach below. When he regained his senses he left the garden and hastened back to town to tell his friend Jason all about it. He knew he had seen a house made entirely of light!

Upon reflection, Marius realized that whoever had built the house, must have died long ago; perhaps shortly after this great achievement. "The man was a wonderful genius," he told Jason,. "Centuries ahead of his time. Imagine it!" Then stricken by the thought of never being able to meet and talk with this genius, and learn the secret of Light-energy organization, he became depressed.

"Perhaps" Jason said, "you could time-travel and find him in the past, you know, while he was still alive."

"In a world teeming with millions of people?" Marius groaned.

"But if he was as famous as you think he was, it would not be so hard to find him. His name would be known for the great work he was doing at that time."

With the help of his friend and his own youthful optimism, Marius' depression passed and he began to envision the great meeting between the two; himself and the artist-scientist, discussing the elements of light, or some such thing. Jason imagined that was the kind of thing people talked about in the twenty first century. So that was when he and Marius thought they might find the genius, several thousands of years in the past.

Shortly after this conversation, Marius and Jason went down to the Sea-of-Silver beach where they expected to see their fathers, who usually went there for their evening walk. They found them sitting on an ancient rock that rose out of the fine silvery sand. Conrad, Jason's father was leaning forward, sand-writing rod in hand, writing something in the sand. Leo, Marius' father, was saying a little impatiently, because he was Heliotrope's foremost Light writer, and reader, "Conrad, why can't you write in Light like any modern educated person?" Leo's own brilliant letters always appeared in the air space above his head.

"We're not all Light-writers like you and your son, Leo. I like sand and I get all the information I want from these ancient grains."

"You get local news. I get information" Leo said. He looked up and saw the two young men approaching. "Hello, what's up?"

"Good evening Leo, good evening father" Jason said politely. "We thought you might be here. Marius discovered something about the Mystery House. He wants to tell you about it."

"Yes I do" Marius said excitedly.

They all looked up and saw the tower and the dome and other intriguing features of the rooftops, silhouetted dramatically against the sky. The pale sun, unable to melt the ice for mankind, at least gave them a sunset now and then. The sky had just turned an unusually lovely pink with silver-edged mauve clouds. Even Leo, who always referred to the Mystery House as a "conglomeration of crazy style of the past," had to admit it was a striking image, while Conrad who often wrote poem's in the sand, said it was pure poetry-a poetic mystery. It was in fact a particularly striking picture, one that Marius and Jason thought they would never forget. The dark outline of a skyline is always striking and this was especially so.

"Isn't it grand? Marius cried. "Father I've only just realized something quite remarkable-the house is made entirely of light! I know you'll find this hard to believe, but it's the truth."

"Indeed" replied Leo. "And how do you explain that?"

"I can't. That's just the point. I need help and I've decided to time travel to the past and find the wonderful genius who created the Mystery House. I will be his pupil and learn all he can teach me about Light energy and construction."

"I'm going too" Jason told his father. "And so are our friends. Only thing is we don't know how to activate the time tunnel."

"Yes. Why does no one time travel? They used to, didn't they? You never hear of anyone traveling these days," said Marius. "Why is that?"

It was true. Time travel was like a myth to some people, but not to Marius. He'd always expected to travel through time one day. There was nowhere else to travel in a world covered with ice, anyway. You could space travel but no one wanted to.

Leo looked at them doubtfully. "I thought everyone knew that. The time tunnel's been lost for five hundred years. You'd have to know a certain secret in order to find it."

"Lost! That's not possible father," Marius cried in protest. "I can't believe it. It's like the energy of the Universe. Nothing gets lost in the Universe. Or it's like water on this planet. Water might change to ice, but it never gets lost."

"That's so Leo" Conrad said. "We're all hemmed in by the universe." He looked thoughtful. "Perhaps a parallel universe somehow—"

"No, I don't think so Conrad. Don't you know your history? The sand doesn't tell you what happened to the time tunnel, does it? Even the Light doesn't tell me about it. Remember those people five hundred years ago who started out on a trip to the past; to that same century you're interested in Marius? They never came back, and the secret location of the time tunnel went with them. It's lost. No one has ever found it. I'm sorry to disappoint you."

Marius refused to accept this. "Don't tell me that! I can't believe it, and I won't believe it. It's so important to me! Father, I must find that man."

"Or woman" Conrad said. "It could have been a woman you know."

"Man or woman. I don't care," Marius thought for a moment. "But I have a feeling it was a man. I must find him."

Leo was proud of his son's accomplishments, at the age of twenty one he had been awarded the title "Son-of-the-Light" a term meaning he was a genius. His beautiful abstract Light sculpture adorned the town square of Heliotrope, and that was because the people themselves had voted for it. Little children played at floating up and letting the Light embrace them. Then at night they had lovely dreams.

"Well Marius" Leo said, smiling at him. "You've always done whatever you set out to do . . ."

"Except for building a house with light" muttered Marius, as though this was everyone else's fault.

". . . so if anyone could find the secret of the tunnel, it should be you. Go to it my son."

Marius didn't waste any time. The next morning he and Jason climbed the steep hill to the top of the cliff where the garden wall of the Mystery House stopped them.

"How do you . . . I mean, why do you come here to search for the secret?" Jason asked. "Do you expect to find it in the house?"

Marius looked surprised. "I don't know. I never thought about it. It just seems to be the right place. Believe me, Jason, I feel as though I was called, to come here, by the house itself."

The house was built on a peninsula that sheltered the bay below, and the garden wall curved away so that from where Marius and Jason stood they could see the ice-covered coast stretching away for miles. Further away they saw the great icebergs rising from the sea. Yet, the water of Sea-of-Silver bay was always warm and people believed this was due to the magical light,

"I know how to open the gate," Marius told Jason. "You go back now. Get our group together and take them to my parent's house this evening. I'll be back by then and we'll make our travel plans."

"That is, once you've found the secret" Jason didn't say "if you've discovered the tunnel," because he had faith in his friend. He had a feeling Marius would find it.

Marius watched him as he started his walk down the hill, then he opened the heavy looking gate that he knew was made of light, not really heavy at all, and entered the garden.

Although, as far as Marius knew, there was no one there to look after the garden, it looked as if it received constant care. On his right was a semi-circular lawn and beds of white lilies, while on his left was a wooded area where the elusive light forms who watched him whenever he came there, lived. He wondered again why the people shunned the hilltop house. He wasn't at all afraid of the elusive light forms. He knew they wouldn't harm anyone. He was aware that they watched him now, but when he turned to look at them, they retreated among the trees and were lost to sight. They moved without appearing to do so.

As he stood, looking about, the white lilies opened themselves, even though it wasn't the right time of day for them to do that, and sent their exotic perfume across to him so that for a moment he forgot why he was there, and thought only of Undi; the sixteen-year old girl he expected to marry one day. Although it was strictly forbidden for him to even touch her until she returned from her three years in-sea where she would learn the ways of the sea and its creatures, the scent of lilies made him feel almost sick with desire for her, just for a moment. It surprised him, for he had never had this happen before. They had not yet developed strong physical feelings for each other, although they were committed to each other. The desire passed and just as well, for he needed to think of nothing but the time tunnel. That was what he had come for. His desire was, at this time, directed toward the genius. He longed for him with the passion of an artist, even more than he desired Undi.

He walked along the path, which would have taken him through an open court to the marble seat overlooking the Sea-of-Silver, had he let it. Instead, he crossed over the lawn to another path that led him to one of the doors of the house. Opening this door he found himself entering an enchanting lobby with a lofty ceiling and pure white walls. On a central table of antique design, was a handsome blue and silver vase filled, with startlingly yellow flowers. Around them fluttered two purple and black butterflies which had followed Marius in from the garden.

He began to feel dreamy, and cool, falling under the spell of the house, and was in danger of forgetting why he had come here. Before he was carried away to a dream land of lilies, he opened a door and walked through to a long narrow space, passing other doors as he went on along this corridor. Spaces and their walls moved, changed into other strange dimensions, opened up, then closed around him. He still felt dreamy but understood that he was passing through dimensional areas, like the ones he had seen when he first came here as a child. Misty forms had made promises then, but had not told him what it was they were promising. He didn't mind now because he was in a sort of comfort zone, where he wouldn't need to find any kind of secret nor look for time tunnels or do anything . . .

It was almost as if the house welcomed him, so long as he didn't try to look for any secrets, especially time travel secrets. It would much rather have him succumb to the irresistible scent of the lilies. He had to call upon his powers to keep erotic thoughts about Undi at bay. The thought of that amused him and he couldn't help giggling a little. He even thought he might be a little bit high on pod juice-but he wasn't.

He made his light headed way along the corridor, over an indoor bridge to another level, where the misty forms merged with misty spaces. While this was happening, he had no sense of time passing, and almost forgot the genius of Old Earth who could build houses of light. He even forgot where he was, but kept on searching for something, throughout the house.

Coming to a door that had an interesting wooden door knob, he took hold firmly and turned it. The door opened and he entered a room with walls made of heavy blocks of stone. A window set deeply into an arched window frame, allowed a single stream of light to enter the room. The floor was of one wide slab of natural stone, with the walls built around it. This suggested to Marius that he had reached the heart of the house. For furniture there was a roughly hewn table and chair, and a wooden bunk with the impression of a head in its pillow.

Marius experienced a sense of déjà vu and was tempted to lay his own head down and leave his own dent in the pillow, thinking "It's the house again trying to trick me" and felt cunning because he thought it was he who was tricking the house, when he saw something he hadn't seen before. Walking across the room to examine it, he saw an opening to another room, or one of those magical spaces.

As he squeezed through the opening everything changed. He lost all those dreamy giggly feelings, and became alert. He hadn't entered another room, or a strange dimension; he'd entered an ordinary cave with a view of the lilies in the garden through the cave's wide entrance.

This, he felt, was the real heart of the Mystery House of Heliotrope. He didn't know why this came to him with such conviction but he didn't question it. He sat still and waited. After a while, the secret was mysteriously and impenetrably conveyed to him on a level he didn't even know he had within himself. It did, however, make him act. He left the cave, crossed the lawn, passed the lilies without noticing their seductive scent, took a flying leap over the wall, and skimmed five inches above the path all the way down the hill until he came to the main road that led to his parents' house. He knew his father would be able to read the secret that had been granted to him as a special favor. The whole day had passed. It was now late afternoon. He was glad to be home.

Jason was there with their friends, a group of brilliant young people like Marius and Jason, who were eager to go time traveling with them, and had their own good reasons for undertaking such an adventure. Their parents were there too.

Marius' mother Elizabeth, whose namesake was Elizabeth the First, of Old Earth, had prepared a good Pod supper, with Pod wine to drink. They all sat and waited to hear what Marius had to say. He didn't really know what he had to say, because he hadn't understood the message. After he and his father had touched each other and embodied, for one blazing second, the abstract form of the secret itself, Leo got the message.

"I'm a little surprised" he said, looking at the eager faces around him, "yet not as surprised as I could have been, because the answer's so simple. It's the magical song from the most ancient people of Old Earth, so far back that we have no idea what they were like except that this was their song. What you and your friends must do, Marius, and Jason, is go to the cave and sit there, close to each other—and this is important, mind you—for if you aren't close, one of you may be left out. So, sit in a very close circle touching in a cross legged position. Then communicate to each other how deeply you long for the song, really more like a chant, to come to you. When you feel you are one with this longing and you feel the song coming to you, you must communicate that longing to those ancient people who have been kind enough to give this information to Marius. Can you do this? If you believe you can, breathe deeply, close your eyes, and silently say "yes", as you let go of the breath. It will not sound like "yes" to you, but don't be deceived, stay with it. It will sound like the first long weird note of the song. It will not be the kind of song you're accustomed to, but you will be able to sing, or chant, the song to its end."

They, of course, all agreed. Then they sat down to the delicious Pod casserole Elizabeth the Third had prepared for them. While they ate they talked about the trip and who would be going. Leo and Conrad and the other parents who were present, all wanted to know the details.

"Eight of us" Jason told them. "Isis and Osiris, Pavarti, Undi, Marius, myself and Eva."

"Hmm, eight of Heliotrope's most brilliant young people." Leo looked at them, "But I see only seven of you. Who is the eighth?

"Tiger Hound," said Undi. "We can't go without him."

"You've heard of Tiger Hound, Father. He's the strange being Pavarti met when she was In-Jungle. Tiger Hound is her name for him" Marius said.

"Yes, yes. I know. He's the handsome animal who has never been tamed. He's a myth."

"He's no myth. He's real. Anyway, Pavarti wants him to come and so do we. We feel sure he has some deep connection with the past. Perhaps he can help us find out how those Old Earth people dealt with the first Ice Age-how they melted it."

"Leave the ice alone. Good God, if the ice melts, we'll all be drowned. Don't mess with that!"

Leo was upset by the thought of all that ice melting. Conrad was more concerned about Tiger Hound's suitability as a Time Traveler.

"Aren't you afraid he'll upset the singing?" He may upset the balance if he tries to raise his voice."

Marius laughed, "You don't know him sir. We have absolute faith in him. In fact his powers are far greater than ours, and his links with the early people of Old Earth are even stronger than ours could ever be." That seemed to satisfy Conrad.

He turned to the women of the group. Eva, the first one, was a bird woman who had spent her three years in the air and the tree tops above Heliotrope's only forest. There she had become bird and lived the life of a mother bird, learning all there was to know about bird life. She had recently returned from In-Air and looked forward to a peaceful and untroubled life with Jason her husband-to-be. He expected the same of her. Little did either of them know that fate had something quite different in store for them.

Apart from all of that, Eva had a namesake whom some people would have said didn't suit her at all. She was sweet, modest, and loving. Her namesake was Mother Eve, a strong primitive earth mother. She had no idea that this would link her to many Old Earth experiences. She and the other three girls had always wanted to meet their namesakes. This was their chance to do so.

Isis, another member of the group was Spirit-Woman. She had a darkness within her beautiful soul; during her In-Spirit period she had entered that dark cave, the cave of the soul. Like her namesake, Isis, who loved the early Egyptian god Osiris, she loved her own living Osiris whose soul matched hers. She, too, had recently returned from In-Spirit. As for Osiris, like his namesake, he had his own soul-darkness and beauty. They both looked forward to finding their namesakes in Egypt when they reached the past.

Pavarti, a beautiful dark-haired girl, was a jungle-woman. While it was true that Heliotrope had no jungle, Pavarti had found hers in a blaze of Light that led her into another of Heliotrope's dimensions. Unlike the spaces Marius had encountered in the Mystery House, hers was nature space, not house space. There she stayed during her In-Jungle period for three years and there she met the love of her life. She called him Tiger Hound because he had first revealed himself to her in the form of a tiger. He too had his namesake, and they asked no more than that they would find bliss when they found their true natures on the great mountain called Kailassa, when they reached the past.

In spite of these exotic prospects before them, they all told Marius that they would help him if they could, to find his genius. The title "Genius", in a way, was his namesake, even though he didn't know it.

Of all the women who wanted to make this journey, Undi was the youngest. She had not yet had her in-sea education and would have been considered too young to go to the past, but she was a strong-willed girl and simply said, "I'm going."

Louise, Undi's mother, was named for Eloise, an unfortunate young woman of the 12th century of Old Earth who had to become a nun after something awful happened to her lover. Louise was understandably nervous about her sixteen-year-old daughter entering one of the vast oceans of Old Earth for three years; she feared, too, that her daughter was in danger of being touched by Marius who, in those unusual circumstances, might forget the rule of no physical contact with a girl not yet returned-from-sea or whatever her in-college might be. Louise fussed a little so that Marius felt obliged to give his sacred promise that he would do the right thing and look after her. It irked him until he hit upon the idea of creating a comfortable dwelling place for her-a few nice rooms perhaps, on some undiscovered island in some enchanted sea. That project appealed to him.

"She will be able to sleep on shore at night for her safety," he said.

"I'm not so sure" Jason said, for once disagreeing with his hero, "Those deep sea monsters never minded if it was day or night when they ate a mermaid."

Well, anyway, Undi will change shape at the slightest hint of danger. She's the niftiest shape-shifter I have ever seen," Marius replied.

Undi's father who happened to be listening to this conversation said, "You're right at that, and don't forget it young man."

"What does nifty mean?" asked Jason.

"It's an Old Earth expression. It means that Undi's a pretty sharp shape-shifter."

"I thought they said "Cool, man", Conrad said with a puzzled look.

"So they did. Everything was cool, but I like nifty. That's an earlier expression" Marius was pleased to be in a position to give this information. Leo, his father, said to Jason, "You see, if you'd read the Light instead of the Sand, you'd know these things."

"Darling, don't be mean to our guest," Elizabeth the Third said to her husband.

"I'm not. He knows what I mean, "Leo said. Turning to Marius, he gave him a warning. "They had a lot of trouble in that twenty-first century. Don't get involved. Just look for your genius, if you must, and learn something about wine-making, for instance. I'd be interested in how they made it. They didn't have the Pod to make their wine; I don't know how they managed." Secretly he thought Marius Son-of-the-Light was the greatest genius and didn't need to rush about looking for any other geniuses.

"And try to find out about those people who left from here five-hundred years ago," said Gizelle, Jason's mother. "If you find them, bring them back with you."

"Yes do, dear. It would be nice. I'd like to meet them. Five hundred years! They probably look just like we do." With that, Elizabeth the Third presented Eva with a package of Pod seeds, "Take these, dear. You never know what your circumstances will be when you step away from the time tunnel. They might save your lives; you never know. Let Pavanti help you plant them and then they'll grow wild. Process them properly and you'll have food, clothing and anything else you need."

Chapter 2

Jason's Fate

You wake up to a perfect day, a day so fine you almost wish you were not about to leave it for some unknown day in the past.

What you don't see is the stranger in the sparkling comic book cloak and shiny looking helmet who calls herself Fate. She wants to change your life. Your life's been changed already because you and Eva got married this morning and you're very satisfied with your life as it is right now.

Dr. Pondu, who believes he knows everything there is to know about Old Earth and the twenty first century in particular, is a luncheon guest on this perfect day. He tells of the horrors of the twenty first century, gives advice and never stops talking. To shut him up we get him high on the juice of the Pod, not the wine but the potent juice from the very heart of our wonderful Pod. It only makes him worse. It affects us too, our parents as well. By the time our farewell luncheon party sets out for the Mystery House up on the hill and we reach the garden wall we all behave like silly little children, forgetting that this is IT, the fantastic IT, and no one knows if we'll ever come back! You'd think we were going to the beach for the day instead to an enormous city that flourished eight thousand years ago.

Marius wants goodbyes to be said in the garden, so for the first time in our lives all our parents and friends come in. They feel nervous when they catch sight of the elusive light forms, watching them from between the trees. Our goodbyes take no time at all. We watched them pass through the garden gateway and start off down the hill. Then you and Eva and the others follow Marius into the house. Once inside the cave you sit close to each other in the circle as Leo has said you should do. You begin the song, which is more like a chant and it makes you feel weird. You think you see the figure of Fate but you can't be sure.

The ancient people of early Old Earth are very kind to you. Before long you feel the walls of the tunnel forming around you and you know the journey has begun.

You don't know what has happened to your comic book stalker but you really don't have time to bother about her. Later you do. You wonder what difference there is between you and your friends and why the impossible thing should have happened to you alone. You are all singing now and things begin to happen.

You will hear things. Among other strange noises you'll hear the long rumbling hum of a billion, million voices, and you'll feel the trembling of a billion, million lives, the crashing of mountains and the upheaval of valleys and all the cries of love and hate and joy and pain, fear and freedom condensed into one long, dreadful, lovely, eruption of sound. Then you will enter No-time and you will hear nothing. That may be the dreamless sleep in which Fate will change your life. You can't tell when it actually happens. How can you tell? You can't!

There are the others, sitting on the floor of the cave. Around them are unfamiliar tufts of shrub, loose stones and earth. They look about them, looking for you, for where you should have been, sitting next to Eva, with Pavarti on your other side. There's only empty space.

They can't tell whether you were left in the cave, or lost in No-time, or if you're floating about in some weird dimension, or whether you are dead. You can't answer Eve when she calls out for you, Jason, before she faints away in shock. You can't even say "Here I am, my love," and you can't faint away with her. You can't do anything.

She recovers and so do the others, but they do not mourn for as long as you'd like, nor as deeply as you would expect, because they have to think of how to stay alive in a cave while outside the bright days and dark nights are rushing by at a terrific speed. Fortunately they have the Pods to eat. You're not even hungry! Centuries come and go while Tiger Hound guards the entrance to the cave, singing softly to himself, and you wait with him, wondering what is going on with you. You finally figure it out. It was that comic book character who calls herself "Fate". She took your body and hid it somewhere in the Universe, leaving you with only your mind. Fortunately for you, it's a good one, one that will be able to stay cool as you go through the ages observing your friends enjoying life or, as the great playwright Shakespeare would one day say, "suffering the slings and arrows of outrageous fortune." You will have to accept your role as observer of all that happens, and after awhile you might get used to it. It mightn't be so bad. You might even become a philosopher. It wouldn't do for your friend Marius because he's a do-er but you'll be alright, you like just sitting and thinking and watching in silence, all alone, because no one has any idea that you are there.

When they woke, they found they had adjusted to the pace of life and were able to make short trips outside and examine their surroundings. They encountered no

*people and only a few strange animals. The House had disappeared or had not yet
been built. When they were settled, Marius and Osiris began to make tools to work
with. They were solid tools, not for light construction, for Marius had not yet learned
the secret. It was going to be a simple shlter made of wood.*

*It was a lonely time, even though they had each other, and a very lonely place.
It was quite a long time before they realized they had been expelled from the Time
Tunnel many centuries earlier than Marius had expected they would be. The
twenty-first century was far away in the future. Osiris figured out that four of our
years would pass by the time we came to it, and everyone was relieved to see that we
were not aging according to Earth time. Sometimes they thought of me and even
wondered whether they would find me waiting for them in the twenty first century.*

I didn't believe they'd find me waiting for them. I simply did not
feel that was the answer to my strange situation. I was with them in
spirit and knew everything that was happening to each one of them,
but I didn't believe anything about waiting for them in the twenty-first
century.

Now that they had adjusted to the passing of time, they were able
to do more and more each day. Eva had planted the magical Pod seeds
and was able to harvest them and use them to meet all the group's
needs. Pavarti, accompanied by Tiger Hound, went foraging for extra
Old Earth food, which they all learned to eat. Undi went down the cliff
face to the water's edge but not yet to enter the sea. Marius sometimes
took her sailing with him in the small sailboat he had made. It would
not be long, I told myself, before she would descend into the unknown
for her union with the creatures that lived in that wide expanse of
water, and she would not be seen again for three years—in time to
spend a year with us in the twenty-first century before returning to
Heliotrope with all the knowledge she had gained. Isis, together with
Eva, revealed her domestic skills, and between them, they made living
conditions comfortable enough.

Chapter 3

Namesakes

None of us had ever crossed Ice Mountain to explore the land that lay beyond those pure white slopes, but now that the mountain was covered with a lush growth of bright, green trees and foliage, they hoped the whole countryside would also be free of snow and ice. This was an exciting possibility and the others suggested to Marius that they should cross the mountain and find out what lay beyond it. He agreed, but so far no plans for this expedition had been made.

Eva couldn't wait. One morning she shape-shifted into her bird body and flew off toward the mountain. I saw her and soon caught up with her.

We flew for several days over a thick, dark, green forest. Eva knew exactly where she was going and her bird-body grew stronger and more forceful as she felt herself growing closer to her goal. There was no snow or ice anywhere. We saw only virgin forest. On the morning of the fourth day, I looked down and saw a pleasant valley with a stream of crystal clear water gleaming in the soft pink light of dawn.

Eva must have known what she would find there: a primitive settlement, with the roughly carved figure of her namesake, Earth Mother.

As she landed she shed her bird shape and revealed an Eva I had never suspected was there beyond her gently sweet womanliness. Taking the form of the primitive Earth Mother, her thighs full and her breasts round and heavy, she settled down to wait for the people to see her.

They came out of the huts. Animals came. Strange creatures came crawling and wriggling from the stream. All were bent on taking part in the fertility rite that would be performed before my wife.

When it was over, I felt as if I had been under a spell. There was nothing I could do, helpless and in awe of my Eva and her queenliness, I tried to say goodbye and then flew back to our camp. I found Marius at work, building another room next to the shelter he'd built for us. They would hardly ever stay in the rooms. They'd all be off somewhere looking for their namesakes.

"And you'll be searching for the genius," I said-or tried to say. As though he had heard me he muttered, "As soon as I finish this wall, I'll be gone. They may do what they like." He was disappointed because we hadn't disembarked from the tunnel in the twenty first century.

Pavarti and Tiger Hound were the next to leave. They went on foot, but after a while, they grew tired of walking, or at least Pavarti did. So Tiger changed shape and carried Pavarti on his back. He had taken the form of a fleet-footed horse, and they traveled quickly. But when they came to the land's end, Tiger Hound sprouted wings and flew, and Pavarti entered the water and made her way like a Fish Woman, although strictly speaking, she was not one. She did, however, have an affinity with all forms of life and all of nature, so she was at ease in the sea.

She sped through the water like a dolphin and rose from the waves at the most southern tip of what was now known as the great subcontinent of India. Climbing up from a narrow beach, she looked about her. Tiger Hound was nowhere to be seen. There were some people, however, members of a primitive tribe of jungle dwellers, dark-skinned, almost naked, with long, black hair. They saw Pavarti, and far from being hostile or afraid, they bowed low and called her by her own name.

A few moments later, Tiger Hound came from the thick jungle and went to her side. The primitive people were evidently in awe of him and backed away, bowing very low and calling him Shiva the Destroyer. Pavarti placed her hand on his head and told them he was both Destroyer and Creator.

He and Pavarti left the seashore and walked away into the jungle, where the leaves of the trees swayed under the weight of huge drops of monsoon rain. The air was moist and sweet with the scent of flowers and thick foliage. Pavarti picked one of the white flowers and offered it to Tiger Hound. As soon as she did this, he changed shape and stood before her in the form of a glorious young man.

"I think I've always known this would happen," Pavarti said. "I've always known you were my beloved and that your Tiger skin cloaked the body of a man." She leaned against him in an attitude of perfect love and trust, and her naked body with its female hips and swelling breasts looked entrancing beside the straighter, harder lines of Shiva's body.

"Yes. I am man at this moment, and you are a woman."

"At this moment?" Pavarti asked.

"We'll change from moment to moment. But as for those jungle dwellers, it is better that they take us for their nature spirits. They will never expect us to grow old, as they will. It's true, too, that we are the Creators and the Destroyers, but so are they. The Life Force exists in everything, Pavarti. You and I will enter into all things. We may love as man and woman, but we may also embrace in all possible forms. If you were a humble stone in the ground, I would still love you."

When he said that, Pavarti was already sinking down to a soft patch of earth, waiting for Shiva's hands to touch her. When he followed, they sank into the ground and became lovers. A huge jungle tree with branches that hung down like roots hid them from view.

Even in Heliotrope, Pavarti had been a serene, mysterious woman with her own reality. Now these qualities in her grew, and her body had grown richer and fuller already. The people had called her by the name of their goddess, and Tiger Hound by the name of their god. So they stayed sometimes in the jungle and sometimes on a high mountain in the north called Kailassa and lived like the gods.

A similar thing happened to Osiris and Isis. They flew to a place where a mighty river wound its way through the Valley of the Nile. When they reached that place, it was the time of full flood, and the Nile had spread its waters over the floor of the valley, carrying with it the rich mud that transformed the valley into an earthly paradise. Osiris and Isis stayed there for some time without revealing themselves, and as the season changed, they watched the water recede and the fresh vegetation spring up as if by magic through the surface of the soil.

They saw, too, that the people had only recently come to this valley and were already at work bringing order to the fantastic wilderness.

Osiris and Isis watched the people for some time and one day revealed themselves in a dramatic fashion. Rising from the soft soil on the bank of the Nile and holding hands in an attitude of love, they swelled up until they were able to seat themselves on one of the high cliffs. They took this unusually gigantic form merely to impress upon the people that they were strangers from another place and time, never to present themselves as gods. But this was how the people saw Isis and Osiris towering above them. Godliness was what they read into the presence of these giants, and they called them by their own names, just as the jungle people had done when they'd seen Shiva and Pavarti.

"They've been expecting us," Isis whispered.

The pair withdrew from their great height and sat quietly on a rock by the river looking at the people, who had stopped their work and were bowing before them.

"Go back to your work," Osiris told the people.

They watched the people until nightfall and when it was dark and the people slept, Isis looked up at the night sky and saw the star, Sirus. "Look, beloved. Let this be our star."

The people accepted Isis and Osiris without question. They called them their nature god and goddess and also their king and queen. Osiris, they said, was the King of the Underworld—that deep dark place they all expected to enter when their life on Earth was over. In his wisdom and majesty, he was to judge them and reward them for the good they had done on earth or punish them for their bad deeds. Isis they proclaimed as a goddess, queen, wife, and mother.

At the time, Isis and Osiris didn't comprehend the enormity of what was being imposed upon them and were not alarmed by it. Isis enjoyed playing her role. But later, they were credited with many more complex and magical powers and were expected to take part in or preside over awesome rites. What else could they have expected when they had made themselves visible—rising from the very soil that brought such blessings to the people?

Osiris was not entirely willing to play his role. He sometimes concealed himself in the form of an insect or a plant or a mouse or even a serpent. The people said that Osiris died every night, and they made up stories about him. He was the moon who came as a beautiful child each month and was devoured by the old moon—the demon, Set. Then he was the young god who was slain in his prime each year. He was the father, son, and husband. He was the patriarch who reigned over men and judged them when they were dead. He was the Earth Spirit, the bisexual Nile Spirit, the bright sun. And Isis they called the Lady of the Horizon, who had begotten herself in the image of the gods.

Osiris went away at one time to assist the people in the cultivation of their fields, and it was said that Typhoon, his brother, gave a feast when he returned. At the feast, he placed the body of Osiris into a box with the aid of his fellow conspirators and he cast it into the Nile. When Isis discovered what had happened, she clothed herself in black and wept bitterly and mourned and swore to find the body of her husband. She found thirteen parts, but one part she did not find.

They sank into
the earth and became lovers

Osiris had not been dismembered by the wicked Typhon as Isis believed. He was sickened by all the violence he had seen and been part of as Egypt and her enemies grew strong and went to war, slaughtering prisoners, torturing and enslaving them. He became the Traveler, wandering alone without Isis through the ages. Everything he saw caused him pain, and he was unable to discover the solution to the dilemma of humanity's existence. In a way, he *was* dismembered—fragmented—for his tormented mind deceived him a thousand times as he searched for means of escape from pain.

By the time he reached Paris in the twenty-first century, Osiris lived in his own world of illusion. His pain was not his alone. It was world pain, and he had a plan. This time, he told himself, he would use his wealth—for he, like Marius, had accumulated a fortune in gold and jewels which he could turn into money whenever he pleased—to stage a great drama of protest. Not only had Osiris accumulated wealth, his charisma and his physical beauty had not diminished and had grown even more compelling, and he gave the impression of wisdom and leadership. Before long he had the youth of Paris under his spell.

Was I imagining this? The youth of Paris? I was afraid of what Osiris might have in mind. I hoped Isis would find him and bring him to his senses. Then I reminded myself that we had many Old Earth centuries to live through before this might happen and I should not look so far ahead.

Chapter 4

The Rock

When I returned from Egypt, where I had observed Isis and Osiris, Marius was nowhere to be seen. Although I waited, prowling about like a bodiless spirit—which, after all was what I was—Marius didn't come back, and I felt lonely. I grew desperate, and at last, I went over the edge of the cliff and down to the beach remembering our last meeting there with our fathers. Even though the beach was much smaller and the sand was darker in color and there were more sharp rocks, I knew that, one day, this would be our Sea of Silver Beach. The cliff had not changed at all.

I began to think of Undi, wanting to see her. She was, after all, my cousin; she was family. My need to see her and know that she was all right was so strong that I entered the water and began to look for her. By nightfall, I found myself a witness to a drama of the sea that we in Heliotrope could never have imagined, for no wind of ours had ever lashed the waves and terrified the sea creatures as this one did.

I was not afraid for myself because I already knew that physically, nothing could hurt me, but I wondered where Undi was. And I hoped she was far below the surface where the movement of the waves couldn't harm her.

Around me, objects were being tossed about chaotically as the waves rose to enormous heights. The wind, rain, lightning, and thunder were fearful yet exciting. I felt alive for the first time since I had realized I was only a spirit. I even imagined I could hear the shrieking of the wind.

By morning, just before sunrise, the wind had died down and the movement of the sea was sensuous but satisfied. There were mountains

the Rock

of water, but they heaved slowly and heavily. Not far away, I saw something being washed slowly this way and that. Two sea creatures were darting in and out and nosing it. One was an ordinary fish and the other was a dolphin. They looked odd together but appeared to be good friends. The object they were interested in looked like a dead female human. The next time it rose on the heaving sea, I saw that it was Undi, and I was horrified when I became aware of what they were thinking.

"It's dead, isn't it?" the fish asked the dolphin.

"It seems like it. But let's make sure." The dolphin made a careful inspection, and the fish followed suit.

Then they both started back in surprise. They had detected a flicker of life.

"A half-drowned human," the fish gasped. "What shall we do? Should we just leave her? She'll die soon if we do."

"Don't leave her, please don't!" I cried helplessly.

It was almost as if they had heard me.

"No, let's not leave her. But I'm not sure she *is* human. There's something about her I don't understand. She's not quite the same as any human I've ever encountered."

"You should know. You are friendlier with humans that I am," the fish said with a shade of reproach in his voice. "The only humans I've ever encountered half tore my gills out with a sharp hook and then left me flapping about on a hard deck until I was almost dead. At the last minute, they decided to throw me back. I hate them! But, strangely, I don't feel any hatred for this one, so perhaps she's not one of them."

"Look at those arms and legs and that head of human hair. It looks like the tail of a butterfly fish, waving about like that," the dolphin observed.

They looked. The hair was like wet gold. The legs were undulating on the swell and looked boneless, as did the arms. They were waterlogged, and there was no life in them.

For some time, they swam around Undi's limp form, protecting it, until at last the dolphin said he thought he knew what she was. What they had come upon, he told the fish, was probably a spirit of the waves, known as an Undi. This seemed like the best explanation, yet even after they had accepted it, they weren't quite sure. Undi had a quality that they'd never before come in contact with. And her particular odor still clung to her in spite of all she had been through that night in the sea. The fish and the dolphin knew that the Undis of the sea were shape-changers, like most nature spirits and were often mistaken for mermaids, but they were hard to grasp when anyone tried to touch them or hold them. They could see that Undi had a solid body, although it was somewhat spongy because of all the water in it, as was theirs. Besides, they knew that an Undi had never been known to die. When the Undis' time came, they turned into fragments of spray and were blown away by the wind. Even so, they were later reborn and returned to other oceans or lakes or any place where there was water.

"This is very serious," the dolphin said. "What is an Undi doing in human form? If the body dies she may be trapped forever and imprisoned in darkness."

It had happened once, so they said, to an unfortunate spirit of the waves who still wailed from that darkness on silent nights at sea. The wailing sounded hollow, as though it had come from some faraway void.

The dolphin and the fish agreed to save this one, and one of them thought of the Rock. The Rock they spoke of was known to very few men, but most sea creatures knew about it. Fishermen claimed to have seen it, but none of them had ever found it and walked upon it, for it was a treasure of the sea and very elusive. I had never heard of it, but I had stopped worrying about Undi. These two creatures could do more for her now than I could.

The fish and the dolphin knew now that only by finding the Rock would they have a chance of saving the Undi—if that's what she was. It seemed that the Rock was the answer, whoever or whatever she was. The fish sped off to look for it, singing as he went.

"Rock, O, Rock. O, Mighty Rock.

Ancient legend of the Sea.

Reveal your rugged strength to me."

Magic words. The fish suspected the Rock was an illusion that appeared in certain lights or that it might even be made of Light itself. Yet the Rock had a reality of its own, whatever it was. He hoped it would show itself, for although he knew the dolphin was guarding the body, he was afraid that some school of sharp-toothed fish would sweep down and strip it to the bone before it was properly dead.

"Come, great Rock," the fish called again.

And then suddenly, he saw it rise in the distance, a dark shape silhouetted against the sky. He instantly transmitted a message to the dolphin. Within a few minutes, his companion was by his side, towing the body by its hair.

"There it is!" he said.

The dolphin saw it as a great hulk of rock looming solidly upward in the cold darkness of the predawn. To him, it looked very real. Yet they both knew it wasn't solid at all, for it was a thing that fantasies, yes, and dreams, too, were built upon. But now it was the right thing for their purpose.

The dolphin pushed Undi's body onto a ledge close to the water. Waves, whom they suspected were sister Undis, washed it onto an even higher ledge, and there let it rest.

As Undi lay on the rocky ledge, the fish and the dolphin waited and watched her. Beyond the Rock, far out at the edge of the sea, something began to happen. A luminous green light crept over the sky and, in some mysterious way, was transformed into the delicate pink flush of dawn. Then new colors appeared, colors that seemed to have no beginning and no end; for as the fish and the dolphin watched, the clear pink radiance was overcome by an apricot glow, which became streaked with splendid orange and scarlet streaks shot with silver and gold. The radiance spread out and rose higher, to illuminate and outline the billowing clouds left over from the storm.

This, too, was sheer magic. Dawn, with all its wonders, was never so colorful. But they could not credit the Rock with this magic. It had come from far away and from some other magician.

Then, as if this unknown wizard had not done enough, celestial music swelled up, and a thrilling song of morning reached the Rock just as the tip of Father Sun's golden chariot made its entrance onto the vast stage of sea and sky. It happened that far away on the coast of Africa, there was a strip of desert, and dust rising from this desert caught the light of the sun and looked for all the world like hanging curtains of gold, which were opening to reveal the drama of Osiris and his rebirth, through Isis, at the dawn of a new day.

Something had to happen. Outwardly, it was the same as any other new day, except for all of those scarlet streaks. But now the streaks were gone and the sky was blue and the clouds white. The sun's rays were now deliciously hot; everything was warming up, and ripples on the sea were sparkling. Other sea creatures had begun swimming around the Rock, waiting to see what would happen to the Undi, for the word had spread. Even though there were hundreds and thousands of Undis in the sea, the fate of this one particular spirit had suddenly become of great concern. Had not the Rock revealed itself for her sake? The creatures of the sea were convinced that this was a very special Undi, which of course, was true. I could have told them that.

She stirred and then became still again. I had never before been privileged to see a Fish-Woman in the sea, and now I realized that, due to my own extraordinary condition, I was in a position to see all that was happening. What made it most remarkable and awe-inspiring was that this great body of water, thousands or millions of years removed in time from us, was the ancestor of our own Sea of Silver. And Undi herself was perhaps a descendent of the earliest water spirits whom we called myths.

She was changing. Her form became cloudy. It still rested, well-balanced on the rock. But as we watched the sea creatures gliding and leaping about in the water, she slowly became transparent, with all of her delicate bones and intestines and organs faintly visible through the skin. Then she faded away from that form and turned into a string of bubbles. I thought she had gone, but the fish knew better. They were not at all surprised when she spoke to them in this form. This was the way, so they said, an Undi sometimes behaved. They were satisfied that she had recovered and spoken to them.

"Well, Brother Fish and all you seabirds and you crabs and periwinkles and you, Brother Dolphin, what is going on?"

The dolphin spoke up and said, "We're here because we saved your life."

"You saved my life! I didn't know I had been in danger."

Undi must have smiled, because several of the bubbles burst, sparkling like diamonds as they did so. Her voice was silvery, like a silvery seashell or the sounds it made or what I imagined it would make. It wasn't like her normal voice, which was smoother and deeper.

"She's alive again. Isn't she marvelous!" the seagulls cried.

"She's gorgeous! Look at the way she sparkles. Dolphin, tell her what happened."

"Oh yes, you were in great danger. You might have been lost forever if Brother Fish and I had not come upon you after the storm. You were floating like a dead thing on the swell."

"Well, I suppose I should thank you, but I remember almost nothing about it. Oh, just a little about a storm perhaps, but that's all. I do thank you, for I'm glad to be alive."

I'd heard that in order to live a life in the sea, Fish-Women had to give up all memories. Memories, they said, carried on from day to day, over a period of time, created fear and desire, and Fish-Women had to be free of all that.

I heard one seagull say to another, "Strange, isn't it, the way Undis forget. They have no memories whatsoever."

"That's why they're always so fresh and new. They never look back. They have no past."

The bubble spoke again. "Well, I'm safe now, and that's all that matters."

But the fish wasn't satisfied. He wanted to know the whole story. "She may have forgotten. We know Undis have no memories, but they do have the power to recreate images for us to look at. It wouldn't hurt her to do that."

"She doesn't have to," a seagull said. "I can tell you what happened. I saw and heard everything. Undi, can you hear? You need not listen. It's much better if you don't."

No one knew whether Undi was listening or not.

The seagull's story was that Undi was sitting on a rock—no, not the Rock—an ordinary rock not far from the Bay of Antibes in the south of France, in the shape of a mermaid combing her hair, when a fisherman came by in his boat and captured her. It wasn't difficult. He just threw a net over her and hauled her aboard.

"At least, I imagined he was a fisherman," the sea gull said, "for who else would go out in a small boat capturing mermaids in a net? He had a small boy with him, who helped him pull her in. That was his assistant, I imagine."

The gull went on to tell them how she had followed the boat and had watched while the fisherman pulled into a little cove and carried the mermaid to his house up on the cliff not far from the beach.

"It looked as if he had been living there forever. I sat on one of the deep window ledges and looked in at them when they went inside. It seemed to me that they knew each other quite well. She called him Marius, and he called her Undi, and they talked like friends, although she was angry with him for having captured her and said he should have waited until she was ready. 'I wasn't ready,' she said."

Now I understood. I remember Marius saying that Undi had come out of the sea once and stayed with him, and one day, she disappeared. At the time, he was terribly upset and worried about her, but he got over it and said that he knew what he would do. That was all he'd said.

But the seagull hadn't finished. Her version of what happened was a little different from what Marius had said.

"This Marius," she said, "suddenly did a strange thing. Well, not suddenly. He waited until she was asleep, and then he took hold of her tail and it came away in his hands. He hid it in a closet."

A youthful crab asked, "Didn't she cry out with pain?"

"No. After all, it wasn't a solid tail such as a fish has. It was just one of her many shapes. She woke up and looked offended and grew a pair of legs immediately. Marius asked her if that meant she was going to stay, and she said she didn't know."

The seagull paused and thought for a moment.

"It wasn't such a strange thing for him to do—taking her tail—for that is one of the time-honored ways of keeping a spirit with you once it has been captured, or even if it comes of its own accord. I once saw another man do the same thing when a small fox came to his house. He took the tail and hid it, just as Marius did. It was a female fox. She stayed with the man until she found her tail. Just for one moment before she left, she let him see her in her female form—a long, slender human form it was, with silky, black hair and a crimson mouth. Then she turned into a fox again and ran off into the woods. The man searched for her all night, but he never found her."

I knew at once that this was an Old Earth folktale. Spirits came to men, and to women, too, in all shapes and sizes, but mostly in the form of beautiful women or handsome men. Usually they tormented people. Sometimes they came from the gods or from demons; they came as poor beggars, sometimes to some old woodcutter's house in the woods asking for shelter as weary travelers. If shelter and food were given generously by the poor woodcutter and his wife, the spirits rose early the next morning and went away leaving a bag of gold on the table. Sometimes the woodsman and his wife would look through the window and see a glorious young man disappearing into the woods. The stories were endless. These spirits are all shape-changers, and I was interested in them, because as I said, Heliotropians are shape-changers. Undi was a shape-changer, but she wasn't a spirit. So I wondered why Marius had treated her as if she were and taken her tail. I would have to ask him some time.

Undi suddenly changed form and wailed, "Oh, he took my tail! If that's true, I'm incomplete. He'll always own a little bit of me." She changed into a little pool of salty water.

They knew then that she'd been listening all the time.

"You didn't seem to mind. You stayed with him for a whole year. I know. I flew there almost every day," the seagull said.

"As his wife?" another seabird asked. "Surely she didn't . . ."

"No. Not as his wife. I never once saw them in bed together. Not that he wouldn't have liked it, but she didn't seem to want to. He was very kind to her, and it was clear that he loved her dearly. But either she wasn't ready for mating, or else she loved him as a friend. She did learn to cook for him, however, and they talked a lot over their meals, mostly about mutual friends. They looked nice together. Her shape, which had been a mermaid shape before he took her tail, was beautiful but now she looked human. And he was an extremely handsome man. I never felt afraid of him."

"How strange," the fish whispered to the dolphin. "Who is this Marius? Have you ever heard of him? Cursed fisherman!"

"No, I haven't heard of him. But I don't believe he's a fisherman."

"Neither do I," the seagull, overhearing him, said. "I thought so at first, but although I went there every day, I never saw him bring back any live fish. He went out often in his boat, and he did have the net, but I'd say, rather, that he went to observe. He was curious about everything in the sea. He had a collection of seashells on the windowsills and a few dead seahorses and starfish and some seaweed, but I don't believe he killed them."

"There are men like that," the other seabird remarked. "They study the ways of all you sea creatures and of us birds and, in fact, all living things."

This made me a little bit sad, for I am, or was, a geologist, and apart from making maps and trying to understand why, in our time, the planet (except for Heliotrope) was covered with ice, I had discovered the fossils of animals and birds that existed on Old Earth. I had occasionally been excited since making this journey into the past, seeing some of these creatures as living beings.

I will not, unless some wonderful thing happens on our return time travel and I get my body back, be able to participate physically in this work again, but I can do so in my mind. For instance, there are no seagulls flying over the Sea of Silver. I found the two who were here, talking about Undi, quite remarkable birds. The one who was telling the tale, in particular, seemed to be very bright. She understood everything. In fact, she was rather a busybody—a bit of a gossip.

She turned now to the little pool of water, which I supposed to be Undi.

When she saw that Undi was listening, she said, "But you grew restless. Oh, yes you did. You went very often to the top of the cliff to look at the sea, and I could tell you were thinking about going back. You didn't let him know how you felt, but inside the house, you prowled about looking for something."

"For my tail, I imagine. Wouldn't you?"

"Why? It wasn't a real tail."

"I know, but he shouldn't have done it. It was not the right thing to do. He should have waited until I came to him in my true form. I resent it, even though I like Marius a lot."

All the creatures looked surprised. This was not the way an Undi usually spoke. A sea spirit is notoriously mindless in this respect.

"Well, he regretted it. He did ask you to forgive him, didn't he? And you said you did. So why did you run away?"

"Oh, I couldn't be angry for very long. I forgave him, but . . . well . . . I don't even remember running away. I don't remember any of this as a matter of fact. When did I run away? And where did I run to?"

"It was only last night. Just as that terrible storm was blowing up. Don't you remember? You had been prowling about all afternoon, and he was out, and then you started to prepare the meal, but all the time you were listening to the wind howling, and suddenly you slammed the pot down on the stove, tore off your apron, and ran out of the house. I followed, flying head-on through the wind. I expected you to go down to the beach and wade in like any sensible creature. But instead, you ran to the edge of the cliff and there you jumped off. There were sharp rocks down below. It's not surprising you lost consciousness, for your new shape was quite solid."

"Exactly. It seemed so, except for being lifeless, when we found her last night," the dolphin told them. "She looked real enough."

"But she had no clothes. She was naked," the fish added.

"Of course. The clothes she had on were torn off her and washed away by the force of the storm. It must have been hours later when you found her. Thank goodness you thought of bringing her to the Rock."

All the creatures suddenly remembered the Rock and its remarkable qualities. But Undi was disturbed, still concerned about the missing tail.

"And I went without my tail. I shouldn't have listened to this."

"I advised you not to."

"I'm even beginning to remember things. What if I should lose my power?"

"Come, it's not as bad as that. You will be blown away and come back as a fresh fragment of spray," seagull said.

The sea creatures tried to comfort her, for they knew that a frightened spirit was a dangerous spirit. I could see that even Undi had begun to think of herself as a spirit.

But her agitation increased as she remembered Marius. "I remember him now. He must have gone out in the storm to search for me. He's like that. He's probably dead by now."

She wept and splashed the sun-dried rocks. "Yes, you're right. His name is Marius. I do remember him. Oh, what have I done?"

They were all shocked. They feared she had become involved with Marius and her life on dry land. She even remembered his name!

Now she herself evoked the image, and they all looked at Marius rushing about looking for Undi. They had expected to see his dead body or, at least, see him utterly grief stricken. But they saw no such thing, for there he was that very same night, making his way through the storm with what looked like a lighted torch in his hand. Along the seashore he went, looking very much alive and strong, almost unaware of the fierce wind that buffeted him about, shouting, "Undi, come back! Where are you, girl? I'm sorry I tried to hold you. Let me explain."

On and on he went, shining his torch on small shrubs and into little caves. "I won't give up. You're my responsibility. I promised your parents. Besides, I love you."

"It hasn't even occurred to him that *I* might be dead. I *did* almost die, didn't I? Oh, leave me alone. I'm going to sleep."

The dolphin said, "That's right. Sleep and forget. Stay here on the Rock, and you'll be all right. We'll all come from time to time to watch over you."

"And I and my descendants will live on this Rock forever and be your companions," said the seagull. She flew to a higher ledge and sat there.

So, I said to myself, *this seagull is smart*. She realized that Undi was no ordinary sea spirit, and that she was to live on that Rock for a very long time.

Undi climbed onto a more comfortable ledge and resumed her true form. She was no longer waterlogged, and her limbs looked very graceful and strong. She left a little water in the small indentation in the rock, and periwinkles, delighted at finding such a comfortable place, founded a colony around its edge. Undi was already asleep.

The fish and the dolphin, satisfied that she was all right, swam off.

"I doubt if she'll ever erase that image from her mind. She'll think she's forgotten him, but one day it will come back to her."

"I agree. He's part of her now, even if she doesn't think about him. But what about him? He's not going to give up, because *she's* part of him too. He'll find her, you know."

"Why worry about him?" the fish replied, somewhat bitterly. "He's a fisherman, isn't he?"

"The seagull said not."

"Well, anyway, he's a man—my enemy and yours too, as you'll find out one day. You and your kind have always been in touch with men, and you think they are your friends but, believe me, they're monsters."

I wanted to tell them that we Heliotropians never killed any of our creatures—the few that were left to us—so closely were we united with nature, but I knew they couldn't hear me.

"Well, he'll never be able to find the Rock."

They swam off, and never went back, although other dolphins and fish who came after them talked about Undi and the fisherman, and they were known to generations of sea creatures who made up stories about them.

Marius had been brought up to believe it was harmful for a girl to be taken from the sea during her in-sea term. He didn't really believe it, thinking it an old-fashioned idea, but he felt a little bit guilty just the same, and remembering his promise to her mother, he began to form a plan to build a shelter for her. He knew where she was, and his yacht took him straight into the uncharted waters where she lay sleeping on the mythical Rock.

It was to be a simple room, or a small house just for her night's sleep, with a tiny balcony where she could stand and watch the sunrise each morning—the Old Earth sun whose rays were so much brighter and warmer than the pale orb that hangs in the sky over Heliotrobe.

The thought of the sunrise and the image of Undi watching the magical colors in the sky affected him so much that this simple shelter he saw in his mind's eye was soon turned into a sparkling crystal palace on the peak of the Rock. He didn't realize this at first, but by the time he did realize what he was doing, he was so pleased that he abandoned himself to it and went on creating delightful rooms furnished with treasures of Egypt and Persia and other exotic lands he had traveled through as he searched for his genius. He simply could not resist all the richness of a structure so unlike the pure white dwellings in Heliotrobe.

In his imagination he saw Undi gracing the rooms and terraces, and shaded walkways that led to lotus ponds, She would learn from her surroundings and become a cultured woman with, of course, a gracious loving nature.

He was beginning to develop what some people might call a Pygmalion syndrome!

He went even further with the design of his palace. Finding his way to the heart of the Rock, he hollowed out chambers where a young girl might gain insight and understanding of her own heart and the hearts of others. Long passages and mysterious spaces were illuminated with deep midnight blues and sensuous ruby red glowing lights. Deeper primeval spaces were lit with mysterious greens, to light her way through the depth of the Rock to the sea each day.

Marius completed this work, and then boarded his yacht, sailing away, exhausted, but more than usually excited and satisfied. He had the feeling an artist has when he believes he has broken through to something new and wonderful. He still didn't realize he had created the palace and everything in it, out of Light! He had found for himself the secret of Light construction and didn't even know it! I hoped this would be the end of his search for the genius.

Chapter 5

The Palace

Undi slept for years, possibly over two hundred. One of the water spirits, who took a special interest because they still thought of Undi as one of them, always played around the base of The Rock. She looked fresh and youthful, even though she was hundreds of years old. She told the newest generation of periwinkles that there had been a big change in the Rock since Undi first fell asleep. The Rock, she told them, had grown larger—so large that it looked now like a small island. Furthermore, she said, about a hundred years ago, a faint glow had appeared on its peak. That glow had increased and grown, and now it looked like a palace made of Light. The periwinkles couldn't see that far, but they took her word for it.

"Will she live there when she wakes?"

"I imagine she will. Someone must have created it for her. She's not quite like the rest of us Undis, you know. She's more like a human woman. She looks like one. And her dreams have changed; she has begun to have human dreams," the water spirit said.

"How can you tell?" asked a young fish who had heard tell of the sleeping beauty on the Rock, which was what they in the sea now called her.

"I hear them, and I see them taking shape. But I imagine she's still a spirit. There are spirits living on dry land, you know, who have the same appearance that she has. They learn how to behave and take care not to be caught. It's possible she will become one of those."

"Why? What for?"

"Who know why we spirits do what we do. We just do whatever seems right at the moment."

"You're talking nonsense," muttered an ancient mussel who had attached himself to the Rock at the water's edge—not even realizing the danger he was in should the Rock ever disappear and become a myth once again. "A spirit is an invisible being—at most, a fragment of spray like yourself, who can't fool anyone. And a woman is a woman, and a fish is a fish, and I'm a mussel; I'll never be anything else, and neither will you. I'm a realist."

"Not so," squeaked a tiny speck of plankton. "We may all be made of the same substance, but we are capable of becoming anything! And we're not always what we appear to be. In fact, we are moments—yes, Moments!—moments of energy. We take form for a moment, enter the scene, play our part, and indulge in our fantasies; and then we change into something else. I honestly believe that we are all part of a being who is all of Time—or beyond Time—and is greater than we can possibly comprehend, and that includes you, Mussel!"

This sudden and energetic statement from one of the least of all sea creatures created a ripple of excitement, for they were the first words ever to have been uttered by a plankton so far as any of them knew. And they were the last, too, for he was on the tail end of a swarm of tiny, wriggling plankton who were already being sucked into the mouth of a young whale. This young whale had been waiting around the Rock to catch a glimpse of the Undi when she awoke. Word had gotten about that she was soon to do so.

So, when Undi did wake shortly afterwards, she did so to quite a large audience. After stretching her limbs and acknowledging all of the sea creatures with a wave of her hand, she began to climb, to the accompaniment of the clamor of the seagulls, the swishing sounds of fish, the clinking of the periwinkles, and the mysterious high-pitched song of the whales.

Seagull, or one of her descendants who looked exactly like her, flew ahead and reached the palace before Undi did. Perched on one of the balustrades made of light so intense that it looked and felt solid—like solid pink marble—she waited until Undi's blond head appeared; Undi had begun climbing the steps from the rose garden to the terrace that ran along one side of the palace. When I discovered that this palace was made of light, I naturally assumed that Marius had created it for her. The seagull seemed to think the balustrade on which she waited was perfectly safe to perch on.

When Undi appeared, the seagull flew to meet her. Together, they entered a long gallery where the light was softer and began looking into rooms, which were all furnished with Light-made tables, chairs, chaise lounges, beds, great jars, flower pots, and little writing desks. I knew it was Marius who had made all these things for Undi's entertainment, and also her education, for each room represented some period of the past. It was as if he were saying, "Look, while you dallied in the sea, people of Old Earth have been creating all these beautiful vases, these sculptured forms, these paintings, and this furniture, which they needed for their homes. See these rugs from Persia, these golden cane chairs from Egypt, and this fragile dressing table from the Queen of Mesopotamia."

The objects faded—came and went. Undi and her companion, Seagull, never knew what they would find when they opened a door.

There were parts of the palace that were composed of what one might call dark light—deep colored light, glowing like rubies and black opals and luminous blue stones, all of which appeared to be part of the Rock itself. There were unexpected corridors and staircases and cell-like chambers where Seagull did not dare to go, so Undi went fearlessly alone. While she was gone, Seagull sat outside in the sunlit terrace and waited. It was odd to speak of sunlight lighting matter up and casting shadows on a terrace made of light itself, but that is how it was. The whole palace was radiant beyond description. And illogical—the whole thing was illogical, and nothing behaved according to the rules.

When she was satisfied that Undi intended to make her home here and was content to wander through the rooms or sit on one of the terraces looking at the sea and sky or try on the dresses made of strange, silky fabric—silken Light—Seagull flew down to let the sea creatures know what was happening on the Rock's high peak.

"She's behaving like a princess, and you—all you water spirits, you simple Undis—should take the forms of ladies' maids and attendants and carry out her wishes. You seabirds and albatrosses should fly above the palace and entertain her with your acrobatics. And remember, all you creatures of the deep, this is a magic island. It is still the Rock, and no one but us with our true understanding of such things, can ever find the way to these uncharted waters."

"Not even Marius, the fisherman who used to search for her?"

Seagull wasn't sure of that. Marius had become a legend to all these sea-folk. Although over three hundred years had passed since Undi was first brought to the rock, Marius never seemed to them to grow older. He had been seen from time to time, and stories about him and about Undi abounded. It was clear that he was no ordinary man, so Seagull could not say with certainty that he would never find his way to the Rock. Perhaps he would never wish to do so. He may have finally forgotten about Undi.

But I didn't believe that. I thought it more likely that Marius had become more sophisticated and satisfied with his work, but I knew from what he had said when I had last heard him speaking about Undi that he cared very much for her. Besides, he probably knew that she was happy and safe, in a dreamy sort of way, living in the palace, so he was not too concerned about her.

Time passed. More Old Earth years flashed by. Even though we had adjusted to those racing years and were capable of acting towards Old Earth people as if a day were a day and not a flash of light and a night were a night and not a flash of darkness (sometimes with the flash of a moon's light), it sometimes happened that we looked around, and while we did so, several hundred years passed. We had to be constantly aware.

But Undi was fortunate; for her, in the sea, time didn't exist. And so the years passed, and she didn't care one way or the other. I often visited the Rock to see her, but, of course, she didn't see me.

One morning, she sat on the terrace and, looking up, she saw Seagull approaching with a small object dangling from her beak. When she was just above Undi's head, Seagull dropped the object into her lap. It was a fragile basket containing a needle, some thread, a small pair of embroidery scissors, and a scrap of silken fabric.

"What's this?" Undi asked Seagull, who had perched herself on the balustrade.

"A gift from a friend. Don't you like it?"

Undi fingered the scrap of silk. "What friend? What a strange thing to send me. Who is this friend?"

"A friend named Marius." Seagull was bursting with the news, but she had promised not to say too much.

She had spotted a pleasure craft one day not far from the Bay of Antibes, and flying down to perch on one of the railings, she suddenly became convinced that the man at the helm was the legendary Marius. She didn't even have to ask; she just knew it.

"Marius," she said as he walked to the railing and stood near her, "after all this time, you have come back! Where have you been for so long?"

She saw he was smiling at her, so she added, "Have you come back to search for Undi after all this time?"

He gave one of his typical laughs, throwing his head back then down again and looking very pleased with everything.

"What time? What is a few hundred years? It was my bedtime. I've been asleep on a wonderful, high, snow-covered mountain in the north of Scotland, where I'm known, when awake, as an irritable recluse who shuts himself in a dark room for months at a time."

That was true. Marius had, at this time, a sort of fortress castle in Scotland. The Time Travelers all, except for me, had to take themselves off to some inaccessible spot for a long sleep every five hundred years or so. They missed a lot doing that, but it was necessary. So that's where Marius had been. But he was teasing Seagull, and she couldn't tell, from the tone of his voice, whether he was telling the truth or not. Anyway, she'd never heard of Scotland, and it didn't matter. What interested her was the legend.

"Is it true that you once took the mermaid's tail—Undi's tail? Have you come to return it?"

This made Marius laugh even more. But then he became serious when he remembered how offended Undi had been.

"Undi's tail? Yes, perhaps I have." Then he had some questions of his own. "Is she happy on the Rock? Has she grown up at all? Is she beautiful, and has she explored all the rooms of the palace?"

Seagull told him the latest news of Undi, which didn't amount to very much because, a lot of the time, she just sat and dreamed.

"Sometimes she goes into a deep sleep and doesn't wake for two or three hundred years. And then, when she wakes, she dresses herself in some lovely dress made of Light fabric and sits on the terrace and looks at sunsets. She says they flash by, but I think she's mistaking them for some gorgeous pink parakeets who live on the Rock."

"Is that all she does? I must give her something to do. Give her this. She's forgotten me, but it doesn't matter. She'll remember everything one day, so I'm not concerned about that. Just say that this comes from a friend. Please don't try to jog her memory. It may harm her."

I felt a rush of warmth for Marius. He was, as always, considerate. And it was true, as I said before, that Fish-Women had to give up their memories while in the sea. Perhaps that is why she believed she was, indeed, a spirit. But that wasn't so strange, for we Heliotropians were spirits, in a way. In most respects, we were the same as you Old Earth people, but our minds were simple. We thought only when we had to. Yet we were capable of deeds you consider possible only in dreams and fantasies. Something must have happened to give us this power—to change us after the second Ice Age, when the sun grew pale and we became the people of the Light.

Well, with a few more words about his gift and what should be done with it, Marius placed it in the seagull's beak, and she flew off with it.

"Marius," Undi was saying thoughtfully. "Who is Marius?"

Seagull wouldn't say any more about him; she'd promised not to, and she wanted to keep her word.

"He's just a friend who thought you might like to do some needlework. Every time you make a stitch, he said, you will come closer to understanding the human heart. Isn't that a nice idea? If you want to be taken for a woman, you must understand the human heart." (We had reached a period in Old Earth's history when ladies made something called "samplers." Needlework was considered a ladylike occupation.)

"Who is this person? I don't know him."

Yet Undi was pleased with the pretty scrap of silk. It was the first thing she had held in her hands since coming to live in the palace that was solid, not made of Light. It was a novelty. She threaded the needle and made her first stitch.

Seagull couldn't help giving her a hint. "Perhaps he is the one who created your palace. He makes pictures with Light. He's been making pictures like that for hundreds of years, ever since . . ."

She wanted to say, *ever since you left him to return to the sea and he ran along the coast looking for you with a torch in his hand.* But she remembered her promise, so she merely said, "Ever since he had a job in a fair, making pictures in a dark tent with a torch in his hand."

It was true. Marius had once had a job like that, but it had been a caprice on his part. Or, perhaps, he had been experimenting with the torch. Whatever it was, he left the fair because those people of the Middle Ages began to suspect him of witchcraft, especially when he moved the torch about very quickly and left an image in the darkness. He had no need of the job, for he was a rich man; so he slipped away like a will-o'-the-wisp before any trouble started, just as Eva had flown away from people who loved her or else suspected her of witchcraft.

"Perhaps it was he who created the palace for you . . ." Seagull watched Undi, looking for some reaction. "He may have wanted you to be safe, in the sea."

Undi replied, "No one created the palace. So far as I know it's always been here. Although," she paused thoughtfully, "they do say I went to sleep, and when I woke, it was here." She had no recollection now of Marius or anything else in her past.

She went on stitching. "Why doesn't this Marius show himself?"

"Ah," Seagull replied, "but he will. He told me to tell you that if you do what he suggests, you will see him."

"What does he suggest? Why is he so mysterious?"

"He said if you go into the darkest room in the palace and sit there, you will see him making images in the dark. He'll make some of his images with Light for you to look at."

"What! One of those rooms deep down near the dark tunnels?"

"No. He said the room is up here. He said you would find it."

Undi thought about it and then said, "Ah, yes, there is such a room—a strange, dark room on this level. That must be the one. How extraordinary!"

It was indeed extraordinary. Halfway along one of the brightest corridors was a doorway made of mist, and beyond this oval-shaped door of mist was a pitch-black room.

"And this Marius says I will see him if I go there and wait? I want to see him right now! Today! All I ever see are you and the handmaidens."

"Don't forget your friends, Eva and Pavarti. You see them from time to time."

Undi looked blankly at her. She had forgotten about Eva and Pavarti coming to visit her. They had been coming more often of late, afraid that Undi might lose touch with reality. But Eva, too, in a way, had lost touch with reality, so I wondered what influence Eva could exert over Undi. They were trying to interest her in going to Paris.

I was curious to know whether Undi had suddenly decided to go to Paris, for as I watched this story unfold, it seemed to me that she was likely to go on living in the palace forever. The sea creatures thought so too. But I heard Seagull say that Undi was going to Paris, as if she knew all about that wonderful city. Apparently, Seagull expected her to leave them quite soon. But, as I said, Seagull was a gossip. The other Undis didn't think so; they usually believed what she said.

"You see, it's as our grandparents and their grandparents said," one of the other Undis told a periwinkle. "They said she would live in the palace forever, and that is what she's doing. Seagull says she has long, golden hair and she eats from gold and silver plates."

"And crystal dishes," another Undi added.

The periwinkle asked, "Real gold and silver, the plates?"

Seagull looked amused. "Well, they're made of Light, like everything else in the palace. But that only makes them brighter. What do you know of gold and silver, anyway?"

"Nothing, except what you've told us," a humble sea snail replied.

"I think she must be made of Light too," a shrimp piped up. "I've heard she's radiant and has the clearest blue eyes ever seen. But they change color; sometimes they're blue and sometimes gray green, and they have dark lashes all around them."

"She does, indeed, sound like a princess," sighed a young dolphin.

"Where does she sleep?" inquired a gentle, little crab.

"Oh, that you should ask! She sleeps in a chamber with walls like watered silk. And in the morning after her long, long sleep, she wakes up and looks at the ceiling, which is like crystal with the sun shining through it."

"Does she ever sing?" asked a baby octopus.

"Sing! Does she sing? Have you ever heard a nightingale? Of course you haven't. But that is what she sings like."

They never grew tired of talking about her. Seagull always had interesting things to tell.

"Do you know what she does nowadays? She goes into a pitch-dark room and looks at images made of Light. It's Marius, the man who used to search for her. He makes images with his magic torch, images that tell her all about the world up there—you know, on land."

"Why does he do that? Does he want her to leave the palace and live on land?" a little shrimp asked.

"I imagine so. He's her friend. He promised her mother and father he would look after her—her mother and father in Heliotrope."

"Where is that?"

"Far away. It's in the future. It's here, but far away in time. You don't understand that, do you? But it's true. Marius himself told me."

The sea creatures gazed wonderingly at her. She was right. It was too much for them to comprehend.

Chapter 6

The Tea Party

One day, several years later, Seagull flew down to the water's edge and called out, "Look! I believe Undi is going to have visitors again." The gull pointed with her beak. "Do you see them? Those two specks gliding through the sky?"

The octopus said, "What makes you think they're visitors? They could be anything."

"Well, they're not birds. They must be visitors coming to the tea party."

"Perhaps they're the two angels," a female dolphin suggested. She was referring to two mysterious beings who often flew overhead and always wore flowing, magic cloaks. The beings just flew above the Rock from time to time—just cruising there in the sky without seeming to have any purpose. All the creatures who had necks to crane looked up at them.

Up on the terrace, looking out as she often did at the sky, Undi saw the two forms and, like the dolphin, she wondered whether they were the two beings who trod the pathways of the sky wearing their long, fluttering cloaks. The beings never landed on her lawn or on the terrace, so now her interest quickened when she realized the two flying figures were heading for the Rock. One of them wore a blue cloak but not like the angels' cloaks. It billowed out like an oval-shaped sail filled with wind. The other one had on a gold shawl that fluttered out from her body like a long, wide streamer, so Undi knew they were not the two angels. As the pair drew closer, Undi saw Seagull flying out to meet them. Leaning out from the balustrade, she waved her own diaphanous scarf.

A faint recollection came to Undi now, of invitations to a tea party she had transmitted to two friends across the ocean.

"In a minute they'll be over the Rose Garden, and I may recognize them." She waited calmly.

They drifted on down, and soon they passed the roses and glided over the fountain. An inkling of their identities was already coming to her, and by the time they landed on the terrace beside her, she knew who they were. It was not that she remembered anything. She just knew them.

I knew them too. They were no strangers to me. The gentle Eva with her child, both of them enfolded in the blue cloak like a mother and child from one of the paintings of the great Leonardo da Vinci, was my own wife. But in the world of so-called reality, she was someone else's wife, and the child in her arms was not mine. And I was not at all surprised to see her with the gorgeous Pavarti, who now looked and behaved like the exotic Hindu goddess of India.

True, Pavarti had changed somewhat, but the change was mostly in her costume and the way she did her hair and the jewels she wore. She had always had golden coffee-colored skin, but now she wore her hair drawn back into a deep braid, with tendrils on either side of her round, smooth cheeks, and she wore heavy ruby pendants hanging from her ears. Her eyebrows, too, looked different. Now they were shaped like long, slender raven's wings, full above the inner corners of her almond-shaped eyes and tapering out on her temples almost to the hairline. Her eyes were edged with the dark eye shadow called kohl, and it made them look enormous; the whites very white and the iris like dark, glowing jewels.

Eva was no less a beauty in her quiet, modest way. Somehow she looked idealized, not quite real, or not quite the simple everyday person I had married on the day we entered the Time Tunnel. However, there was no doubt about who they were, and after the first shock of seeing them land on the terrace, I was not surprised. What did surprise me was the child.

As soon as they landed, Undi laughed with joy and said, "Eva! And Pavarti! My dearest, darling ones. How happy I am to see you. And you have brought your baby, Eva! What is his name?"

Eva drew back the blue cloak to reveal the face of her baby. He looked as if he had been born a mere two days ago.

"Roland," she said proudly. As she said that, the marvelous grace and charm and tenderness a woman is capable of shone out of her. Her whole being at that moment expressed the true selflessness of motherhood.

Then I saw that she too, in a way, had lost her memory. It was not so much a loss of memory as a lack of awareness of who and what she was and where she had come from. In a flash, not uncommon in my experience of story-unfolding, I saw her as she was in her own home in Paris, with all the strain of her daily life. More than that, I was aware of the change in myself as, for the first time, I found myself possessed of a dual awareness—of the female as well as the male. One might say I entered into her and became one with her and understood the reasons for what I considered her unreasonable behavior. What I saw was that Eva had willingly accepted the fears and illusionary thinking—the human sickness we had been warned against before embarking upon our time travels—because, from the moment we had entered into Old Earth human society, Eva had wanted to be like other people. Most of all, she had wanted to be a mother and to be what is considered an average person. She did not want to be—at least while we were living in Old Earth time—a Heliotropian with the powers we possessed.

Yet that had not stopped her from transporting herself through space in Pavarti's company, dressed in the blue robe of the idealized mother in a Leonardo da Vinci painting. *So*, I said to myself, *there is conflict in Eva and something is wrong.* Even the child in her arms was an illusion—a sort of phantom. The real child, Roland, was no longer a babe in arms but a young man of nineteen attending an art school in Paris who had reached an age where he was likely to slip from his mother's grasp.

Undi was sitting at a small, white tea table pouring tea like an English hostess. She was behaving elegantly. I wondered whether she had learned about English tea parties from Marius's images. I think he thought it was time for her to leave the sea and learn something about the world—English tea parties? Was this his idea of what went on out there in the world? I wondered. Pavarti, too, was behaving like an Indian guest at an English tea party. Even Eva, in spite of her Madonna-like appearance, looked as if this were her usual occupation, except that most of her attention was given to the bundle in her arms.

Undi offered cakes to go with the tea. "Please take one. They're quite fresh—straight from the kitchen."

"Oh, Undi! I know your kitchen. You simply give an order to some Botticelli angels," Pavarti said, "and these delicious cakes appear."

"Actually, my handmaidens . . ."

Pavarti chose the Dream Cake, although it was the one Undi had meant for Eva, and after the first taste of it, she closed her eyes rapturously and sighed. Her expression of bliss made me remember what it was like to eat something truly delicious.

Undi smiled with gratification. "Eva?" She offered her the plate. "Come, leave your baby for a moment and have one of these. And drink your tea."

Pavarti took the cake that had been meant for Eva, so Eva took the one that Pavarti should have had.

Eva did as she was told and took the cake that had been intended for Pavarti. Not that it mattered, but Undi had her ideas that such and such a cake should be eaten by such and such a person. Eva's face was almost comical. She too sighed and fluttered her eyelids, and when she murmured, "Marvelous!" I said to myself, *Only women could behave like this over cakes.*

Undi chose one for herself. It was called Apricot Rapture and, as far as I could make out, it was little more than a mound of apricot and almond flavored cream on a base of soft sponge cake. The effect on Undi was even more pronounced. Her eyes closed and her lips parted (after she had swallowed) and her breast rose and fell beneath the silky light fabric of her bodice which was, I must admit, a most adorable shade of green.

"Oh," she sighed, opening her eyes and looking at her friends. "I'm in pain! No, not bad pain, but a sweet, longing sort of pain. I'm longing for something. I thought it was the cake, but it's something else. It's as if I'm suddenly full of rapture and expectancy, as though something is going to happen." She took another spoonful of cake.

"What you long for is the rapture of love," Pavarti told her. "Isn't that so, Eva?"

Eva stopped in the act of swallowing and then opened her mouth and closed it. She murmured doubtfully, "I don't quite know what you mean. Undi's still a virgin; how can she know?"

"That's just it. She doesn't. She's been In-sea for such a long time, and she's beginning to long for the love and the attention of a man without knowing it! It's perfectly natural, if that's the way she is going to go."

Undi, of course, was terribly intrigued by what they were saying about her. A man! In Heliotrope, a Fish-Woman, unlike a Bird-Woman, did not necessarily build her life upon domesticity and the daily love of one man. She would certainly need love, but only from time to time. She was a seeker, a dancer, or even a creative artist of some sort and was capable of spending long periods alone in contemplative reverie. Or she could spend hours in a form of meditation, looking at such things as flowers or leaves or a grain of sand, gazing at the sea from a high cliff.

In the sea, Undi had learned about the primitive life forms and about evolution, and she delighted in these studies. But at the core of her being, there was the image of a man, and that man was lover, husband, child, and very often, an image rather than a reality. Undi was capable of love and tenderness, but so far, she had not even dreamed of love.

Moments later, looking at Eva doting over the child, Undi was disturbed by the sight. She saw the baby merely as a bundle of squirming, pink flesh with fierce little fists attacking his mother's face. She marveled that, to Eva, he was the most wonderful, all-absorbing thing in the world. Her whole attitude suggested adoration.

"Eva," she said, "you haven't told me how you came by this baby. Who is the father and what is his name?"

Eva gazed blankly at her. She had forgotten the father! She tried to recall him, and in her confusion, she replied, "Oh, there isn't a father yet. The baby's only just been born."

Undi cast a quick glance toward Pavarti—a look of concern—and murmured, "I understand, Eva. At the moment, you can think of nothing but the baby."

Eva looked relieved. "Yes, I'm proud of him. He's only two days old. Do you think he's too big for his age?"

"Oh no, just perfect," lied Undi. She had no idea how big a two-day-old baby should be. But it hardly mattered, for suddenly, she saw him in his own time and space, and he looked quite different because he was not a baby at all but a young man, and this was the truth of the matter. She didn't want to upset Eva now by pointing this out to her. She would find out for herself soon enough.

My poor Eva! I was grateful to Undi for her tact. There was no point at all in making Eva unhappy. She had come to the palace to escape from that. Seagull, who was poking about near the archway that led to the terrace, understood what was going on. She could see into Eva's mind, and she could tell that Eva was in distress and that this visit to Undi's palace was a respite from some pain or emotional disorder she suffered in her life.

The baby was awake now, and his head wobbled from side to side. Undi relinquished the vision of him as a young man and again took him at face value. Still repelled, she watched a pink tongue appear, dripping saliva. Then she heard a burp and saw an astonished expression appear momentarily in his eyes. Eva thought this was marvelous, but Undi didn't like it at all; nor did she like the odor of him.

Then, surprisingly, she became aware of a feeling of compassion for the helpless little creature. She could feel tenderness rising in her breast. Her hand went up and she felt the rise and fall of her deepening breath. She felt it in her lips and her eyes and her whole face, and she became aware that she wanted to hold and kiss the little creature. Her face felt like a flower on a long stem leaning forward to shake life-giving dew on the face of the child.

Pavarti was watching and smiling. "Yes, you saw clearly. He lives in Paris, and is really about your age. To Eva, he is an illusion. The tenderness you just felt is part of the rapture of love. You should go to Paris, Undi. That is where you'll find him. You ought to fall in love with Roland." She turned to Eva. "Don't you think so, Eva? Your son would be just about her age."

Eva didn't seem to know what Pavarti was talking about.

They had finished their tea and were sitting quietly listening to the sound of the waves beating against the rocks below. They stayed like that for some time, until Pavarti rose from the couch and said she was going. "I can't bear to be parted from Shiva for very long." She sometimes referred to Tiger Hound as Shiva.

"Eva will stay a little longer with me," Undi said. "Won't you, Eva?"

They all paused again to enjoy the essence of something precious they'd been conscious of all morning. It was hard to define, but it was there.

"I'm sorry to leave. It's not often we are together like this. I wish Isis were here too." Pavarti's smile faded as she thought of Isis and her long search throughout the ages for Osiris. But the charm of her surroundings captivated her again, and she smiled with pleasure. They were in a wide, spacious chamber opening onto the marble Light terrace with its balustrade where Seagull usually perched. The long, low couch she'd been reclining on was a delicate beige color, and above it on the wall was an embroidered wall hanging, depicting pale green seaweed and apricot—and blue-striped fish. There was also the tea table and chairs that looked as if they'd come from a pharaoh's palace. That was all the furniture the room had in it, but the floor was tiled with beige and silver tiles studded with turquoise gems. And near the arched windows, which were wide enough to pass through onto the terrace, there were several Persian blue jars with large, exotic plants growing in them. The leaves of these plants had irregularly shaped holes, and the sunlight passing through them created enchanting patterns on the wall.

"Your palace is a radiant jewel, Undi, and so are you. You're very beautiful now. It seems only a short time ago that you were begging to be allowed to come with us. Isn't it time for you to leave all this and start your life as a woman?"

Undi looked confused.

Eva gazed blankly at Pavarti for a moment, but after a pause she said, "Yes, Undi, you should join us in the real world."

She looked as if her own words had surprised her. They surprised me, for none of us were living in the so-called real world. Undi, who was supposed to be an In-Sea student, was living like a fairy princess (and I blamed Marius for that). Pavarti and Tiger Hound were living in Kailasa—home of the Hindu gods—and visiting Paris now and then in the guise of a rich, young Hindu couple. And Osiris, who had devoted himself to great causes throughout the ages, was now living as a superhero with a group of young people ready to do his bidding, while Isis was the eternal tragic figure searching through the years for her lost love. Marius himself had become a great creative artist and a builder, but I considered that, in creating a magical life for Undi, he was not doing her such a great favor.

But then I stopped and thought, *How can we behave like normal Old Earth people (if such a thing as "normal" exists)? We don't really belong here, and anyway, we have been living through the centuries since the Stone Age, and no Old Earth person has ever done that. So how can we call our life here a "normal" life?*

Undi gave a strange little laugh. "Isn't this a real world?" She looked around the room and then at the sparkling sea. Yet she considered their suggestions. "All right, I'll come. But only when I say so. I want it to be the right time, moment, or day—or whenever it strikes me."

Pavarti left them, and Undi turned to Eva and asked her whether she'd like to use the bathroom. "For the baby, I mean. Perhaps you need to attend to him in some way. Come along. I have everything in there. It's a wonderful room."

As they walked out of the morning room, I saw Undi look back at another woman who'd suddenly turned up and was sitting in one of the chairs. At first I didn't know who it was, but when she turned her head,

I saw the noble profile of Isis. I also saw that she was in great disorder, emotionally as well as physically, and I couldn't help comparing her distraught appearance with the cool grace of her surroundings. Her black hair was uncombed and unwashed and her face, in spite of its fine bone structure, which never changed, was drawn and haggard. It was not the first time I'd seen her in this condition, so I wasn't surprised. Undi knew who she was, but she must have decided to let her rest in the pleasant, airy space while she and Eva went on to the extraordinary place Undi called her bathroom.

On the way, they passed through several galleries and open terraces. They could see the sky and the sea and the tips of the pines that grew further down the mountainside and also the elegantly cultivated rose garden.

"Undi, I feel happy here." Eva seemed surprised by her own lightness of heart. Poor girl, she'd been robbed of all her children. Time had taken them from her. It was no wonder she clung to her phantom child.

"Do you know, there is a lake on the far side of the island," Undi told her, forgetting that Eva had been here many times before. "It has lotus flowers growing in it. Imagine that! I'd never even heard of such a flower until this Marius showed them to me in the dark room. He makes pictures with Light, you know." She danced along the colonnaded walk, feeling light and precious. "Lotus. That's what they're called." She stopped suddenly and looked out at the sky. "Look, Eva. Come here."

They stood still, looking at a flock of pink parakeets. The blue sky was streaked with them, flying past. But then the two girls had to avert their eyes. There was a round ball of fire in the sky—the hot Mediterranean sun. I could hear them thinking, or saying to themselves, "But it's too red. The sun should be a pale silvery color, and the sky should be pale heliotrope." They were remembering the sky above our own city in our own time.

Then the memory passed as they turned into a cooler, shaded corridor.

Chapter 7

The Bathroom

The palace itself was timeless. The Rock rose from unchartered waters, and no one knew where it was. I wondered whether Marius had indeed created it with Light, or whether Undi herself had sung it into existence. Some of our women are very strong singers. They can sing something into existence that lasts for a long time. This made me think of the Tunnel. We had sung it into existence, expecting to need it for only a short time, but as I suddenly realized how long we'd been here and how many centuries had passed, I almost lost consciousness. It happened sometimes.

When I recovered, Undi and Eva were already in the bathroom and Eva was enjoying herself immensely.

"Undi, the floor!" she was exclaiming. "It feels like layers of the finest silk. It's heavenly to walk on. It's like the softest marble, yet it's not marble."

"I told you you'd like it." Undi looked pleased.

"The walls! What makes that wonderful light? It's blue—no, it's not. It's green. And it's silver. Do the walls themselves make it? It's coming from the stone, isn't it?"

True, the walls glowed with this mysterious moving Light.

"It's underwater Light. Look, the ceiling is the same."

Eva looked up and was fascinated. Reflections and shadows and subtly glowing colors moved slowly across the surface of the ceiling.

"Oh, Undi. It's like a grotto. It is a grotto, isn't it? I saw one once . . . It's deep, isn't it? It's so mysterious. I can hear something. What is that sound? That sound is going right into me, Undi. It's filling me up."

Undi could hear faraway sounds, too, but not the plaintive music that Eva heard. Undi looked as if she heard sounds of her own. Water was lapping somewhere against rock.

On the far side of this wide chamber, or this grotto, was an opening in the wall. Water, like water from an underground spring, flowed from it and made a melodious sound as it splashed into a giant conch shell on the floor. Coming from the natural opening in the rock wall like that, it reminded me of the sparkling water that gushes forth from fissures in rocks to cool the cucumbers and the bottles of Retsina and the feet of travelers in the mountains of Greece. As it flowed over on one side of the huge shell, it continued on along a narrow channel that got lost among some shadows. It had a scent of pines, and as it splashed and flowed, it carried with it faint sounds, mingled with silence, which are so often heard in forests or deep woods—sounds like rustling leaves, bird calls, whispers and little cries, and other odd sounds made by scurrying insects and small animals.

Eva stood still, listening to these subtle suggestive signs that life existed somewhere beyond the walls of Undi's bathroom. She was looking at her baby and holding him a little bit away from her so that he, too, would be able to hear them. But there was a faraway expression in her eyes, as though she heard the voices of her other children and as though Roland wasn't enough. Children's voices were stealing through her entire being until she was beside herself with an unbearable nostalgia. From far away, faintly came the sounds of very young ones, laughing and calling from the far side of the woods.

In the center of the room, Undi was sitting on the edge of her own pool. She was listening to sounds of her own. Turning to Eva, she said dreamily, "Yes, you'll hear many voices in here. I hear my own voices. Mine invite me to depths you've never been to, Eva. You're a Bird-person, not a Fish-person like me. But I suppose yours carry you to heights I've never been to, so that makes us even."

Eva went over and looked into the pool. At first glance, it looked like a marble pool with fresh water because of the marble rim around it. But then she saw the color change, and she realized this was seawater. She looked inquiringly at Undi.

"Yes, it *is* the sea. You're right. It's very deep. It goes right down through the heart of the Rock to the ocean. I don't know how deep it is, although I go there from time to time." She let her hand play about in the water. "Don't you think it's remarkable, Eva? I mean all this. I didn't know when I was fourteen that In-sea would be like this. I never heard of anyone having a palace and a Rock and a bathroom like a wonderful grotto. It's so . . . luxurious."

"It is, indeed. And it combines a sort of civilized elegance with . . . what should I say?"

"I think of it as a civilized elegance combined with a primeval mystery. I'm glad it affects you like that too. When I come in here, I become aware of feelings and longings I've hardly realized I have in me, and sometimes I feel so . . . fine. I hardly know what to do. Sometimes it seems that I'm afraid to wait and see what will happen. Eva, I see myself hovering on the edge of something. But I always stop it from happening. I dive in and go back to the sea."

Eva was startled by this confession. But then she grew thoughtful and looked about her. "Undi, is there some other space here?"

"Another space?"

"Or another time? I feel as though I could enter into another space, with another kind of time . . ."

Undi looked as if she was waiting for Eva to say more about this, so Eva went on. "I'm all right, but I feel strange. I think I'm hovering on the edge of something myself. It's also a very nostalgic sensation. I can hardly bear it, but it's wonderful."

Undi looked delighted. "I told you. It's a wonderful bathroom. Sometimes I feel almost displaced—removed, but in a lovely, dreamy way. I wish sometimes that I could resist diving into the pool because it washes away all those unrealized sensations."

Eva stepped closer to the pool and Undi said quickly, "No, you mustn't dive in, Eva. It might carry you away to deep water, and you might drown. You should use the water that flows from the spring. That's your bath."

"I may not even bathe," Eva replied, "but I will wash the baby. Is that all right?"

"Of course. Over there you'll find towels dried on the branches that grow on the pine tree on the side of the Rock; you'll find everything you need. Put the baby down on that couch. It's softer than it looks because, you know, everything here is made of Light. So don't worry about it being hard for him." She gestured toward a shelf on the wall.

"And over there you'll find scented soaps and lotions and powders. And, oh look, there's a sandalwood fan. Fan yourself with it. You'll love it. It perfumes the air."

Everything around them radiated with a silvery light that kept on changing to a blue-green light and back again. Yes, it *was* as though the light came from the walls themselves. I would have felt out of place had I had my own male body because it was as if this room and all that was rising in it was female and feminine and mysterious. I wondered what Undi was up to, bringing Eva into such a room—this chamber where uneasy longings were evoked.

Eva was, or she had been, a simple soul, like all Bird-Women, a domestic soul. Circumstances had inflicted pain on her that she would never have had to bear in her own right time. I wondered whether this had created a greater depth of feeling in her. Not that she was without feelings of love and tenderness—she was capable of strong emotions, but at home, they were all understandable emotions. Here there were strange, exotic things going on. Had some mutation taken place over the years spent here in Old Earth time? I felt uneasy. What if I should recover my physical self and claim Eva as my wife and we should take up where we left off? What would I find?

Undi's head was full of fantasies that even she would not have entertained under normal conditions in our own time. True, Fish-Women were not like Bird-Women. They loved but spent much of their lives in a blissful state of contemplation of the Light, trying to understand its mystery. They never arrive at a full realization of Light because they also desire the love of a man. But they are predictable. We know exactly how they will behave. Here, I found some new element in Undi, and I didn't believe I knew at all what her life would be here or how she would behave. I worried about what her influence on Eva would be, and since I could do nothing about it, I felt frustrated and angry, as any husband might when he sees his wife stray into realms he cannot enter.

This wasn't a permanent state; I merely felt like that while I was in Undi's bathroom observing Eva's behavior. I reminded myself again that all I could do was observe and, at most, be curious about what would happen. There was nothing else I could do. I just had to put aside my disquiet, but it was not an easy thing for me to do.

After putting her baby down on the soft couch, Eva straightened up to speak to Undi only to find that she'd slipped away. Eva guessed what had happened when she saw the widening circle on the surface of the water in the pool. So she turned her attention again to the child. He was lying on his back, behaving as any baby would, looking up at the ceiling and gurgling with pleasure as the light and the shadows changed from silver to a mysterious green and the shadows moved slowly about. To Eva, of course, he was a baby. She could touch him and hear him and look into his eyes. She imagined him storing up these impressions and this experience for the enrichment of his life. Tenderly, she washed him and changed his diaper and settled him down to sleep.

When he was asleep, Eva looked at her own image in the mirror. She examined it carefully and curiously, as though she didn't quite believe it was her own. It began to recede and grow smaller and, turning, it moved into shadows. At the same time, the tinkling voices of the children grew louder, although still far away. She saw her image making its way through woods, where the trees were fine and silvery like our trees at home. Eva followed, passing through the walls of the cave. The ground she walked on was soft and mossy and, over her head, leafy branches met to form arches; it was as if she were passing through a dimly lit cathedral with shafts of light streaking down through spaces between the leaves and the branches.

Eva realized now that she was following her own true self. She watched her true self walking slowly and tried to catch up with her, but there was always a distance between them. The image moved slowly and gracefully between the tree trunks, sometimes half hidden and sometimes in full view.

Eva began to feel anxious. She wanted to catch up now that she knew this charming, mysterious creature was herself, but she couldn't bridge the distance between herself and her image. She had the feeling that something was about to happen and she would miss it if she didn't become one with her true self.

"I'm sure something is about to happen," she whispered, not wanting to speak loudly in the silence and the deep shadows of the woods. The children's voices had grown silent, and there was only an occasional rustling sound.

She didn't expect anything to happen outwardly, only between herself and her image. So when something else happened, she wasn't really prepared and received a shock, for it came with great suddenness and from outside herself. There was a brilliant flash of light, which at first she took to be a flame. For a moment, she was terrified. But then she saw that it wasn't a flame and no one was attacking her. It was not even directed at her, but rather, it was as if a shutter had opened to reveal a brilliantly lit space, an open glade flooded with light that was stronger than sunlight, stronger than flame. The shutter stayed open just long enough for her to take in the scene. She had time to see that the glade was alive with children, and her emotions were deeply stirred when she realized that these were all the little ones she had born throughout the centuries. They looked up from their games and gazed at her for a moment and then turned away. But as they turned, they stopped being children as Time took possession of them. They grew old and faded away even as she looked at them.

It was a cruel thing for Eva to have to face, for she had never seen her children become adults. She had always had to leave them. I wanted to comfort her, but there was nothing I could do. The image vanished, and Eva looked about her as if dazed.

Her true image looked around, gazed sadly at her, and then disappeared into the depths of the woods. Eva retreated back through the trees and through the wall of the grotto and back to where she stood looking at herself in the glass. This time she saw Undi standing behind her, wet and dripping with seawater and naked. She looked clear and pure, but there was a faraway light in her eyes that startled Eva.

Neither of them moved. Undi's eyes met Eva's in the glass. "I'm sorry. I disappeared, didn't I? I hope you didn't mind, Eva."

"No, I didn't mind." She hesitated. "I . . . I liked being here with the baby. But something happened. I'm not sure what it was."

"You're not sure?"

"No. Anyway, it was nothing." Eva turned away so that Undi would not see her eyes.

"Something *did* happen. What was it? Tell me."

"I thought I caught a glimpse of my true identity. I was walking much too slowly. The children were growing too fast." Then Eva looked puzzled. "What children? What am I talking about?" She changed the subject. "What did you do? No need to answer. You went down to the sea, didn't you? I'm surprised, though. I thought you had finished your studies, Undi. I thought you lived here doing nothing—a life of ease."

"No, not quite. That's what Seagull thinks, but it's not so. There's so much to learn here. Nothing's as simple and easy as it is at home." She, too, stopped, wondering what she meant by "home." She'd forgotten Heliotrope again. "Do you know what I've been going into today? The question of sacrifice."

"Sacrifice?" Eva looked puzzled. Sacrifice didn't exist in Heliotrope.

"Not only sacrifice," Undi told her, "but compassion. I've also discovered the meaning of the word *compassion*. I thought of it when I saw a certain kind of fish."

These were questions she would never have brought up at home. They were Old Earth considerations. Heliotropians never bothered about such philosophical questions. It was as if they had all been solved long ago and we had, in fact, forgotten about them, except for my father and Leo, Marius's father. But they didn't speak to us about them, so neither did we.

"What certain kind of fish?" Eva asked, looking puzzled.

Undi tried to explain. "There are certain kinds of fish of a species that existed long before humankind appeared on the planet. These fish are exactly the same now as they were then, and they don't know that life on Earth has advanced to this point—where man walks about like the Lord of Earth. So they still go about like the prophets they were millions of years ago. They bear on their faces all the signs of the future, and even though they themselves do not suffer—because as far as they are concerned they know and feel nothing of what is written on their poor faces—they do express all the pain and anxiety and the sorrow and the greed and the violence and the fear that mankind is afflicted with. It is written in their faces. It's odd to see them swimming about as though nothing is wrong."

"It would be odd," Eva replied, looking disgusted. "What do they look like, I mean apart from all that? Are they horrible or repulsive? I don't like the sound of them at all."

"I told you. They have no idea they're prophets. They're innocent, but they're like ugly little children who aren't ugly at all because they're pure. That's what I mean about feeling compassion. I feel great love for them. You should be able to understand this, with your love of children. Have you ever noticed them? I mean the fish."

Eva looked startled. "No, no exactly." Although we Heliotropians never kill and eat living creatures, she found herself thinking of a fish in the kitchen with glassy eyes, waiting to be cooked, and smelling strongly. She knew she didn't like the odor at all, but she also knew that she knew how to cook a fish! She had learned to do that as the Old Earth years had passed.

Undi read her thoughts. "Oh, I don't mean a dead fish! I couldn't bear to eat a dead fish. You don't, do you, Eva? They look even more like prophets when they're dead."

Eva again envisioned fish she had seen with pulled-down mouths and soured and bitter-looking, tragic faces, fish with jutting jaws and sharp teeth and bulging eyes. She envisioned a shark and hated what she told herself was its mean look; she recalled the beady eyes of an octopus, which Undi could have told her was the gentlest of creatures; and she thought of the cunning look of a crab. I wondered what she would think and feel if she were to see all the strange deep-sea monstrosities who slithered and crawled and glided and waited in the mouths of their holes on the ocean floor or around seaweed forests. These creatures would probably seem repulsive to her. But she herself felt compassion for Undi because she thought this was how she saw the human race.

"But, Undi, people aren't all like that." She wondered how she knew. The only people she could remember at the moment were Undi and herself. "Some people have sweet, smiling mouths, and they look delightful and happy."

"That's true. I know that."

I wondered how *she* knew because she, unlike Eva, had never lived among Old Earth people, and she knew almost nothing. There were both talking from an inner source of knowledge they weren't consciously aware of.

"Some of them are happy most of the time," Undi continued, "and beautiful all of the time until they grow old and die. But humankind is not happy. Don't ask me how I know. Or say the Dolphin told me. Or Seagull. She's wise. Oh no, my darling, the world is full of suffering and those fish carried the marks of it long before we humans were even thought of." Undi gazed into the looking glass and examined her own angelic face with its soft, shell-pink mouth and smooth cheeks; her marvelous, changeable eyes, green at the moment and very, very light; and her sweet eyelids. Oh, she was a delicate beauty without a doubt, but I had been an observer on Old Earth throughout the ages, and I had seen beauties like that whose angelic faces had become sad and ravaged because they had dreamed of perfect love and had been destroyed by their own desires and never ever found the love they imagined awaited them in someone's arms.

I wondered whether Undi would expect such a love from Roland when she came Back-from-Sea. I wanted to tell her that such a love was hard to find, and she should not expect it. We had all been contaminated in one way or another. Our old professor at home had warned us against such contamination, had he not, before we entered the tunnel. "Beware of seven deadly sins," was what he'd said. Not that he really understood them. I think he thought they were germs or viruses of some sort.

I was trying not to think of Undi in this way. She was so lovely I didn't like to think of her being destroyed by desire. And she was so sure of herself! That might change too.

"Of course," she was saying, "there are the most gorgeous fish down there. They're breathtaking, Eva. I can't begin to describe them all. And there are the noble dolphins and the great whales. They foretell something, too, of the nobility of the human race. But my heart really goes out to those poor ugly ones—the innocent ones whose faces bear the marks of humanity's pain."

She knows about the suffering of humanity, I thought. *But she doesn't see any danger for herself.*

Eva appeared to be listening, but she gave no indication that she understood or cared about the fish. She was, however, concerned about Undi and wondered why she went on talking about them. "She's been In-Sea too long. I don't talk about birds all the time."

"It's mainly the larger fish. The smaller ones have expressions I haven't fathomed yet. I will, though. I change size and join schools of those small ones, you know. I identify with them. They are all cruel. Even those smaller ones are ruthless. I see them killing or even eating their victims alive. It was horrifying at first to watch the wriggling victim disappearing down the throat of some larger creature. But today, when I saw the smaller fish, I saw *myself* being consumed. I experienced the terror and the horror of having some poison injected into me so that I became paralyzed yet remained conscious while my flesh was devoured. Oh no, I wasn't harmed. I know we can't be harmed. But it almost harmed my mind to even think of such a terrifying thing happening to anyone. But then a strange thing did happen. I saw myself as the sacrificial victim, and it became clear to me that this was a most important realization. As I imagined myself in this moment of terror, I underwent a transformation and experienced bliss. Just before I saw myself being consumed and bringing life to some other creature, I submitted to what I knew to be a law of life, or of nature, and as soon as I had submitted to this law, I knew joy, almost as if I had at last reached the supreme moment in life, which is to give one's life for the good of another. And I saw that there is no escape from nature's law and that sacrifice is really bliss."

Eva was looking at her with a sort of distaste, suspicious of her and what she was saying, and I wasn't surprised. Even Undi didn't understand what she herself was saying.

Can she be a sadist? I asked myself. *She's telling herself that pain will produce bliss.* Then I thought, *Perhaps it does.*

Eva was disturbed because such ideas never entered our heads at home. We had no illusions, and we never deceived ourselves. Our minds did not have to deal with the suppositions Undi put forward.

Even though she has lived in the palace Marius created for her and has not had to deal with the world like the rest of them, she has changed, I said to myself.

Undi was still talking. "That wasn't all. I went on to another state today. I was still aware of what was happening. I must have been, or how could I tell you about it? That was also frightening at first because I became so small and all the life forms around me were so small that, for a while, nothing was recognizable. I mean time, space, and dimensions as we know them didn't exist. When one becomes as small as that, nothing can be measured. Existence was nothing more than a blossoming—a faint movement—and there was no concern for what was and what was not. We just blossomed in and out. Yet we were perfect forms performing a sort of dance. Do you understand what I'm trying to tell you, Eva?

That wasn't all. Undi had even more to say, "I entered into yet another state where nothing was being absorbed by anything else— no dance, no movement, nothing." She thought about that. "No, it's not quite true. There was silence. I could hardly recognize it because, how could I, when I had nothing to hear with? Yet I knew it was an astonishing silence and it existed in an astonishing stillness. Then, Eva, I almost ceased to exist because it wasn't possible to be as still as that with no change at all taking place . . . ." Then Undi looked at Eva with the strangest expression I have ever seen, and her eyes were almost as transparent as water—the palest green eyes I have ever seen. And she whispered in a way I have never heard anyone whisper before, "And it was the beginning and the end, and it was the dream . . . . and at the end of the dream . . ."

"Undi, please, don't. You don't know what you're saying. I don't want to hear. Look, dearest," she held out her child, anxious to have Undi return to what she considered her normal behavior, "here is my child. Hold him. He's clean and sweet now. I washed and powdered him. You can hold him for a while."

Undi looked at the bundle Eva was offering her. She suddenly became her gracious, charming self, and her eyes darkened until they were like deep blue-green sea. "Oh, Eva, what a precious gift. I will. I want to hold him. But not now. He's not old enough. I'll embrace him when he appears to me in his true shape and in his right time. Then he'll be tall enough to hold me, too, and we can love each other as Isis and Osiris do."

Eva looked puzzled. "But he's a baby. He'll always be a baby. Take him now."

"No, not now. I'm sorry. Forgive me?"

"Of course, Undi dear." Eva wasn't really sorry because she had almost regretted what she'd said. She wanted to go on holding the baby herself—not give him to anyone else to hold.

Undi took her by the arm. "Come. Are you ready?"

And after glancing around to see whether she'd left anything, Eva allowed herself to be led back to the corridor. When they were outside, Undi told her she had something to show her. She said it seductively, and I wondered what she was leading Eva into now. They walked along the corridor, and Undi stopped before another misty door. These doors were made of mist or fog, yet they were solid until one tried to pass through them. Then the thick fog yielded. They passed through this one, and I again went with them. But the room we entered was in complete darkness. It was so dark that Eva could not see anything

66

at all. Her eyelids felt the weight of it so she closed them. She was frightened, and her legs wouldn't move. She imagined herself standing at the edge of a bottomless pit, which she would fall into if she were to move.

"It's all right." Undi sounded amused. "Nothing will harm you. On the contrary, you might be delighted as I always am." She pushed my wife forward. "Just walk straight ahead. That's right. One step after another."

And to my surprise, Eva did as she was told, and Undi, although she didn't actually walk away, was no longer there. She had left Eva alone in that awful darkness. I was angry. I tried to make contact with my wife, but her mind was closed to me. I would have guided her out of the room had she responded, but there was nothing I could do. She just kept on walking forward like a sleepwalker, still holding the baby.

Suddenly she uttered a shriek, and I saw why. A hole—a shutter like the one she'd seen in the woods—opened, and an eye, a strong, round, glittering eye looked out at her. The face it belonged to was not visible because the eye filled up all the space. It looked at Eva for about thirty seconds before it disappeared. Eva, as though entranced, moved forward to look into the lighted space. Inside, far away now, was the owner of the eye.

What is he doing, frightening her like that?

But Eva wasn't frightened anymore. In fact, she looked pleased, just as Undi had said she would be. She stood there looking down into his space where he was swinging his arm about, making a picture of stars. He was making a Light picture of a starry night. He said, "Hello, Eva. You're not afraid, are you? Let everything go and fly through the starry night, back to Paris." The eye belonged to Marius.

Undi never came back. She had left Eva and made her way to the edge of the lake, looking for lotus flowers and their huge leaves. I went down to the edge of the lake because Eva had disappeared, and I thought she might be with Undi. Although Pavarti had said she wanted to join Shiva, she was there but not Eva. Pavarti had changed shape and was now nothing but a slimy root in the mud.

This didn't stop Undi from speaking to her. "Look, Pavarti, there goes Eva."

Pavarti sprang up instantly, in the form of a perfectly formed white lotus. "Why, so it is. And it's nighttime. Where is she going, floating past the moon like that?"

I saw my wife with her child in her arms and her blue cloak billowing about her like a silken sail, floating past the huge moon.

"I don't know where she's going," Undi answered Pavarti. "Back to Paris, perhaps. I left her in the dark room. Marius must have painted that starry night for her."

"Oh, that Marius! He's a genius. He can paint anything he likes." Then Pavarti turned into a pink flamingo and stepped daintily onto a mud flat. She was joined by another flamingo, whom I took to be Tiger Hound, or Shiva as she called him. They walked away together, and Undi, suddenly remembering Isis sitting alone in the morning room, made herself very light and flew up the side of the mountain to the palace. I sat alone at the edge of the mud flat, asking myself what was happening to everyone.

Chapter 8

Isis

hen I returned to the Palace, Isis was still there. She was sitting at the table resting her chin on her long, graceful hand. She still looked haggard, but it was clear that she was not quite as distraught as she had been.

Sitting down beside her Undi offered tea, but after one disinterested glance at the teapot, Isis shook her head. After another moment's silence, she looked at Undi and asked for gin. She left her cake untouched but looked around for a cigarette. Undi could see she was in no mood for such mild pleasures as tea and cake, but since she had no cigarettes to offer, she sat still and waited to see what Isis would ask for next. Instead of asking for anything, Isis took a small white paper package from her pocket, opened it, and sniffed the contents.

"Cocaine," she said, apologizing to Undi because she didn't have enough to share. But then she found there wasn't even enough for her own need, and she became visibly disturbed. She kept screwing her hair up into a scrawny bun at the side of her head and undoing it again to let it fall to her shoulders or where it would.

No matter what she does, or how awful her state, she's still a noble creature, I observed. Yet it was a sad thing to see such a woman brought so low. She looked slimmer than usual, and her fine bones were barely covered. But they were such delicate and lovely bones that one could not help but find them exciting.

"Poor Isis. What's wrong?" Undi murmured, knowing quite well what was wrong. She moved and went to sit in the chair close to Isis and put her arm around her shoulders. "Darling, why are you so disturbed? It's all right here, you know."

Isis leaned against her then moved away. "I don't know. Yes, yes, I do. Everything is moving at such a terrible rate, and I can't keep up with it."

This was a condition all members of our group, except for myself, had to deal with. Isis and Osiris had adjusted like the others to the speed with which the planet turned and days flashed by. But now, whenever Isis used cocaine, she lost her power to do this and everything about her raced by at a terrifying rate.

"It will slow down if you sit here quietly." To help her, Undi herself sat very quietly, almost as if meditating. But she noticed something that shocked her. "Isis, darling, you have a bruise on your face. What happened?"

"Someone hit me," Isis replied. She said it without shame or bitterness.

"But why are you so disheveled and dirty? It's not like you." Undi said this so lovingly that far from resenting it, Isis felt soothed.

"I had no money and nowhere to go. Someone hit me."

Undi looked up at the blue sky. Images appeared in the clouds. There was Isis, dressed in very stylish and elegant clothes. She looked remote and secure, with an inner light shining through her beautifully made-up face. I remembered that Isis had been, ever since the beginning of this century, a much sought after fashion model. Recently, in New York, she had been the highest paid model, and her image had appeared on all the most important fashion magazines. She had also traveled to exotic places for photo shoots against superb backgrounds and stayed at the most expensive hotels, in the height of luxury. Isis had maintained this lifestyle, on and off, since the days of the great designer, Schiaparelli, in whose fabled creations Isis had stunned the fashion-conscious world. Periodically, she would disappear from the scene, only to return again and become famous under another name. She rose like the Phoenix, and no one recognized her. No one ever knew how low she had fallen or that the new and radiant being whose face and body appeared on the covers of magazines was the old Isis who never died. Yet there was evil at work—the Earth sickness we had been warned about—and Isis had grown fearful.

"I never stop. I'll never give up, Undi, never. I'm afraid to stop."

"What happened this time? Why have you fallen so low, Isis?"

"People once said I was a nymphomaniac. Now they say I 'sleep around.' It's just a different way of saying the same thing. It's because I am always searching for Osiris, and I mistake other men for him, Undi. Sometimes I feel humiliated. I feel guilty."

"Is that why you have the little, white package?"

"Well, one of the reasons. It usually helps, or I think it does. You know what it is. It's cocaine. I fell from great heights because of this drug. People began to see they couldn't depend on me, and I felt desperate. I could have escaped this time before it took possession of me, but for some reason, I didn't, and now no one wants me as a model. I went to an agent who found work for me in a dingy, little place upstairs in a wretched building in New York—a sort of theater. I had to walk along a narrow ramp pretending to dance, but what I was actually doing was undressing myself. I removed a piece of clothing with every step I took. They called me a stripper. Other girls and women were doing it too. The men sat below. They stared up at us and tried to see between our legs. Isn't that disgusting? At the time, I hardly knew what I was doing. Some girls spread their legs out wide so that the men could see. On certain nights, the men were allowed to come close and touch them."

Images were in the sky again—Isis in the dingy upstairs strip joint, for that's what it was, on West Forty-third Street in New York. She was on a ramp, just as she had said, taking off her clothes. But it wasn't really disgusting because the lighting was soft, and Isis looked like a goddess. She removed her clothes with the utmost grace and she looked far beyond the men who were all looking up intently. They threw dollar bills, and Isis pushed them into a little pile with her foot and later picked them up and tucked them into the top of one of the only garments she had on, her stockings. Later still, one of the men waited for her outside and she mistook him for Osiris and went away with him and then, when he touched her, she screamed and ran because she saw he was not Osiris.

The images grew dark. There was the owner of a small bar, on some side street, hitting Isis on the face because, he said, she owed him money for cocaine. He opened her purse and took her day's earnings.

And then she was at a party in a large house owned by some gangster, somewhere beyond the city. Something was happening in every room. Isis was in one of the rooms with a man, and it was as if she had awakened from a dream, for she again realized that this wasn't Osiris and was saying, "Who are you? What do you want?" Struggling to free herself, she said, "I don't know you. Let me go."

And the man was saying, "You asked for it, baby, and you're gonna get it."

And from the same party, two men drove her away and raped her, leaving her on the roadside near a bridge.

"Oh, yes. It was exactly like that. Two policemen came and took me to a hospital because I had been so roughly handled," Isis told Undi. "They questioned me, but when they left the room, I got up and walked away before anyone saw me." She looked away and smiled in the secret, mysterious way she sometimes had. "Then I was sickened by the whole thing and just wandered about. I must have seemed mad to the passersby because I was moaning and muttering to myself. I had no money and nowhere to go except to the park, but even there, I wasn't allowed to rest. So at last I changed shape, and no one saw me, and I flew away and came here."

"I'm very glad you did, dearest. It's not the first time, is it? I'm always glad when you come."

They sat still, and gradually the sound of the waves soothed Isis and she regained some of her composure. She shook out her rich, cloudy hair and her face became radiant again.

"You look lovely now, Isis." Undi felt even more drawn to her than to Eva or Pavarti, I could see that. Perhaps it was because the true Isis was our mother, our radiant symbol of spiritual renewal. Undi would not remember this, I was thinking, because she had not been aware of such things. When we left Heliotrope, she had a childish mind. But now she surprised me by saying something that indicated the depth of her intuition.

"I know what you're thinking, Isis. You've forgotten who you really are and who Osiris is, and you blame yourself somehow for his disappearance. But it's not so. And besides, you had done all you could to find him—to save him. I believe you sometimes wonder whether you are right to have embarked upon this long search. It makes you feel guilty. You feel guilty because, for his sake, you're in danger of destroying yourself. But I don't believe that will happen. I believe you will triumph."

"How can I be triumphant if I never find him? But you're right, Undi. I do feel guilty. Sometimes I wonder what I did that was wrong— what we both did. It wasn't entirely our own doing. They claimed us as their gods when we revealed ourselves to them in the Nile Valley. Even his descent into the underworld every night and his return in the light of day did not seem so unreal. It was like our own Light Festival happening every morning, so we accepted it. And I enjoyed it, Undi. I must confess. I enjoyed being their queen and their goddess. I even enjoyed waking him in the mornings and telling him it was time to be reborn. It was like a beautiful game. 'The women are waiting with garlands,' I would say, 'because you have returned from the Underworld.'" She smiled at the memory.

But then she looked almost craven. "And now I search for him but cannot find him. I must bring him to life again, but I can't find him. It is because of my search that I feel guilty and forget who I am. I am trapped in an endless cycle of loss."

Undi wouldn't allow this. She, herself, was suddenly radiant and joyful. "Isis, forget your pain. Let us enjoy the day. It's such a wonderful day. At any moment, the pink parakeets will fly by. Come, smile."

So Isis smiled. It wasn't one of her secret smiles that made her attractive to men because it suggested pleasure in store for them but a pure smile in response to Undi's own sudden childishness. She willingly accepted the suggestion that she should enjoy the glorious day, as though that was her reason for coming to the Rock. Like Eva, she removed her shoes and, at Undi's suggestion, she took off her soiled clothes and allowed one of the handmaidens, who had appeared as if by magic, to drape her in fragile Light fabric, which made her feel sensuous and alive and happy. She and Undi, ridiculously happy and fragrant, ran like two young girls—virgins full of expectancy— along the corridor to a terrace all wide and sparkling like crystal in the sunlight.

Yet, here, as though she had spent the small amount of strength that had welled up in her, Isis sank down onto a low couch and looked very tired. She was deathly tired all of a sudden, and her face grew thin and pale and expressionless, and she looked like an animal prepared for sacrifice. The great artery in its throat is opened, and as its life's blood gushes forth, it sinks curiously with open mouth and protruding tongue into the nothingness of death. I've seen it happen. She looked like that.

She was not dead; she was empty. The cells and fibers of her body felt nothing—no pain and no discomfort and no pleasure. And most of all, her mind was empty. She had given up, and her power was absent, and there was a great emptiness where her will had been, forcing her on through the ages! And she was not alone. It was hard to understand, but Undi, who at first had been alarmed and had tried to hold her and bring her back from this emptiness, grew as quiet and empty as she was. Her caressing hand, too, gave up and lay still and she, too, became an empty vessel. There was no movement—nothing at all around them but the fragrance and an essence that had been there all day.

The state they were in could not last. Movement and change had to take place. In a moment, they would return to consciousness of themselves—that was the most likely thing—and their minds would again become active. Isis would again be filled with the accumulated mind matter—the memories and anxieties of the ages, which like mist, penetrated every crevasse. It would enter like the tide down below that was about to fill the small holes and cracks in the rocks and all the indentations with water and would fill them again and again so long as the tide rose and fell. There was not a moment to spare if a miracle were to happen, if some chance happening, or a miracle, were to bring about a change and alter the course of events—if, as Pavarti might have said, Isis were to step for a moment from the wheel of Karma.

With but a second to spare, before they could stir and wake and be no different, a miracle did occur! Something unexpected and simple and very surprising took place. A bird, a nightingale from far away Albania, far from its nest, happened to fly by, quite unaware of the two silent figures on the terrace. So there was no design in this. In fact, I had the impression that this was something that had nothing to do with anything on Earth or in heaven. It simply was. Humans tended to believe that all things and happenings sprung to or from their own center, but this didn't. It was pure chance that caused this bird to fly by. It opened its beak, and out of its tiny throat came jewels. I saw jewels, but in actual fact, they were the priceless notes of its song. I visualized them rising like a string of precious pearls and fresh, sparkling diamonds and lovely, glowing rubies. They rose in the air and defied gravity, and the sound was clearer and more beautiful than any sound I have ever heard. Yet they were also like a manifestation of the essence that had haunted the corridors and the rooms and the terrace that day.

Then the miracle happened. Instead of passing away to their own spaces through some opening in the sky, the jeweled sounds were drawn *down*, into the emptiness of Isis and Undi, just as air is drawn into lungs that have emptied themselves one moment past!

In that moment, Isis and Undi became one. And they were also the nightingale and its jeweled song, and with the scent of dewy roses about them, they became a single being. This single being that had a single name, Isundi, rose on a sudden breeze and turned into a radiance of some sort—a being made of Light. And it stayed like that until the nightingale had flown away and reached Albania later that afternoon.

When it alighted on the first tree it saw in Albania, Isundi returned to the terrace, and Undi and Isis became themselves again. It was as if the planet had turned once without them and their feet had returned to a new meadow. Isis was like one reborn. Undi, too, had changed a little. Perhaps it was like the end of her life on the Rock. I wasn't sure about that. But Isis had truly changed, of that I was sure. A change like that cannot be anything but miraculous.

They walked slowly back to the room where the tea things were still on the table. Suddenly, they began talking about what Isis should do.

"I'll certainly go back to one of the great cities of the world," Isis declared. "The question is which one?"

"Choose the first one that comes to mind. It won't make much difference, will it?"

"Not really. It's just that, in some cities, I am still known. Not New York. I won't go there. That's where I've just come from. Berlin?" She thought about Berlin for a while. "Well, that's a possibility. But not Mumbai again. It's too soon for that too."

"What about Copenhagen? They have a statue of a mermaid . . ."

"You're the only mermaid I need. No, I don't want Copenhagen. I suppose it had better be Paris. Eva lives in Paris now, does she not? I have to choose one of the important cities, Undi. I have the feeling that Osiris will be in Paris, drawn there perhaps to do something of importance. Yes, I'll go to Paris."

"Isis, I'm afraid I have to say this, and I know you won't like it, but why don't you stop searching?"

"Oh no . . ."

"Listen, it's time to be still. How will Osiris ever find you if you are always moving from place to place? But it's not even that. You must let your mind be still and stop creating a present based on fears from the past. Do you understand what I'm saying?"

Isis looked scared again, but this time it passed quickly. "Undi, my whole life will be worthless if I give up my search."

"No, it won't. Don't ask me how I know. I just know that you have to let it all go and *be nothing*. I mean don't hope or ask for anything. I know now exactly what you must do. I just thought of it. What you must do, Isis, is find yourself a spinning wheel and place it on a balcony where you can sit all day and spin so that people passing by can see you."

"What a strange idea! I don't know whether I remember how to spin."

"It will come to you."

"Who told you all this? How do you know? What makes you say such a thing?"

"I don't know. But I'm sure it's a good thing to do. I don't mean you should sit *all* day. No, you will find employment again as a fashion model and you will even become famous as you were before. People will adore you, and your picture will be in the magazines, and you will earn a lot of money, and you will have a very stylish apartment. You will even go to other countries to have pictures taken of you in front of places like the Parthenon or the Taj Mahal or leaning over a white balcony in Belgravia—that's in London—but it won't make any difference. You will really be on your own balcony, spinning. And when you return to your own apartment, you will calmly take the thread in your hand again and go on as if you had never left off."

Isis was astonished. Yet it wasn't unusual at all for wisdom to come out of the mouths of babes like Undi. I was not surprised when Isis suddenly grew calm and looked at her situation in an entirely new light.

"Of course! That is exactly what I must do. Undi, you're my dearest friend, my sister. I love you for what you've just said, and now I'll say something to you."

"To me?"

"Yes. Listen. You must leave this Rock and the lovely palace and come to Paris with me. We can be together, you and I, and Eva too. Wouldn't you like that?"

"Well, I must admit I have been thinking about it, Isis. I will come, I promise, but not just yet. Not today. I must wait for the right day— the right moment when something tells me when and where to go." She went to the window and looked up for the two angels, thinking they might be flying about overhead as they sometimes did. Then she turned back to Isis with a delighted smile. "Did you know that I'm promised to Eva's son, Roland? Eva offered him to me, but when she did that, she thought he was a baby. I know he's not. When I come to Paris, it will be to meet him. Oh, of course, you and I and Eva will be together often, but most of the time, I'll be with him. We'll be in love. Pavarti has said so."

They embraced, and Undi watched Isis float through the wide arched windows and over the rose garden and turn into a cloud of mauve mist as she began transporting herself to Paris.

Chapter 9

Paris

he two streams of black smoke from a burning building on the Rue de la Grande Chaumière were carried by wind blowing strongly in the direction of the Montparnasse Cemetery. They passed over the rooftops of the Rue Delambre like two snakes, and then, suddenly changing direction, sped toward the Rue de la Gaité where Eva had an apartment. She'd had many apartments, not all of them in Paris, but that's where she lived now with her son Roland. I wondered whether she had seen the smoke—whether she was standing on her tiny balcony gazing up at the sky.

Then I remembered that Eva would have left home by now, and so would Roland. By now he should have been at the académie, where he studied painting, and Eva should have been in the Metro. Or perhaps she had left the Metro and was already walking along the Rue de la Paix toward Maison Gustav where she worked as an alteration hand. Whenever I thought about this job of hers, I felt irritated because it was unnecessary for her to do that kind of work. *Doubtless*, I thought, *she will soon be pinning up hems and shortening sleeves for women who would fall over with shock if she revealed her true self to them and let them know what kind of power she really possessed.* I couldn't understand why she did it, and I didn't want to become irritated, so I forced myself to stop thinking about her. In any case, she never knew what I was thinking, even though she may have sometimes thought about me.

She couldn't have forgotten me any more than she could forget Heliotrope. I looked up again at the burning building. It wasn't really in flames, but there was certainly a lot of smoke. It kept on gushing out of the two attic windows, yet there was no sign of a fire on the lower floors. The fire engine was expected at any moment. Madame Leguine, the wife of the proprietor of the Café des Grande Poissons, had given the alarm.

She was in her doorway now, looking anxiously in the direction of the Boulevarde Raspial, while her husband and Monsieur Maurice sat calmly inside the café drinking Cognac. At least they tried to sit calmly, and I must say, they almost succeeded. But M. Maurice must have been concerned about his own business premises. His restaurant was only two doors away, right next to the Académie de la Grande Chaumière, next to the art supplies store, which was on the ground floor of the burning building.

"It is almost ten minutes since I telephoned the fire department," Madame Leguine said, turning back to her husband and M. Maurice. "I was the first to realize there was a fire, monsieur. You know what a sensitive nose I have. I actually smelled it before the smoke became visible. I telephoned immediately, didn't I, Henri?"

"Thank God you did, madame," Maurice replied soberly. Usually he was a jolly man, laughing and joking a lot with his customers, artists and intellectuals of Vavin and Montparnasse, but now he looked serious. I didn't blame him. I had followed him into the café a few minutes earlier. He'd been walking briskly along the Rue de la Grande Chaumière with a big basket of vegetables from the market, which was probably intended for the luncheon that day. But, happening to look up, he'd seen the smoke and rushed straight across the street and into the café with the intention, I felt sure, of calling the fire department. Of course, Madame and Monsieur Leguine told him to sit down and wait because they'd already done so. Monsieur Leguine then opened the bottle of Cognac, even though it was so early in the day.

Some of the students from the académie had already come down from the ateliers and were standing outside the café, looking up at the attic windows. I half expected to see Roland, but he was not among them.

The two men finished their Cognac and, leaving their glasses on the table, went to the doorway to join Madame Leguine. She was a thin, wiry, little woman with lots of energy. Monsieur Leguine was overweight, as so often happens—a little, thin wife and a large husband. They were kind people. I happened to know that Madame Leguine often gave Roland a free coffee, being well aware that he hardly ever had money in his pocket. That was another thing I couldn't understand about Eva. It was not at all necessary for her to be so tight with money. She could have been very well off, rich like Marius and Osiris. Not like me, of course. But then, I didn't need money. Without my body, I didn't need anything. But she did. Or even if she didn't, Roland did. It was not at all necessary for him to be always prowling about in a state of penury, unable to take a girl to the movie if he wanted to. He wasn't my son, but I cared for him and sometimes wished he were mine.

"Look, it's still coming out," Monsieur Leguine said, meaning the smoke.

"It is indeed," replied Monsieur Maurice.

The narrow street was filling up with spectators. For the most part, they were residents of the street and students of the académie. I again looked in vain for Roland, feeling sure I would recognize him. Two people came and joined Monsieur and Madame Leguine on the pavement. One was an old lady named Madame Rose, and the other was her companion, Monsieur Raferé, her good friend. A very old man, Monsieur Fouroux, also joined them, and they all stood outside the café where they had a good view of the attic windows of the art supplies store. Monsieur Fouroux was a scholar of magic symbols and demonic characters and the like. He had a small musty bookstore at the end of the street, almost too dark inside for anyone to see what was on the shelves. Sometimes, he lit a red lamp, and in that glow, the customers themselves look diabolical.

These people knew each other well, having lived and worked here all their lives. They knew all about the great old days of the not-so-distant past when Montparnasse was one of the art centers of Paris. True, Madame Rose came from the South of France, but she'd been living here long enough to be considered a native. She and Monsieur Raferé worked at the Académie de la Chaumière. And as I said, Monsieur Maurice ran the Restaurant Renoir. He and his father before him had been dishing out excellent beefsteaks and fried livers at prices reasonable enough for poor artists for many years, and they often accepted paintings in lieu of payment; the walls of the restaurant were covered with very fine works of art. Indeed, some of those painters were now famous. Madame Rose, for that matter, was said to own a very valuable work of art, a painting given to her in her youth by the handsome and tragic young artist, Modigliani. She had never, of course,

madame Rose and Monsieur Rojere

mimi and Frou-frou

considered selling her treasure. Why should she? She lived simply, and her needs were few. I imagine she continued to work at the académie not because she needed to but because it was her life. The same might be said of Monsieur Raferé.

Observing these elderly people, I realized, as I often did, that life was really too short. Or else, one lifetime wasn't enough. But Madame Rose seemed to live her life wisely, and so did Monsieur Raferé. There was something about them that gave the impression, or it did to me, that they lived in a timeless world and, also, they seemed to share a secret about it. Old Monsieur Fouroux too lived in his own world. He had to be well over ninety, but I didn't believe he was at all concerned about his age or even his physical state. He was completely absorbed in his books and his research into the occult. He was the oldest resident of the Rue de la Grande Chaumière which was, of course, centuries older than he was—an ancient street indeed—and he made his way along it when he had to, like a very old tortoise, with his head and neck emerging from his wide coat collar, almost at right angles to his body, always looking downward.

I watched him. Standing there outside the Café des Grande Poissons, he had difficulty in tilting his head up so that he could look at the smoke. His back was bent from pouring over his old books. So he really couldn't see the attic windows. But as I moved in closer, curious about what was going on in his weird but active mind, I perceived he could see something else that struck him as odd. All the time, the firemen, who had at last arrived, were at work, climbing their ladder with a hose, two of them, while two others, who had broken the lock on the door downstairs—or perhaps someone inside had opened it for them—were entering with axes, a woman had been looking out of the third-floor window. And it was she whom Monsieur Fouroux looked at now, as though there was something unusual about her. It was true; she did look odd. She leaned against the window pane, scratching her chin idly as though nothing was wrong, and gazed down at the spectators in the street with a blank, dreamy expression on her face.

She attracted my attention too. I wondered whether she could be a Heliotropian. There were quite a few of them, going about the world you know, hiding their identities. They were shape-changers, like all Heliotropians, and could almost always escape danger by turning swiftly into something else, like small insects or birds that could fly out of harm's way. I had no reason for suspecting that this woman was a Heliotropian, except that she appeared to be without fear. But that really wasn't enough to go on. She most likely was just an ordinary woman.

I could see that Monsieur Fouroux, gazing up at her, did not think so. He thought she looked like a sacrificial victim, and because of her blank, dreamy expression, he suspected she had been sedated for the Rite, whatever that was to be. At any moment, he was thinking, she might withdraw from the window and reappear on the roof with arms upraised in ecstasy while flames consumed her.

No such thing happened. The old man went on looking at her, while everyone else looked at the firemen on the ladder. They'd reached the top. She wasn't a pretty woman. That wasn't why he looked, although he still appreciated a pretty woman almost as much as he had when he was only eighty. It was just that there was some mystery attached to her and the way she went on gazing at all the people in the street.

The proprietor of the art supplies store behaved oddly too. He'd appeared in his doorway at last, and he, too, was scratching his chin. After looking defiantly at everyone outside the Café des Grande Poissons, he withdrew, closing the door behind him. The firemen were still inside.

"Look at that! He's been inside all the time. And we thought he was out—away somewhere. We need not have been so concerned on his behalf." Madame Leguine felt as though she'd been wasting her concern or her sympathy. "Why is *he* so unconcerned? You'd think there was nothing wrong at all. But there you are. I suppose it's not my business."

"I know how I'd feel if it were my building that was on fire," Monsieur Maurice said. "Look. Is all that water necessary? They're flooding the whole street. I can't see any flames. Perhaps he's in a state of shock. They've been strange, these two, ever since they took over the store. They've never responded to my advances. Have they to yours?"

"Not a bit," Madame Leguine said. "They've been here for six weeks now and have never spoken a work to either of us, have they, Henri?" Still, she looked as if she were sorry for them—the man and his wife, who was still leaning out of the window. "It's horrible to think of the condition of their stock. It must be very wet by now."

The fears of the residents of the street were soon put to rest. The fire had not even spread to the lower floors of the building, but the water had. The building had been thoroughly drenched, and now the firemen were packing up and preparing to drive off, leaving a big mess inside on the first floor and quite a few puddles in the street. The woman upstairs gazed down at them, and taking a hairpin or something from her hair, she extended her arm. Delicately taking aim, she opened her fingers and let whatever it was fall. It landed in the water and floated about for a while before it disappeared.

My attention was drawn to those puddles. I had the feeling they meant something to me in particular. Yet I found that hard to believe. They were the concern of the whole street, not mine, surely. I didn't live or work here. I was an outsider. This was a very tight, little community, here on this short, narrow street. Yet the feeling persisted. I thought at first that I had been drawn there that morning because of Eva. Sometimes I haunted her, staying close to her for days without her being aware of it. But, I reasoned, if that were so, why wasn't I waiting about on her street? Why was I here? Was it something to do with Roland, her son? Was it because I wanted to observe him at his art studies? My reason for being here wasn't a matter of great concern to me. I was curious, that's all. I'd come to this street that morning without knowing why and had waited. The fire had broken out, and here I was, looking at all the water and wondering what it had to do with me.

The crowd was thinning out. Madame Rose and Monsieur Raferé stepped cautiously over the puddles and returned to the académie. The Leguines went back to the café and started pouring wine and hot coffee for people who felt the need of refreshment. Monsieur Maurice took his basket of vegetables back to the Restaurant Renoir and gave them to his sister, who was the cook, reminding her to prepare the fried liver and the beefsteaks, while he himself gave his attention to the salads and the tarts.

And the old scholar, Monsieur Fouroux, shuffled back to his dark den and switched on the red light because he couldn't stop thinking about fire spirits and sacrificial victims. The more he thought about the woman, however, the more he began to doubt, for she had not, after all, gone up in flames. In the devilish, red glow of the lamp, he leafed through heavy books, searching for answers. He came to the conclusion that those two people were the kind of beings whose sole purpose was to create certain situations, sometimes out of pure deviltry, and to make things happen. "In this case," he muttered to himself, "they have set fire to a building in order to make firemen come and fill the street with water." But he didn't find that very interesting. "Something else will surely happen. Perhaps I should go and warn everyone."

But he kept on turning pages and forgot all about his neighbors.

It was true, however, that the water was behaving abnormally. I noticed it, although no one else seemed to be aware of it. It should have flowed away along the gutters by now. Instead, it remained on the road in the form of puddles. And it looked green, like seawater. It stayed well on into the afternoon and, in fact, was about the only sign left of the fire. On the outside, the building was unmarked. The afternoon students, when they arrived, would not have noticed that anything was amiss had it not been for that water. The proprietor had closed the door after the departure of the fire engine and had not been seen again. He was there, to be sure, for a little boy had peeped through a crack and had seen him. The boy told the Leguines that the man was inside the store, all by himself, sitting on a box, sniffing away at the damp, horrid odor of wet drawing paper.

"What about the woman?" the child was asked, and he said he knew nothing of any woman.

I could have told them. The woman was still upstairs in her bedroom on the third floor. She had withdrawn from the window and was looking at her reflection in her silent mirror. Calm and indifferent, her eyes looked into themselves and she saw nothing. I no longer wondered whether she was one of the missing Heliotropians, for Heliotropian women never see nothing. If they were to look at themselves in a mirror (which they never do, as a matter of fact), they would certainly see something, for they were exotic-looking creatures. They didn't have to do anything to make themselves gorgeous. They simply were. Eva for instance, was not only beautiful; she was adorable. Or she had been. Now she seemed bent upon destroying her natural beauty by wallowing in anxiety and worries she appeared to take delight in.

Just before one o'clock, the afternoon students, unaware of all that had happened, began to arrive—to dawdle in the lobby or to talk to each other on the steps of the building. Some were early and some late. Among the early ones was a man I had never seen before. As soon as

I did see him, I had the feeling I should be seeing even more of him in the future. His name, I soon learned, was Georges Albertine, and he had made an effort to be early so that he could find a place to park his car. He was fortunate, for he had found a space right outside the académie. I followed him into the building.

Madame Rose was sitting in her usual place in the corridor.

"Ah, Monsieur Albertine!" she said politely.

"Good afternoon, Madame Rose," said Albertine, who was equally polite. "Would you be kind enough to give me a slip for the life class?"

The sense I had gained over the years as a disembodied spirit let me know that Undi would soon return from In-Sea and that this man would fall in love with her. I didn't want this to happen. First of all things were complicated enough with Marius being away such a lot chasing after his genius. Then there was Roland, a student at the Academy. Isis and Pavarti had talked her into believing he would fall in love with her so there was going to be something brewing in that direction. Looking at M. Albertine I found that I liked him and didn't want him to be hurt as only an older man could be by falling in love with a young girl like Undi. In fact, I could see it right now. He would soon experience the sweet pain of love for her, poor fellow. I felt sorry for him.

I realized that he was one of the casual students who paid by the day and not by the term as Roland did. He handed the money to Madame. Rose and she put it in a tin box on the table before her. Madame Rose sat at this table every day except Sunday, taking the money and handing out slips for the drawing and painting classes. She also engaged the models and gave them kindly advice, warning them against certain men—impostors who gave the names of well-known artists and lured young models into poky little rooms and did not pay them. Neither she nor Monsieur Raferé was a director of the académie, but Georges behaved toward them as if they were. I could see he had great regard for Madame Rose in particular. He admired her enormously; that was clear. And I did not blame him, for she was a most distinguished old lady, with her white hair drawn back into a classical bun and her fringed Spanish-type shawl worn over a long, black, silk dress. She had a firm profile and was very self-possessed. Most people liked her and felt flattered when she spoke to them. Monsieur Raferé, her colleague, was not quite like that. He was self-possessed, to be sure, but he was gentle and almost humble, although he always seemed to wear a secret smile. He and Madame Rose, in fact, often exchanged secret smiles.

The charming old lady handed Georges his life class slip. "Here you are, monsieur. Thank you." She smiled at him. "We haven't seen you for two weeks. I hope you've been well?"

"Very well, thank you. Business kept me from coming, that's all." It wasn't true. Instead of coming to the life class, where he was obliged to pay attention to anatomy, Georges Albertine had indulged himself by staying at home and painting his fantasy scenes, which were to do with a slim, blond dream girl, whose image he had created for himself.

"I regret having had to miss classes, but it won't happen again." *Not for a while at any rate*, his inner voice whispered. I heard it. He had this inner voice, which seemed to amuse him, but he never heeded its advice. His closet was cluttered with paintings and drawings of this dream girl, and he almost believed she was real. He paused. "Er, what happened in the street today, Madame Rose? There's water everywhere. It's like an ocean."

"An ocean, monsieur?" she smiled. "Let's say a small lake. But don't worry. It's all over now." She cast a quick glance at Monsieur Raferé, who stood nearby, holding a cat in his arms. He was a few years younger than Madame Rose, who must have been about eighty-five.

Returning her glance and making it secretive, although it wasn't—I mean, it had no reason to be—he said soothingly, "Nothing but a few oily rags smoldering in the attic. Isn't that so, Frou-Frou?" He was talking to his cat but looked up and smiled at Georges.

I found out that both he and Madame Rose were of the class of people who could talk to cats and dogs and even inanimate objects. They both had this ability to a marked degree. There was something magical about them. It was not a pose. They were very matter-of-fact, very real people, and that's what made them so satisfying, I suppose. Yet they had their magical quality too. The two cats, it was clear, adored Monsieur Raferé, and he loved them dearly.

Apart from standing in the corridor frequently, doing nothing, Monsieur Raferé looked after the ateliers. He kept the stoves alit and put easels away and looked after furniture that had been used in paintings—couches, for instance, like the green couch they had in the life class that day. And he was the one to go to if you wanted anything. He, too, gave friendly advice, but that was usually about the school itself, not about suspicious characters. He had few beliefs and few opinions, but he had an elfish sense of humor. Most mornings, he went over to the café on the corner of the Rue Delambre for a glass of warm wine, which he drank standing at the bar. It made him feel mellow and amiable, and he came back to the académie with a faint smile on his lips. Once, he had been a painter of scenery in a theater, and his attitude was always professional, as well as kindly and polite. Nothing disturbed him, nor Madame Rose either.

I considered them highly sophisticated and had the impression that had a group of Australian aborigines walked in carrying their sacred bark, Madame Rose and Monsieur Raferé would have simply taken their money and directed them, without comment, to the still life class.

Georges still wasn't sure of what had happened. He regarded Mimi, the other cat, for a while, as if he thought she might tell him and then went on his way. At the end of the narrow corridor, he came to a flight of stairs, which he began to climb. Halfway up, he came to a landing, where a door suddenly opened. He encountered the secretary of the académie, Monsieur Jacques, who bobbed a silly sort of curtsy and then realized his mistake. He had mistaken Georges for another silly fellow like himself with whom he usually exchanged curtsies. He and the fellow would meet, place their fingers to their chins and bob up and down. Now he suddenly realized he looked ridiculous, so he pulled himself up and looked cold and haughty, trying to make Georges feel inferior. Georges was unaffected. He'd hardly noticed the curtsy, and anyway, he was still puzzling over the water.

"Has there been a fire, Monsieur Jacques? Shouldn't something be done about the water? My car is standing in the middle of a lake."

M. Jacques raised one eyebrow and said nothing, while Georges waited for an answer. None was forthcoming, so he went on his way, wondering whether information was being withheld and, if so, why.

Once inside the atelier he forgot about the water and became absorbed in the task of setting up an easel and arranging his paints and other materials. The class he had chosen was an oil painting class with a nude model. Only the model was not yet here. Georges was the only person in the room except for myself. I had followed him. Roland came to this class, but sometimes he went to the still life or the abstract painting or the class where a very old man taught the principals of cubism; he was said to be the last of the cubists.

I wonder whether he'll be here today? I asked myself.

It was no use trying to communicate with Georges. All he could think of was choosing the right spot to set up his easel. This was one of the reasons why he'd come so early. It was a Monday, the first day of a new pose—a new model. You chose your spot and you had to stay there for the next two weeks, so Georges wanted to be sure of being in the right place, where he would have a good view of the model without being too close to her.

She'd not yet arrived, but Georges believed he knew what she would do when she did enter the room. She would walk in and eye the students if they were already in the atelier and then go to a screen beside the model's stand. Behind it, she would disrobe, and it would shake about while she did so. It seemed to Georges that models could not wait to take their clothes off, and they did it in a frenzy. Once they were up on the stand, naked, in a world of their own, gazing inward or else going to sleep, they became queens—the center of everyone's attention.

Yet Georges was apprehensive. He hoped the model for that day would not be the fleshy kind with large breasts and full thighs. Thinking about such women, as Rubens had painted floating about near heaven, for instance, he wondered how they could possibly stay aloft on clouds with all that weight on them. His ideal woman was slim and ethereal, with a wistful, dreamy expression in her eyes, like the Botticelli Venus. Yet she was also stylish and wore expensive clothes, even though at times she looked like a nymph from the forest. He dreamed of such a girl and had painted many imaginary landscapes with nymphs like that idling away their lives by lakes or under trees. Actually, those landscapes were very pleasing and fresh, but Georges hid most of them in a closet. Even though he had plenty of money, he wanted to be known as a highly paid portrait painter of rich and fashionable people. The nymphs and the landscapes belonged to his secret life.

He chose a spot halfway between the door and the model's stand, not wanting to be too close to the model, whoever she might be. There was a handsome, green couch on the stand, and he wondered whether they were to be given yet another reclining pose.

90

"I don't mind," he was saying to himself. *"I have nothing against reclining poses. But I've been coming here for a month now, and each time, I've painted a model in a relaxed, sleeping position. I wouldn't object to a standing pose."* Then he reminded himself that he had missed the last two weeks. *"Perhaps they had a standing pose while I wasn't here."*

He liked the green couch and couldn't help thinking how well it would look in his own studio in his mansion. He lived near the Bois de Boulogne. Recently, he had cleared one of his best rooms of its furniture and had refurnished it with a model's stand and a magnificent antique chair for his prospective clients to sit in while he painted their portraits. He also had a most impressive collection of lengths of cloth—velvets and silks and brocades—and some rugs and wall hangings with which to construct his backgrounds or use as voluminous shawls around the shoulders of his female models. He even had a crimson velvet jacket and some silken shirts for male clients who might want something out of the ordinary in the way of a portrait. He imagined his female clients posing for him in the chair or on a stool, in costumes that resembled taffeta tents flowing away from their shoulders, their bare necks decorated with ruby necklaces. But so far, he had no clients. In fact, he had only recently, since his retirement, started to paint—something he had always wanted to do.

Taking a stool, Georges put it beside his easel and placed his expensive box of paints on it. He was about to open the paints and squeeze his colors onto his palette when he remembered that the master had told him not to do this until he had been given the color chart. He hoped to get one today from the massiér, but the massiér was not yet here. Georges was getting restless. Unwrapping a large, white stretched canvas, he placed it on the easel. Then he took his brushes from the paint box and stood them up in a glass jar and set out his oil and turpentine and his paint rags. He was ready, except for the color chart. With nothing else to do, he thought he might as well go over to the Café des Grande Poissons for a glass of wine.

When I come back, he told himself, *the model will have arrived. And I will get the color chart from the massiér.*

Yet he lingered. Two others had drifted in, and they, too, began staking their claims to a bit of floor space. That reminded Georges to put his mark with strips of tape on the floor where the easel stood, and he realized he had no tape. Then the massiér came in, and he forgot again as he watched the massiér get out his basket of old shawls and lengths of silk and old curtains and artificial flowers and select a dusty, pink strip of silk to drape over the end of the couch. He also took out a handsome but worn piece of embroidered Chinese silk, which he arranged, trailing from the head of the couch to the floor and, changing his mind, threw it back into the basket.

"It is an antique couch," Georges observed, *"much too good to have paint splashed on it."* He coveted it. *"It will become ruined if it stays here."* He again thought it was just the right kind of couch for his new atelier at home.

"The model is late," someone said.

The massiér, whose job was to see that everything was in order, arrange poses and announce rest periods, and maintain peace and quiet, grunted and looked irritable. Georges didn't like to ask him for the color chart. *I'll ask him when I come back.*

"Well, where is she?" someone else asked, meaning the model.

The massiér's dark eyebrows drew together. His eyes, which were tormented looking to begin with, seemed to flash dark sparks. I learned afterwards that he came from a certain part of the South of France where the minstrel wind blows and where people were passionate and excitable, with that same tormented look. Yet he was a kindly young man when things were going well. Today, he felt that things weren't about to go well. He was waiting for the model so that he could arrange the pose.

He knew what he was supposed to do, and it irritated him when an American woman named Ethel, who had just arrived herself, said, "Where is the model? You do have to arrange the pose, you know."

And when he gave her a fearsome look, she refused to be intimidated and went on. "Well, you won't let us do it, and it always takes you such a long time."

To make matters worse, a French girl gave her opinion. "Yes, you're right, Ethel."

Georges lingered to listen to this. He would not have said anything himself because he still felt like a newcomer, but he was glad someone had spoken up.

The massiér hissed, "Still time."

"Perhaps she'll rush in making the usual excuse that none of the clocks in the quarter are right. That's the usual excuse." It was a young Englishman who bleated like a sheep.

Another American woman, Babs Widgery, said, "Well, that's true, isn't it? If I were to depend on those clocks, I'd go crazy. Not one of them agrees with the other." Babs was a very amiable woman, who was not really concerned about anything, not even the clocks. "Don't worry. I imagine she'll be here soon" she said.

Ethel said in a nasty sort of voice, "I hope she has her own watch."

"I guess she has, although now I come to think of it, I've never seen a model posing with a watch on," Babs answered.

"Poor girls," Georges felt bold enough to say, suddenly sympathetic. "They work hard for a few francs. I don't suppose they can afford watches."

"Oh," Ethel sniffed. "I think they do very well. They earn more than a salesgirl."

"How do you know that, Ethel?"

"I asked a salesgirl at Bon Marche how much she earned."

"Some young girls won't pose privately, you know," the young Swiss woman said, "so they have to depend on the schools. Poor girls, they would be at the mercy of all the men if they posed privately."

"I thought it was the other way around—the men were at the mercy of the models."

"Ethel! How can you say such a thing? I'm surprised."

"Oh, Babs. You're such a charitable person. You're right. I shouldn't say things like that. But where is she? The afternoon will be gone before we get started."

The life class that Georges had chosen to work in had a master who came twice a week. When he came, the students all had to stop working and stand behind him while he made corrections and demonstrated on someone's canvas. Very often, the one who owned the canvas had to stand there and watch his or her beloved brushstrokes get scraped off or painted over.

"Don't be upset. You are not here to paint a masterpiece," the master would tell them, "but to learn how to construct the form" or some such thing. Very often, I discovered, the model had to pose, standing if she had a standing pose, for well over an hour if the master forgot to observe the rest period. The model came every day and held her pose for forty-five, then thirty, and then fifteen minutes interspersed with five minute rests. But halfway through the afternoon, there was a fifteen minute rest, announced by the massiér, during which most of the students would go down to the Café de Gros Poissons to drink coffee and chat.

It was a mixed class. Some students were young, but some of them were in their forties or fifties. Georges was just over fifty, and Monsieur Moitessier, a local resident who lived not far from Eva on the Rue de la Gaité, was a little over sixty. An old Russian with a greasy, broad-brimmed, black hat and a stained waistcoat could have been eighty or eighty-five.

The young students were all French, but the slightly older French girl, Solange, and the young Swiss woman, were in their thirties, as was the young English bank clerk, who came every summer for a painting vacation. The other students had christened him "Carrot" because of his red hair. On Thursdays, a German woman named Ursula came but not always to the life class. Sometimes she chose other classes; she liked the abstract class and the still life. Once, when Georges had looked into the still life atelier, he had seen an Australian girl named Doreen painting a cabbage as large as the back of a bus. Its size shocked him. Another painting—actually, three canvasses called Triptych—puzzled him because they were all completely black, and the young English student whose work it was had ridden his bicycle over the wet surfaces and then walked about on them in his sneakers and told Georges that he was going to rename the work and call it "The Unimportance of Being Ernest."

Georges said that the work was "very interesting and profound," and I think he said this because he had been told that the young Englishman was a lord, and this thrilled him. He had great respect for the English aristocracy and hoped to paint portraits of them.

"You have a most interesting head," George had told the young lord. "I wish you would do me the honor and permit me to paint your portrait one day." Georges was free with Old World courtesies when he felt it necessary.

Roland, of course, was a regular student, and at the moment, he worked mostly in the still life and only occasionally in the life class. Lately, he had missed some of his classes, and he often wandered about

looking troubled. Eva didn't know about this, but Monsieur Moitessier, who was fond of Roland, was concerned about him.

Well, Georges was feeling restless. He still had not asked for the color chart, and the model was not yet here. He still wanted to go over to the café for his wine, but he wanted to hear what was being said.

Carrot was asking the massiér in his irritating, knowing way who their model was to be. "Who have you got penciled in?" Somehow, the way he said it was irritating, not only to the massiér but also to everyone.

"Jeanine," snapped the massiér. "Is that all right, eh? Yes?"

"We had her two weeks ago. Too skinny," grumbled Monsieur Moitessier, the local resident.

"Too skinny! Too skinny! You want an elephant, eh? Or a hippopotamus?" hissed the massiér. He was a serious art student who, due to lack of funds, was obliged to take this job in return for free tuition. Sometimes he resented it.

"She could be a giraffe for all I care," Babs Widgery piped up. "Anything, so long as she gets here and gets up on that stand."

Her friend, Ethel, giggled but stopped giggling when she saw that Babs was serious. "I don't mind what I paint," Babs said to the Swiss girl.

They went on to speak of the model and what sort of pose they would like for the next two weeks, but still Jeanine didn't come and they began to fidget and make jokes and get out of hand. The massiér had to call for order. But then a more serious note was struck when someone mentioned the latest sensation in the art world. I guessed they were speaking about Marius.

"An artist named Marius who is said to paint his pictures entirely with light," one of the students was saying. "His work is said to be fantastic."

"I know. I've heard of him. But who is he? Has anyone ever seen him or met him? Marius who? I don't really believe it, you know. There must be some sort of trick." Ethel said.

I could have told them there was no trick. I could have told them the truth, but then that was my problem. I could never tell anybody anything, because I couldn't speak. Even if I could, they wouldn't have believed me.

Nothing like Marius's work had ever been seen before. It was quite true that he painted with Light. But he'd been working in secret, hiding himself in his ateliers in remote places wherever he chose to live, mostly in Europe and in the north of Scotland and, lately, in the Old House, where he'd been building an atelier, very secretly.

"I know. It's difficult to imagine him taking light from the sky or from some inner source or wherever he takes it from and—poof!—just using it. But that's what he's supposed to do, and I for one am prepared to believe it," the Swiss girl said with great conviction.

"But have you ever seen him?" Ethel asked.

"Perhaps he's a lightning conductor," Babs giggled and then wondered whether such a thing was possible.

Monsieur Moitessier grunted. "Nonsense. I believe in good, old-fashioned paint."

He was preparing his canvas, and after that remark, he ignored the rest of the conversation. It was about creativity and where it could lead. Georges, agreeing with Monsieur Moitessier, lost interest and left his fellow painters to their discussion, which had grown noisy, and went downstairs and over to the café for his wine. Inside the café, he sat near the window looking out at the art supplies store and then at his car, which was parked outside the académie. He realized there really had been a fire, and that accounted for all the water. He wondered what it was like inside the store. Damp and unpleasant, he imagined. He felt sorry for the proprietor.

But as he visualized the shelves stacked with drawing paper, soggy cartons of charcoal and crayons, soiled painting kits, and stacks of canvases, it occurred to him that he might get some bargains. Wealthy as he was, Georges Albertine liked a good bargain. He was a thrifty man and lived simply, although he had a weakness for antiques and did not mind spending money on them.

A gentle breeze ruffled the largest puddle right by the back wheel of his car, but he didn't notice this because he was looking up at the front of the building. The woman was still there, looking just the same, except that she wasn't scratching her cheek. She turned away from the window, and Georges looked down in time to see the proprietor turning away from the door just as he'd done before and closing it behind him. Georges wasn't particularly interested in those two people. He continued to look down and saw that the water was behaving strangely. It had started to ripple and foam. That's what really interested him.

"*The breeze, I imagine.*" Then he found himself contemplating the grains of sand on a beach.

"*A whole world in a grain of sand and an ocean in a drop of water. Very interesting.*"

He wished he could see a drop of water through a giant microscope. What monsters he might see!

Lost in thought, he did not notice Madame Rose and Monsieur Raferé come out of the académie and look up and down the street. He closed his eyes for a moment, imagining life forms that might even now be swelling to gigantic proportions and reproducing themselves in the miniature ocean near his car. He imagined them taking over the world. The thought made him open his eyes, and to his surprise, he saw Madame Rose and Monsieur Raferé holding out their hands to a young woman in a wet green dress who was poised gracefully right in the middle of the puddle. She had her back to him so he couldn't see her face. But I recognized her at once. It was Undi back from the sea! Madame Rose and Monsieur Raferé led her into the académie and that was the end of that. Georges finished his wine, paid for it, left the café, crossed the street, tried to peer through the window of the art supplies store, saw very little because it was dark inside, and decided it was time to return to the académie.

"Your model has arrived," Madame Rose said as he passed through the corridor.

"Jeanine?" he asked somewhat surprised because he hadn't seen her enter.

"Oh no, not Jeanine," Monsieur Raferé smiled. He stroked Mimi and looked mysterious.

"I can't imagine what has happened to her," Madame Rose said. "She's usually so reliable. No, this is a new one. You'll like her. Her name is Undi. She says Undi means sea spirit. Quite a fanciful young lady. Hurry now. You've already lost a lot of time."

Georges was puzzled. There was something about the way they smiled at each other. And why, he wondered, had they been outside on the street helping the model out of a puddle?

Chapter 10

The Abduction

Someone had had the temerity to remove Georges's painting materials and stack them up behind the door. He couldn't believe it at first, but when he did so, he was angry and would have stalked out had someone not moved at that moment, affording him a clear view of Undi lying naked on the couch. He stood there, at Monsieur Moitessier's elbow, shuffling about and occasionally bumping his arm, unaware of anyone but her.

"Merde, I was just blocking in the left breast," growled Monsieur Moitessier. He turned and glared at Georges, but Georges took no notice of him. At last, the massiér announced the long break, and all the students put their brushes down and, one by one, left the room. Monsieur Moitessier was one of the first to go. He was going down to look for Monsieur Jacques, the secretary, and tell him about Georges being such a nuisance. He hoped the secretary would do something about it.

Georges waited until the room was empty, except for himself and Undi, and then he approached the model's stand. He stood looking at her, thinking how odd it was that she should be asleep during the long break, which was mainly for the benefit of the model. *"If she wakes when the break is over,"* he said to himself, *"she'll feel cheated."* He thought about waking her but didn't quite know how to go about it. Looking around, he noticed the massiér's basket of props and draperies, and he took from it the piece of Chinese embroidered silk. Going over to Undi he covered her with it, and she surprised him by waking and pulling it around her body as she stood up. She didn't look at him, but as she put her hand out to steady herself, he took it and helped her down from the stand, and together they left the room.

When the long break was over, the others began drifting in. They waited for the model, but she didn't come. Neither did Georges Albertine. Carrot went downstairs to look for her, and after a few minutes, he rushed in again with the news that Undi had been seen getting into a car with Monsieur Albertine.

"Oh no. Not Monsieur Moitessier. He wouldn't do that," exclaimed Babs Widgery, whose hearing wasn't good.

"What wouldn't I do?" inquired Monsieur Moitessier, just entering the atelier.

"Run off with the model. Not you, Monsieur Moitessier. That new man. Carrot said he saw him shoving her into his car."

"No, not I. No such luck," Monsieur Moitessier said dryly. "Much as I'd like to run off with such a pretty girl. No, it wasn't I, but I did see her driving off with that nuisance, Albertine, who stood behind me for the last half hour. What's happened?"

"Monsieur Albertine? I can't believe it."

"I wonder whether she went out into the street naked. Her clothes are still here. Look." Ethel was poking her head out from behind the screen. The other ladies jointed her, uttering exclamations of surprise when they saw Undi's clothing.

"My goodness," Babs Widgery said. "These models can afford better clothes than I can. Look at the quality of this lace, here on this slip. I've never seen anything like it."

The others smiled, knowing that Babs was enormously rich and could easily afford handmade lace on her underwear. Monsieur Moitessier sniffed, while a younger man who'd followed the ladies held up a sweet little bra, mostly lace, and said, "Charming." He was French.

"There can be no doubt," the massiér chimed in quickly before they could blame him for the whole affair. "No doubt at all that they have gone to a hotel on the Rue Delambre to make love and have no interest in art whatsoever." He snatched Undi's bra from the young Frenchman. "That's the way models are nowadays."

"Nowadays!" snapped Monsieur Moitessier. "That's the way everybody is and was and always will be! Merde. And I had only got as far as blocking in the left breast." He looked angry, yet there was the suggestion of a memory of something pleasurable in his eye.

The Swiss girl, whose name, I think, was Elvera, shrieked "My God! How funny!" She laughed uproariously. "With him, what's his name, Albertine or something? I still can't believe it."

The whole class was upset, but no one regretted Undi's sudden departure more than the Green Couch. She was a beautiful, old couch, who had once graced an elegant salon in the heart of fashionable Paris. Although she was not a human being she had absorbed energy and character, drawn from at least two of the individuals who had used her most often—the lovely courtesan, Camille, and her old Aunt Mieu who, in those days, had taken over the care of Camille's luxurious apartment. So she had feelings, and she knew what life was like. Some years ago, she had found refuge in the Académie de la Grande Chaumière.

Happy as the Green Couch had been when they brought her upstairs that day, the prospect of spending two weeks in the life class hadn't excited her too much. The classes at the académie, to tell the truth, bored her. She appreciated a great painting, but she had little patience with the crude, tormented work of the students. This wasn't to say that she didn't hope to come in contact with a young genius one day. It would be nice to become the subject of some famous work of art. In any case, she told herself, it was good to be in a light room once again, free of the dust sheet that always covered her in the small room under the stairs. Lately, the only people who paid any attention to her were Madame Rose and Monsieur Raferé and the two cats, Mimi and Frou-Frou. She didn't care for the cats because they sharpened their claws on her legs.

"Fate is strange, is it not?" she remarked to a washstand and basin that stood by the wall behind the model's stand. They were a popular pair, especially when the massiér decided upon a pose in the style of a Renoir, like "Dancer Washing Her Feet," or that kind of thing. "Only yesterday I was beginning to think I'd never see the light of day again. Not, mind you, that I was so delighted when I realized they were bringing me into the Life Class. Oh dear, I thought, the same old thing—same old nude models crushing me to death. At least Jeanine doesn't weigh much. Not like Babette. Babette imagines herself to be a petite, little miniature, but she must weight hundreds of pounds. Does she still pose here?"

"No," replied the water jug. "But I know exactly what you mean. 'Model Reclining.' 'Dancer Washing Her Feet.' 'Woman at Her Toilette.' Same old thing, as you say. Still, it's better than being in the abstract class."

"Oh, my God! Shocking what they do to you there! I mean, if one is a washstand, one expects to look like a washstand, don't you agree?"

"I certainly do. But, you know, when that model came in here this afternoon, I was agreeably surprised. I was, in fact, quite thrilled. I could tell at once she was no ordinary human being. There was something about her that enlivened me very much. It was exciting because, even though she seemed to be in a bit of a daze, I sensed something immediately. In fact, she communicated with me and wanted to know whether I was comfortable when she lay down on me. Consideration came naturally to her."

"That was, indeed, very nice of her."

"Exactly. How many people ask you if it's all right when they flop down on you? And, you know, it was strange. I could smell the sea—a fresh, delicious odor of the sea—and I at once knew who she was. I'm absolutely sure of it."

"Who was she, dear?" the washstand asked. "Don't keep it all to yourself."

"My dear, don't you recognize the Botticelli Venus when you see her? You saw her, didn't you? Wouldn't you swear she looked exactly like the Venus? Camille—you know, my late mistress—she had an excellent copy of the painting hanging in her salon. The duke promised her that, if it were possible, he would buy the original for her. Nothing was too fine for her, he used to say. Meanwhile, she had the copy painted because she imagined she looked like the Venus. I couldn't see it myself for Camille had dark hair, and she wasn't as tall as the Venus. But I never said so. I wouldn't have hurt her for the world. But this girl now could be the Venus herself. And another thing I noticed. She weighed almost nothing. It wasn't because of her weight that I was so aware of her, I assure you. No, it was just her presence, if you know what I mean."

"Oh, indeed. Some people just have it."

"Anyway, I feel upset. I can't imagine why she let that man carry her off like that. You saw what happened, didn't you?"

The washstand and the water jug said they were absolutely dumbfounded when it happened. "A puzzling affair, I must say. I wonder whether she'll come back."

As you can imagine, I found this conversation amusing. I realized that so far as Undi was concerned, the Green Couch must have been very sensitive. Her experience as a couch in the salon of a young woman like Camille must have taught her much. She, herself, must have listened in on many interesting conversations. Many lovely arms must have rested on her carved wooden ones. I wondered whether she had any morals. I'm sure she had a wealth of what was known as practical good sense; I don't know how many times since then I would hear her urge Undi to be nicer to Georges instead of sighing over a penniless student like Roland. She really belonged to a world of the past, where social position and money mattered. I knew those values really didn't matter so much any more, but to hear her speak to Undi, you would think they were still just as important. These old people (and old couches) don't seem to realize that there's a new spirit abroad in this century. When one has lived through the ages and observed the changes in manners and values and clothing and almost everything, without any real change taking place in human behavior, one becomes hopeful when a new spirit is abroad as it is now. But it's happened before without bringing about real freedom in man. We're free in Heliotrope, but we're not as interesting, on the whole, as Old Earth people.

Anyway, the old couch was quite beautiful with her green velvet covering and her fine carving. And she was soft and comfortable, too, with something about her that invited confidences. She had a kind heart and also a certain flightiness about her that I found attractive.

The massiér did his best to satisfy the class. He arranged Undi's lacy slip and green dress, which was quite a different shade from the velvety moss green of the couch and stuck a few artificial flowers into a vase which he placed near her back legs.

"You still have an hour left," he told everyone, "so you had better do a still life."

Monsieur Moitessier snorted and scowled but set to work, as did everyone else. They were not very enthusiastic, however, but stood before their easels, dabbing and scraping as quietly as they could. An occasional sigh or a whisper broke the silence, and once Carrot heaved a big sigh and quoted Brancusi. "To see far is easy, but to arrive is hard, very hard," he said aloud, causing the massiér to snap even more loudly, "Quiet! Silence!" Those were the only voices that were heard during the remaining hour.

Roland

Chapter 11

Roland

At four o'clock the class was dismissed. No one was to touch the couch or the rest of the things on the stand. Tomorrow was another day. Perhaps she'd come back, and perhaps she would not. Who could tell? The students began to pack up, scrubbing off the smeared paint and cleaning their palettes, carefully placing their brushes and their paints in their boxes. Easels were left for the massiér to put away, but he would do that later.

Everyone except Babs Widgery and Monsieur Moitessier left the room. She smiled at him, and held up her canvas with a long green smear on it. "Well now, I do declare, I never would have thought of making an abstract of this."

The Frenchman didn't answer her at all. In his opinion, she was not a serious painter. And besides, she wasn't even French. He waited until she had left the room and then went over to the stand where he stood gazing at the underclothing on the green couch. He made no attempt to touch them but just stood there, saying, "Umm, umm, well, that was a pretty girl. What a pity."

The room looked empty and dreary and would have been colorless had it not been for the rich velvet of the couch and the radiant silk of Undi's dress. All around, on the walls and the floor were smears and splashes of old paint that had turned gray. He could not help observing this and wondered why it was that when a lot of colors like that were blended haphazardly they looked gray. He reminded himself that this was a very old building and he liked it that way. Considering this changed his mood, although I couldn't see why it should have done so. But he was no longer grumpy and cross, or even sorrowful.

As his thoughts returned to Undi, he merely felt softened and regretful because she'd gone. He looked at the green dress and murmured, "Green. The color of youth."

"Ah yes, youth," whispered the couch, trying to convince herself that one is as old as one feels.

Thinking of youth reminded Monsieur Moitessier of Roland. He was fond of the young man—a boy, really. At least, that's what he was to Monsieur Moitessier. M. Moitessier suspected that Roland suffered the usual pangs of youth because at times he behaved as if he carried a great burden on his shoulders—or at least, in his mind. When he wasn't in one of those moods, Roland worked quite hard at his painting, and Monsieur Moitessier believed the boy had great talent.

He found himself wishing that Roland had been there that afternoon. He suspected that Roland had no sweetheart, and it struck him that he and the lovely model would have made a good pair. Not that he was thinking of marriage for the boy. It was just that he had an idea that Roland was in need of some feminine company. He didn't believe the girl had started something with that fellow Albertine, who was old enough to be her father, and was convinced that there was some other explanation for what had happened. Perhaps, he told himself, she hadn't gone off with him at all. Yet, had he not seen them with his own eyes? He was shrewd enough to see that Georges wasn't really a ladies' man so it was a bit of a puzzle and really none of his business.

What would Madame Vergé have to say about it, he wondered? He often met Roland's mother on the Rue Delambre and on the Rue de la Gaité where they lived. Last time, she'd given him a piece of her mind on the subject of art, Roland's art in particular.

"You encourage my son, don't deny it. You talk very grandly about art, but you don't have to live by it. You're past sixty, if you don't mind my saying so. You're retired now, and you can afford to dabble in such things. And that's not how you made your money in your youth. Yet you encourage Roland to study painting instead of some sensible profession like law or medicine. He's wasting his time at that académie. And do you know what the latest is? Paper sculpture, if you please! How long will that last?"

Eva was giving way to pent up feelings, or she would never have spoken to Monsieur Moitessier like that, I'm sure. But as she spoke, she suddenly remembered she was a Heliotropian and she realized she might outlive Roland by thousands of Old Earth years. That was too much. She immediately rejected the memory, and having done so, she returned to her attack on the startled Monsieur Moitessier—Gaston. His name was Gaston. "Spilt glue and scraps of torn-up paper all over the bedroom floor. What security is there for him in that?"

Monsieur Moitessier didn't like being told he was over sixty, sixty-four, to be exact. But in these moods Eva was formidable. He realized how much younger she was than he. He judged her to be in her thirties. She'd married young so he had heard. She was not bad-looking, he told himself, and she was the lad's mother. He liked her, and he did sympathize with her point of view. Yet, art was art.

"Madame," he expostulated, "are you or are you not a Frenchwoman? A Parisian? Think of the glorious tradition of painting in this very quarter. How can you adopt this materialistic attitude?" But he knew only too well how she could. Was he too not a realist? Would he have carried on his father's hardware business if he were not a realist?

"Materialistic," Eva almost shrieked. "I'd like to know who would look after us if I didn't go to work all day." She suddenly realized how her behavior must seem to her neighbor, Monsieur Moitessier, and she turned away but not before he had seen her blush and tears come to her eyes.

"Well, perhaps you're right. I wouldn't worry too much, Madame Vergé. If I get a chance, I'll talk to him. Perhaps he'll consider taking up another career that will give him more security. And he can still go on with his painting."

I couldn't help thinking that all this was unnecessary. As a Heliotropian, Eva could have easily accumulated wealth over the centuries, as Marius and Osiris had done. She could have made life very easy for her son, and I didn't know why she hadn't done so. I wondered whether it had something to do with her wanting to forget all about Heliotrope and to be truly an Old Earth person. As such, she could watch her son grow up, reach maturity, marry, and have children and make her a grandmother. At times she did succeed in forgetting or blocking out her memories. But denying the truth to oneself, as Dr. Pandé, our Heliotropian counselor, might have told her, was one of the diseases of Old Earth. Many people didn't know what the truth was. Eva did. She simply hid it from herself. At least, that's what I sometimes thought.

Monsieur Moitessier knew that Eva worked in one of the most famous fashion houses in Paris, and he honored her for it. Yet he expected more understanding of her. Security was very important to be sure, but he believed that man couldn't live by bread alone. He admitted to himself that, in Roland, he saw what he would have liked to be himself. As a young man he had dutifully followed his father's footsteps and had spent his early years working in the business his father had built up. It was clear that Roland had no intention of putting anything before his painting. Although he secretly admired Roland for this, he believed he understood Eva's concern.

He knew something of her family life because he had lived on this street even longer than she had. They were neighbors. He remembered when her husband had killed himself. They said it wasn't suicide, but the rumor had persisted. The story was that Eva had come home from work one evening to find the young maid hysterical because Gerard Vergé, a quiet, cold, and secretive fellow, had drunk some poisonous brew and had died soon after doing so. The maid had actually seen him swallow it. If it had not been so tragic it would have been comical. He had known Vergé, Eva's husband, who imagined he could paint. His painting was not thought much of, but like Roland, he devoted himself to it entirely, while Eva went to work. She used to go off every morning while Gerard stayed home and mixed paints. He used all sorts of unconventional mediums. In fact, Monsieur Moitessier thought he spent more of his time experimenting with these mediums than he did painting.

He'd had a book about the cave paintings of India, and in it, he had read of a certain green—a poisonous-looking green it was too—that had been arrived at by one of the painter-monks while working on the walls of Ajanta, when he had left yogurt and something else in a copper pot for weeks until it turned green. Gerard tried the same thing, which he had once shown to Gaston Moitessier. Then he added something else to it that must have been deadly. And then he drank it! That was the story. They said it was a mistake and that he had intended to drink his glass of wine. The maid said that he seemed very preoccupied with something and had put his hand out and grasped the mug with the mixture in it, instead of the wine glass, and tossed it down quickly before he realized what he was doing. It must have tasted awful. He tried to spit it out, but it had already gone down.

Monsieur Moitessier thought it was a likely tale! He never quite believed it. Roland had been a baby at the time, Eva an adoring mother. She never seemed deeply attached to Gerard. Bewildered, she left the funeral arrangements to Gerard's brother, Roland's uncle, and continued to go to work each day. But at the time, it seemed to Monsieur Moitessier that a change came over her. She became withdrawn and looked scared. After a while, there were a few suitors, but she rejected them. Gaston was interested in her himself, and he had been younger then by fifteen years. But, of course, so had she, so he'd hesitated, just as he hesitated now. All he could do was take a friendly interest in her and Roland and let them know that he was at their service if they needed help.

"Strange," he said to himself. "She has never shown any sign of age in spite of having worked so hard. Quite wonderful. Some women age so quickly." He knew she had kept the maid, Carmalita, for about seven years, but then Carmalita had gone away, and Eva had managed on her own. A brave little woman and a true Frenchwoman—even if she had no patience with painters. And still pretty. He liked her and was a little bit provoked by her inaccessibility, even though he'd had at least two mistresses during the last fifteen years. He liked young widows, especially when they had sons. The sight of a young widow caring for a son excited him, although he didn't know why this should be so. He wondered what sort of a wife Eva had been.

I could have told him—not from my own experience of her, alas, for our marriage was never consummated. But I have observed Eva with her husbands over the years, and I should say that she has never really been in love with any of them. All she wanted was the children. So I have never really been jealous, although I sometimes wished the children could have been mine too. Sometimes she became fond of her husbands, but knowing that they would be gone long before she was, I suppose, she never took them very seriously, especially as we had been warned by Dr. Pandé against forming attachments. Some inspired gratitude in her, but I do not believe that she ever submitted to any of them out of genuine desire or love. That was probably what was really wrong with Eva—that and having to part with her children. Throughout her life on Old Earth, Eva has given birth to many children, poor girl.

She certainly had not loved Gerard Vergé, and I think he must have known it. He was one of those men who were already full of despair and anguish, although outwardly he seemed cold. I imagined he wanted to be loved, and when he realized Eva didn't love him, he became even more miserable. The sad thing was that painting didn't love him either. An art has to love you for you to excel at it. That's what Marius says. So Gerard must have been quite wretched sometimes. Eva must have realized this, but she couldn't give him any comfort. So that's why I think she didn't believe the story about him drinking the painting medium by mistake. Perhaps she has been consumed with guilt and that's why she tried so hard to forget her own true identify. Fortunately, something would happen later that was most unexpected and would change her life in the most extraordinary fashion. I was glad about it, even if it left me out.

Monsieur Moitessier stopped thinking about Eva, and his thoughts were again taken up with conjectures about the model. It occurred to him that he didn't know the nationality of the young lady. She had not spoken to anyone, not even the massiér. Perhaps she was French, but even if she wasn't, she could be forgiven for that because of her youth and beauty, which, in his eyes, excused many things. An ugly woman, as his mother used to say, should never have been born. This, of course, showed a lack of compassion on the part of his mother and on his part, too. But he was, after all, what has become known as a male chauvinist, or so the ladies of the painting class believed, and he sometimes seemed intolerant. But there was more to him than that, it seems to me. I detected a sense of humor and a certain warm and sensuous charm. If I were one of the female members of the class, I think I'd find him very interesting. I even detected an earthy sexual quality in his nature.

He was thinking now that Undi might be a nice companion for his young friend, Roland. He was genuinely concerned about Roland. He suspected the lad might have become involved in some sort of revolutionary movement. Lately he had observed that Roland often had to run off to some sort of meeting, and his work was suffering as a result. So he was concerned, not only for Roland's sake, but also for Eva's.

Regretting he was not closer to her, he could, he told himself, at least give Roland the benefit of an older man's experience. "You need a nice companion. At your age, you should be carefree and happy," he would say to Roland when next they had a glass of wine together.

Just as he was about to turn and put his canvas in the rack reserved for regular students, the door opened and a young man burst into the room. He looked excited. His fawn-gray eyes were alert, and his finely shaped lips were smiling. Brown hair, which could have been stringy and unwashed, but wasn't because it was clean and shining, with a few silky strands dangling over one eye, hung down almost to his shoulders. Monsieur Moitessier looked at him and remarked to himself, *There's no doubt but that he's a romantic-looking youth. Velveteen pants. Must be new. And a white shirt with a dark vest—not bad. Every inch a Bohemian.* He smiled at the youth. "You look like one of the artists of the Romantic era when Paris was at its best. Where did you get the beret?"

Of course, I knew this must be Roland. After all, he was only nineteen and the fact was that I'd been away with Osiris and had never seen him before. Osiris was in Paris now, you know, and I was concerned about him too. In fact, the only one of our group I didn't have to feel concerned about was Marius. He was in Paris as well. They were all coming together, as though something was about to happen, and I divided my time and attention between all of them.

To get back to Roland, Monsieur Moitessier said to him, only it was more like a statement than a question, "What have we here?" He could see very well that Roland had a large, white canvas under his arm.

"A canvas," Roland replied, looking around the room eagerly. "Where's the model? She's gone, I suppose. I was hoping she'd still be here so that I could get a feeling for what I'm going to do tomorrow." He held up the large canvas for Monsieur Moitessier to see. "Look, Monsieur Moitessier. It's the largest canvas I've ever had. I went into the art supply store, and there was a notice telling people to take what they needed. I took this and some paints. You should go and see for yourself." He looked around the room. "What's the model like? Merde, I wanted to see her. Madame Rose said she is charming. I hope she's not too charming. It can be distracting . . ."

"Ah, Roland, don't be so excited. The question may never arise so far as she is concern. Yes, she was a lovely girl, and she was very good to draw. You would have liked her very much. But I'm afraid she's gone."

"Well, I'm coming tomorrow. I couldn't come today . . . er— something I had to do—but tell me more. Is she blond or brunette?

I had something in mind—radiant, light colors. Does she have good color? I wanted the canvas to be flooded with golden light and the model to have golden hair."

"Beautiful color, if you like painting silk dresses and panties. Me, I like what's inside them."

"I don't understand. Have we a costume model then? I expected a nude. I planned to paint a large nude."

"No, no. We *had* a nude, but she ran off after the first hour and left her clothes behind. They're on the green couch. Since then, we've been painting a still life." He made a typical French sound in his throat, which expressed disgust.

"Too bad you weren't here, Roland. You might have stopped her. She ran off with a man who was much too old for her." Monsieur Moitessier took his paint box and walked toward the door, thinking what a pity it was. Such a girl might draw the boy away from the revolutionaries he was involved with. One revolution in France had been enough.

Roland looked excited. "Too old for her? How interesting! She must be very pretty. She must have great appeal."

"More than pretty. Like nature itself, yet with it, she had a sort of sophistication—poised and self-possessed. Ah, well, that's the way it goes. Perhaps we'll have Jeanine tomorrow after all. See what happens. Good-bye, Roland. Or would you care to come and take a glass of wine with me?"

"Not today, thank you. I want to attend the late-afternoon drawing class. Tomorrow, perhaps?"

When Monsieur Moitessier had gone, Roland put his new canvas under the model's stand, pushing it well back so that no one would see it and take it. Then he sat on the edge of the stand and looked at the couch. "What a fine couch. That graceful curve along the back! And a wonderful color. I like the carving on the wood too. Magnificent!"

"Oh," gurgled the couch. "What a lovely young man. He must be new."

"Yes. He's nice, isn't he? Talented too," the water jug whispered.

New students came and went, and sometimes the couch never saw them. She liked Roland's appearance and his presence. He was touching the green dress, and on his face, was an expression of awe. He'd never touched such fine fabric before. "What's this? It's lovely."

"That's her gown," the couch said huskily.

"Her gown!"

"Yes. Can you imagine her leaving it behind?"

Eva would have been delighted to hear him responding to the couch. "You are like my father," she sometimes said to him. "My father often had visions and he could talk to things. You are like that."

"What a wonderful shade of green. I'd like to paint that."

"Yes, it makes one think of the sea, does it not? Like the waters of the Mediterranean on a warm day."

Roland gazed at the dress. Then he noticed something else. "And what are these? He slipped his hand into a black stocking so sheer that it made his flesh darken only slightly and shimmer inside the fine mesh.

"Hmm," the couch mused. "I didn't notice those before."

"I didn't know girls wore things like this." The girls Roland knew wore pants or long skirts with heavy shoes. Most of them couldn't afford finery. Some of them wore miniskirts but not *gowns*.

"Oh, yes they do. Those who care."

Then they both noticed a delicate odor above the fumes of the paint and turpentine in the room. It was a subtle fragrance.

"Scent! That's a new scent. She smelled like the sea before," the couch told him. "Something quite unusual has been happening here today. That girl was no ordinary model."

Roland slipped his hand out of the fine mesh of the stocking. "Was she very beautiful? She must have been. What happened?"

"Oh yes, she was beautiful. But there was something else about her, a light. She was radiant, and she weighed almost nothing. It was that special quality that made me so aware of her. I'm sorry you weren't here, young man. What's your name?"

"Roland."

"Ah yes, Roland. You know, I feel something special in you too. It's a pity the Botticelli Venus has already been painted, for if it had not been, you might have painted her today. She looked exactly like that lovely girl."

"The Botticelli Venus? Really? Did you say she took a reclining pose? There's nothing very unusual about that. It's been done a thousand times. But that doesn't matter. As you say, I might have done something entirely original with an old, familiar subject. I believe I have that power in me. Sometimes I believe it, at any rate. At other times, I hate what I've done—mere dull copies of the works of great men. Sometimes I think I should never even look at great paintings, especially of the past. It's so difficult to give up the past and do something original." He looked downcast, but as his gaze returned to the green dress on the couch, he brightened. "A model can be a great inspiration. Something mysterious happens sometimes."

"Indeed it does."

"Have you any idea why she left like that? Was she kidnapped? Why walk out and leave her clothes? No one does things like that."

"She did. But that's not quite true. She didn't walk out entirely naked. He had the decency to cover her. He came up to the stand during the rest period when everyone else had left the room, and he wrapped her in a long piece of embroidered Chinese silk. That's how she left. She seemed to be in a trance—not at all normal, I should say. But she looked very nice in the embroidered silk. A girl like that can wear anything. The washstand and the water jug said they were dumbfounded when it happened. None of us could understand it."

Roland looked at the washstand and the jug with new interest. He'd painted them so often that he was sick to death of them. But now he saw new possibilities in them. Suddenly he thought of something. "How will she make it stay on?" He laughed. But then he thought about Georges Albertine, the old idiot who'd carried her off. "What could she be doing with a man like that? I mean, he's very old, isn't he?"

"Not so old. Not a bad-looking man at all. Not young like you, of course."

"Look, I think I'll go downstairs and find out what happened. I have to know whether she's coming back tomorrow. I mean, I need to have a model tomorrow, don't I?

"Good-bye, madame," he said as he started off toward the door. Then he paused and looked at the couch with some surprise, for it had suddenly struck him that he had been holding quite a long conversation with a piece of furniture. And yet, it didn't seem so odd. He remembered now that he used to talk to things when he was a child.

The Green Couch was just as interested as he was in having Undi come back. Something told her that Undi might provide some means of getting her out of the académie. It was just a feeling she had, but as she sometimes said, "I like to trust my feelings."

"Well, good-bye, dear," she said to Roland. "And don't forget to tell Madame Rose that everyone in this atelier wants her back. No one is angry with her. They have only praise for her and blame her abductor, that Georges Albertine, if that's his real name."

Downstairs, Madame Rose and Monsieur Raferé were just about to leave. It was after four, and they usually went out for a little break before coming back for the late-afternoon drawing class in the ground-floor atelier.

"I didn't engage her, and neither did Monsieur Raferé," the old lady said in answer to Roland's question. "She just turned up. I must say, though, that in all my years here, I have never heard of a model doing that—walking off with one of our most respected students. I can't really believe they went to a hotel in the Rue Delambre."

"Neither can I." Monsieur Raferé stroked his cat. "And neither can Frou-Frou, can you Frou-Frou, my pet?"

"Monsieur Albertine looks like a man who could wait—at least until the class was over. Don't you agree, Monsieur Raferé?"

"Oh, I imagine so," he replied. "Although one can never tell. Anything is possible. Too ardent, perhaps. Oh well, I'm sure someone else will turn up tomorrow, Roland. Jeanine may come, and there's always a model or two waiting around for work. Don't worry."

"Of course. But she's the model I want," Roland insisted. He didn't consider himself as one of those part-time students because he was so deadly serious about painting. So he referred to the other students as "They". "They", he said, "all want her, as a matter of fact, so do I. Please don't engage anyone else until we see whether she comes back tomorrow."

"I understand. Well, if she comes back with a reasonable explanation, I don't see why not, do you, Monsieur Raferé?"

Roland went over to the Café des Grande Poissons to sit and wait for the late-afternoon class to begin. The proprietors knew him. Sometimes Madame Leguine gave him free coffee, knowing he didn't have very much money to spend. She did so today. He sat there thinking about his new canvas and the model, mainly concerned with the composition he had in mind. But then the image of Monsieur Albertine disturbed his thoughts. He'd never seen Georges, and now he imagined him to be about eighty. Old idiot! He was rich; that was it. Was it possible, he asked himself, that the lovely, young girl had gone with him for his money? This was a sexually exciting thought, although Roland didn't realize it.

Although he imagined he despised money, Roland was intrigued. What sort of a girl would go with an old man because he was rich? She'd have to be beautiful. It was a classical situation, really—the beautiful, young girl; the rich elderly protector; and the poor, young student—himself. Suddenly, the model whom he'd never even met became more desirable than some of the young girls he knew who would have been more than willing to go to bed with him for nothing. He couldn't help wondering what she and Monsieur Albertine were doing right at this moment. Was he seducing her with food? Food and wine in one of the fancy restaurants? This made Roland feel jealous and resentful, for that was something he would never be able to afford—not until he started selling pictures, at any rate.

I was interested in his images of the older man, the young girl and the student. Undi could have had Marius if she wanted a rich man—but no. Perhaps she was to be drawn toward this typical classical Old Earth situation—a drama. With Marius, there would not have been that kind of drama. She knew him, and he was a friend, and there was no intrigue with a friend.

Then Roland imagined a scene such as his mother had once described to him in a moment of resentment of her own. An elderly man, she had said, sitting there at the spring showing with a young girl, pointing with his cane at the model gowns as they were paraded before him on the richly carpeted floor. Roland, far from being shocked, had been intrigued. He saw Undi, sitting beside George, greedily accepting clothes that she would never be able to buy for herself. It was the only glimpse Eva had ever vouchsafed him of the world of fashion and wealth, where she played her part as a mere backstage fitter and alteration hand.

The only other glimpse Roland had of luxurious living came to him from the movies. About once a week, if he could raise enough money for a ticket, Roland went to see an early movie. Last week he'd seen old Adolph Menjou in a penthouse overlooking the rooftops of Manhattan trying to seduce an innocent Ginger Rogers, who wanted to go on the stage. The week before, he'd seen Joan Crawford, also choosing the rich man instead of the poor one and coming to an unfortunate end. He never let his friends know that he went to see movies like this. They would have laughed at him, and he supposed they were right to do so. When he wasn't sneaking off to see one of those, he went with his friends, if he could, to see films like *The Andalusian Dog* or Eisenstein's *Alexander Nevsky* or Man Ray's experimental films or Charlie Chaplin's *Modern Times*. It was just that those early Hollywood movies held a certain fascination for him. They portrayed wealthy people on ships or in spacious country estates or in smart town houses or impossibly large New York apartments, unless they were poor immigrants, living in tenements downtown in the slums.

An even more voluptuous image entered his mind. He imagined Monsieur Albertine sliding his hand along Undi's thigh and pulling down the shimmering, black stocking.

Roland pulled himself up. Leaving the café, he crossed over to the art supplies store, and as the door was still open, he entered and helped himself to some drawing blocks and several packages of charcoal. While he was at it, he took some drawing pens and black ink and a Japanese brush and ink to go with it. Then, seeing that it was time, he returned to the académie and took his seat in the downstairs drawing atelier.

Chapter 12

Georges's Fantasies

"Have some of this wonderful tart," Georges said to Undi, pressing her to eat food she didn't know how to eat.

"Madame Guyot, the tart is excellent. Mademoiselle is in raptures," he called to his femme de ménage. That lady, with her neatly coiffured head and good, plain face, appeared in the doorway of the dining room. She had looked out several times, to see how they were faring. Undi fascinated her. Never before had a young lady wearing a silken Chinese wall hanging come to dinner. She hoped the large, antique broach Georges had given her from his collection of Celtic jewelry would hold the robe in place. Undi had wound it around her body in the style of an ancient Babylonian robe and pinned it at the shoulder.

"Now," he said when they had finished eating, "let us take a stroll around the salon." He looked at her. "This piece of stuff. Is it safe? Do you need another pin? Tomorrow, we'll get you some clothes from the Rue Faubourg St. Honorie."

He was pleased when she answered him for she had hardly spoken except to murmur her thanks now and then. He had quite taken possession of her. In her confused state, she offered no resistance. Even in Heliotrope, a Fish-Woman had to be given time to come Back-from-Sea. Without meaning to, Georges had taken advantage of her.

"I have clothes. I left them behind the screen. I want to go back and get them," she said faintly.

Georges, however, had made up his mind to take her to the House of Gustav Roché, the stylish fashion house where Eva worked. Georges knew Jules Mason, a young man who was head of public relations in the same house, and he hoped that Jules would see to it that they were given special attention. Thinking about this, he became excited, and he realized, with pleasure, that he was a rich man and could afford to buy whatever she wanted. He rarely spent money on clothes, wearing his own until Madame Guyot reminded him to get new ones. He was fond of his old, tweed jacket with patches at the elbows. As for his socks and underwear, Madame Guyot simply went out and bought those herself and gave him the bills.

They strolled about in the large salon, tripping over things Georges had let fall to the floor. Madame Guyot always said no one could keep up with his messiness. Now, as she was clearing away the dishes, Georges called her again.

"Madame Guyot, what are you doing? Stop fussing over the dishes."

She could be heard, scraping plates, even from the salon. The noise ceased, and she came to the doorway again. "What is it now, Monsieur?"

"Do you like mademoiselle's robe? It's a princess's robe from the Forbidden City in China. Do you like it?"

"Formidable," Madame answered. "Does she always wear such robes?"

"Oh no. She's wearing it today, just for a whim."

"Not many young ladies could get away with it, Monsieur. Very original."

Georges was delighted. "Mademoiselle is staying the night. Please make up the Polish bed, and tomorrow morning, please have fresh croissants for her breakfast."

Outside, it had grown dark. They had eaten early because Georges had insisted that she needed food. In spite of his delight, he was a little uneasy, sensing something in her that he couldn't put into words. Even though it was dark, it was too early to go to bed, so he made her sit in a chair that looked like a throne, large and imposing and highly decorated with heraldic beasts and lion's claws and told her he had something to show her. Still passive and confused by the strangeness of her surroundings, Undi did as she was told, while Georges went away to his atelier, which had once been a smaller sitting room, just off the salon. There was a very fine archway between the two rooms. Over the arch were the fifteenth-century wooden angels—two of Georges's treasures.

When he returned, he carried a great stack of his drawings, and Undi was obliged to spend the next two hours looking at sketches and watercolors of the landscapes with the dream nymphs and maidens I already told you about.

"You see," he cried, "don't you see? You! They are all of you, my princess. Why do you think I took you away from that model's stand? You do not belong there. You belong here. You are exactly the woman—the girl—I have always dreamed of. Yes, indeed! I'm quite overwhelmed. It's a miracle how you just walked into my life."

He was, indeed, deeply moved. Tears almost came to his eyes. But Undi only gazed dreamily at him and said nothing. To tell the truth, she was wondering how it had happened. Her intention had been to find Roland at the académie, or, rather, her instinct had guided her to the Rue de la Grande Chaumière. And she wondered what she was doing here, in the house of this strange man. She didn't dislike him, but she wasn't at all interested in him. True, the maidens he had drawn did look like her, but that was of no interest to her, either. If Georges's feelings for her were as deep as he believed, he had good reason for feeling uneasy, for he could be easily hurt, as an older man can be by a young and beautiful girl.

He turned to her from where he sat on the low stool in front of her high chair, his drawings on the floor around his feet, and looking into her eyes, he suddenly surprised her by saying, "What I want is to enter into you through your eyes and wander about in the landscape of your soul."

Leaning forward, he took her face between his hands and said, "Open your eyes and let me look into them." Never had he behaved in such a way toward any woman, and later, when he remembered what he'd done, he was surprised and wondered how he could have said and done such a thing. But at this moment, he was not aware of his odd behavior.

Undi responded as a cat does. She allowed him to look into her eyes for a few moments and then calmly turned her head and looked at something else in the room.

He gave a deep sigh and stood up, believing for the moment that Undi had actually allowed him to see into the depths of her being. Yet a little while later, his desire to look deeply returned, and he felt uneasy again. His doubt passed as he led her about the room, pointing out some of the small figurines and pieces of jewelry he kept in cabinets. He also led her into the atelier and showed her the rich silks and brocades he kept there in an antique chest. He was happy simply because she was there, and he became quite entertaining and charming, saying amusing things and, without realizing it, forcing her to become aware of him as a man. His confidence returned and so did his delight because Undi actually looked at him and smiled.

Undi had nowhere else to go, and she was very tired. When he led her to the huge, ornate Polish bed with its embroidered canopy, she climbed up and stretched out and fell into a dreamless sleep almost at once—not the long sleep we Heliotropians needed every few hundred years but a short nap that lasted until morning.

When Georges saw that she was asleep, he stood beside the bed looking at her. Finding satisfaction in this, he drew up a stool and sat down so that he could continue to watch her in greater comfort. He even drew back the silken cloth and looked at her body. But he made no attempt to touch her. After a while, his mind became active. Ideas began racing through it like wild horses. One after another, they came and went, until he suddenly imagined he had found solutions to all the problems that had plagued mankind. Questions of a deep philosophical nature presented themselves to him, and he was able to solve them all. He suddenly believed he understood the riddle of the universe. And then he saw that he would know how to deal with problems of a political nature—with foreign policy and domestic problems, problems of inflation and unemployment and student protests and all that sort of thing.

And when he had dealt with that, he saw that he had his own life to deal with, and he saw how easily he would be able to reach his own goals. He was a brilliant portrait painter, and he saw how he would go about getting clients. He saw himself at social gatherings, at the races, and at English garden parties making contacts with English nobility and famous actors who would be falling over themselves to have their portraits painted. He even saw Prince Philip and the queen herself sitting in his studio with all his silks and satins swirling about them.

Dream girl

Undi, dressed like a queen herself, was beside him at art shows and openings, while crowds stood around them as he gave his opinions of modern artworks and could make or break modern artists with merely a shrug. He saw all sorts of things and felt powerful and potent. So excited was he that he hardly knew what to do. In the end, he didn't do anything except close all the windows and make sure the front door was locked and take a last look at Undi before going off to his own room.

Madame Twujot

Chapter 13

Georges and Undi Go Shopping

onsieur Raferé made a mistake. When he heard that there had been no word from the model, he took it upon himself to have the furniture removed from the life painting atelier and returned to the room under the stairs. To tell the truth, he didn't like the idea of the couch getting paint on it and the washstand and jug getting cracked, and that was why he acted too quickly. He was just telling Madame Rose about it, and she was scolding him a little, saying he shouldn't have touched anything, as the pieces were being used as still life when in walked Monsieur Albertine, large as life, and asked for the model's clothes.

Madame Rose had always believed Georges was a gentleman, and she hadn't changed her opinion. Now she didn't know what to do. She was more in favor of giving him the clothes. Monsieur Raferé wasn't so sure about that, but she whispered to him that, since Monsieur Albertine was well off, it was hardly likely he would want to steal a model's clothing.

"Why not? He stole the model, didn't he?" They had retired to the room under the stairs, leaving Georges in the corridor.

"*Stole* is a strong word," Madame Rose replied. "Anyway, that's why he wants them now, I imagine. He wants her to dress properly and return the Chinese silk." She flicked a fleck of dust off the couch and examined the jug for cracks.

The couch whispered, "Oh, my dear, has the Venus come back?" She had been very cross with Monsieur Raferé for having her moved back into the dark room.

Just then the secretary of the académie put his head around the doorway and asked what was wrong.

"It's Monsieur Albertine asking for the clothes of the model he ran off with yesterday."

"Ha! That one. You mean to say they've been in the hotel room all this time. What energy! Well, is she coming back?"

"I don't believe so, Monsieur Jacques."

They returned to the corridor, where Georges was being entertained by Frou-Frou as she gamboled with an India rubber on the floor.

Monsieur Jacques addressed Georges. "This model, is she coming back today or not? How can people paint in the life class if you're always snatching the models away?"

Georges regarded him scornfully. "The model is very ill. I took her to the doctor while you people were all in the Café des Grande Poissons. It was a matter of life or death, or it could have been. And why 'always,' pray. Have I ever done it before? Is it a habit of mine?"

"Of course not, monsieur," Madame Rose said gently.

But Monsieur Jacques sniffed. "She looked healthy enough to me."

"Perhaps, but one cannot judge by appearances. The poor girl has not fully recovered, even now."

"Even now, eh?" The secretary gave an unpleasant wink. "At least you could have taken her away in her own clothing instead of wrapping her in the life class draperies."

Georges controlled himself very well. "Where are the clothes now?"

"Where are the model's clothes?" Monsieur Jacques asked Madame Rose.

She looked at Monsieur Raferé, who answered, "In the small room under the stairs."

"Oh, very well. Go and take them. I hope Mademoiselle will have recovered by this afternoon. I'm sure she'll be well enough."

Madame Rose rolled her eyes at Monsieur Raferé. Her look said plainly that it wasn't Monsieur Jacques's job to worry about models.

"Certainly not. I've made myself responsible for her until she is well again." Georges turned to Madame Rose. "The poor child was on the verge of starvation."

"Child! A girl like that? Never," Monsieur Jacques replied and walked off.

Just then, the door opened, and Undi walked in.

"Undi!" Georges cried. "I told you to stay in the car until we reached the doctor's office."

She helped him by saying, "I needed water. I feel faint."

"You see," Georges said to everyone. "What did I tell you! Water, quickly!"

Water was brought, and Undi was made to sit down, while Georges went up the stairs to retrieve his paint box and materials from the atelier. Looking round for the Green Couch at the same time, he was surprised to see it was no longer there. This strengthened the desire he had to possess the couch, and he decided to ask Madame Rose about it when he went downstairs. He wanted it for his own atelier. Undi would pose on it only for him.

Gathering up his materials, he returned to the corridor. Monsieur Raferé had taken Madame Rose's place at the table. Undi was nowhere to be seen.

"They're in the room under the stairs." The old man smiled gently and stroked Mimi, who was sitting on his lap. "It's just there, monsieur, at the end of the corridor."

"Monsieur Raferé," Georges said, "would it be possible for me to buy the green couch?"

"That's a matter to discuss with Madame Rose. The couch belongs to her, does it not, my Mimi?"

"Not to the académie then?" Georges was surprised. "Do you think she would sell it to me?"

The old man shrugged. Actually, he was not so old. It was just that he had something elfin about him—he was a shrewd, old elf with both feet in the real world. "It is a beautiful couch. I've always said it was a pity to keep it hidden under the stairs. I've tried to protect it, you know. Offer her a good price, and she may oblige you."

In the room under the stairs, Undi and Madame Rose and the Green Couch were chatting—talking about their ages.

"I'm a hundred years old, but I don't feel it," the Green Couch told them.

"And you don't look it," Undi replied sweetly. "But what's a hundred years? If you reckon by Old Earth time, I should say I was five thousand years old," she giggled. "I don't feel it, either."

"Get dressed, my dear," Madame Rose said.

Undi began to pull on the black mesh stockings. The Green Couch complained to Madame Rose about the dust sheets. "I don't like them. I hate being covered up like that."

"I imagine not. But I only do it for your own good."

"And the cats scratch me."

"I know it. What can I do? I can't hurt Monsieur Raferé's feelings. He loves his cats."

"I'd be glad if I could leave the académie. I'm not really of any use to anyone here." She turned (not physically, of course, but as a couch turns) and asked Undi, "You don't need a couch, do you, dear?" Then, realizing how ungrateful this may have sounded, she added, "Not that I don't appreciate your rescuing me from that hairdressing salon, dear Madame Rose . . ."

Madame Rose looked sympathetic but said nothing. She had sometimes considered taking the couch up to her apartment or selling it, should she get a good offer. It was not practical to take it upstairs because she had no room for it. She, too, loved the couch but not at all sentimentally. Still, she was too practical a woman to give the couch away for a song! She expected to get a good price.

She returned to the corridor to relieve Monsieur Raferé and was very surprised to find Georges Albertine waiting to make her a far better offer than she'd ever hoped for—much more than she'd paid the hairdressing salon where the couch had been in danger of getting hair dye and other stuff all over it.

"Monsieur, you have asked at a most propitious moment," she responded. "I agree." But then she remembered the life class and asked whether Undi would be coming back to fulfill her engagement for the rest of the two week period.

"No. I have taken the responsibility of looking after that girl. She needs rest. I'm sorry, Madame Rose. I'd like to oblige you, but she cannot pose here."

If Madame Rose suspected that Undi was perfectly well, she said nothing. Monsieur Raferé called a carrier he knew of, and Madame

Rose went back to the room under the stairs to prepare the couch for the journey.

"Oh, madame! It's hard to believe! Where will I be going, may I ask?"

"A very nice home. You're going to the house of a Monsieur Albertine."

"That kidnapper! Not with Undi?"

Madame Rose smiled. "I believe you'll be seeing quite a lot of her. In fact, I'm sure of it. He has taken her under his protection. She is living in his house at the moment."

"Oh, I see." If a couch could smile, the Green Couch would have done so. This was something she understood. "And when will this happen, Madame Rose? Oh, but I'm sorry, in a way. Now that it's happened, I believe I shall miss you and Monsieur Raferé."

"I, too, shall miss you. Carriers will come for you today. I'm sorry, but I have to cover you up very well. Be prepared for a bumpy ride and put up with it, as I know you can. Be glad you're going to the home of a gentleman."

Georges put his head around the doorway to take another look at his treasure. He stroked the carved wooden back and seemed very satisfied and backed out again, telling Undi to hurry and meet him at the car.

The carrier came sooner than anyone expected—two carriers, in fact. They began to cover the couch with yet another dust sheet. By now she was very excited, indeed.

"Good-bye, dear friends," she cried in muffled tones to the water jug and the washstand. "It does seem as though my life is changing at last. Oh, my dears, I wish so earnestly that you were coming with me."

"Ah, yes. So do we. If only Basin were here. But she's gone, broken long ago. That's fate. But we're happy for you. One never knows what's around the corner. It's wonderful!" The washstand was a generous old dear. She had a sense of humor too. "What will they say when they come to class and find that *we've* been taken from the atelier as well as you and the model? Perhaps they'll have to drag us up there again. It's time they did another 'Nude Washing Her Feet.' Won't that be a joke on Jeanine should she turn up. She hates those feet-washing poses."

"Yes, yes. But, oh, to be in a real house at last. I'm so excited. Perhaps I'll be there within the hour. Good-bye, good-bye!"

But the couch was to be disappointed. While Georges and Undi were on their way to the Rue Faubourg St. Honorie to go shopping, the Green Couch, instead of being driven straight to Georges's house, there to be received by the forewarned Madame Guyot to whom Georges had telephoned, was taken to a storeroom in some outlandish part of Paris to await the next stage of her journey.

This had all come about because Madame Guyot had insisted upon Georges taking Undi back to the académie to get her clothes. "Lovely as she looks in that Chinese stuff, Monsieur, she cannot go shopping on the Rue Faubourg St. Honorie like that. It would cause the wrong kind of sensation. She is just not properly dressed."

She often spoke to him like this, and he often admitted she was right. He admitted it this time. He wasn't a fool, only an eccentric, and he knew how people were supposed to dress. In fact, fashionably dressed people intrigued him. He wanted Undi to be fashionably dressed, even though he wanted to go on thinking of her as a nymph or a princess.

"Oh, very well." But that meant he would have to go back to the Académie de la Grande Chaumière, and he didn't want Undi to go anywhere near that place now. He was glad they had gone, however, because of the couch. *"Was it only last night,"* he marveled, *"that I planned all this?"*

Last night, he had gone to bed feeling apprehensive, afraid that he might wake up and find Undi gone—afraid she might have slipped away in the night, even though he'd locked all the doors.

But no, she had still been there when he'd crept out in the morning to look for her, hoping she'd still be asleep so that he could examine her while she was unconscious. But she had her eyes open and was gazing at the two wooden angels over the archway that led to his atelier. They were fifteenth-century angels—very old—with outstretched wings, long robes, and gently amused smiles on their wooden faces. They reminded Undi of the two angels who often flew over the Rock, except that those two were sisters, whereas these were brothers. At least she supposed they were brothers. Georges saw that she was looking at them, and he was glad she had at last shown an interest in his possessions.

He had wanted to look into her eyes again, but this time she prevented him from doing so. In some mysterious way, she barred his path. He sighed and said, "Yes, quite right. We must get you up and go out shopping. Shopping for the right clothes takes a lot of time. I never do it for myself. But for you, my princess, I have all the time in the world."

They had breakfast, and with Madame Guyot's help, Undi took a bath, folded the Chinese wall hanging around herself once more, and off they went. As they came downstairs, a young woman came out of the ground-floor apartment. Georges had had the ground floor converted into two separate apartments, one for Madame Guyot and her husband and the other for a gardener who never came, so he had rented it to this young woman and her husband. Georges liked having them around. She was a model for her husband, who had suddenly become successful as a new "space-age" designer. She wore his clothes, partly because they suited her and partly to advertise them. This morning, she was wearing a pair of sequined black pants, very tight, and a shiny silver T-shirt with a pair of breasts silk-screened on the back. Around her neck was a metal collar connected by electric cords to a sort of space helmet that had a visor over the eyes. She said, "Good morning," and looked at Undi through the two glassy bubbles in the visor.

Georges was thrilled. "Isn't she marvelous?" he said to Undi as they got into his car. "Her husband's a young, new designer. They'll be moving soon to the Avenue Foch. He gives her a new costume to wear every day." He giggled. "But don't worry. You won't look like that. We're going to a more conservative house—modern but conservative. I don't want my princess to come out of it looking like something from a spaceship." He gave directions to Madame Goyot's husband, Yves, who was acting as chauffeur for the morning. "Académie de la Grande Chaumière first, Yves, and then the Rue Faubourg St. Honorie."

In the back seat of the car, he suddenly became spiteful, digging his fingers into Undi's arm and whispering—or hissing—"Why didn't you let me look in your eyes this morning? You've changed. I thought you were docile like my little sister, but I suspect you have a mean streak in you."

Undi drew back in surprise.

Then, as swiftly as it had happened, it passed. He didn't seem to realize he had done it, but I could tell by the way she rubbed her arm that his pinching fingers had hurt her.

It was a cool day, not really spring yet, so Georges wanted her to have a lightweight suit to finish up the season.

"My mother sometimes got a lightweight suit to finish the season," he told her. But he was laughing in an odd way.

I didn't know whether he was laughing at himself or his mother or what. Perhaps he was simply excited. All the new spring shows were over, but he wanted to get something for Undi from the spring collection.

"You do know what the collection is, don't you, my princess?" He told her, "All the new clothes for spring."

I think he was very happy now, not only because of the shopping expedition, but because of the Green Couch. He imagined it was already on its way to his house, and was elated by that prospect, as well as by the whole morning's adventure. This was the first time he had ever gone shopping with a woman—at least since he had become an adult.

"We're going to The House of Gustov Roché," he informed Undi. "You've heard of it—you must have. Princess Gisla gets all her clothes there. You've heard of *her*, I'm sure. They'll know how to dress my princess too."

Undi said nothing. She'd never heard of any of these people, and she wasn't even curious about them. She agreed with Georges about the spring suit because she was feeling cold in the green silk dress. It had been made from one of Eva's fabric Pods, which Seagull had, surprisingly, dropped into her lap just as she had dropped the little sewing basket, and Undi had stretched out the fabric herself. To her surprise, it had turned green. She liked it very much, but she realized it wasn't suitable for this cool weather. She had no objections to make when Georges proposed buying something for her to wear.

Yves Guyot stopped the car before the imposing front door of The House of Gustov Roché and listened while Georges told him where and when to pick them up. They got out of the car, and Georges led Undi into the ground-floor salon. He'd never been there before, of course, but he tried to look as though he had. He fully expected Jules Mason, who, I am sure, had other things to do, to come down from his office to meet them; but he was to be disappointed, for Jules Mason was busy elsewhere. He was an important and influential young man who was always busy. The downstairs vendeuse was not particularly warm, but she did, at least, call the upstairs vendeuse to tell her Georges and Undi were on their way. When they stepped out of the decorative little elevator, an elegant, middle-aged woman was waiting for them. She greeted them gracefully and took them into a room that had very stylish-looking furniture. It had a cream suede couch with golden legs and an oval-shaped table with golden legs and a suede top. There was a golden clothes rack, and mirrors with golden tops and bottoms lined the walls. These mirrors attracted Undi immediately, not because she particularly wanted to look at herself but because, when she did so, she saw that her reflections went on forever. This was due to the way the mirrors were placed, so that each image was reflected in the next mirror and so on until, I suppose, it reached eternity.

The vendeuse went away to get the clothes that Georges asked for—the spring suit; a long, formal gown; and a casual outfit, which he left to the sales lady's discretion.

"You can see she's a woman of taste," he whispered to Undi.

They looked through the doorway and caught a glimpse of her as she appeared between racks of garments in a room across the hall. Normally, she would have called a model girl to show the garments while Georges and Undi sat on the suede couch, but Georges had told her he wanted Undi to try each one on herself. "She's just as beautiful as your model girls. More so."

So the vendeuse took Undi into another small changing room and brought her back in the lightweight suit. Georges said it was charming. A particularly delightful shade of blue, it was a tweed with a narrow miniskirt and a long jacket. Undi stood in front of the mirrors and watched herself disappear into the mist of eternity. She experienced a sensation of being transported—not in the normal way we Heliotropians practice the art of transportation, which is a simple affair of transmutation, but as if she were gliding through mirror-space to the misty dimension reflected therein. It reminded her of her grotto and the misty walls of her bathroom.

The vendeuse took her away again and gave her the casual outfit, a pair of jeans and a T-shirt with a golden heart on it. She put on these two garments but was not very interested in anything that was given to her; nor was she particularly interested in what Georges and the vendeuse were saying. She felt impatient and curious about something she expected would soon take place in the mirror-spaces.

Georges sensed nothing. He went on talking about the hostess gown—that's what he called it—and asked her to try it on. He liked the jeans and the T-shirt and ordered them with an extra blouse. Off Undi went again to the changing room and came back wearing the long, silvery velvet gown. Georges said it was too long. Yet he wasn't sure about that. He didn't know whether the gown should reach the floor or should be ankle length.

The vendeuse picked up a golden telephone and asked for an alteration hand to be sent at once. Georges settled himself more comfortably onto the couch, while Undi turned again to the mirrors. The alteration hand came and asked her to stand on a small raised platform, while she knelt on a low stool and prepared to pin up the hem of the gown. She had a small pincushion hanging by a cord around her neck, and she began taking pins from it as she went inch by inch around the hem of the long, silvery-gray gown, pinning it up.

Looking at her reflection in the mirror, Undi saw that the attractive woman was her friend Eva. She and Eva had always been close friends, Eva being a Bird-Woman and Undi a Fish-Woman didn't make any difference. That had nothing to do with friendship in Heliotrope. They'd always been close, but now Eva either didn't recognize Undi or else she didn't want to. Unconsciously, however, she must have known who Undi was. They looked into each other's eyes in the mirror and then saw their reflections sliding away until they were lost in the mist. But they saw something else in the mist. They saw themselves in Undi's bathroom. Eva was holding the baby, offering him to Undi, and Undi was looking at him, only he was the young man. To her, he was not the baby, but the man.

"He's almost twenty years old, Eva—not a baby at all. You'll have to let him go now. It's time you faced up to the fact that he's a young man and you'll have to leave him, just as you've had to leave all the others."

Undi regretted saying this to Eva, even if it were true.

"Oh, no, I didn't mean that, Eva. That's not what I meant, not at all. All I said was I'd hold the baby when he was old enough. I said I'd hold the man and not the baby. That's all I said." She said this silently, looking away from the mirror, or trying to, but she couldn't, for they were within the mirror space. Undi remembered everything, and she was trying to make Eva admit that she, too, remembered. But Eva couldn't bring herself to do that. She had wiped it out of her conscious mind.

"What about the starry night?" Undi was saying. "You remember that, don't you? It was such a gorgeous night. You floated down through the night among the stars. You must let yourself remember that at least."

Eva's fingers trembled, and she stuck a pin into her thumb. She was being drawn, whether she liked it or not, into the starry night Undi was talking about. I hadn't entered the starry night with Eva that other time, but this time I did. We were carried along together like thistledown on the balmy air. Her blue robe was billowing out like the sail of a white ship, but it billowed slowly, and she moved her arms and legs slowly, and I followed her. We were like dancers in the dream sequence of a movie. She pulled the edge of her robe around the child's head to protect him from the night air, although it wasn't necessary for the night was warm. The cloth formed a shell-like hood around his face.

At first, we were high above the clouds and could see the moonlit hills and hollows of the cloud landscape below. It stretched away invitingly, making us want to walk and run on the pure, white surface. Eva set her feet upon it and took a few joyful steps in slow motion, holding the baby away from her body and letting her head fall back so that the breeze could caress her throat. But the cloud landscape was not solid, and she passed right through. I followed, fearlessly, easing myself through the cloud on which she'd been running, for unlike Eva, I was weightless, and a weightless being such as myself didn't sink through the mist of a cloud. We were not subject to the laws of gravity. To pass through that cloud, I had to make an effort, willing myself to do so.

Eva was floating about upside down, floundering about, and trying to right herself. She floated sideways, catching glimpses of the moon through a break in the clouds and then spun round and saw something far below, more brilliant than the stars themselves. Before she could identify this vast object in the darkness, the clouds drifted in and blocked her view. She turned anyway and floated with her face toward the endless night with its creamy moon and twinkling, white stars above the clouds again.

Her phantom child could see them too. He had no way of measuring distances, which babies cannot do, so his little fist kept shooting out as he tried to grab at the stars, which he imagined were right in front of his face. Eva allowed him to do this, for she wanted him to see and remember forever.

What she could see far below puzzled her. It was like a vast ornament made of precious jewels. It looked like a huge diamond pin attached to smaller ones by long strings of moonstones that spread out in all directions, where they were joined to even smaller round ones and square ones studded with diamonds and lined with gold. There were rubies and zircons and emeralds. They all flashed and sparkled, as if they were lying on the great bosom of a woman who sighed and moved. Sometimes, though, they looked like sequins flashing on her black chiffon veil.

"Don't you know what they are, Eva?" I asked and on this occasion, I actually got through to her.

She said, "No, I don't want to know. They are lovely as they are."

After a while, I told her, "It's your city. It's where you live." She had never seen the City of Light before, so radiant and so beautiful, from such a height. Nor had she ever had a moment of glory such as this, with the child in her arms and the sense of her own loveliness.

She was close enough now to make out the long avenues and their flashing red and green lights and the white lights on cars that were moving up and down the boulevards and turning off onto little, winding streets, stopping and starting at corners. The long, silvery-black snake that wound its way among the brilliant jewels now became the Seine with its many gracious bridges, brilliantly lit; its gold and white statues; and its little boats and silent barges resting tenderly on the surface of the water. The tall thing she had seen revealed itself to be a metal tower, and here and there, a stone tower rose up or some church appeared in a square of light. She could see people in the streets, and some were leaning over balconies, looking at the night and at the stars.

Below her was the Notre Dame. It looked like a small church, but as she drew closer, she saw it was enormous. She could see people standing in the spaces all around it. She passed on, over avenues and circles and squares filled with bunchy trees, all soft and dark, and as she dipped and turned, she saw the attic windows of Paris, and sometimes she saw lovers kissing at the entrances to the metros.

"They can't see us, can they? I don't believe they have any idea we're here. I'm invisible. Look, baby, we're invisible. No one knows we're here." She felt complete within herself and with the baby.

I noticed that her blue robe was flying away, and underneath it, Eva was wearing one of her everyday dresses. The baby was asleep, and I could see her looking about for a place to land. At last, she saw the roof of the Arc de Triomphe de l'Étoile, and that was the landing place she chose.

It was cool, almost cold, and as her feet touched the stone, I heard her saying, "Oh, how heavy I feel." She was feeling the weight of her whole body. She walked to the edge and looked down. She saw a man coming out from under the Arc, waiting with his dog on a leash to cross the road, which is a difficult thing to do just there, with cars rushing around the circle the way they do, and she said to her son, "Look, my son. Look at the man with his dog."

But the child was asleep, so she let him be. He, too, was heavy, and she wished she had some soft place to lay him down. She opened a narrow door in the thick wall and discovered a staircase going down, so she stepped in and began to make her way down in the dark. With every step, she grew dreamier and dreamier. Before she had reached the bottom step, she was asleep, and if it had not been for me, leading her in her sleep, I don't know what would have happened. There was no longer a baby in her arms, but that didn't surprise me. I had known something like this would happen.

I followed her into the Métro, and when her train came, I entered with her. At Edgar Quinet, she got out and made her way up and out into the square, and then she crossed, and walked up the Rue de la Gaité to the apartment where she lived. Inside her own apartment, she walked along the hall and looked into Roland's room. He wasn't there, but the room was a mess. Then she was back in the House of Gustov Roché looking at Undi in the mirror.

"You see, Eva. Now you remember, don't you?" Undi said. "Now won't you say you know me?"

Undi's image
to eternity

I expected Eva to smile and say yes, for to say nothing was to deny the profound loveliness of her journey through the starry night. But she said no such thing. Gathering up her pins and her kneepad, she gave no sign and even looked angry because Georges had changed his mind again about the length of the dress. Undi didn't seem to mind. She looked at Eva for a moment and then turned away, as if she were thinking of something else.

During the drive back to Rue Guttenburg, Georges told Undi about his plans to give a big party.

"A Saturday, I think, don't you? You will wear the long hostess gown, my princess. No—don't object. In that gown, you look like a queen. No, you're too young to be a queen, but you will look wonderful. I'll invite a lot of people to meet you." He was having a fine morning.

Undi had chosen a silk tie from the men's boutique, and he had taken off his old tie and put it on.

"Aren't you pleased, Princess? I am. We must do this again." He had never before felt as happy as he did when Eves Guyot drove them back that day to the Rue Guttenberg.

Chapter 14

Undi's Independence

bout two weeks later, the couch was delivered. Madame Guyot, with eyebrows raised, gave Georges the news when he returned to his house one evening with Undi.

"Do you need another couch?" the good lady asked.

"Yes, Madame Guyot, I am collecting couches now. Are you pleased? Do I have your permission?"

"Of course, monsieur. You have it. You just missed the carriers. I gave them a tip, and I have their bill." She still had it in her hand.

"Quite right. Give it to me. It's a valuable couch. Well, they took their time, but at last it's here. Come, Undi. Let us see what sort of condition it's in."

Georges and Undi mounted the stairs, followed by Madame Guyot. The couch was waiting in the front lobby of his apartment, terribly flustered and eager to talk.

"Now," Georges said, "where shall I put it?"

"Oh, wherever it is, move me softly. Make him move me softly, child," the couch whispered to Undi. "That ride! But, my dear, it's all been ever so exciting. I was taken to a storeroom and placed near a thirteenth-century writing desk. Imagine! Rather a crude piece of furniture in some respects, but he had such quaint ways! Interesting too. Such a memory of things past. All those years and so much in his life. Male, of course. In fact, we had quite a flirtation and were becoming serious about each other by the time those men came and separated us. Oh, my dear girl, parting is such sweet sorrow. And how those carriers banged me about. You should tell someone about it. Where am I, for goodness sake?"

"This is Monsieur Albertine's house. You remember him. He's the one who took me from the académie while I was half asleep."

"Oh yes. That kidnapper! He's the one who bought me from Madame Rose. Well, it looks like a prosperous home. It could be worse."

While they talked, Georges busied himself preparing a space for the couch in his studio. "There. Right up there on the dais." He disposed of the matter quickly because all he could think of was Undi.

Just when he had been so happy, she'd run away from him, and he had been in a very unhappy state of mind for the last five days. He had just found her, quite by chance, coming out of the building on Rue Tilset where she had rented the room in an apartment owned by a queer-looking man named Monsieur Raymonde.

"Undi, where have you been all this time? Tell me. Why don't you tell me anything? I'm your friend. What have I done except be kind to you?"

"I don't mind telling you," Undi replied, smiling at him. "I've been at the académie where you first saw me. I thought you'd know that."

"No, I didn't. Why didn't I think of that! I would have gone there to look for you. I'm very surprised I didn't think of it." He looked puzzled. "But where did you sleep? You didn't sleep at the académie, I'm sure of that. You must have slept somewhere."

"I slept in a garden. I found a nice garden with a statue—a huge woman's face on a pedestal—and the ruins of an old building. There were people and cars all around and a café and buildings nearby, but it was quiet in the garden, so I slept."

Tears came to Georges's eyes. He was shocked and hurt because she had preferred to sleep in some public garden rather than in his house. I could see that he was now deeply in love, and I felt sorry for him.

Undi must have felt sorry too. She murmured coaxingly, "I see that I've hurt your feelings. I didn't mean to, you know. But you see, Georges . . ." Somehow she didn't know how to tell him that he had tried to possess her, so she just said, "I'm like a creature—a cat or a bird or a crab or an octopus. I like to go on my own and roam about in the night—to take in the quietness and the stars."

"Male cats do that," Georges flung at her. "Were you searching for a male cat?" She didn't answer, so he asked, "And what did you eat? Can you truthfully say you were alone all that time?"

"I can."

I could tell she thought of Roland as she said that, wishing that he had been with her.

"Then what *did* you eat? Did you have any money?"

"I ate nothing."

"My God! No, I can't believe that! You must be hungry. Undi, my princess, I want to make a society lady of you. I want to introduce you to people. How can I do it if you go about like a flower child, sleeping in parks and posing nude for artists. You will have no social position."

To Undi's surprise, the Green Couch agreed with him. "He's right, my dear. There's something in what he says. It would be foolish to give up your chance of a good life just to live the life of a nymph or whatever you are."

"You'll never find a friend like me in Paris," Georges muttered.

"What he says is true," whispered the Green Couch. "It's hard for a girl all alone in Paris to find a good man friend. Did I ever tell you about my mistress, Camille? She died young, poor sweet thing. She died of consumption brought about, in the beginning, from sleeping in parks and not eating enough. What a lovely girl! Fortunately for her, she was taken up by a rich gentleman just like Monsieur Albertine and eventually became the mistress of a duke."

Undi smiled. "I don't need to become a Duke's mistress, really I don't. Besides, I'm in love."

"A poor student. I know him." The Green Couch heaved. "A charming youth. But what can he offer? Don't lose your head, my child. If you do, *you're* lost."

"I cannot become lost. I'll always be safe."

"In any case," the Green Couch went on, as though Undi hadn't said anything, "a spirit has another destiny. That's what you are, aren't you? You can't even expect to find ordinary love. That's not for the Botticelli Venus. So you may as well be nice to Monsieur Albertine and accept what he offers while you're here. It won't hurt you."

"What is that secret smile on your lips? You've been completely absorbed in your own thoughts and haven't heard a word I've said." Georges looked suspicious. "What did I say?"

"You said you'd like to paint me sitting like this on the couch. You're going to hang the green velvet you have in your hand from the top of the screen behind the couch and add that long, blue chiffon scarf to lighten the green. Do you know what I think, Georges? I think a soft gray would be better than the green."

"How clever! And I thought you weren't listening. Are you sure? The gray chiffon! I've lots of it. I can cover the whole background. Yes, you may be right." He fussed about with his chiffons and satins and velvets, feeling happy again for the first time that week. He was quite convinced that Undi had come back to stay. "I'm including the full length of the couch. It will make a wonderful composition."

"Oh, wonderful! I'm sure he'll do me justice. And you, too, my sweet girl." the Green Couch gurgled.

"The Green Couch is pleased."

"The Green Couch? Are *you* pleased?"

"Of course."

"Then we'll rise early tomorrow and start work immediately."

"But I can't. I won't be here early in the morning. And I will be at the académie tomorrow."

There was nothing Georges could do to make her stay. They ate in silence. Only once did Georges press more of Madame's soufflé on her. When the meal was over, Undi said she was tired and would like to go.

"I can't sleep with you. It's not correct. It's no more correct than sleeping in the park. I have a room of my own now, and I must go back tonight. What will they think?" She didn't really care what anyone thought, but this excuse came to her suddenly. She thought it was something that he would understand.

He did too, but it only made him wonder whether he ought to suggest marriage. This was something he had never ever considered. He was one of life's natural bachelors. He made one last effort. "Look, I will have one of my rooms transformed just for you. You can stay here as my tenant only; of course, I wouldn't charge you anything. That would make it respectable. Yes, you are probably right."

His efforts were all to no avail. Undi asked for the rest of her clothes. Madame Guyot packed them for her in a small valise. Then Undi asked Georges if he would drive her back to her new home. Or did he expect her to go alone? He agreed, miserably and drove her back to the Rue Tilset, a narrow street not far from the Etoile. It was lined with high walls that hid the courtyards of nineteenth-century houses and apartment buildings. The apartment Undi was going to was on the fifth floor of the oldest building on the street.

When they reached the huge front doors of the courtyard, they sat for a few moments in his car.

"I don't like this place," he muttered. "Look, my princess, come back. I will even spend the night in the hotel near my house. I don't want you to stay here."

"No. I have accepted the room, and I will stay."

"Then give me the telephone number."

"As far as I know, there is no telephone."

"What! No telephone? What sort of a house is this?"

He got out of the car, opened the door with some difficulty, and walked with her across the court. Undi asked him to be quiet, so he humbly stopped talking altogether. She could hear the croaky, little whisper of a cement maiden saying, "You're back! You're back! How happy I am!" The cement maiden was a statue that graced the fountain in the terrible cement courtyard. On the other side of the court was a doorway. Inside was an iron lift in an iron lift shaft and a dingy-looking staircase winding its way around it. She would not let him come any farther.

Before she stepped into the iron lift, Georges said, "You know, I've invited all those people for Sunday. Come on Sunday. Shall I come and get you? No, I'd better not. Take a taxi. Come early and wear the gray hostess gown, for you are to be my hostess. You won't forget, will you?"

"No, Georges, I promise."

With that, he had to be content. She even gave him a little kiss, which I thought was not wise, for it only gave him hope.

"Come early and spend the afternoon," he said.

She said yes, but unfortunately, Georges had asked everyone to come on Saturday, not Sunday, so I was afraid he was going to be very much disappointed.

She entered the lift, and Georges walked back across the court. It was nine o'clock in the evening. The concierge was sitting at her window as he went past. She had just let the cat out. She looked at him curiously, and he looked at her.

144

"Madame, I am a friend of the young lady who has just come here to live—Mademoiselle Undi. I would be grateful, should there be any small service she may desire, if you would oblige her."

He slipped a large note across the windowsill, and after a quick glance at it, she scooped it up with her square hand and bestowed a grudging smile upon him. "Certainly, monsieur. You may depend on me."

But she had, of course, every intention of reporting the matter to Monsieur Raymonde, the owner of the whole building. He and his sister had rented the room to Undi, although, so far, Undi had not seen this mysterious sister, if, indeed, she existed. There was something about the way Monsieur Raymonde had spoken of his sister that made Undi wonder about her.

Outside on the street, Georges shook his head slowly in a kind of disbelief and got back into his car.

During the week, not hearing from Undi, he paid a visit. He had to ask the concierge which apartment she was living in, and this caused him some embarrassment. He was even more embarrassed when, after running the gamut of several pairs of eyes of other tenants, he reached the fifth floor and pressed the bell of apartment 5A. It was answered by a man of about his own age. The man looked at Georges suspiciously and said Mademoiselle Undi wasn't at home. Georges had expected a woman, and the sight of Monsieur Raymonde threw him into a state of confusion. Monsieur Raymonde stood there, and he, too, was suspicious.

He had told Undi he would not allow any male visitors. "Imagine how I would feel," he told her, "if I came upon a strange man in my hallway."

"Please tell her I expect her on Sunday," Georges muttered, again giving the wrong day. Then he hurried down the stairs, too embarrassed to wait for the iron lift.

He was in such a state over Undi that he quite forgot he had invited everyone else to come on Saturday, and later that evening, he and Madame Guyot made a list of all the food and ordered it to be delivered on Sunday. He really didn't know what he was doing.

The Couch

Chapter 15

Georges' Party

The following Saturday, I had one of those experiences I often have when I find myself least expecting it. This time, I found myself in a vehicle with five people who were on their way to Georges's house. At first, I didn't know whose house I was going to or who the people were. They were attractive and very lively—in the mood for a party. I hovered above the head of the driver for a while and then drifted back to hover above the heads of the backseat passengers.

Then it was that I realized Isis was one of them. She was sitting next to the young man Georges knew, who worked at The House of Gustov Roché—Jules Mason, the brilliant young public relations man whose father was Georges's old friend. On his other side was a young black man in an elegantly tailored white denim suit, whom Jules referred to as Robert. His name was Robert Dunstan, Jr., and he was a fashion designer from New York. The two people in the front were Australians who had driven up from the South of France that day and had not yet had time to have the mud splatters washed off the vehicle, which was a station wagon. Their names were David and Helen Westworth, and they were spending a yearlong vacation on a yacht in the Mediterranean.

Isis was the only one of this group who wasn't talking or giggling or squeaking or making some sort of noise. From what I could see of her, she looked gorgeous in a long, black dress, with an interesting pair of earrings that dangled almost to her shoulders. I was glad to see her so well composed and elegant.

The others were all talking at once and giggling and arguing about the best way to get to Rue Gutenberg. David was driving and, as he'd never been to Paris before, I wondered why he didn't want to follow Jules's directions.

"Turn right at the next corner, I tell you," Jules was saying, "and then go straight on."

"I've done that already."

"No, you haven't. That was another corner. If you'd done what I told you, we'd be there by now. Just go straight. I mean, turn to the right and then go straight. You'll come to the lane at the back of Rue Gutenberg."

Rue Gutenberg, where Georges lived, was somewhere near the Bois de Boulogne.

"I know, named after the man who invented printing."

"David, do as he says," said his wife.

"Just do as I say. How often do I have to say it?"

"All right, but it won't help."

"Just try, David, for Pete's sake."

"There, I've tried. Down here, you say? Gee, I passed here before. I must have missed it."

"Yes, you see? I can see the house already. It's not exactly on Rue Gutenberg, but behind it. You have to drive down that narrow opening . . ."

"I can't. It's too narrow."

"No, it's not, David. Do as he says!"

"That's what it's for. That's right. You see? How do you think my father's old friend, Georges Albertine, manages with *his* car?" Jules said.

"He doesn't drive a station wagon. He's probably got a narrow, little French car."

But he tried, and the station wagon passed along the passage with almost no difficulty and came out on a back driveway near a group of trees. Jules had been wise to bring them the back way where there were no other cars. Others had all come the front way and were parked in front of the house.

"This is it. Stop here."

"You see, David? He was right."

"Yes. You see, you should always listen to Papa Jules. Get out, everyone."

They got out, and I with them, following along close to Isis. There was an air of great reserve and mystery about her, which reassured me. *It's possible*, I said to myself, *that the jeweled notes of that nightingale stayed with her.* I was thinking of the nightingale she and Undi had heard that day in Undi's palace. Jules and Robert were being very nice and respectful toward her, and this made me hope that all was well. She looked composed—not happy exactly but composed. The fact was that although that experience—the nightingale's song—had had a profound effect on her, she had to guard against slipping back. It made her seem reserved.

They all began making their way around the side of the house toward the front entrance—all except Helen, who wandered off to look at something leaning against the wall of a gardening shed. When she saw what it was, she shrieked for David. He came running at once.

"Helen, what is it?"

Helen indicated a ghastly white form that was leaning against the wall of the shed and then began shrieking with mock horror. It was one of those plaster figures with all the muscles exposed. Georges had bought it for his studies of anatomy, in which he'd lost interest after a week, and then given it to Yves Guyot, who was supposed to have put it in the shed. The sinewy face of the ghastly creature had a lean and hungry look, accentuated by the shadows of evening. Around it were an assortment of plaster limbs, noses, and broken fragments of ears and fingers. Helen started looking through this collection for the missing part of the creature's anatomy, but David led her back to the path. It wasn't much of a path because of the ivy that had crept over it and then on up the sidewall of Georges's house.

On the front lawn, Jules, Isis and Dunstan stood in foot-high grass looking at two stone heads on low pedestals that were hardly visible because of the grass.

"This one is Marie Antoinette, aren't you, darling? Isn't she wonderful? And that one is Evangeline." Jules had been here before, and he knew the statues.

Evangeline looked like an abstract sculpture. Her only distinguishable feature was a protuberance in the middle of her lovely, smooth, egg-shaped face. They both looked like ladies of quality who had fallen on hard times and were obliged to live outside in the garden while other people rented their house.

Jules, whose mother had been English and spoke English perfectly, spoke to them in that language. "Good evening, ladies. You're both adorable. Are you, by any chance, Mister Albertine's sisters? Shame on him, leaving you out like this."

David and Helen were standing before the front door, pressing the bell that would make the door spring open.

"Jules, come on. We've pressed the bell. The door's opening. It'll close in a minute."

Jules joined the others, and they all entered the lobby. Inside, there were two doors belonging to the downstairs apartments. Gigi, the model, and her successful space-age designer husband occupied one of these. The Guyots lived in the other one. A wide staircase led to Georges's upper floors.

"Are we all here?" asked Jules. "Come along, up the stairs."

"Are you sure it's all right?" Helen murmured. "We weren't invited, you know."

"Nonsense. He'll love it."

"What's upstairs?" Robert pointed to a narrow staircase that led to the attics.

"Probably a maid's room. Everyone in Paris has a maid's room. Here we are." He pressed a bell, and they waited with that feeling of anticipation people have when there's a party going on inside.

"Now, I told you, he wants us to meet his girlfriend. She's a princess or something. I think she comes from Tibet."

"There are no princesses in Tibet. At least, I don't think so."

"Well, I don't know. Perhaps she's Chinese. He said something about her wonderful robe from the Forbidden City. Her name is Undi."

When he said that, Isis started and said, "Undi!"

But there was no time to ask her if she knew who Undi was, for they heard the door being opened.

Georges stood there looking pleased but puzzled—apprehensive, delighted, hospitable, and confused, if so many expressions on a face at one time were possible.

"Jules, how wonderful! Come in. Did I really ask you for tonight? I must have. Everyone else is here, so I must have. Come in." He looked them all over. "And your friends! They look most interesting. Come, don't stand outside all night."

The group entered and stood in the entrance hall.

"You did say Saturday, didn't you, Georges?" Jules asked. Then he turned to Isis and said, "It is Saturday, isn't it, my love?" He and Robert had been visiting all the nightclubs and bars for the last few nights, and he hadn't had much sleep. He wasn't sure what day it was.

Georges answered. "Yes, it is Saturday. I'm sure. It's all very embarrassing. I thought I had invited everyone for tomorrow night, but they've all come tonight instead. A large crowd, as you can hear."

A babble of voices came from the salon. Georges looked helpless. There was no one to do anything for him. He had given Madame Guyot and her husband the night off, and they'd gone to the skating rink.

"I'll find a place for you to hang your coats." Georges was glad to be able to say something useful. He opened the door of a closet and found it was stuffed full of canvases. "Oh," he said and went away to get coat hangers, even though Jules called out, "We don't need them, Georges. We don't have coats."

He looked at his friends and giggled. "Crazy, isn't he."

Looking through the doorway to the salon, the new arrivals saw that their host had been waylaid by a lady sitting in the deep, ruby red chair. He was bending over her, and his face had assumed the expression of a courtier at a ball bowing over the hand of a duchess. He was listening with the utmost attention while she explained something to him. With every word she uttered, his face went into fresh contortions of wonder, incredulity, and delight. When she paused for breath, it was his turn.

As Jules and the others entered, they could hear him explaining something to her. "It is my intention," he gushed, "to paint ladies like you with all their finery and their jewelry. Yes, their diamonds and pearls. Rubies too. Have you any rubies, dear Madame Renault? You must wear them, dear lady."

The lady's husband, standing beside her chair, gave a sad and weary smile when he heard this. He looked like a businessman or a banker. Georges had certainly gotten together an odd collection of people, and I wondered how he had managed it because a lot of them laughed at him for his funny ways and didn't take him very seriously. He was eager and innocent, in spite of the way he sometimes gushed insincerely when he had hopes of getting a client, preferably a rich one. It was not that he needed the money, not at all. He just wanted to pass through the ranks of the rich in order to reach the famous. His own wealth helped sometimes, but not often.

Jules and his friends moved further into the large room, where the oddly mixed crowd of people were sitting and standing about. They seemed to find each other amusing and to be enjoying each other's company, in spite of the fact that they'd been given nothing to eat. Georges had ordered a lot of fascinating party dishes, but they hadn't been delivered. He supposed they would arrive the next day, and he wondered whether he could keep the party going all night and serve them for luncheon. On the other hand, the drinks had been delivered twice, so the guests were making up for the lack of food by drinking more than usual.

When Isis entered the room, she stood still and took stock of the antiques, the tapestries, the angels, and the fine Persian carpet on which she stood. Georges had inherited some of his furniture from his grandmother, but he had a taste for antiques and attended auction sales regularly.

"Look at those beautiful curtains, Jules," Isis remarked.

Jules looked at the lofty windows. High and long as they were, the curtains were longer and trailed onto the floor in rich, velvety folds that looked like red pools of spilt wine. Isis observed many things in the room that Undi had not even noticed. She felt at home here with these objects of the past. Their richness corresponded to the complexities of her own being. Sensing Undi's presence, she thought about her friend now and could not help comparing the luxurious heaviness of the velvet curtains, for instance, with the light, transparent quality of everything that she knew existed in Undi's palace on the Rock. She looked at the tapestry on the far wall, over the Polish bed, with its thousands of stitches that had bewildered Undi because of their busy, nervous quality but intrigued Isis. A rich creation of an early period, the surface of the tapestry simmered with what looked like a million tiny snakes but were stitches going this way and that, forming themselves into medieval ladies and their knights, black-robed monks, an old cow, distant hills, blue skies, clouds, church steeples, peasants in fields, a castle on a hill, leafy trees, and cavalcades of superhuman aristocrats on their colorfully decorated horses, all making their way toward a radiant sun—an orb of scarlet and golden threads.

Above the doors on the long side of the room, Isis saw the angels, which Georges valued more than his tapestry. They were delightful, wooden beings with their fifteenth-century lips turning up at the corners to form half moon-shaped smiles. The feathers of the outstretched wings, faintly colored with traces of pink and gold, were finely carved. Wooden hair held in place by wooden headbands must once have been a golden yellow, for traces of the paint still clung to the angels' pageboy bobs and curled fringes.

Isis couldn't help wondering how Georges had come by these treasures. People often asked him this question and didn't quite believe him when he replied, "I found them a long time ago in the cellar." It was true. He had found them, rotting away in his grandmother's dark cellar, and had claimed them and had them restored; he had not had them repainted but had had the wood treated to prevent further damage. There was a certain careless disregard about the way his antiques were displayed. It wasn't that he didn't value these things; he loved them. But he could not avoid clutter. So his Persian rug; the large, throne-like chair Undi had sat in; the hand-carved table; small statuettes; the cabinet full of rings and broaches and necklaces; small stools and side tables, with their magazines and art books; and the great, old Polish bed all looked as if they had been deposited about the room casually.

The guests were making quite a lot of noise. Isis suddenly remembered another party she had been to in a loft in Lower Manhattan, which she would have really preferred to forget. She saw herself with a half-empty glass dangling from an unsteady hand, leaning against a man she'd encountered only a moment ago. She remembered how she had closed her eyes with rapture because, she imagined, she had found what she had been searching for. As she leaned against him, she was rudely awakened by a shriek of laughter. Opening her eyes, she'd seen a heavyset young woman standing before her saying spitefully, "Oh, I know you. You're a nymphomaniac." It hadn't stopped her from going home with the man. Once inside his apartment on East Sixty-first Street, they'd had to have another drink, and while he was pouring it, she'd seen that he wasn't Osiris after all. She'd felt terribly tired. There had been a stupid argument and a struggle, until he'd given up and flung himself onto his bed and left her to find her own way out. She'd wandered through the streets until she'd reached the bar where she knew she could get cocaine.

It was the same old story repeated over and over again in her life, until now. Now everything was different. She had taken Undi's advice about the spinning wheel and spent many hours sitting before an old spinning wheel she'd found in an antique shop. Tonight was one of the few times she had gone out with Jules after her day's work with the photographer. She had agreed to come tonight to please Jules. Isis was one of Jules's top model girls. Jules saw her every day, and a tender friendship existed between them. I was glad she had a friend like that, who presented her with no problems.

He was bisexual. He liked women for their beauty. In fact, he was not such a social butterfly as he pretended to be. He worked intensely during the day and made it his business to be seen in all the smart restaurants and clubs at night. In this way, he used up most of his energy. He didn't have much left over for sex. Women felt comfortable with him.

He had seen the Polish bed and wanted Isis to sit on it. "Sit on this divine bed. I want you to be seen as much as possible. You should go out more often. You're supposed to be seen in all the smart places, but you hardly ever are." He wanted everyone to notice her and talk about her. She was one of the most elegant and glamorous models in Paris, and he wanted everyone to know she was employed by the House of Gustav Roché. He looked at her affectionately as she sat down.

"Darling, you look divine." He genuinely admired her. The long, black gown she was wearing with such flair was a Schiaparelli model he had lent her from his collection of famous designer's clothes. "I can't give it to you, darling, but you may wear it whenever you wish."

He sat beside her on the Polish bed. No one else had dared to mount the steps and sit on it. Jules felt the mattress and looked longingly at the bolster. He felt frightfully sleepy. He and Robert had been up late for almost a week, and he now imagined them lying their heads down and drifting off to dreamland on Georges's antique bed.

"What a lot of people, Jules. Does Monsieur Albertine really know all of them? I thought you said he knew almost no one."

"I gave him a list. Actually, they're a pretty dull lot. Don't you think so?"

"No, they're people. I can see why he's lonely. He's different. But he does seem to have some friends. Where is his princess, Undi? I believe I know her," Isis said.

"You do? She doesn't seem to have arrived yet. Perhaps she's not coming. He doesn't look very happy, does he? What is she like? It's hard to imagine him with a princess in a robe from the Forbidden City." Jules giggled his infectious giggle.

They watched Georges coming in from the hallway. He was on his way to a pantry, looking for food to give his guests.

"Let's go and help him," Isis said. She wasn't awfully happy sitting on the Polish bed. She didn't particularly wish to be exposed like that. People were looking at her and talking about her. She stood up. "Perhaps he's looking for more glasses."

"All right. And you can tell him you know his girlfriend. There can't be too many Undis in Paris."

They found Georges in the pantry perched on a stool, looking for crackers on the top shelf. He passed down several packages to Isis. "I'm very distressed. I ordered a lot of food. It hasn't been delivered."

Looking up at him, Jules said, "Never mind. Everyone seems happy. What happened to your girlfriend? Isn't she coming?" Isis nudged Jules when he said this, but she was too late.

Georges looked stricken.

"Are you sure you told her to come tonight? Perhaps she'll turn up tomorrow?" Jules tried to make up for what he'd said.

"By a very strange coincidence, I happen to know your friend. She's a very close friend of mine," Isis remarked.

"Of yours?" Georges looked down at her in surprise.

"Yes. Undi. She's new in Paris, isn't she? I know her well. I'm sure she would never let you down deliberately. There must be some mistake. I'm inclined to agree with Jules. She might have mistaken the date."

Georges looked amazed. "You may be right. In fact, I expected everyone to come tomorrow night. Everyone may have mistaken the date."

"Or you may have," giggled Jules, in a frivolous mood. He seemed bent on upsetting Georges.

"Jules, will you take those glasses and the crackers?," Isis said. "I'll look after Monsieur Albertine. Come." She led Georges away after a quick glance at Jules. "Let's talk about our friend, Undi." Georges allowed himself to be led into the hallway. "What's in here?" They'd stopped before a doorway.

"My atelier. You're very kind. You know Undi? How extraordinary." They entered the atelier, and he led her to the Green Couch on the dais. "Let's sit here."

The Green Couch was pleased. She hated being left alone. "Well, at last!" she exclaimed. "I was wondering when someone would come." She gave a gratified sigh as Isis and Georges settled down on her velvet body. She knew from experience that when two people left the room where the party was taking place and came to sit on her, she would overhear something of interest.

"I don't know why I'm so sad," Georges said mournfully. He was a little bit drunk.

Isis gave the impression of strength. She invited confidence, so Georges talked about himself. In a little while, he was saying things he'd never said to anyone else. He even told her about his sexual problems. "I am inhibited. I don't believe my parents never made love. I don't know how they got me. I think they found me. So I have put lovemaking right out of my mind." He looked at her, suddenly realizing what he had said. But she showed no sign of embarrassment, so he went on talking. "I've fallen in love with this young girl, Undi, but I have never—wouldn't dream of—not unless she . . . But it's not a physical attraction exactly. I want her love, yes, but I want something much more than that." He found it difficult to say what he did want because, to tell the truth, what he wanted was impossible.

Then he even shed a tear. It hung on the edge of an eyelash, while two or three more moistened the cornflower blue of his eyes. "Oh, I know I'm just an ugly man . . ."

"Ugly! What nonsense. You're not ugly at all. If something would happen this evening to make you feel happy, you'd see yourself quite differently."

Georges blinked at her and felt better.

"I'm sure Undi will turn up with some perfectly reasonable explanation. You may have made a mistake, you know. It may not be her fault at all."

Georges was beginning to feel quite cozy. "She's a beautiful girl, isn't she?" But then he looked sad again. "She couldn't love me. I don't see how she could."

"She may not be *in* love, but she will appreciate you and love you for your kindness. I know her. She's a good person."

"You know her! Yes, of course. You know her. She is a friend of yours. How wonderful. I was under the impression she had no friends in Paris. How do you know her? Tell me. I'm surprised. You look like a woman from another world—the world of fashion and society, and yet, not that exactly. Fashion and society are not the right terms for you. You're extremely beautiful and mysterious too. You have allure." He was looking at her more intently, almost forgetting his own anxiety. He was curious too, trying to picture Isis and Undi together—the princess-nymph and the goddess in the Schiaparelli gown. Although he called Undi his nymph and his queen or princess, reason told him that she was a humble working girl whom he had elevated to the rank of princess. Had someone told him she came from a poverty-stricken but aristocratic family, he would have gladly let himself believe it. It would explain why his princess had to earn her living as an artists' model.

"Don't forget," the Green Couch whispered to Isis, "she's falling in love with that youth, Roland. It will break his heart if he discovers she's having a love affair."

"It doesn't matter very much. Roland will be dead and gone long before . . ."

"What! He's so young," the Couch exclaimed.

"Everyone we meet grows old and dies. Lives are so short here on Old Earth. We're like you; we have much longer lives." She paused to think about what she'd said. "*But perhaps not*, she thought. *He is, after all, Eva's son—half Heliotropian. Her other children have all passed on, but this one may not.*

"It's sad," she said, "to watch them come into the world and pass on so quickly."

"Yes, it *is* sad. I miss my beautiful Camille. But what about Monsieur Albertine? He's quite a nice man. I've found that out. And he's rich. She should be nicer to him."

"But not too nice. She belongs with us—to Marius. He loves her, and she'll be his in the end. Monsieur Albertine couldn't possibly understand Undi and what she is. If she tried to explain, he wouldn't believe her."

"No, I don't suppose he would," agreed the Green Couch. "She's no ordinary girl."

Isis looked at Georges with such compassion that he almost sobered up—not that he acted as if he was drunk, but he was.

"Life is too short to be wasted on anxiety and fear of not being loved. You believe the worst of her because she didn't come tonight . . ."Isis began.

"Not only tonight. You don't know what happened. We went shopping. We bought clothes for her to wear this very evening. Then she ran off the next day, and I didn't see her for a week. I was distraught. I thought she must have come to grief of some sort. Then, on Friday morning, I happened to be buying a newspaper on the Rue Tilset to see if there was anything about dead girls, and there she was, coming out of a building—an apartment building that looked . . . Well, I can't say what it looked like, but it gave me a bad feeling. I called to her, and she came over to me and got in the car as though nothing had happened. I was most upset. She told me she'd rented a room in that building."

"A room? Just one room to live in? That doesn't sound like Undi."

"She could have stayed with me. I certainly would not have forced myself upon her. She did come home with me, and we had dinner but she insisted on going back to that ridiculous room . . ."

"That's right," the Green Couch whispered to Isis. "I tried to reason with her. I told her that Georges was a very nice man and a wealthy one and that she should try to be nicer to him. It was then she told me she was in love with Roland. I told her she was behaving like any idiotic girl who thinks she's in love. Do you know what she told me? She said she'd slept in a park; I imagine it was that small church garden in St. Germaine de Près near the entrance to the Métro with that work of sculpture by Picasso, a big female head—rather strange. I told her she'd never have any social position if she went around like a flower child, sleeping in church gardens. And she said she wasn't interested in social positions. What can you do with a girl like that?"

Georges had no idea that Isis was talking to his Green Couch.

"I drove her back to Rue Tilset," he went on, "but she wouldn't let me come up to the door of the apartment. She wouldn't even give me the telephone number. She said there wasn't one. What sort of apartment is that? No telephone!"

"That doesn't sound like her at all. But I'm sure she'll come, even if she comes tomorrow. Believe me, she would never wish to hurt you. I'll speak to her and tell her you have been unhappy. That's something she would never want—to make someone unhappy."

Georges looked at Isis gratefully. He no longer felt so guilty about his impotence, and he was already feeling more like a reasonable-looking human being.

He wasn't an ugly man. True, he had a strange smile that opened his mouth as if he were expecting something to swim into it and that stretched pale, pinkish-beige lips across slightly uneven teeth and opened his cornflower blue eyes wide so that he looked a little bit mad, but I wouldn't say he was ugly. He was a gentleman from a good, middle-class Swiss family. I thought Isis had done well to restore some of his confidence. It was not what she had said so much, as the beauty and graciousness he saw in her.

He looked at her with even more interest, wishing that Undi would be as kind as Isis was. He wished she would talk to him as Isis had done and take an interest in his feelings. But he was no longer suspicious. He softened and felt a wave of warmth and love for Undi and wished she were here, looking lovely in the gray gown. He felt gentle and resigned. Then he sighed and wondered why, with all the women there were in Paris, he should have fallen in love with this young girl.

"Let's go, madame," he said to Isis. "Come, let us take a walk into the next room."

They took a walk around his atelier and then passed into the salon. He escorted her to a love seat made for two. Gigi, the model who lived downstairs, occupied one space, so Georges bowed to Isis and left her sitting in the other. They knew each other, the two women, and sat together for a little while, talking about the spring shows, until Gigi's space-age husband came for her. They were going on to another soiree in an apartment owned by someone named Marcell on the Avenue Foch.

As her eyes followed Gigi and her husband, Isis saw Osiris!

Marius had talked him into coming to this soiree, just as Isis had been talked into coming by Jules. Marius must have known Isis would be there, but he hadn't said so to Osiris. All he'd said was that Osiris should come. Marius was really making a sacrifice; just at the moment he was deeply involved in the work of his upcoming exhibition of Light paintings that would take place in the sky above Paris, and he really didn't have time for parties.

"Why? You know I don't go to soirees anymore," Osiris said when Marius asked him to come.

"Neither do I, but we're both going to this one. Don't ask questions. And bring your young friend, Roland."

"Who is this man, Albertine? Why should I meet him?" Osiris asked.

"I don't know him, and he doesn't know me. I told you not to ask questions. We're gate-crashing, busting in."

Georges didn't even notice when Marius and Osiris and Roland entered with another group of guests. Anyway, he wouldn't have objected. He liked having attractive and interesting people at his soirees.

This was Roland's first fashionable soiree. He looked about eagerly. Marius, knowing he was Eva's son, took the opportunity of examining him, while Roland had no idea who Marius was. Marius may have wanted to meet the boy, or his intention may have been to bring Isis and Osiris together. Perhaps he, too, expected Undi to be here. It was hard to tell with Marius. Perhaps all those concerns may have motivated him. In this room, with all these people around him, I saw Marius in a new light. He had become stronger, taller, and his personality overshadowed everyone, even though he made no attempt to attract attention to himself. I felt proud of him.

Roland saw Isis and went over to her. He had met her through Undi. "It's a surprise, meeting you here, madame. Are you surprised to see me? I came with my friends, Osiris and Marius." He pointed them out. He need not have done so because she and Osiris were staring at each other.

"Indeed! I am surprised." She turned away from Osiris to smile at Roland then turned her head again and went on looking at Osiris.

It was Roland's turn to look surprised. "Do you know him?"

"I've known him for a long time."

She spoke in such a peculiar tone that Roland, who was sensitive and perceptive, understood at once that there had once been or still was a very close relationship between her and his friend.

Her tone and the radiance in her face affected him deeply, and the strong emotion that flowed across the room as she and Osiris looked at each other formed an aura around him and all the people near them. He couldn't put it into words, but he was fully aware without understanding it that something was happening.

What Marius had said was true—the time of The Light and The Love Tryst was almost upon them. For the next two months, had they been at home in Heliotrope, Isis and Osiris would have become more and more sensitive to each other and to everything around them, and the people would have been affected, just as Roland was now, only a thousand times more so. Even if our fathers, enlightened wise men, did not believe in the Love Tryst, Isis and Osiris would be swept into it as if it were an act of faith.

Isis was still looking across the room at Osiris, and he was looking at her, but they made no move toward each other. Then Jules, Robert, David and Helen were there, surrounding Isis.

"Are you ready, darling? We're going on to Marcell's, if that's all right with you?" All the people in the fashion world knew Marcell.

Isis rose from the seat and went with them. Walking toward the door, she continued to look at Osiris until it was no longer possible unless she were to turn her body and walk backwards. She didn't do that. As if in a trance, she followed her friends out of the room.

Several days later, Isis met Roland by chance. Their meeting was near the Madaline. She invited him to have tea with her and took him to a charming little Salon du The she knew of. She knew he would speak to her about Osiris.

While they waited for the tea, she asked Roland about himself and his work at the Académie de la Grande Chaumière. He told her a long story about his father's paintings and how his mother had hidden them after his father's death and had told him never to enter a certain room—little more than a closet. He used to think about that closet and feel resentful. When he was about seventeen years old, he found a key, tried it in the lock, and opened the door. For a moment, he was sure he saw a blaze of light and a night sky full of stars, but then it was only an illusion in the dark interior of the closet. He discovered not only the paintings but also his father's painting materials, which he found to be in good condition. When his mother came home that evening and saw him standing before the easel, painting the bowl of flowers on the small table in the lobby, she had to sit down and be fanned and be given a glass of water because she was so overcome. She thought she'd seen his father's ghost!

Isis listened to this story with patience, knowing that sooner or later Roland would speak about Osiris. It was amusing to hear about Eva and how she'd had to be fanned, but Isis was in no mood to be amused. At last, Roland told her that, while at first he had been excited and happy about studying at the académie, he was now very troubled because Osiris had made him aware of the awful state of the world and he wondered whether there was any purpose in working toward anything.

He told Isis about the pollution, the corruption in high places, the destruction of the rain forests, the melting of the great ice peaks, and all the other terrible things that were destroying the planet and its oceans were too depressing; Osiris was planning a protest spectacle such as had never been seen before, which would climax with a number of them setting fire to themselves in the Place de la Concorde. Osiris and two saintly disciples named Ki and Sylvester would be the first. Others would do the same thing during the weeks that followed. Roland said all this in a matter-of-fact way. That made it even more horrible for Isis to listen to. She was shocked and felt she must do something to save Osiris.

Madame Renault and her long suffering husband.

Chapter 16

Gathering at Golfe Juan

olfe Juan, which in our time would be called Sea-of-Silver Beach, because of the silvery mauve color of the sea, was now, in the twenty first century, a seaside village frequented in the summer by vacationers from other parts of France. It was never lively, nor as fashionable as some of the other bays and villages along the coast but there were charming old villas where good, even luxurious, accommodation was available. A train line, edged with tall slim palm trees and short round ones ran all the way to the Italian coast, passing Monte Carlo on its way.

The house that Marius had built, and was still building as if it was a work in progress, stood on a high cliff overlooking the Mediterranean. Further along on the cliff there were a few white villas owned by people who came in the summer from other parts of France, or from other countries. They didn't bother Marius and he didn't bother them.

When he first started to build the house, Marius expected us all to live there, but as members of our group began to live the lives of their namesakes; they found themselves in other places and other situations, which I usually observed. They came to the house only on special occasions.

At this time they were all in Paris. Marius kept his small yacht "Ondine," moored in the bay. When he was not traveling the world in search of his genius, whose existence I'd began to doubt, he returned to Golfe Juan and added more rooms, or staircase, or garden courts, or something new and wonderful to the house. The only two people who shared it with him at this time were Madame Do-it (his name for his femme de ménage) and the young boy, Reynard, who helped him in many small ways.

I, too, lived in the house much of the time, but in a lonely sort of way because, of course, they were not aware of my presence. I had grown accustomed to that kind of loneliness, but lately it had become, shall I say, irksome. Often, when I was away observing the adventures of my friends, my impulse was to say something, to utter an exclamation, or to express my opinion until I came up against the wall of their complete unawareness of my presence. This was so, especially as at this time when Osiris was gathering the young people of Paris around him and forming a group whose aim was to stage a dramatic event in protest of what he called world crimes. I wanted to make my voice heard but I couldn't and that could be frustrating.

The most pleasant moments were when I went for a sail along the coast with Marius in the yacht, Ondine, Undi's namesake. This day we sailed a little way toward the bay of Antibes where Marius was able to collect a few odd creatures to put his large fish tank. He studied these creatures and made images of them in Light. Beautiful and fantastic they were too, in gorgeous colors and patterns such as you see on fish and butterflies and insects, creatures we had too few of in Heliotrope; it was a treat to see them here!

When we returned to the bay, clouds on the horizon were turning scarlet and orange with streaks of radiant pink. Up on the cliff top the Persian blue dome and the high walls and tiled tower of the house were silhouetted dramatically against the sky, just as the Mystery House had been when we last saw it from Sea-of-Silver beach, with our fathers.

Marius was bending over securing the dingy. That done, he straightened and turned, looking up as if following my gaze. It was at this moment that Marius and I were almost able to communicate with each other. What we saw almost blew us away. Marius was even more blown away than I was. He yelled, "What a fool I am".

Then he looked around almost as if he'd seen me and shouted, "Where the hell are you, Jason? You're supposed to be my friend. Why are you never here to tell me what's going on?" And I shouted back, "I'm here! Why the hell can't you see me? I'm going crazy. Why can't you hear me? And tell me what's going on?"

"Merde," he yelled. With that he leapt into the air, flew up the face of the cliff and landed on one of the balconies, and I followed.

I hadn't finished, "You see, you've been running all over the world looking for a genius who didn't exist. It's been you all the time."

Then he raced through all the corridors of the house and up and down staircases, calling for Madame Do-it and Raynard. She came running, with Raynard in her wake. "What is it monsieur? Who has been killed?" she cried dramatically. The poor lady could not take in what he was trying to tell her. How could she? She had never suspected she was working for a crazy man from the future who was building a house made of Light under her very nose. Raynard had his suspicion but he was still a child so he kept it to himself.

Now, Madame Do-it, clever lady that she normally was, took the opportunity of suggesting to Marius, that he take a longer break. "Take a break, Monsieur. It's not enough to go sailing alone for half an hour. Enjoy the summer as all sensible people do. Invite those lovely friends of yours in Paris. Take them sailing. You have that delightful yacht. Why not use it with your friends?"

That calmed him. It was just what he wanted. Raynard helped him send messages to Eva, Isis and Osiris, Pavarti, Tiger Hound and Undi. They sent them on what was at that time called the Astral Plane. We, in Heliotrope, called it Space-Thought. We sent thought messages when we needed to communicate.

While we waited for them to come, I spent time reflecting upon the mystery of the house. Nothing had been explained, except that Marius was the genius who had built it and the other genius didn't really exist. How had it survived throughtout the ages? Why did it seem to be alive, with those mysterious spaces within its walls? And how did it glow sometimes, and seem to move? And most mysterious of all, how was it that the time-tunnel could be found there and nowhere else? And who were those elusive light people who inhabited the wooded area of the garden? And why had Marius forgotten that he had built it? And he still didn't know how he did it. It looked and felt so solid. Madame Do-it had no idea she was walking about on floors of Light everyday, and when it moved or glowed she thought there must be an electric storm taking place somewhere.

I had a feeling those elusive light forms in the garden could see me, or what there was of me to be seen, but they were too shy to let me know it. They could have answered all those questions, I told myself, but they chose not to.

There was just one thing that gave me cause to be concerned. I had noticed that when Marius was sending out his messages, he had hesitated several minutes before sending one to Undi. I knew what was wrong. He had learned of Undi's ambiguous relationships not only with Georges Albertine, but with Roland as well. He was not exactly jealous, because that wasn't in his nature, but he simply didn't want or couldn't bear to see her, I think he was shocked and hurt. She wasn't the Undi he knew, the sixteen-year-old untouched princess on the rock, but some twenty first century girl doing what was permissible to her. Just the same, he sent the message asking her to come, because he realized that no matter what she did, she was one of us.

"Anyway" I said to myself. "She's sure to come, the same as the others will come and we'll see then how Marius feels when he sees her." As for myself, I was wondering how I'd feel when I saw Eva. She was having more than ambiguous relationships. She was taking husbands.

I suddenly felt lonely and depressed. The depression stayed with me until the next day when they all began to arrive. As soon as I saw Eva's sweet face and heard the magical sound of Tiger Hound's voice, and heard the joyful sound of Brutis barking to welcome them, I felt better.

Isis was the first to arrive. Even without his invitation, she would have come to see him that weekend, so urgently did she need to talk to him about Osiris.

She rang the bell on the red gate in the high stone wall like any normal Old Earth visitor and was admitted by Raynard. Marius was in the garden with his enormous hound, Brutis. The dog bounded forward when he saw Isis and would have knocked her to the ground if Marius had not called to him. Brutis obeyed the call but tore off into the park in a vain attempt to catch butterflies made of light.

Eva was the next one and Isis had to curb her impatience because Undi followed straight after Eva. Raynard was only mildly surprised when they floated over the wall instead of ringing the bell. He'd seen people flying over the wall before. For Pavarti and Tiger Hound, however, he opened the gate. Pavarti, looking gorgeous in her white and silver sari and her turquoise jewelry, made her graceful entrance with Tiger Hound in his glorious human shape. He looked like a brilliant young "Oxford returned" Indian in his white summer suit and spotless white shoes and his silver-sprinkled pastel pink turban.

"The last time I saw him, he looked like a poor farmer," Undi said. "I don't know how Pavarti can deal with all those changes."

"Well, she changes with him," Marius said. He took them into the house and told them what had happened. Of course they were very pleased and excited and congratulated him.

Later, he led them through the park to the edge of the cliff, where they sat on one of the marble seats and looked down at the beach and Marius's small boat bobbing about in the bay.

Isis sighed. "It's hard to believe that this is the same beach where your father and Jason's father used to sit and talk to each other, where we played as children."

"They still do. Sit and talk, I mean," Marius said.

They all sighed, thinking of me, Jason the unbodied. I'd almost forgotten my own name. I hardly ever heard it spoken.

But Isis wanted to speak about Osiris.

"I wish Osiris was here to see this. It's so beautiful. Marius, is he coming? Why isn't he here?"

"I invited him. I don't know. He hasn't answered."

Isis could no longer remain silent. She told them what Roland had said about Osiris.

Tiger Hound, whom Pavarti called Shiva, laughed in what seemed to Isis to be a heartless way. "Ah, so Osiris is going to take his own life," he said.

"Why do you laugh? Don't you understand what he intends to do?" Isis turned to Marius. "It seems to me that you know about this. What is going on? What is Osiris doing in Paris?"

She regretted not having spoken to Osiris at Georges's party, and she wondered why they had let the moment pass.

Marius looked thoughtful. Recalling a conversation he'd had with Eva a long time ago in Venice, he suspected that Osiris had become suicidal, and he didn't believe his friend's condition had improved. He believed Osiris had only managed to disguise his condition.

At that time, when he'd met Eva in Venice, Osiris had also been living there; he'd been an importer of silks and brocades and precious gems, and he'd owned a little palace overlooking the Grand Canal. He'd owned his own ships. He'd lived alone but was sought after by the matrons of Venetian society, who believed him to be a bachelor. They could not understand why he took no interest in their daughters.

Marius, who was known everywhere and was always a success in society at this time, had been invited to a feast given in honor of the father and uncle of Marco Polo, who had just returned from the court of the Great Khan, and at this feast, he had met, not only Osiris but Eva as well.

During the course of the evening, Marius and Eva had walked out onto a small balcony and stood for a while, looking down at the gondolas gliding away along the canal.

Mostly they'd talked about Osiris, and Eva had expressed her doubts about the state of his mind.

From where they stood, they could see Osiris in the crowded Venetian reception room, handsome as ever, and dressed in the rich silk and velvet that was fashionable for men at that time. He was standing by an enchanting marble fountain in the center of the room, aloof and impervious to the expectations of the ladies who vied with each other for his attention.

Eva was also dressed in rich silks and jewels, as befitted a gracious matron who was the mother of two young boys. Conscious of her position in society as the wife of an important merchant and playing her part with dignity, she had, at the same time, not forgotten who she really was—a Time Traveler from Heliotrope. But to Marius, there were already signs in her face of the sorrow she had borne throughout the ages, when her loved ones had begun to realize there was something about her that was alien to them. At times she had been taken for a witch because she never appeared to grow older. Only by taking her bird form and flying away had she escaped death. Now she knew she would soon have to leave her husband and these delightful boys before they, too, grew uncomfortable in her presence. They would soon turn into old men and die, while she remained young and beautiful. She dreaded leaving them, but she dreaded even more having to watch their love for her turn into something more akin to fear and suspicion.

However sorrowful she may have become, her sadness had been sweet and gentle, and she had understood it. It was not then the suppressed thing it was now—the cause of her bitterness.

"That was hundreds of years ago. It's now the twenty-first century. I believe Osiris is at the point of despair," Eva had said to Marius. "It doesn't surprise me that he avoids Isis, and I think it's just as well he does so because it would be torture for her to be near him if he were unable to love her. How could he, with all his guilt? It would be impossible for them to be as they once were. For that, they have to be open and free with each other and live only for that moment and for each other."

"Indeed, you're right." Marius hadn't thought of it like that.

"Osiris was already destroying himself with guilt and regret at that time. I am very concerned about what happens now, Marius. When I try to speak to him, he will not face it at all, not even for me. And you know how open and kind he always was with me."

"Did you speak to him?" Isis asked eagerly, longing to hear news of him even if it was of the past.

"Oh, yes. We talked but said nothing of importance at that time. He was glad to see me, and I to see him, but he wouldn't let me get close. He didn't behave like himself at all. But he was well and looked very well."

Isis looked down at the sea and said, "Marius and Eva, you are mixing up the past and the present. I too am interested in what's happening now. Osiris is suffering from 'world pain.' He's not about to seek enlightenment under a tree as Prince Siddhartha did until the cause of all pain was revealed to him and he became the Buddha. Osiris couldn't do that. He wouldn't enter into the pain and let it transform him. Instead, he invents a thousand ways to avoid his pain. He might as well weigh himself down with a thousand bricks. He reads too much too."

"He's intelligent. He should know what to do," Undi said.

"Intelligent! Of course. We're all intelligent. It doesn't always help. I've discovered that." Marius looked at Undi and said, "He's her lover. He should be doing what he does best—making love to her."

He made Undi blush but she said to Isis, "Yes, Osiris still loves you, Isis, of course. How could he not love you? But I think he's taken a wrong path. He'll find his way back, won't he, Marius?"

Marius thought of the time he had met Osiris in Jerusalem. "You know, I saw him in Jerusalem at the time of the Crucifixion. He was tormenting himself even then. He felt guilty because he wasn't the one up there, suffering the pain of death. I told him he shouldn't even think such a thing. He had no right to be so presumptuous. We may seem like gods to some people because we can do things they only dream of, but we're not. He played the god in Egypt. He died every night and became the rising sun or some such thing every morning. Only it wasn't real. He didn't really die every night; he did it only symbolically, and that was his shame.

"Then what does he do? He makes his way through a troubled world full of god-kings and fertility gods who sacrifice themselves or get torn to pieces for the common good. And if I know Osiris, he's too sensitive not to be affected by all he saw at that time. In Jerusalem, he sees the Man up there dying the real death on the cross, and three days later, he hears of the Resurrection . . . . It's an odd thing to say, but I had the impression that day that Osiris was envious. He would have welcomed that death on the cross himself—especially as all around him, on almost every hill, such executions were taking place."

"Oh, please, don't say that," Isis cried, tears springing to her eyes. "It's my fault. I'm the guilty one. I made him stay in Egypt. I enjoyed it, but he was never happy. That's why he's cut himself off from me. He must hate me!"

"Forget the word *guilt*! You're taking too much upon yourself. In spite of your perfect union, Isis, which I'm sure you'll have again when this is all over, Osiris is responsible for his own actions. I'm hoping this will all pass."

"That's what I've told her," Undi said, putting aside the huge, green leaf she'd been fanning herself with. "I never allow myself to feel guilty—not about anything." She cast a sidelong glance at Marius. She did feel a little bit guilty, remembering the wonderful palace he had made for her on the Rock and she'd never once thanked him for it. She suddenly wondered what it would be like to love Marius. She put that thought aside, for she knew she desired Roland. Isis and Eva had said so.

"It's time! It's time we were together. If we were together, he'd forget the past," said Isis. She suddenly looked glad, as if the solution was perfectly simple.

"It certainly is time. Do you know how long we've been here?" Marius asked.

Isis cried passionately, "I know. Haven't I searched for him throughout the centuries?"

"Yes, you have," Marius said soothingly. "But Tiger Hound and I will see that he's all right. Don't worry about it, Isis."

When the weekend was over, I traveled part of the way to Paris with the two young women, hoping for a sign that they sensed my presence. Of course, they didn't. I felt depressed as though the shadow of death was flying along with us.

Undi was telling Isis about her relationship with Roland. She was saying that, contrary to what some people believed, Roland had never so much as touched her hand, even though he seemed to like her. It wasn't what she had expected. "When I left the palace," she said, "I expected him to make love to me, but he never has."

"He's involved with all those people around Osiris. He's troubled and confused. How can you expect him to think about love?" Isis told her. "Osiris expects him to kill himself."

"But you expect Osiris to think about it."

"So I do," Isis replied sadly. She was wondering what Marius had meant when he'd said it would be all right.

I wondered too. Osiris had suddenly shut himself off from everyone. He no longer had any relationship with any one of us but sat in his private room all day and left all the arrangements for the sacrificial drama to Isobel. It was to take place the following Sunday.

I couldn't bear the thought. I left the two girls and returned to the Old House to sit in the cave where we had sung our way into the Time Tunnel. I tried to sing my way back home to Heliotrope and our own time, but nothing happened. I just sat there like a fool for several hours, feeling lost and lonely. It was the first time in all the years we had spent on Old Earth that I had been really miserable.

The Old House

Chapter 17

City of Light

The following Sunday, Georges was reasonably happy again. He and Undi climbed the stairs to the Sacre Coeur to find a good place where they could stand and look at the sky. Georges didn't believe he was going to see anything remarkable, but he'd come just to please Undi.

Almost as soon as they found an empty space by a stone wall overlooking Montmartre, it began. What happened was that flecks of something that looked like snow began to fall, and within the space of a few minutes, the whole of Paris was a sparkling fairyland. Rooftops; parks; the Eiffel Tower; the Tuilleries and its statues and trees; the Louvre; the Petit Palace and the Grande Palace; the Seine and its lovely bridges, boats, barges, and banks; the Notre Dame and the Trocadero and the great railway stations; the Gare Montparnasse; Gare d'l Este; Gare du Nord; and the Bastille—all glowed. Even the bookstalls along the Left Bank and the fountain not far from the Beaux Arts and the Beaux Arts itself and everything else as far as the eye could see—and I could see it all because I was high up in the air myself—was bathed in this radiance. I knew it wasn't snow, of course, but flecks of light that Marius was flicking away from his fingers. It was easy for him to do this, but Georges kept fussing and saying it wasn't possible.

"There must be some explanation for this," he said several times.

Yet there they were, right before their eyes—those big, white snowflakes. They even flickered over Georges and Undi, so that they, too, sparkled like everyone else all around them. It was extraordinary because no one was getting wet. Then, as soon as everything was bathed in the brilliance, it became clear to all the enraptured people who were

175

out that day that they were composed of Light. Undi realized what they were and tried to tell Georges. Of course, he too saw that it was Light, but that only added to his confusion. People were running to lean over the wall where Georges and Undi were standing, up near the Sacre Coeur. There were a lot of people—a big crowd. When Undi looked around, she saw Isis and Roland standing right next to Georges. Isis had been waiting for her to see them, but Roland was lost in wonderment and hadn't noticed her.

One snowflake flashed like a light, making both Georges and Roland blink, and while they did so, Isis and Undi slipped right through it and came out onto the terrace of the palace on the Rock.

"Come, quickly," Undi said urgently, and taking Isis's hand, she ran with her to the room of darkness. She wanted to see Marius making his pictures of Light over Paris, but they were a fraction of a second too late. All they saw was the spotted hound chasing a butterfly made of Light in his spacious garden. "That's his dog," Undi whispered.

"I know," Isis whispered in reply. "I've seen Brutis."

"So you have. I forgot."

They turned away, and Undi looked at Isis with a question in her eyes. She was a little bit jealous because Isis and Roland had been together.

Isis explained. "You're probably wondering why Roland and I are together. It's all right. We met by chance walking up to the Sacre Coeur. He told me more about Osiris and all about his plans for their sacrifice. You know, they really believe that the planet is being destroyed."

"How can it be? Heliotrope wouldn't exist if that were so. Doesn't Osiris think of that? If the planet were to be destroyed, there'd be no future, yet Heliotrope is the future. Perhaps Heliotrope is a dream left over from Old Earth time."

Isis looked thoughtful. She was thinking about Isobel. Roland had told her about this girl named Isobel who was always at the meetings. He said she was a strange girl who could see into people's minds.

Roland had said in describing this young woman, "She saw into my mind once and sent a message across the room, which I heard as distinctly as if she had spoken aloud. She told me that the situation was getting worse and worse and we must do what Osiris wants. She works in a large building somewhere outside of Paris, where research is done all the time. Those mysterious people who are always referred to as "They", know many alarming things that are being kept secret from the public. She says she came upon this information by chance when she discovered an enormous computer in the basement of the building. It has all the facts stored in it. It's supposed to be a secret—and she thinks she's in danger because she found out about it."

"Oh, dear!" Undi looked concerned, but she couldn't comprehend what Isis was saying.

Just then, they heard a distant rumbling. Down below, huge waves began to leap up and beat upon the rocks. The palace quivered and flashed like a thousand diamonds. It was as though the storm was telling them that even the palace and the Light itself were in danger. The storm died down and the sea spirits, who, like furies, had been leaping high into the air, sank back and turned into tired, gentle little specks of foam.

"Let's go back." Isis, too, had been shuddering, but she was calm again. "It's all right. We'd better go back."

Time began again. Roland and Georges had finished blinking, and Undi and Isis were back with them, leaning over the wall as if nothing had happened. But, of course, something had happened, and now something else was taking place. The snow that had been a sparkling blanket of Light—the first picture of Marius's wonderful exhibition ever to be seen—now broke up into a million silvery fragments that radiated upwards and changed into a million bluebirds that flew about with a fluttering and a sweeping this way and that, until they rose higher and higher and became part of the sky itself.

The snow, the bluebirds, and the whole picture had been so full of radiance that everyone standing on the terrace and on the steps leading up to the Sacre Coeur, including Isis, Roland, Undi, and even Georges, forgot all fears and doubts and became idiotically happy. They all streamed down and filled the streets, the cafés, and the parks, until Paris was full of the sound of their voices. It was a Sunday that people would remember for a long time.

The first of the series had been a great success. The critics, even though they couldn't explain the phenomenon, raved about the new art form. All of Paris raved with them, and Frenchmen were able to hold their heads up again, believing the glory of Paris as the art center of the world had returned. Even though the pictures had been exhibited in broad daylight, the Light used in the creation of the works of art was so brilliant that they stood out against the sky, almost as if it were night. The strange thing was that the pictures appeared early in the morning and lasted into the night. Another extraordinary thing was that people accepted the phenomenon without asking any questions. It was as though, suddenly, everyone believed in magic. This wondrous Light brought forth by Marius was the same brilliance we experienced in Heliotrope on the day of our festival.

MONDAY: A Still Life.

Lilac jacarandas and green vines of Light climbed the huge iron supports of the Eiffel Tower, sprouting upwards and out until a wide umbrella of the most heavenly violet flowers spread out above the tower. As the day wore on, new buds and leaves opened out, and the giant still life reached higher and higher into the sky. It had no particular meaning—it wasn't meant to. But it did have in it the wonderful color of a Heliotrope sky.

TUESDAY: An Abstract

That's what it was at first. The Parisian sky was a typical gray that day, so Marius chose it as a background for his Abstract in Luminous Blues. Through the patterns of blue, however, there emerged streaks of delicate pink, strong orange, harsh black and brown, and small touches of creamy white. This brilliant composition of Light hovered above the Boulevardes Montparnasse and Raspail, the Rue Delambre, and the Rue de la Gaîté and extended as far as the Montparnasse Cemetery.

On this Tuesday, Roland, looking up from the small balcony of his mother's apartment, became very excited—even more excited than he had been on Sunday and Monday, and called Eva to come and see it. She came to the balcony, looked up, and said quite calmly, "Oh, yes. Another one. It's Marius, the great artist who makes picture with Light. You remember him, my child. He painted the starry night for me."

Roland stared at her and would have asked her what she meant if he hadn't been so intent upon looking up at the picture again. He would recall the remark afterwards but would be unable to make anything of it, so he'd forget it.

Eva herself merely looked a little stunned and then said, *"Now what did I mean by that?"* The picture gave her a sense of déjà vu, and she continued to look at it as she walked along toward the Metro Edgar Quinet on her way to work.

Something was happening to the picture. The streaks of vivid color began to move about and take on another form, as though the abstraction was reverting to the artist's original conception. As Eva looked up, she saw that it became a picture of two people on a luminous blue bed, making love. They never stopped moving. It was an image of tender sensuous love. Two people could be seen quite clearly, caressing each other and exploring each other's bodies, enjoying their closeness. It may have shocked a few people who looked up at it, but, after all, they were not obliged to look. As I watched *The Lovers*, I found myself wishing I had my body so that I could do what they were doing.

Well, Madame, and what do you think of that?"

Eva looked around and saw her neighbor, Gaston Moitessier. He was looking at her with such a mischievously amorous expression that she was staggered by his boldness. She muttered something and hurried off, but when she reached the entrance to the Métro, she turned again and looked back and saw him still standing there, smiling and pointing to the picture in the sky.

Sitting in the train, she couldn't help marveling at Marius's skill, even though she prudishly chided herself for having been so interested in the subject matter. She thought of poor Gerard, her last husband and Roland's father. He hadn't understood much about making love and had never aroused passion in her. So she wasn't really aware of what she'd missed. Now, she suddenly realized she was still young enough and became uncomfortably aware that a certain desire had stirred in her. She often had dreams that troubled her. Only on very rare occasions would the dreams be pleasant ones. Most of the time, they were jumbled and ridiculous. Her sense of dignity was offended. Poor Eva. This trouble of hers made me feel protective, but there was nothing I could do. I could only observe, as usual.

Suddenly, as she looked at her fellow passengers, the thought came to her that other people who lived alone as she did might have similar desires—old maids, or men, perhaps, who had no wives or mistresses and didn't frequent brothels (she blushed at the thought, for Eva was remarkably puritanical; she'd never been anything but a respectable matron) or young people who were tormented by their own sexual energy. She lowered her eyes as she realized she was looking along the compartment, seeking out certain types of people, wondering whether they, too . . . Then she had the horrifying thought that they might look at her and recognize her as one of them. She knew that some people lived celibate lives. Suppose they wondered? Her neighbors? *Oh, mon Dieu, suppose Gaston Moitessier thinks of me like that!* She was ashamed.

But as the day wore on, her embarrassment passed and she became absorbed in her work, only occasionally stopping to look out of the window at the brilliant light in the sky. A little seed had been planted, however, and she didn't forget the picture of *The Lovers.*

WEDNESDAY: A Seascape

This was another Light image that appeared to have no meaning. Marius painted anything that appealed to him at the dawn of each day. Perhaps this one was for Undi. There was a wide, tempestuous seashore with high cliffs curving down to a windswept beach where a pale yellow skiff lay on its side with white seagulls flying above it. The colors of the sky and the cliffs and the rocks and the sea were silvery gray, pink and putty-white, and rust and blue.

Undi saw it when she came out onto the Rue Tilset that morning. She was on her way to Rue Gutenberg to spend the morning posing on the Green Couch for Georges. The sight of the seascape and the rocks and the white birds disturbed her and made her wish she were back in her palace. She wished she were in her bathroom so that she could dive into the pool and become one again with the sea. But she resisted the impulse and hastened on to Georges, to tell him all about the seascape.

"Today, he's produced a masterpiece. It's drifting down toward the Tuileries. Oh, Georges, why won't you stop painting for one morning, just one morning, and come out and look at the pictures like everyone else?"

After seeing the first picture, Georges had retired to his own atelier to paint his own pictures.

It was true that everyone else was out in the streets or leaning out of windows or balconies. Even Monsieur Raymonde, Undi's landlord, had surprised her by expressing an interest. She was surprised because she had seen very little of him, and he had an air of secrecy when she did see him. As for his sister, Undi had never even met her and had begun to wonder whether she actually existed. But then she, herself, had been out every day and came home late and went straight to her room. Sometimes she didn't come home at all but spent whole nights lurking in some old garden or sitting by the Seine under one of the bridges. No one ever saw her. She had been with Georges every morning and at the académie every afternoon. Georges continued to shower gifts upon her, and she accepted. He was grateful for a smile and a light kiss.

Naturally, everyone at the académie was very excited by the pictures in the sky. Since Monday, very little work had been accomplished, as people stood about in groups on the Rue de la Grande Chaumière, talking and looking up at the sky. Monsieur Moitessier; Doreen, the girl who was working on the enormous cabbage; Carrot; Mrs. Widgery; the young lord who was painting the three canvasses; and others all went over to the café to talk about "the new technique." Some were enthralled by it, and some resented it as people do when they resist something new. Roland found the picture exciting and terrifying. He was not ready yet to discard everything he had believed in order to plunge into the unknown, which was what Marius's art was to him. No one had asked him to anyway. Marius had not set himself up as a teacher or an authority. He was simply being himself and doing what he wanted to do.

Madame Rose and Monsieur Raferé went out to have a look. They had lived through the impressionists, cubists, pointillists, and the primitives; the Fauves, futurists, abstractionists, Dadaists, pop artists, and minimalists; and now they looked forward to living through the era of the Lightists. Monsieur Raferé went first, taking the cats out to see it, and came back to report to his colleague that it was "not bad, not bad at all." Then Madame Rose took a short walk to the pavement and looked up at *The Lovers* and came back nodding her head. "Yes, in art, anything is possible. I remember Pablo Picasso telling me that in 1928."

Roland had been at the acadèmie on Monday but not on Tuesday. He spent the day with members of the group, rehearsing with them for the performance they were to give the following Sunday. It was to be as soon as that! What a strange week it was—so much taking place, and it was now only Wednesday. A remarkable thing was happening. The Light pictures made people feel that something new was being opened up which they could accept—fresh hope for humankind—and yet, here was Isobel going ahead with plans for the self-immolation, not only of Osiris but the two young men, Ki and Sylvester, as well. The members of the group were behaving as if they were to give a performance of an ordinary street theater. No one mentioned the sacrifice. They worked on the mechanics of what was to happen. It was amazing how quickly they had pulled the drama together. They all knew their parts, what they had to do before and after the play they were presenting, and how they would make their escape when the police came, as they surely would. Isobel was firm and asked for complete obedience. No one was to stay behind to see what happened to Osiris and Ki and Sylvester once their fires had been lit. There was still no communication between Isis and Osiris. If she wanted to ask a question, she had to go to Isobel.

Undi said to Georges, "But it's something you should see, Georges. Why are you so stubborn? You'll be sorry. These pictures won't be here next week. You can't buy them and hang them on your wall. They're made of Light. They have no permanence, except in your heart and mind."

"I don't believe it," Georges muttered. "Besides, I was almost killed yesterday when I went out. Everyone has gone mad. The streets of Paris are dangerous."

It was true. On Tuesday afternoon, Georges had gone out to sneak a look at *The Lovers* on the luminous blue bed. He had intended to go to the académie, just to be involved, but he knew he would see Undi posing on the stand, naked, with everyone looking at her, and he didn't want to see that. He imagined Roland would be there—don't think he hadn't noticed how they had looked at each other and smiled while walking back from the Sacre Coeur on Sunday. He was jealous, not only of Roland, but of the images in the sky and Marius, the man who had created them.

So, instead of going to the académie, he'd walked all the way along Boulevarde Raspail and finally made his way to Serves Babylon. On the corner, he noticed two young gendarmes gingerly examining a parked car. They appeared to be in some doubt as to what to do about it, and Georges realized why. Fortunately for him and the two gendarmes, they all moved away around the corner, and some sixth sense made them duck just as the bomb inside the car exploded. That was the second bomb that day. The first had gone off in a courtyard where journalists who worked for the French radio parked their cars and stood about chatting each day before going into the building. Several people had been hurt. This sort of thing had become almost a daily occurrence. People became accustomed to hearing about "another plastic bomb, the work of terrorists!" It was all part of the intricate pattern of the wide tapestry of the city.

The week was like that—full of creativity, violence, a certain tension, and an expectancy. People looked forward each day to a new picture over Paris, but at the same time, rumors of Sunday's big street drama had been circulated. And people were interested in that also. The French were proud of their tradition of theater art and their small cabarets and street performers. Somehow there was the feeling that this was to be linked with the pictures of Light—a performance of some kind with live actors, a fusing of drama, painting and Light, free for anyone passing by in the street.

And in the place where she worked by day, Isobel the Inscrutable, made frequent visits to the giant computer in the dungeon. It was an oracle. She was accustomed to oracles, for she was a high priestess. She knew when they spoke the truth. Going down to it, where the elevators couldn't go, where it was dark and secret, was like going to the cave to seek the terrifying dark-robed oracle of ancient Greece.

The machine didn't speak in riddles like that oracle. It intoned, to be sure, but in clear statements. It made indictments against humankind— its wars, its revolutions, its treachery, its crimes, its assassinations and its kidnappings. These were only headlines. It gave dates and details of horrible deeds. It detailed the pollution and depletion of all the Earth's resources—the poisoning of the rivers and the destruction of seabirds and the fish, the wildlife, and the coral in the sea. It told of miscalculation and bungling on the part of scientists and doctors and economists the cunning of politicians and statesmen and dishonesty in high places. There was indifference to suffering or much fuss made about packages dropped for starving Africans—packages that were often stolen by undeserving people, while others were forgotten. Child abuse was taking place in civilized countries. The oracle intoned on. Hunger, animals' habitats destroyed, rainforests, destruction of the ozone. Draughts, hurricanes, and misused government aid. Unemployment, drugs, torture, quests for power, fraud. Adulation of the wicked. Rewards for the wicked and the immoral. And on and on the oracle intoned. It listed mass suicides, madness, despair, and fear, all culminating in the War of the World that would end it all. Isobel spent hours listening to it. It gave exact figures, names, and locations. She even saw her own name under the heading of petty crimes, along with the names of her friends. She saw lies and small acts of cruelty and, most of all, the self-destruction and the frittering away of precious life. She saw fear in all its shapes and forms.

"But, Machine," Isobel asked, "surely there is another like you that tells the good news. Are there no messages of hope?"

The machine answered, "I'm not programmed for that. I am the doom machine."

Isobel's machine told her that the world would come to an end quite soon if nothing was done. She whispered to herself, and at night, she scattered leaflets filled with terrifying information for the public. She looked into the future and saw many like herself, scattering leaflets, fighting their way through mobs and barricades, and taking part in meetings or dying in foreign lands; they languished in filthy jails or appeared on talk shows. She talked and talked and talked, and that was unlike Isobel, for she was a silent person and a mystery woman. Even I didn't know what to make of her. She never said anything about the simple fact of love. She tried with all her might to make it known to the world that it was doomed. And, of course, she was in love with Osiris and would do anything he asked of her. But now he was as unmoved by her as he had been by the presence of Isis at the meetings.

It was springtime, and the city was coming to life. Here and there, groups of unhappy workers and discontented students made their voices heard. But flowers still bloomed in the Luxembourg Gardens and in the Tuileries and the Jardin du Plantes and in window boxes. Lovers still kissed in the streets of the Left Bank and at the entrance to the metros. People discarded winter garments. Spring shows opened. Women still thrilled to the new styles, as though nothing else mattered.

Eva and Jules were busy in the Maison Gustov Roche, together with all the other people in the fashion world. Undi was restless, and Georges took her to Versailles for dinner. Monsieur Moitessier called on Eva with the pretence that he had not seen Roland lately and was concerned about him. Monsieur Raymonde allowed a cleaning lady to do the hall carpets in his apartment where Undi lived. This was most unusual! There was a faint movement from the room that was supposed to be his sister's. He asked Undi to pose for him while he took photographs. He looked furtive when he said it because he wasn't interested in art—only in images of naked girls. Madame Rose had a blue vase with spring flowers on her table at the académie. Monsieur Raferé went over to the Dôme and came back in a delightful mood— just a little bit drunk. Crowds filled the sidewalk cafés—the Dôme and the Coupole and the Select. The skies became bluer and bluer and the spectacular exhibition of Light pictures continued. Children played at being Light artists and waved lighted candles about in dark rooms, making their parents believe they were potential geniuses.

Thursday: On the Seine

A great violet barge, all radiant with Light and rippling water teeming with silver and gold fish, drifted about in the sky following the course of the Seine, pausing when it had reached the edge of the city and then drifting back again until it was above the Pont Alexander III. As the day progressed, the colors changed. At midday, there were apple greens, blue, and deep plum, and when evening came, the picture of the deep rose and dark blue barge and the apricot and violet water with its black fish glinting like sequins on a woman's gown drifted up and finally turned into distant stars and planets in the night sky.

Georges was not getting on well with his painting. He had a commission to do the portrait of the banker's wife. He didn't have to wrap her in one of his satin drapes after all because she wore her own opera gown, which looked like a tent. She also wore her emeralds and had her hair done in a high beehive shape. He started well, but his client upset him by asking if he could do her in "Lightism." He felt that Undi was drifting away from him, and he was convinced it was because he couldn't make love like a younger man, while, really, all she talked about were the paintings in the sky, and she seemed so distant. He brooded over this, and the Green Couch felt sorry for him.

Yet Undi came for his sittings and even let him look into her eyes. He thought about his villa in the South of France and wondered whether he should take her there. Now that, at last, he had a commission, he felt a perverse impulse to go away and leave the banker's wife sitting in her tent on his highly decorated model's stand. Yet he couldn't make up his mind. The lure of worldly fame as a society portrait painter was still attractive, and he made no real effort to pack up and go. He told himself he couldn't get away because he had to finish the portrait. Yet the thought of taking Undi to the South of France kept nudging at him.

FRIDAY: Children

Marius must have been in a playful mood. Sketches in Light of children and their pets appeared all over the place. Someone walking along the Avenue Foch might suddenly find this brilliant little outline of a boy and his dog dancing before his eyes. Or a bicyclist on the way to work might pull up sharply because of the little girl with her white mice who was hopping up and down on the top of a stone wall. Six children riding a baby elephant startled a cabinet minister on his way to see the president. A toy giraffe, with a boy of fourteen on its back, swam sedately around in the air above the pond in the Tuilleries. All were brilliant little outlines of jiggly Light. Children in flocks, like birds on their way south, kept flying under and over the Arc du Triumph. Pet silkworms followed, floating gloriously on mulberry leaves. Eva, softened by the sights of so many children, promised to go out with Monsieur Moitessier as soon as the spring show was underway.

All the while, Isobel conducted rehearsals. Twenty young people from schools of acting, from art schools, and from music schools, were brought together for the final rehearsal of the dramatic street theater. And fifteen more were making the final technical arrangements. Roland was among those, with Roco, the Japanese in charge of costumes; Eddie Zimmerman, in charge of music and all the sound effects; and Mohammed and the others who comprised the inner group. They were the only ones who knew what Osiris intended to do. I couldn't help thinking that it was going to come as a great shock to all the others should he succeed in setting fire to himself and to Ki and Sylvester. At the last minute, they were all going to be told and plans were being made to get them away from the scene quickly. Osiris had made arrangements to hand over the apartment to Roland. Roland had told him he did not intend to kill himself. "I'll find other ways to help save the world." To his surprise, Osiris had agreed, but he asked Roland to keep the apartment open and keep the group together.

Isobel was busy in the apartment. With the help of an accomplished cook, she was preparing food for the whole group. Undi was trying to understand how they could sit there talking about the play as if it were just a regular production. Isobel had explained it all to her. Isobel had spent several hours with her, telling her all she had learned from the oracle. It was the only time Isobel had ever spoken to her.

Is everybody mad? Undi kept thinking about sacrifice. She was thinking about creatures that killed and ate each other and the bliss she believed the victims experienced as they submitted to the laws of nature. Once she had seen a host of tiny predators attack a large fish. The fish had writhed about in the sea, trying to escape, until its agony was transformed into bliss. At least that's what she believed. She imagined she saw its life passing into the lives of its attackers, nourishing them. *Is that what's going to happen to Osiris? Whose life would he be enriching and nourishing?* I didn't blame her for asking these questions. *Will he be transformed into the Light? Or will he just burn up and be seen no more? Will he rise again like the Phoenix?* She reminded herself that Marius and Tiger Hound had said not to worry, but she had no idea what they'd meant by that. Neither did I. As for Isis, she sat nearby as though in a trance. Her attitude puzzled Undi. *If it were I, I'd be screaming at everyone*, she said to herself.

Masks and costumes were all ready, waiting in the storehouse at the chateau Osiris owned outside of Paris. Banners and posters had been distributed to work groups, and the posters were already exposed around Paris. The banners would be hung on Sunday, near the site of the performance. Roland was completely dissatisfied and wanted to tear all the posters down and remake some of his banners. No matter how fine everyone said they were, he groaned and said he'd stay up all night making new ones. No one took any notice of him because they knew it would be all right. The posters would stay where they were.

Eva wasn't there, of course. No one had told her anything. If she had known what was going on, she would most certainly have gone to the police. Or she may have taken to her wings and flown away. She had, however, become extremely restless and worried and irritable with Roland as the day of the sacrifice drew closer, as though she sensed something.

In the next room, Ki and Sylvester were sitting quietly on cushions on the floor. That was the way they usually sat. Undi kept looking at them and at last went into that room and sat on the couch and watched them. She supposed they were meditating. They were still and silent. She had the impression, and so did I, that they were turning into flowers and that, as Ki and Sylvester, they no longer needed to exist.

Undi could see Osiris in his private room, just sitting there. As a child, she had not looked at him too closely. She had been in awe of him, knowing he was a person of importance. So she had not been aware of how handsome he was and how the light filled his face with radiance. She noticed it now and wondered at it, thinking it odd that it should be there, even when he planned to put an end to his life. In fact, nothing had changed in his face, except for the contours of his cheeks. His face was thinner. His cheekbones, like those of Isis, were noble and fine and now they were more prominent, making him look even more fascinating then he had looked before. He was tall and slim and carried himself like a prince. It was not surprising that, in many of the countries of the ancient world he'd passed through after leaving Egypt, he had been chosen—sometimes even captured and held until he consented—to be their king and to sacrifice himself, as was the custom in some primitive kingdoms. He had always escaped by changing into a hawk or some such creature. In one such kingdom, he had seen an old king, when his time came, sacrifice himself for the good of his people, slowly cutting himself to pieces and setting fire to his own funeral pyre one moment before he fainted away. Osiris had always felt disgust when he was obliged to bear witness to such a deed. Yet now he was prepared to take this heroic step himself, and he did not feel any disgust. As she thought about this, Undi was now both fascinated and horrified.

Roland came up to her, still complaining about his own banners. I suppose he was hoping she'd say they were wonderful. But if she did, I said to myself, he would wonder how much her opinion was worth. He tended to be superior where women were concerned. But perhaps he was right, insofar as Undi was concerned at any rate. She really didn't know anything about banners. She said just what Roland, and I too, thought she would say.

"But, Roland, I think they're wonderful." Then she added, surprising us, "I have an image in my mind too. I see it as if it were on

Isobel the priestess of self-sacrifice

a banner like your images. I see a great wheel of life and death as big as the planet Earth, with all the creatures of Earth consuming each other until nothing is left but bare, dry rock."

"That's an interesting image," Roland said generously, "but more like a movie than a still picture."

I could see he was interested in her and in awe of her because he still thought she was the mistress of a rich man. They were friendly, but this thought had kept him from making love to her. Now that he had earned some money for designing the banners, he didn't feel quite so much like the poor, young student. He was not at all what could be called rich, but it made him feel somewhat bolder.

It seemed to him that the situation was even more interesting now that Undi had come to join them in the last week of Osiris's life. She was obviously concerned with something besides money. He smiled at her, and she responded with one of her gentlest Fish-Woman smiles. They drew closer, and when Isobel brought them some food, they shared one plate.

SATURDAY: Tiger in the Sky

Marius painted a gorgeous, brilliantly striped tiger in the sky over the Trocadero. It had eyes like fire; a lean, strong body; and a long tail that lashed about. Sometimes it faded and became almost invisible, and then it would blaze out again until it almost blinded people who looked at it. Toward evening, it raced across the sky and crouched down as though it were stalking the setting sun. It was still there at sunset, waiting and crouching, and when the sky grew dark and night fell, it remained in its crouching position until the next day, which was Sunday, the day of sacrifice.

For Roland, Saturday brought a full realization of what was to happen on Sunday. He quite forgot about his posters and banners and about Undi, for this was the day when the unbelievable sacrifice was to take place. So far, his world had been a safe one, with only the minor irritations and tragedies of a middle-class environment. Young men like Roland didn't accept the notion of the violence that would become a way of life thirty or forty years later. All he did was get up in the mornings and go to the académie or wander about looking for his friends at certain locations. And all he consciously worried about was the cost of his paints, his relationship with his mother, or whether Adolph Monjou seduced Ginger Rogers in the old movies. Whatever else was eating away at him was well hidden in his unconscious, but even that wasn't very much. His moods were more an affectation, which he would outgrow several years later.

Now, as he looked up at the tiger in the sky, he felt truly afraid for the first time. The tiger itself exerted a power over him he couldn't understand. He associated it with what was to happen to Osiris. And while it remained in the sky, he felt powerless to back out. He had to stay with Osiris until the end.

Tiger waited in the sky.

Chapter 18

The Old King and the Spring Queen

An audience consisting mostly of passersby had formed a circle around an open space near the Trocadero. In the center of the space was a tree made of three-ply wood and canvas, and behind it was a small platform with a throne-like chair on it. A beautiful queen sat in the chair, and a very old man so gnarled and wrinkled that he looked like a tree trunk himself, prowled around the tree. He was the Old King of the Sacred Grove. He was thin, but he looked strong and alert even though he knew he was about to die. The young king would come to claim his right to the sacred tree and they would fight. This was the ancient way, and it had to be.

The queen sitting on the throne was also waiting for the Young King. She was the Spring Queen waiting for her beloved, who would overpower the Old King and bring new life to the grove.

To reach the old man, the Young King was to be led in by masked mimes dressed in black. They could have been demons, the good mimes and the demons being dressed alike. There was another character called the Wanderer, who wore a simple costume consisting of a loose white blouse and dark pants that made him look like a romantic poet. Unlike the mimes or demons, he did not wear a mask, nor did he wear a crown. The audience was expected to know he wasn't the Young King but a sort of mystery character who had never before been heard of in the old myth.

The members of the audience who were familiar with the ancient myth of the sacred grove knew what was to happen, or believed they did, while others who didn't know the old tale watched with interest or enjoyed the sight of the Spring Queen in her golden dress decorated with a pattern around the skirt of new, yellow corn cobs.

I expected the play to proceed in a reasonable manner, telling the tale until it came to the sacrificial scene, but this wasn't so. Osiris, in his deranged state of mind, had written crazy scenes into his play. In fact, it all seemed crazy to me.

The Young King, who should have challenged the Old King, didn't do that at all. There was the Old King standing at bay, desperately prepared to defend his tree even while he knew what the outcome should be, while the Young King seemed to find him ridiculous. This wasn't right. It was insulting to the Keeper of the Sacred Grove—the Old One. It was as though the Young King had never learned the proper way—or else he had forgotten the Old Sacred Ways.

Eddie Zimmerman, the musician, entered the scene, but instead of singing, he tried to prompt the young man, saying, "Fight, fight!" and hissing at him. This made noisy members of the audience shout, "Go on; fight the old man!"

The Young King then leaped about, striking aggressive poses at the empty air, laughing derisively but never making any attempt to attack the Old King. He behaved more like a clown then a heroic figure bringing new life to the grove.

It was even more confusing for the audience than it was for me. New characters representing an audience of the ancient play were dressed in an odd assortment of costumes of the twentieth century so the members of the real audience weren't quite sure who was who. It was like a play within a play, but even this make-believe audience was puzzled by what was happening. They now thronged the street while others leaned out of windows of building, wondering whether the Young King had forgotten his lines and was improvising until he regained his memory. He should be fighting the Old King by now, they must have been saying to themselves, so that spring would come and the corn would grow.

The Old King was frustrated and angry and, worse still, he, too, was thrown into confusion. He appealed to his subjects, "One of you. Come up here and take the place of this dolt." He looked around wildly and saw the queen on her throne. "If you don't, the Spring

Queen will die." No one seemed to know whether this was an idle threat. But no one came.

The Young King leaped up onto the platform and then was helped down by mimes. But those mimes could have been demons. They all looked alike. They grabbed him and tossed him around among spring dancers who had entered, expecting to do the dance of the new corn. Demons kept crowning him with the ears of an ass. It was clear now that they *were* demons. More of them came roaring in on black motorbikes. Two came hauling a broken-down vehicle, which could have once been a car. They dumped the Young King in the back seat. The din they made was awful.

The Wanderer then mounted the platform. The Spring Queen turned away and hung her head. Then she pointed to the Old King. I supposed she meant that someone had to fight him first before they could be happy together. But she was already wilting and dying.

The Old King leaned disconsolately against his tree trunk. He was no longer a king. Now he looked like any old man filling in time and feeling nothing but irritation because the play wasn't going the way he had been led to believe it would.

Far away in the palace dark room, which seemed to have relocated itself into the mysterious new studio Marius had recently built in the House, our four Heliotrope ladies were seated comfortably in what looked like a box at the opera, watching the play. They behaved as if this were a perfectly ordinary theatrical production and seemed to have no idea that it was going to end in a ghastly sacrifice of three men. If they asked each other where Tiger Hound and Marius were, it was only because they thought it would be nice and fitting to have male escorts beside them. All they had for company were some of Undi's handmaidens from the crystal palace on the Rock. These young ladies sat sedately behind Isis and Undi.

As the play progressed, however, a certain uneasiness began to creep into the remarks of our four girls.

"I expected to see Tiger Hound in this scene," Pavarti said. "I wonder what's happened to him."

"Well, yes, it is getting close, isn't it."

"Close to what?" Eva said. She looked puzzled. "I have a feeling something's about to happen, but I can't imagine what it'll be."

194

"No, how could you? No one ever told you."

"Told her what?"

"I don't know."

"Look," Undi said, "It's getting to be suspenseful. I think Marius should be told about this."

"I think so too. Wasn't there something he had to do?"

Isis turned and looked at the handmaidens with the question in her eyes, but they had no answer for her. They, too, were puzzled by what they saw on the big round hole in front of them.

The members of the technical unit and all the other helpers and the make-believe audience were walking around and around in a wide circle that acted as a gravitational field for all the characters in the play. Gradually they were all drawn into it. Even the motorbikes and the old car moved slowly and quietly now, around and around.

The Old King and the Spring Queen

"Look," Eva said, as they all gazed through the hole in the dark room. "They're making three pyres. What are those for?"

"I don't know," Isis replied. She looked scared, yet she still didn't remember what the three pyres were for.

Undi said, "We don't know what's going to happen. We're just looking." Yet they felt uneasy, and Isis said at last, "I'm surprised that Marius hasn't come."

"And Tiger Hound. Where's Tiger Hound? I wonder why they don't come."

"What's happening now, Eva?"

"Look for yourself. Osiris is speaking to the Old King." Eva moved aside so that Isis could see clearly. The hole in the darkness grew larger, and there was room for all of them to see through it.

"Look, it's the Wanderer," Pavarti whispered. "He's telling them something. Look, he says the demons will strike again and again and destroy the Sacred Tree. But he will defeat them. He says there's nothing a demon hates as much as a hero, a man who'll sacrifice himself for the Sacred Grove."

"Who will be the hero? I thought it was that Old King. He doesn't look like a hero. Why am I whispering?" Undi said

"I thought the Young King was to be the hero," said Eva.

"Wait", cried Isis. "It's Osiris! He's the Wanderer and he's asking the Old King if he is prepared to die. He says he will take the Young King's place and fight to the death."

"What does the Old King say?"

"He says, 'You must be crazy!'"

They all looked at each other, unable to believe that the wretched, old man had spoken to Osiris in that manner.

Osiris, or the Wanderer or whatever he wanted to be called, asked the Old King whether he was prepared to do the deed himself. "If you won't fight, are you prepared to kill yourself?" he asked. "It has to be done. The Old King must die."

"Get out of my sight," yelled the Old King. "I told you you were crazy, and you are." Then the irritable Old King went and hid behind his tree. I didn't know what he did after that. Perhaps he left the stage altogether, slipping away at the back of the platform. It was confusing. You couldn't tell whether this was the correct script or whether the old actor had just walked off.

Mimes came and lifted the Wanderer. They carried him and held him aloft and made sure everyone on the stage and in the audience had seen him. Then they presented him to the Spring Queen. Even she didn't seem to follow the script properly. It was hard to believe that, just when the Wanderer was about to sacrifice himself for the Sacred Tree, she should be made to simper and say, "Oh, my hero," but that's what she did. She and her throne were carried off, and the Wanderer was placed on a pyre in front of the tree. Perhaps this was all part of the plan. His sacrifice was to be an integral part of the play and at the same time an integral part of the reality of the world beyond the boundaries of the performance space. Maybe that was why the play was so crazy—maybe it was meant to show that the world had gone mad.

Some of the players had slipped away, like the Old King. There was a flight of steps on the far side of the square. Some of them had gone that way. Roland had not gone with them. *The Tiger* was still there in the sky, watching, and Roland was under its spell. He had to stay even if he didn't want to. He returned his gaze to the ground because he couldn't bear to look at the Tiger. Nor could he look at Osiris, for although Undi had told him that Osiris would be saved, it seemed that the drama had to go on to the end.

It wasn't a great surprise when Ki and Sylvester suddenly turned up. They came from behind some screens and quietly seated themselves on the two other pyres. The pyres were composed of corn and wheat sheaves. I didn't know where they had come from or who had provided them, but there they were. They were not very big. When Ki and Sylvester sat down, they were close to the ground in front of the platform where Osiris sat. There was the circle of players and some of the audience moving slowly around, wanting to look but not daring to do so because they sensed the moment was near. Osiris looked stern and unyielding. I didn't like his expression very much.

Something happened to me. Suddenly I was fed up, sick of it all. I wanted to be back in my right time and my own place, in Heliotrope. I even wanted Eva or my mother. We Heliotropians never wanted our mothers, not in that way. We liked to be close to them at the time of the Festival, but we didn't cry like babies for our mothers. I didn't cry, but I was sick of everything. And as for this play, it all changed before my eyes. I thought Eddie's music was too loud and Jacques, singing away with the mike in his hand, looked idiotic, jiggling about and twisting his lips. The demons were rotten actors, just people without talent in masks. The mimes were self-conscious and precious, and there was Osiris sitting up there looking so pious, about to save the world.

As if that wasn't enough, Isobel turned up! The high priestess! She'd be better off, I told myself, if she would lose weight and cut her hair. She walked across the performance space and mounted the platform, her flowing robe flapping about in the breeze.

The audience was looking puzzled. They sensed something. They'd have been pretty dumb if they hadn't. On the far side of the street, two policemen sat in a police car. They were aware of the unrest among the audience. I was hoping they'd come over and stop the play, but they didn't.

Isobel stood over Osiris. I caught a glimpse of Roland's face. He looked horrified. I imagine he knew what was in the handsome blue jar Isobel bore so reverently. The horror of it struck me too. The jar was full of the inflammable liquid she intended to pour over Osiris! It was real then! She raised it and started to pour. Osiris closed his eyes so the liquid wouldn't sting them. When she had finished, she went down to Ki and Sylvester and poured the rest of it over them. They looked pained, as if the odor and the physical act were objectionable to their delicate sensibilities. They would rather have burst into flames spontaneously or by the power of the mind. As the liquid flowed out, as a matter of fact, it looked silvery and sparkly, not at all lethal. It looked more like the water of eternal life. I half expected Isobel to raise her arms, as old Monsieur Fouroux had expected the woman at the window during the fire on the Rue de la Grande Chaumière to raise her arms while fire consumed her—the sacrificial victim. She didn't do it, but what she'd done already was fanatical enough and quite horrible.

Marius and Tiger Hound had still not appeared, and now Osiris was taking something out of his pocket, which made a slight rattle like matches in a box. It *was* a box. He opened it and took out the match and scraped it along the side of the box. The realism of this act was horrifying. It made me feel sick. But I had no time to feel sick for the match ignited. Just then there was a flurry of something black. It was Death, no longer a shadow but the creature himself! The dark figure swept across the platform and disappeared from sight behind the Sacred Tree. Osiris hardly noticed. He carried the burning match very carefully to his breast. Ki and Sylvester had done the same. The flames shot out simultaneously. There was a shriek. At exactly the same instant, flashes of brilliant light from some other source made it impossible for anyone except me to see what actually happened. It was the Tiger.

He sprang upon the first flames that leapt from Osiris's body and consumed them. He also made a fearful sound. I could see then that, although it was *The Tiger of Light in the Sky*, it was also Tiger Hound as Shiva. But at the same time, before anyone could make a move, something else happened. I saw two figures coming down through the clouds and I recognized them as the two angels who trod the pathways of the sky over the Rock, never doing anything in particular except fly back and forth in their magic cloaks. They streaked down like two silver arrows, snatched Ki and Sylvester, and streaked back again before the dazzled eyes of the spectators could blink. When it was clear enough to see, all the street audience saw in the place where Ki and Sylvester had been sitting were sweet-smelling flower petals, some of them still fluttering in the draft caused by the angels. Osiris had vanished, too, but on his mat were singed leaves and scraps of burnt cloth.

People were shrieking and pressing forward, while others tried to push past them and rush toward the avenue. The police rushed over from the other side of the avenue and tried to calm them down. When the commotion had died down, they examined the burnt mat and looked at the flower petals. But there were no bodies—nothing—so what could they do? The most they could try to do was arrest members of the cast and the technical crew, but Osiris had received permission from the authorities to use this space for the performance. If the crowd yelled and shrieked, it was part of the show. In the end, everyone was declared free to go. Isobel had already disappeared with her empty blue jar—a flapping blue robe speeding away down the avenue.

Roland and other members of the group waited until the police had gone and then returned to the Trocadero, hoping to find Osiris and Ki and Sylvester. When they never came back, Roland returned to the apartment, where he waited in vain for many days before going home to Eva.

Chapter 19

Secrets of the Rue Tilset

Undi sat in her room waiting on Roland. Although the sun had not yet set, it was dark in the hallway. It was a gloomy hall at any time of the day, but at this hour, six o'clock in the evening, it was positively spooky. Undi hadn't noticed this. She was already dressed in her bright, little room. She looked happy and excited, yet when I observed her more closely, I realized she was also very tense. It was the first time she and Roland had a date to take place privately, in her room. The clock in Monsieur Raymonde's study ticked away about twenty minutes of the late afternoon, and by the time she had combed her hair and touched up her makeup, it was almost half past six.

As the clock chimed the half hour, she went to the window and looked out. There was no one in the court below except her friend, the Cement Maiden, in the fountain. She heard the husky whisper, "Not yet, not yet, not yet." The words soothed Undi, and she turned away and went across the room to sit on the edge of her bed and attend to her fingernails. She was using nail polish now, and, in fact, she had used quite a lot of makeup. I wanted to tell her that it was all quite unnecessary. Her skin was still radiant, and her lips were a natural shade of pink. But I could see she enjoyed using the blusher and the eye shadow and the lipstick and the coral nail polish she was applying as she sat on the bed. Yet she was still listening to the ticking of the clock. At fifteen minutes to seven, she again went to the window.

This time she withdrew quickly because she saw the concierge. Going over to the mantelpiece, she picked up an earring and began screwing it on, but after looking at herself in the mirror, she took it off again. It was one of a pair Georges had given her—gold with small diamonds hanging like teardrops.

She gazed moodily at herself for a full minute and then turned away and took off her dress. It was one Georges had bought for her. I sensed she didn't want to wear it for Roland, for I knew that was whom she was waiting for. She hung it up in the closet and took out the sea green silk. It still looked as light as air, and I was glad when she put it on. So was she. It made her feel more like herself. Although she was ready now, it was difficult for her to sit down and relax. The clock was still going ticktock, and the rhythm of it was getting right into her. *Ticktock, knock knock.* She was saying it silently, but when she realized what she was doing, she stopped. *Anyway, he'll ring the doorbell. He won't knock.*

Then, to my surprise, she lit a cigarette. Georges had given them to her the night before in a fancy restaurant. A cigarette girl had been standing by their table, and Georges, dear fellow, had looked utterly delighted and bought a packet of mauve cigarettes with gold tips, which he'd handed to Undi, saying, "For my princess." And she'd replied, "Thank you, your grace." They were playing games!

Ah, I thought, *if he could see her now, waiting for a young man!* The clock wasn't saying "ticktock" anymore. It was saying "Ro-land, Ro-land." Where, I wondered, was Monsieur Raymonde? And where was his sister, Mademoiselle Raymonde? I caught another glimpse, this time of Monsieur Raymonde dozing off in a train speeding north, but of the sister, I saw nothing. I wondered if he had invented her, perhaps to make Undi believe someone was always at home—to stop her from inviting young men over while he was away.

Undi's eyes now had an expression I'd never seen in them before. She was looking at something that hadn't happened yet—at Roland's arrival at the front door. She envisioned him pressing the doorbell. She was like a doe at the waterhole, alert and ready to spring up and speed toward the door.

"Undi," I wanted to ask, "what has happened to you? You're a Heliotropian. We don't wait like that for doorbells to ring." But, of course, I couldn't reach her.

She was talking to herself. "It's like being blind. I can't see him coming, and I can't see the minutes passing. But suddenly, I'll be filled with the sound of the bell—a loud, sharp ringing, and it will be like a Roman candle bursting throughout the apartment."

Yes, I thought, and there'll be such a clamor! It will fill the silent hall and startle all the inanimate objects. Chairs will leap to their feet, cups will fly off the shelf, and the heavy sofa will heave and clutch at its heart. Photographs on the wall will jabber and point their fingers. Beds will thump on the floor and the pages of books will turn over furiously. And there will be Roland like the child Buddha emerging from the lotus. What a way to picture him!

It was now a few minutes past seven. People didn't come at five past or ten past seven. They come on the dot. So where was Roland? Undi was listening even more intently. The organs in her head that had been created to hear things—sounds, spaces she had only a while ago tried to empty of everything so that they would be ready for the bell—started to fill up again with noises that were of no use to her, like creakings from an upstairs apartment, the scuttling of a mouse, a distant fire engine, even the sound of a moth beating against a windowpane. She tried to get them out of her ears, but they wouldn't go. Footsteps in the court below! She rushed to the window. It wasn't the one she was waiting for. She couldn't see who it was. Suppose it was Monsieur Raymonde coming back to trick her?

Downstairs, the Cement Maiden whispered, "Someone's coming, coming, coming. Pitter-pitter pat. It's a little boy, a little boy. Go back, Undi, to the edge of your bed. It's only a little child."

Then, there it was. The shrill sound of the bell; the sudden clamor now filled every corner and cranny of the silent apartment. Now, like the doe at the waterhole, like the dancer leaping on stage, she leaped! She reached the hall and sped onward, then stopped. Something strange had happened. So dark, darker than it should have been. But Undi couldn't wait to turn on the light and she started off again. There was another loud ring and just as she had imagined, or was it I who'd imagined, all the inanimate objects clamored and cried and flapped their legs and arms. "Answer it!" they cried. "Answer it," as if she wasn't making an effort.

Then she composed herself and tried to walk in a normal manner along the long, dark hallway that now looked like a tunnel. At the corner, she stopped again and stared in amazement. Something very odd indeed had happened to Monsieur Raymonde's wide front hall. It had become very long and very dim and grimy with age and did indeed look like a prison! So that was it. I had known it all along, although I didn't care to say so. Undi was peering ahead, trying to see the front door. But that had changed too. It was now terribly high—so high that the top of it disappeared into the dark, gray mist of the ceiling. And it appeared to be made of iron or lead, rather than glass and wood. The chains and locks were still there. They'd become enormous.

Yet, in spite of all this, Undi could just make out an outline of someone on the other side of this door. It was not possible to see who it was, but, of course, she believed it to be Roland. Who else would she imagine it to be? Unless it was Monsieur Raymonde. Somehow, she had to cover the distance before he went away. He had rung three times already. He might think that was enough. He would surely go if he thought no one was going to answer. She set off again, walking as fast as she could without actually running. For some reason, she believed there was a reason for not running. She didn't know what it was, but she knew she mustn't run.

Before she had gone very far, she noticed that two figures were seated, one on either side of the hall table. The table was enormously long, so long indeed, that it stretched away into the distance, making the two figures far from each other. She recognized them. They were Monsieur Raymonde's parents, looking exactly as they did in the photograph in his study. She felt nervous about having to greet them as she went past. She didn't want to be impolite, but she didn't want to be obliged to slow down. She never seemed to reach them, anyway.

After hurrying along for what seemed like an age, she noticed there were many more doors opening onto the hallway. They even sprang into the wall as she looked ahead and, as she passed each one, she was aware of it opening a little. She was also aware that, once she had passed each one, the narrow opening widened and eyes looked out at her. In some, heads were actually thrust forward. She knew she was being watched—observed. And who knew but that she was being followed.

"Whatever it is or whoever they are, I must not allow myself to be distracted. I must get to that door." As she said this, the bell rang for the fourth time. There was an impatient note to its pealing. "Oh, don't let him give up. Please!" She hoped the iron lift would delay him—break down between floors so that he would have to wait.

She broke into a fast trot, and as soon as she did this, she became aware of the greater activity behind her. Looking around, she saw that the hall was filling up with women. Their eyes were almost eating her! I'd never seen such eyes—eager, greedy, sly, demanding. Some were just sad, though, and overanxious. Such hungry eyes. But why? Undi didn't stop. She hurried on, and women strained away from their doorways, ready to rush after her. I realized that each one imagined or hoped the bell was ringing for her. So did Undi!

"But he's not for you. He's for me. He's promised. It's all prearranged." She called this out over her shoulder.

It was a shock when one of these phantom figures, as I supposed they were, answered in a loud aggressive voice, "Oh, no! Not for you. He's for me. I've been waiting." The voice came from far behind Undi, yet it swelled up as though the woman was coming closer. Undi looked back and saw the woman straining to get ahead of the others. She increased her own pace and hurried on.

Why did she ever enter such a madhouse, I wondered for about the fifth time. I could tell Undi was wondering the same thing. What had all these women to do with her and Roland? Was it just because he was a man? Or was it because happiness and freedom had been denied? Undi remembered a Light picture Marius had made for her in the dark room of her palace, a picture of a young girl and a youth gliding about in an underwater paradise, full of love, light filtering down through the clear water. They played like children, but they were also lovers. *Nothing*, she thought, *could be further apart than these women and myself. But I can't help it if they're starved. I've no time for compassion. I must get on. This is becoming nightmarish.* She didn't seem to know anymore why she so desperately longed to reach the front door. The reason had disappeared, and only the horrid, weird business of trying to get to the end of the hall remained. And then she couldn't even think about that because she had reached the part of the hall where Madame Raymonde was sitting, in her black taffeta gown.

The matronly lady turned to look at Undi. So skillfully did she turn that not a single crease appeared in the pin-tucked bodice. She looked so stern and disapproving that even the women who followed fell back a pace and gave Undi the advantage.

"*She's the cause of all this,*" I said to myself. But immediately I knew it was too easy to blame the poor lady. Her eyes were hungry too, if one looked attentively at them. Besides, what was I blaming her for? Oh, yes, for the women. Undi went on, gliding now, like a dreamer. The length of the table was extraordinary. Undi glided past and past and didn't reach the other end of it for a long time.

When she did so, she came upon Monsieur Raymonde, Sr., himself. He was sitting very straight and looked uncomfortable in his stiff, starched collar, but that didn't stop him from looking like a jovial outdoorsman. I'd seen men like him sitting around on their white verandas in the heat in India, cooling off with their whiskeys and sodas. To Undi, he looked more human than she had first thought. There was something about him, one had to admit. He had an air of adventure and courage, like men who had gone in search of the Nile at the turn of the century.

Anyway, I could see that Undi was wondering whether the old man could help her. She was thinking he might be able to restore the hallway to its normal length and then get back into his picture frame and take Madame Raymonde with him. This would enable her to reach the front door and open it with an easy normal sense of well-being. The feeling she had now was far too frantic for her liking. So she leaned toward the old man—he wasn't so old, in fact, but she, being still very young, thought he was—and was about to ask him, when he put his hand out as if to pat her on the bottom and gave her a knowing wink, almost a leer, which horrified her far more than it need have. I saw then that he, too, was to blame, if there was such a thing as blame. And he, too, was in the plot to prevent her from reaching the door. But why? What was the plot and what was the reason for it?

Then another possibility presented itself as Undi looked back once again and saw the women gaining on her. She wondered if one of them, or perhaps all of them, was the sister who'd never yet been seen. Appalling thought. Was she a monster who had split and multiplied herself and had to be kept under lock and key? And had Undi somehow let her get out? It was awful. Undi herself began to feel frightened, as well as frantic. Was she, too, being sucked into one of the rooms in this endless corridor? Was that what desire would do to her?

Just as she looked up again, the door of a closet opened, and to my surprise—for I *had* seen him in a northbound train, remember—there was Monsieur Raymonde himself, behaving in a very suspicious and mysterious manner. He put his head out, looked around furtively, and then made hissing noises to attract Undi's attention. When she looked directly at him, he beckoned to her, bubbling over with whatever was on his mind. I noticed his face particularly. It looked to me like one of our Pods, all pulpy with deep lines dividing it into parts, which were either sinister or cherubic. The only difference was that our Pods, when in full bloom, glow with a radiant glow. Monsieur Raymonde glowed with dampness. This was due, I imagined, to the intensity of his emotion. Whatever that was, it must have made him feel hot.

He was so insistent that Undi paused and hesitated, even while she looked toward the door. The shadowy image was still there, visible through the door. It was like an X-ray picture.

"What is it, Monsieur Raymonde? Quickly. I'm in a hurry."

"Come in here, Mademoiselle Undi. This way. I'll show you a quicker way."

"Really? Truly?" She didn't ask, a quicker way to what. But then, she wasn't in quite her right mind either. Her mind was clouded by desire, something Dr. Pandé had warned us to beware of before we left Heliotrope.

"Yes, you're expecting someone, aren't you? Come then."

"Yes, I am expecting someone. Then you don't mind? It's only a young boy from the académie. An artist."

The bell pealed again, and both she and Monsieur Raymonde put their heads out of the closet (for she was in there with him by now). They could see the figure moving about. She wanted to get out of the closet and run on again. At the same time, there was a fearful flutter among the women. I saw Undi flutter in response and make another effort to leave the closet.

Monsieur Raymonde restrained her and held her back. "I can't have strangers and intruders coming in by the front door. You come with me. I told you I'd show you a quicker way."

The closet was actually an entrance to a winding staircase with a chamber at the bottom of it. It was either a chamber or a dungeon. Undi remembered then that he'd mentioned another entrance to the apartment, so she started to follow him down the stairs, thinking she'd emerge into the courtyard and catch Roland before he left. But when Monsieur Raymonde paused and looked back at her, she thought she saw something in his face that looked evil. There was a dim light directly over his head, which made him look like the mad doctor of an early black-and-white movie. I saw it, even if she didn't. But she did see it. It made her suspicious.

She slowed down. "What is this staircase? Where does it lead?"

"It's an escape to the world, my dear." He laughed and he even *sounded* like the mad doctor. But then he added, "It's a fire escape—just a fire escape. Come along."

I was trying to make her hear me. "Don't be such a fool, Undi. Go back."

Yet, even though she, too, was suspicious, she didn't turn back. *That*, I thought, *is the story of many a person's life. Yet again, some turn back when they shouldn't have. So the thing is, I suppose, never to have to make a decision but to know instinctively what the right course to take is.*

Monsieur Raymonde was making weird, little grunts. They could have been the sounds a slightly corpulent man might make going cautiously down a dark stairway but, on the other hand, they could have been the sounds of a man plotting a crime with an innocent victim within his grasp.

Anyhow, Undi went on down the steps with the Mad Doctor Raymonde, as I shall always call him, and looking down, she saw the concierge and her friend, Madame Frou-frou, waiting in the chamber below. They were chattering quite loudly, and I heard them talking about Undi. Madame Frou-frou was saying, "She's pretty. That's what they want. Don't spoil her appearance. He'll want to take pictures."

"Pretty, indeed. It depends on what you like, doesn't it."

I gathered that the concierge had her own ideas about beauty. But I could see that Monsieur Raymonde may have been right when he'd said this chamber was an escape to the world. Every inch of wall had a passageway leading from it. There was a big, dangerous world out there, and Monsieur Raymonde, little man though he may have been, was a link in a chain of petty human foibles that were linked to small crimes that led to even greater and greater ones. One of the passageways actually did lead to the courtyard, but the two ladies blocked the way to it. All Monsieur Raymonde was interested in were his pornographic photographs. He was getting ready to take Undi's picture, and the ladies had black stockings and whips and other paraphernalia ready to use as props.

Undi turned and ran up the winding staircase. She reached the closet and burst into the hallway, just in time to hear the bell ring again. The figure outside appeared to be hopping about with impatience or indecision, almost disappearing and then growing closer, as if trying to peer through the crack. Only there wasn't any crack.

The women were still there, but they hadn't made any progress at all without Undi. I realized she had somehow tapped into their existence, wherever they lurked in this apartment, and they couldn't make a move without her. Off she went once more, trying to disregard them.

One of them called out, "Open it. He'll go. Open the door, you little beast!"

"I'm going as fast as I can. But he's mine, not yours. You've had your lives. Leave me alone." I was surprised to hear a note of anger in Undi's voice. She was fed up with these women—no longer afraid. But she changed her tone when one of them grabbed her green silk dress and slowed her down. Another tried to catch hold of her hair. Women tumbled out of doorways, and the hall was like a river of female flesh with female desires and longings; all their pain rose to the ceiling in the form of a dreary, gray mist. Instead of making it easier by pushing her forward, they were fighting with each other and grabbing at her at the same time and holding her back. She was striving to get free of them and trying to run forward, but all her movements were in slow motion so she was getting nowhere. Heavy weights held her back, while the figure on the other side of the door grew fainter and receded again until it was no longer there. She could make it out, going and shrinking into a faint blur and then disappearing until she knew it was too late.

"Let me go! Let me go, you bitches!" she actually screamed. It was unheard of language for a Heliotropian, yet it had force, and I wasn't altogether shocked. Undi needed a little force in her.

A faint voice came from the closet. "Mother, Father, stop her. Don't let her open that door. She's a disgrace, bringing her lovers in the front way. She's a whore, a slut."

And the old man's voice came back mildly, "Son, son, come now. That's no way to have fun."

There was a sudden push, and she was jammed against the door at last. The blur was still outside. There was still time. She shrieked hysterically, "Just a minute! Hang on! Wait . . ." And she began fumbling with the locks and the chains.

Of course the door wouldn't move. The key was in the black box and there was nothing she could do but stay there, wedged against the door, weeping with frustration while the crush became even denser and she was pinched and punched wherever the awakened horde of women could get their hands on her.

"Oh, what can I do? I can't let him in. He'll go, and I'll become a prisoner here like all the rest of them. Let me be! I hate you all! You bitches! You bitches!"

Just then, quite a different kind of hand touched her, and a very gentle, different, calm kind of voice reached her ears. "Move aside, all of you. I have a key. I've had it for a long time now, and I know just how to use it."

All the women disappeared! I could hardly believe it. Undi stood there, trembling. In their place stood a miracle—Mademoiselle Raymonde! Mademoiselle Raymonde! She was a gentlewoman of about fifty, with a somewhat ironical smile on her serene face. Cool, calm, and quite devoid of any sign of concern. No fuss whatsoever. She inserted the key and gave a peculiar kind of twist and a special kind of pull; the iron box opened, the chains slipped away, and the locks sprang open. She stood back, while Undi turned the handle and opened the door. There on the doorstep stood Roland with a slightly sheepish expression on his face because he had, in fact, been on the point of turning and going downstairs without even waiting for the lift.

"Come in, dear boy," Mademoiselle Raymonde said. She stood right beside Undi, and he couldn't help being taken aback. He'd come there with a sense of guilt because he knew about Monsieur Raymonde not allowing male visitors, and here was a sweet and gentle lady inviting him to enter. She and Undi looked odd together.

"I was just about to go out," Mademoiselle Raymonde said, as she drew on a neat pair of gloves that matched her conservatively tailored spring suit. She then adjusted the veil that covered her straight-brimmed hat and all of her dear, kind face. You would have thought she was in the habit of going out like that every day.

"I am Undi, and this is my friend, Roland. I'm so glad to have met you at last," Undi murmured, all sweetness again.

"And, of course, I am Mademoiselle Raymonde. Eloise." She smiled from behind the soft mist of her veil, a subtle smile, which could have implied that she knew how much they were longing to be left alone. "Oh, my brother was going away for a few days. Did he tell you that, Undi?" And after a quick glance at Roland and another little smile, she stepped out onto the landing and rang for the lift. They gazed at her as she stepped into it. Then she was gone.

About an hour later, this charming creature came back. I was fascinated by her. Not only did her seemingly serene expression, much more in evidence now that she had removed her veil (I had even followed her into her room), but her odd behavior capture me. It struck me as being odd because whatever action or movement she achieved was so light, and yet precise, that she seemed to defy gravity. She showed no interest in what might be happening in Undi's room, which was actually right next to her own suite of two rooms—one of which was a bedroom with a connecting door to the next room, which she used as a workroom. She did not even pause when she entered this room; nor did she stop with an expression of listening near the wall between herself and Undi. Yet I knew that she was quite aware that Undi and Roland were there.

She had a few little packages in her handbag. Taking them out, she untied the string and removed the paper without tearing it and folded it and placed it in a box with other folded papers, all colors and sizes. The contents of her packages were lined up neatly and lovingly. Yet they were mundane articles—a white plastic bottle of paper glue, some stiff drawing paper, and last, several yards of electric wire, very fine, with tiny bulbs even smaller than ones that might be put on a Christmas tree. They were lined up on a shelf near other such things, like scissors, slim little sticks of wood of different sizes, paint brushes and a small paint box, small jars, and large sheets of cardboard. She did, in fact, look at all these things most lovingly, touching them gently and making sure that there was a small space between each article so that each one could be seen clearly. On a lower shelf was an extraordinarily large stack of fashion and art magazines.

Going back to her bedroom, she opened a closet before removing her hat and jacket and skirt and blouse. The skirt was hung by two loops from a hanger and the jacket was fitted onto the hanger so that the shoulders would keep their shape. The blouse was hung in another section of the closet, while the hat was returned to its box, which was then tied with a wide, satin ribbon and placed on the top shelf. She

Miss Raymond had 'the key'

even took off her outdoor shoes and put shoetrees in them before they, too, were stored away in a box on the floor. Then she put on a large apron type of dress that crossed over at the back with two long strips of material drawing it into the shape of her figure which, by the way, was quite an attractive one.

Now she was ready for something, and I, still fascinated, wondered what it was. She must have had dinner at some little restaurant while she'd been out, for she took from her bag another precious little package—a small piece of cake that was wrapped in two colored paper napkins. This, she put aside. Perhaps she would go to the kitchen later, I thought, and make herself some coffee and have it with her cake.

I found out about nine o'clock that evening that she didn't need to go to the kitchen because she had her own little kitchen in a sort of closet in the workroom, with all the things necessary for making her own breakfasts and small snacks. Without invading her privacy too much, I went into her mind—a very easy thing to do, for it was a clear, open mind with almost nothing to hide—and found that Yves, her brother, had gone to the trouble of having this tiny kitchen installed for her some time after their parents' death and had had the large dining room table from the dining room they hardly ever used brought in so that she could use it as a work table. In many other little ways, he had been thoughtful and kind. They lived separate lives, but his feeling for her was protective and deep. I hadn't thought of him like that. I found myself almost liking him.

I could have been in Undi's room, observing Undi and Roland make love. It was, in a way, a momentous occasion, for it was very clear that this was her first love, apart from Marius. But she looked upon Marius as a sort of father figure, and he had never made love to her, even when he had captured her centuries ago. So Roland was her first love, and this seemed fitting. But I had no intention of intruding upon them.

Besides, I could imagine what was happening. I was sure that Undi would enter into the whole experience with the greatest enthusiasm and receive great pleasure and also a sense of wonder. I didn't believe that very young people thought or felt very much love when they had their first experience. It was usually a physical experience. At first, the sight of a young man with a strong erect penis might even be frightening, but that fear should pass. So I didn't pry.

214

Moreover, I was much more interested in Mademoiselle Raymonde, whose first name was Eloise. I decided to think of her as Eloise. I wondered whether she was going to paint a picture. And what was she going to do with those little electric wires? What was it that made her so content to live alone in these two rooms? How had she achieved such serenity? And how was it possible for two people such as her brother and herself, so very different, to have come from the same parents?

While I was pondering these questions, she had set to work, but in a way I hadn't expected. She was leafing through magazines and seemed to be looking for something specific. Her complete attention to what she was doing brought Isis to mind—Isis sitting alone in her apartment, spinning. She, too, had achieved serenity, although I suspected that there were still some demons within Isis that she would have to deal with sooner or later and that she would not reach Osiris, wherever he was, until she had confronted them or, in some way, been delivered from them. Her serenity was real enough, so long as she devoted herself to her chosen task. So she spent most of her free time at the spinning wheel. Now she would be longing for the mystery of Osiris's disappearance to be solved; yet she stayed with her spinning wheel and had faith. It wasn't easy for her.

Perhaps it was so with Eloise, yet I sensed that her serenity was complete. She had created for herself her own world. I would not have been at all surprised if she had opened a door (which seemed to have no purpose because I could not imagine where it led to—it was on the side of the room that overlooked the court) and stepped through it to a wide meadow. I could even see the scene—a wide lake, white columns of an open pavilion, an emerald lawn with leafy trees, and young women in white Grecian-like garments, all bathed in the pink shadows and soft light of sunset. A sublime, untroubled world.

But, no, nothing so miraculous. Her world was in her work. She found what she was looking for in the pages of the magazines, and taking the scissors, she carefully cut out the images she wanted. I had already noticed what looked like ordinary cardboard boxes lined up on the top shelf, but when she took one down and placed it on the table and looked intently into it, I saw that it had a tiny peephole on one side and some of those tiny electric wires coming out of the top. As soon as she lifted her head, I slipped in and looked through the peephole myself.

"So this is her private world!" I said.

Inside the box, which was about nine inches high and twelve inches wide, was a fantastic landscape, far more fascinating and surrealistic than the one I'd imagined. But there were no people, and that's what she was doing now—making little stand-up figures from images she had cut out of the magazines. When they were ready, she lifted the lid of the box and placed them all in position. They stood around or sat on marble seats or leaned against white columns and leaned over rose bushes. Beyond the borders of the enchanted garden she had made of paper and paint and cutouts, there was a perfect blue sky, and the lid of the box was also blue on the inside. But she seemed to have captured time too, for the sky deepened on one side, as though night had fallen; the shadows were deep and mysterious, while far away on the left side, the sky was a gorgeous sunrise pink. When the little people were all in place, she put the lid on the box and switched on the tiny electric lights that she'd placed skillfully inside. She looked through the peephole once again, and I am sure that I saw her shrink, like Alice, and become small enough to pass through to the world inside.

Yet she was still there at the worktable. She looked up at the other boxes lined up on the shelf, and just as I had been sure she shrank and passed through the peephole, I now felt sure she said to me, "Take a look. You'll agree, I think, that my worlds are boundless, and there's no limit to what one can create." She was the only person who had spoken to me for centuries. It was wonderful!

I took a look, peering into the boxes one by one, and saw all the other fantastic worlds she had created. When I looked through one of the peepholes, I saw someone as curious as I, just inside the hole, a little to the right so that only half of the face and one bright eye was visible, looking out at me. It gave me quite a start.

Then I thought I might as well look in on the lovers in the next room. They had finished making love and were sitting on the bed, eating Georges's candy and smoking his cigarettes.

The Cement maiden.

Chapter 20

What Eva Saw in Her Looking Glass

onsieur Moitessier took Eva out for dinner as he had promised himself he would. They went to a very good restaurant he knew of, and throughout the evening he put himself out to be attentive to her. By the time the dessert came, Eva felt relaxed. It had been difficult for her at first because she had thought she'd given up dining out with men.

Over coffee, they talked about Roland. "The young lady he's friendly with is charming. I think it's good for him to have a friend."

"I only hope he won't think of taking her seriously," Eva replied. "Suppose he got some silly idea into his head about marrying her."

"Oh no, of course. He's much too young."

"Girls like that can get around men. All they can think of is getting a man." Eva looked worried.

"Do you know the young lady?" Monsieur Moitessier asked.

"If she's the one I think she is, yes, I do," Eva said darkly. "I'm afraid I don't approve of her. There's some mystery about her."

Monsieur Moitessier studied Eva's face as she drank her coffee. He thought she needed softening up. He wondered how he would manage to do that. He didn't dare invite her to his apartment, afraid he might scare her off. But he was in no hurry. After all, he'd known her for a long time. He didn't know why he'd suddenly made his mind up to court her, but now and then the Light picture Marius had painted of *The Lovers in the Sky* came back to him. He realized it had rekindled his interest in Eva.

Nor had Eva forgotten those Light images, but she tried to make herself believe that Monsieur Moitessier's only interest was in Roland. "You have some influence over him, Gaston. I hope you'll use it. Point out to him that he cannot become seriously involved with this girl. He wouldn't listen to me, even if I said anything. We used to be so close, but now he seems to regard me as his enemy."

Monsieur Moitessier—Gaston—was afraid she was going to start up again and said to himself, *Someone should stop her mouth with kisses.* He was delighted with the idea and hoped he'd have the opportunity to do it one day. Or one night. Nighttime would be better!

"I hope for his sake that he never brings her home to my apartment. I'm afraid I might be impolite to her," Eva said nastily.

When she returned home that evening, she went to her room and looked at the photograph of Gerard, her dead husband. She hadn't really looked at it for a long time. After she had examined his face for some time, she went over to her dressing table and sat there. Looking up, she saw her own face in the mirror. It was easy to sit there gazing at herself because she had one of those kidney-shaped dressing tables with space for her knees. She didn't often spend time like that, but she did so now. Just as she had examined Gerard's photograph, she now examined her own face. It looked unfamiliar to her, but that was because she hadn't sat right in front of it like this for a long time, either. She wondered whether Gerard would recognize her if he came back now. But, of course, he would. Her face was still young-looking and firm, but her lips were a little thinner—not as generous as they once had been. After looking at them and trying to bite them a little to fill them out with red blood, she wondered if she had allowed herself to worry too much about Roland and that girl. She had forgotten that she would soon have to fly away and leave him, and she worried about money. She didn't want him to spend it on Undi.

She looked too often into a canister on the kitchen shelf where she kept small change. That was ridiculous because the amount of money she kept there wasn't going to make them or break them. She realized that it was at those moments that her lips tightened. And then she knew she looked mean every time she saw Roland with a girl. She looked like that at her work sometimes. She resented certain things, and sometimes she suspected people of things—idiotic things, like taking her pins. She recognized that some of her own actions were simply the result of fear. But didn't she have things to be afraid of, like the future, for instance, or getting ill?

What good did it do to fear them? There was no point in all this anxiety, I told myself, because Roland would do what he wanted to do, and then grow old and die, and she'd find someone else to worry about.

She kept on looking at her face until she couldn't see herself. It looked like another person's face, and she wondered if she had been letting another person's nature creep over her during the last fifteen years. This face wasn't the face of the real Eva. It couldn't be. The real Eva had a face like a tender flower. This one was harder, and it had lines. She experimented. She closed the mouth tightly and saw what the trouble was. It made a difference to the look of the whole face. She tried to smile, but the grimace frightened her. Supposing her beauty should vanish altogether! She knew she'd been beautiful when she married Gerard. But she wasn't thinking only of her physical beauty. She was thinking of the radiance she had once possessed.

Of course, she worked hard—fourteen years at the same job. No one could find fault with her, working so hard to support her son. That reminded her of the small inheritance from his uncle, which she was supposed to use for his education. She'd never told Roland about that. There was really no excuse for the way she grudgingly said she had no money to pay his fees. But that was because she still hoped he would go to study law. She was keeping the money for that, and that was why she had kept it from him.

"Remember how I came home that day and found him painting?" she asked her reflection in the looking glass—that unfamiliar person who didn't look like her. "I've skimped and saved for his sake, not my own. In a way, I have sacrificed myself, and his father's relatives know that." She paused to take time to resent Gerard's family (except for the uncle who'd left the trust fund), but she wasn't as concerned with them now as she was with herself. She was examining herself, not them. "Security. It is so important." But then she had to admit that, when she came to think about it, really think, it was a very shaky thing, security. It could vanish overnight. "If I were to build a house, it could be wiped out by fire or an earthquake, and so could the insurance company. So it really doesn't exist. Yet a mother has to make some provision for her son."

I could have told her it wasn't that exactly. The canister in the kitchen, for instance, contained a few francs, yet she behaved as if it were a fortune.

"Have I lost my sense of proportion?" She remembered how she had doled out a few francs to Roland and expected him to buy paints with them. She'd done so because she didn't want him to be a painter. The thought of the académie constantly irritated her. Yet Gaston was sympathetic toward Roland. He thought Roland was a good painter and showed promise of becoming greater. He sympathized with her too, and she was beginning to wonder what his intentions were. Everyone knew he had had a mistress for ten years and the woman had died. Did he want another one? Eva knew he'd always liked her, but now his manner had changed. What did he want? She thought of the unaccustomed boldness of his behavior; it was as though he had come to a sudden decision to court her. She realized how far she had retreated from life. She'd forgotten how to behave with a man, and if Gaston Moitessier had not been an old acquaintance, she wouldn't have even gone to dinner with him. But she knew he was fond of Roland. The thought of taking a lover—well, she couldn't imagine it. Yet, his hand on her arm had been warm and firm. She suddenly blushed as she pictured him holding her body, touching and caressing her breast.

But that girl who was so disturbingly familiar, who had actually come into her home and spent the night! The two of them sneaking in like that! And she'd recognized her too. She was the one who had bought the suit. Or rather, that man, Georges Albertine, had bought it for her. She gasped when she realized that her son was sleeping with another man's kept woman. Of course, this was the girl he had been spending his nights with! Jealousy overcame her other resentment against the girl when she imagined the intimacy that must exist between them. He would tell her his secrets and his hopes, and perhaps he would go to her when depression overcame him, as it often did.

"When he was small he was secretive, but he came to me. Then, when his father died, a slow change began. I think he turned to Josephine more than to me, but I didn't mind that. She was a good friend." Josephine was Eva's maid. Eva realized how much she had missed that girl, and worried about her too, when she'd gone to marry a soldier in Algeria. *"Now, it's as though he has*

no one to talk to in this house. He spends his time, when he's at home, playing with those paper things in his room. He thinks I don't understand his painting."

Thinking about it for a moment, she realized she hadn't tried very much. "I didn't understand Gerard's painting either. But then, he had never been successful. How am I to know? Roland said once that he needed to create. If all he could do was copy others, he would give it up. He is only beginning. I should give him a chance." It was hard for her to consider this. Give him a chance, and his youth would be gone, what with spending his time at the académie and then doing his military service. She had carried a child and cared for him. Wasn't that creativity? Had she succeeded? Was it time now for her to let go of him?

All the time she was talking to herself and looking at the face in the glass, she had the impression that something was moving inside her, not such a physical sensation as when the baby had moved inside her but another stranger sensation. It was like an upheaval. And she imagined that what was moving was her true self, trying to find its way out, just as if it were being reborn. It would happen only if she remained outwardly still and continued to look relentlessly at the face in the glass. So she did that, and while she looked directly into those eyes, they began to get dark and she found herself looking at a starlit night. And flying through the night was a lovely woman with a child in her arms!

"Why, that's me!" She began to remember everything. "That's my true self flying through the night. Oh, how wonderful that was. How lovely the city looked from up there. And all those stars." How happy she felt, knowing that that lovely person was herself.

She imagined she ought to stop looking at that vision and get ready for bed. But she kept on looking, trying to fix the picture firmly in her mind so that she wouldn't forget it anymore. Then she saw her face in the glass again, and it was her true face. It was the gentle face that had looked back at her in Undi's bathroom. She was suddenly transported to the palace, and Undi was there with her. But this time she had no baby in her arms, and she felt deliciously free.

"Something marvelous has just happened to me, there beyond the mist. You know—the other side of my life."

222

Undi looked very interested and asked what it was.

"I was looking at myself, my inner self, you know. And I saw a little of the truth. Oh, I know I didn't go into it very deeply. There are some things I can't understand. But I knew that I had lost touch with my original self. And suddenly, this evening, I looked into the looking glass, and there I was. Oh, Undi, I was so happy. It was like being reborn. I became beautiful again."

"Eva!" Undi exclaimed. "What a lovely thing to happen. I knew it would, you know, but I couldn't push you. Not that you weren't beautiful always. But I know just what you mean—your spiritual beauty. Strange, how a face can change—especially over there in what they call the real world. Funny, I call *this* the real world!"

"I suppose it's a matter of opinion. I certainly feel more like myself in this world." Eva sounded comfortable with herself. "But you always look radiant, Undi, no matter which world you're in."

"I'm not sure about that. Sometimes I've done things that weren't very nice. I've been thinking about that lately. Now that I've come Back-from-Sea, I can see that one has to be careful. The world might change one." She looked thoughtful, but looking out at the blue sky, she couldn't help putting all her doubts aside. "I feel wonderful today. That's why you find me here in the palace. Look, we must forgive ourselves and celebrate!"

"Oh, yes. I feel like celebrating too, Undi. What are your Botticelli Angels going to give us this time?"

"Tea? No, I've changed my mind. It must be something more special than tea." She clapped her hands, and one of the loveliest handmaidens came into the room with a bottle in her arms. She was followed by another with two glasses. They put them on the table and then flew out of the window.

"We'll drink this. It's something very rare. In fact, it's the only one of its kind. It was made by a Benedictine monk, and something went wrong with it. But it was wrong in the right way, if you know what I mean. It was so wonderful that he sealed it up and never made another like it. After that, he turned into a bird and was never seen again. It's ours. We'll drink to our true, beautiful, unique selves."

As Eva drank, she suddenly thought about Gaston Moitessier standing in the street and pointing up at the Light picture in the sky.

It was just a sudden image of him, as a matter of fact, and it passed as quickly as it came. She and Undi went on sipping their drinks and enjoying the sight of some pink parakeets flying outside, toward the bluest of skies.

Chapter 21

Gaston and Eva

Students were preparing to put away their painting materials for the summer. There would be no painting classes, only a summer drawing session in the late afternoon, until the new term began. They cleaned their palettes until the brown wood glowed and then threw away their paint rags, many of which had been torn from old bedsheets. Gaston Moitessier looked at his latest painting and felt fairly satisfied. He even gave a grunt of acknowledgement when Mrs. Widgery complimented him.

"You've made enormous strides," she sighed. "I wish I could say the same for myself."

He made a sympathetic noise, for he'd softened toward her. She had given Roland four very large canvases, saying she wasn't going to use them. "Next term, I'm going to do small still lifes. I can give them to my friends for Christmas."

Roland had been very happy when he'd received these canvases. Monsieur Moitessier was pleased.

"She's not such a bad sort, after all."

Leaving the atelier, he stepped over to see what was going on in the still life class. The Australian girl, Doreen, was still at work on her colossal cabbage. He wondered if she'd ever finish it. Someone else had a half-finished "Refrigerator Interior." He didn't make any comment. To tell the truth, he felt humble. These were all quite young students painting—if it could be called painting—what they called "real life." He smiled, imagining them setting up their easels in his hardware store and painting what they saw on the shelves. *"Me,"* he said to himself, *"I'd rather go on painting pretty women, like Roland's mother for instance. I wonder what they'd think of that."*

He knew, however, that youth had the right, even the duty, to change things in the world if they could. Roland was still in the atelier putting his paints away.

"Roland, my boy, we haven't had that glass of wine together yet. What about now? Are you free?" He had something to say to the boy.

Roland was free, so they went over to the Coupole and found a table at the far end of the terrace.

"Hmm, getting worse every day," Gaston grunted, looking round at the crowd, among whom were many foreigners. Although Montparnasse and the surrounding area had been inundated by foreigners for as long as he could remember, Gaston always made that remark when he went to the Dome or the Coupole. The waiter came, and Gaston ordered the wine. Settling back in his chair, he looked at Roland. He was fond of the boy, and now the fatherly interest he had in him was even stronger, owing to some unexpected development in his relationship with Eva, which had given him cause for further satisfaction last week.

He thought Roland looked glum. He wondered what was wrong. Or was it just an expression that many of the young men wore on their faces these days?

"Where's your sweetheart?" he asked. "I haven't seen her lately. Everything all right?"

Roland told him that Undi had been busy working as a photographers' model, and that was why she hadn't been seen at the académie lately. Monsieur Moitessier raised an eyebrow but didn't ask what kind of photographers they were. "What are you doing for the summer?" he inquired.

"I don't know." Roland looked even glummer at the thought of staying in Paris while almost everyone he knew would be going away.

Gaston didn't quite know how to proceed, for Roland wasn't giving him much encouragement. He wanted to talk to the boy about his future. He felt he had the right to do so now, after what had happened.

"How is your mother?"

"She's well." Roland still looked gloomy. But then he looked up and caught Monsieur Moitessier's eye. "She's quite well. She bought a new dress at the place where she works, you know. It looks good on her."

Gaston smiled. "What sort of dress?" He seemed to know already. His smile said so.

"A deep blue velvet. It's quite elegant and sexy too." Roland looked as if he were surprised at what he had just said. He cast another glance at his old friend and suddenly realized that Monsieur Moitessier was interested in his mother. He was sitting there, tasting the wine that had just been brought to the table and looking as if he were tasting the thought of Eva in a sexy dress. His eyelids were dreamy, and a slight smile hung on his face.

"You know, I've always been fond of your mother. But, of course, I've always had the greatest respect for her. Your father was alive when I first met her. But lately . . ." He looked at Roland and somehow he felt more confident.

Roland wondered if he had understood Monsieur Moitessier, and then he felt sure he hadn't. Yet he was interested and surprised. He took a sip from his own glass and let the thought of his mother and Gaston Moitessier flow down with the liquid. Then another thought struck him. His mother had surprised him very much a week ago by going away somewhere for the weekend, but had told him nothing more than she was going to visit some friends in Normandy. He had gone out on Friday evening, and when he'd come home, she'd been gone. Then, on Sunday, when he'd come home late, she had already returned. He and Undi had taken advantage of her absence and enjoyed a whole night together on Saturday. Now, with Monsieur Moitessier sitting there looking so pleased with himself, Raymond wondered whether Eva had been with him! He couldn't really believe it, for he knew his mother never had anything to do with men. Until now, he had taken that for granted, but now he suddenly saw her in a different light, and it startled him.

The ice was broken and Monsieur Moitessier felt free to talk to Roland about himself. "You know, Roland, your mother is right to feel concerned about you. A painter's life is a hard one. Take me, for instance. I am a practical man. I have made a lot of money and I'm very comfortable, but if I had started to paint when I was a youth like you, I would have nothing. I'm not sorry. I've enjoyed my life, and now I am still enjoying it. Oh, yes, I realize we're not all alike and each man must do things his own way. You're young and a little impatient, and I don't suggest you should do as I did. That's your affair. No, no, don't say anything. I have been thinking a lot about you, my boy, and I must say, I share some of your mother's concern, even though she doesn't believe it. She says I encourage you. Well, I do. You're a good painter, and I do encourage you."

Roland looked interested and would have spoken, but Monsieur Moitessier held up a hand. "But you have to plan things. Now, as I see it, few painters make a living; some are lucky if they manage to stay alive, am I not right? Well, some are prepared for that, and they accept the hardship. That's all right if they are prepared to live without a family, a wife and children, and a normal life. But if they want all that too; well, it's no good, Roland. What are your ideas on the subject?"

"I . . . haven't considered marriage," Roland said, thinking that Monsieur Moitessier was referring to himself and Undi. "I want to paint. That's what I have decided upon, you know."

"Hmm. Have you considered learning some sort of trade, for instance? With something else behind you, you could at least earn money while you went on painting. You might consider carpentry, for instance, or plumbing, eh?" Monsieur Moitessier understood such trades because he'd had dealings with these tradesmen and their tools in his hardware business. "The world may be facing a global financial crisis. You should be be prepared. It wouldn't hurt, you know, to be able to make a few francs now and then. Give you a sense of security."

Even as he said this Gaston saw the worst side of things. He envisioned a world full of unemployed plumbers and carpenters. He didn't say so to Roland, not wanting to discourage him.

Roland, on the other hand, experienced a moment of optimism, inspired by a play he had heard of. He00 said, "Some people say the world has always pulled through by the skin of its teeth. In your opinion, Monsieur, in these terrible times, is that possible?"

"Oui, peut etre," Gaston replied and he made that special French sound, clearing his throat, as he wasn't quite sure if he meant it.

Roland, who was a reasonable youth in many ways, considered the idea of being a carpenter, and then he considered being a plumber. Neither of those trades appealed to him very much, although if he did have to make a choice, he believed he would prefer to be a carpenter.

"I tell you what," Monsieur Moitessier said, reading his thoughts, "why don't you go away for a month or two, to the South of France or somewhere where you would enjoy yourself and have a carefree summer vacation. Think about what I have said. The world is changing fast. Paris is changing, and you have to make some provision for the future, believe me. So think about it."

As Gaston thought about the state of the economy he wondered if he should spend all his money while it still had value.

Roland felt dismal again. Having to think about the practical side of life made him feel drained of all inspiration. Yet he realized that something *did* have to be done. He thought about Undi. Not that he wanted to marry. They had never even discussed that. But he knew that if he had money, their relationship would be a different one. She seemed interested in worldly things now.

"I would like to go away, certainly," Roland told Gaston, "but I don't think I would be able to afford it."

"That's what I was coming to, if you will allow me. If you would accept (and I have discussed this with your mother), I would pay the cost of your vacation, train fare, accommodation, and some extra for a little pleasure. Your mother and I spoke about it the other day."

Again, Roland looked surprised. His mother had been much nicer, sweeter, and gentler during the last couple of weeks, and he had not failed to notice it. But he had not expected any money from her for a vacation. Now, here was Monsieur Moitessier offering to foot the bill!

Gaston watched the expression of surprise passing over Roland's face. "What do you say? Would you like to take your sweetheart with you? How are things between you? Are you serious, or is it just a casual affair?"

"Oh," Roland seemed to come out of a well of deep consideration. "Oh, we are close, but . . ." Roland and Undi were still lovers but were finding it difficult to have any privacy and this fanned their ardor. Then he remembered that Monsieur Moitessier had just made a generous offer, and he should answer him. "It's very kind of you, and I don't know quite what to say. I had thought of hitchhiking somewhere on my own. But I wouldn't expect Undi to do that. It would be very nice if we could go together."

He couldn't bring himself to say he loved Undi and, in fact, the word *love* hardly ever came up. They were lovers but had not spoken about love. So he just cast another glance at Monsieur Moitessier, and one of those flickering smiles that often passed across his eyes and

Gaston Moitessier

231

lips told the older man that Roland was still a little cautious, a little secretive, and whatever existed between him and Undi was not going to be brought out into the open. Well, that was as it should be. It was their own affair. He merely wanted to know if the boy would like to get away for the summer and take his sweetheart with him.

"Your mother knows of a charming, old villa close to the sea at Golfe Juan where you can have a good accommodation, if you're interested in the South. She'll tell you about it. Two old cousins of your father own it. She knows the details. I don't."

Roland brightened. It would be nice. He could paint, and he and Undi would be able to go for walks. "I would like that very much, thank you. I would really look forward to that." But then he thought of something. "You know, Undi is earning enough money now to pay for herself. I wouldn't expect you to pay for her too. She wouldn't expect it, either."

"Well, whatever she has can be spent on pleasure. You'll want to go out and spend a little money, won't you? So let her take money with her if she wants to. I will pay your expenses with a little over, just in case you need it. I want you to enjoy yourself."

Roland could hardly believe it. He had been to the South of France only once, as a small boy. He felt shy.

But Gaston could see that he was excited and grateful, and he was satisfied. It was a funny thing. He had never had children of his own, and he did not regret this. But he had always been attracted to women who had boy children. Not girls. No, to him, a woman was also a little girl, but for some reason, the sight of a woman with a son aroused protective and also erotic feelings in him for the woman. His mistress of ten years had had a son, but although Gaston had tried to win him over, the lad had never responded, and now that his mother was dead, he saw nothing of the young man. Roland was quite a different type of young man. Gaston felt that they were close.

He sipped the rest of his wine and thought of Eva. He smiled a secret smile and felt warm. For some time, he had pondered over the question of what to do about Eva. He had not felt as confident as he pretended to be because of the difference in their ages, and also, he didn't quite know how to approach her because of her seeming indifference to men. She had never been to his apartment, and he had not been to hers since her husband had died. So what was he to do?

Suddenly, he'd had an idea that he quickly put into effect. An old friend of his, whose husband had been his comrade in the French Underground during the War, lived in a fine seventeenth-century chateau in Normandy. It had been badly damaged during the war, and Francoise had spent a large part of her fortune and her time having the chateau restored after the death of her husband. She was fond of Gaston, and he felt free to ask a little favor of her. So he made a telephone call and explained the situation to her, knowing that she loved a romance.

"Certainly. Bring her here for the weekend. Come this weekend, if you can. Next week, I'm having a lot of guests, but this weekend, I'm all alone. I'll be very glad to see you."

"It's more sudden than I expected," Gaston replied, "but I will suggest it to the lady. You'll like her. She's a pretty woman."

"I'll put you near each other in the old wing. It's a little drafty, but it's romantic. And when she hears the ghost, she'll run to you for protection."

Gaston knew the chateau. He had stayed there on several occasions. The prospect pleased him, and as Francoise had said, the old wing was certainly romantic.

Somewhat to his surprise, Eva had accepted the invitation on short notice and even bought herself some new clothes at lower-than-cost price, as was her right where she worked. On Friday afternoon, when Gaston got his car out of the garage and called for her, he was gratified to see her wearing a chic summer skirt and blouse with a handsome three-quarter length knit coat, which he found very attractive, and a neat pair of shoes. She carried a good leather bag, which she hadn't used for years, just large enough for a change of clothing and her underwear. In the bag was the velvet gown that she was to wear for dinner. He put the bag next to his own in the back of the car, and off they went.

They'd arrived at the chateau at sunset, and Gaston was pleased. Eva would be able to see it in the evening light. It was a fine example of seventeenth-century architecture, set in wide fields, gardens, and with woods stretching away into the distance. Standing at one of the windows of the gallery upstairs, one could see hills and fields and the steeple of an old church in the far distance. On either side of the chateau were two rows of very old trees, heavy with branches and leaves, that extended as far as the iron gate and stone wall and a narrow moat that no longer had much water in it. Gaston had seen all this before and intended to show it all to Eva on the morrow.

Francoise, his friend, must have seen them coming. She and her two spaniels were standing on the front steps, waiting for them. The two dogs ran to Gaston when he got out of the car, and he patted them affectionately.

"Welcome." Francoise smiled at Eva and then led them into the spacious entrance lobby, larger than Eva's own salon. There were large doors on either side of it. Francoise opened one of them and said to Eva, "This is the Sale du Dais. I hardly ever use it. It's much too large. I have smaller, more comfortable rooms through here." She led them into a smaller salon beyond the Sale du Dais. "I will show you over the chateau tomorrow when you will be able to see it properly. Now you must have something to drink."

After dinner, the trio sat in the salon and chatted. The two ladies seemed to like each other, and Gaston felt gratified. Francoise was particularly hospitable toward Eva. At ten thirty, she led Eva and Gaston up the grand staircase to the second floor.

"I am giving you the old bedrooms in this side of the building. This was not damaged by the bomb, and the rooms have hardly been touched for a hundred years, except for the plumbing and electricity I had installed. The other rooms at the end of this corridor have been restored, but they are not even furnished properly yet."

She showed Eva into a very large bedchamber that was furnished with solid, antique furniture. There was a four-poster bed, a dressing table, and an old-fashioned wardrobe, along with several upright chairs, an easy chair, and a table. "And look at this wallpaper." Francoise called Eva's attention to one wall of the room that was covered with hand-painted wallpaper. "It's a hundred years old, and so is this door." It was the door of a small closet that jutted out at the far end of the room. The door had a design of twining branches, leaves, and birds. Inside the closet were a bidet, a wash basin, and a toilet.

"I'm sorry there's no bath. But there is one at the end of the corridor," Francoise explained. "Now, will you feel comfortable? I hope so. You need not feel nervous. Gaston will be right next door." She cast a sly glance at Gaston, who was standing in the doorway.

Eva smiled and went to look out of the tall window.

And Gaston thought, *She's looking at the garden. I'm glad there's a full moon tonight.*

As he left the room with Francoise, he looked back and imagined that Eva looked small and a little bit lonely. He regretted having to leave her all alone in the large chamber with its high ceiling. He was touched. She looked young and helpless.

In his room, Francoise smiled and told him to make himself at home. "I don't have to explain anything to you. You know where everything is. That's your bathroom over there. Goodnight, Gaston, and good luck."

When she had gone downstairs to her own chamber that she had had restored just for herself, Gaston waited a while and then went to Eva's door in his dressing gown. He knocked and called, "Eva."

He heard a small voice say, "Yes, Gaston."

"Are you all right? Is there anything you need?"

"No, thank you, Gaston. I'm perfectly all right. Good night."

He smiled to himself. In no hurry, he intended to spend the whole of tomorrow courting her. He imagined that, in the woods where the ground was carpeted with blue bells or strolling through Francoise's sweet-smelling garden or walking across the fields to see the old farmhouses that were all part of the large estate, he would be able to get close to her. And he had great hopes for tomorrow night. If he didn't succeed by then, well, the ice would be broken and there'd be another opportunity. He would see to that.

Gaston had decided to ask Eva to marry him, but he also wanted to have her as a mistress for a little while first. He didn't want to start off as a newlywed, with Eva feeling shy, and he, too, for that matter, climbing into a nuptial couch, knowing what was supposed to happen and perhaps failing each other. He felt like this because of the difference in their ages. Besides, he believed that sex—love—out of wedlock was more romantic. He wanted that first, before they settled down. *If she'll have me.* He reminded himself not to take her for granted.

At about twelve thirty, just as he was about to close the book he'd been reading and put his light out, he heard a trembling voice calling from the hall. Going to his door, he looked out and saw Eva, clad in a Japanese kimono of pale beige with delicate pink and white flowers on it, looking anxiously out of her doorway.

"Oh, Gaston, I saw your light on. I couldn't help calling you. I know it's silly of me, but I'm scared. Every time I close my eyes, I hear footsteps. Something—someone—is creeping past the door. Oh, I'm so sorry to bother you, but it's frightening. Don't you hear them too?"

Gaston knew about those footsteps. They scared everyone at first. But he also knew they weren't footsteps, only the old wooden boards at this end of the building creaking rhythmically. They sounded exactly like someone walking stealthily along the gallery and entering one's room. It took quite a while to be able to ignore them.

"Poor little one; she's frightened," he said, putting his arm around her protectively. The feeling of her shoulder and the soft sensuous silk of the kimono thrilled him. It was a very old one that she had treasured throughout the years. It was made of the finest hand-painted silk; padded with some very light, fragile stuff; and lined with an even finer silk, although Eva had forgotten when and where she had gotten it. She had kept it carefully preserved in tissue paper, sandalwood, and a linen bag since the early days of her marriage. This was the first time since that she had worn it, and the feeling of it was so delicious that she, too, was thrilled.

"Come," Gaston murmured, "it's nothing—only the old boards. I have just the thing for you—some fine, old cognac. We'll have some, and you'll feel better." He kept his arm around her and led her into his room.

It was like hers, a large chamber with the two wide windows. There was a couch and a table at one end of the room. He had already had some of the cognac, and his glass was on the table. "Let me get another glass." He found one on the old-fashioned dressing table and brought it back.

Eva was still standing, as though waiting for him, so instead of inviting her to sit down, he put the glass down and took her into his arms, enfolding her in a warm embrace. Then he kept one arm around her while he brought the other one around and lifted her face with a gentle hand and kissed her on the lips. Eva stood passively, letting him do it. When he did it a second time, though, her lips responded, and her body made a little undulating movement as it settled closer to his. He couldn't quite believe it! It was so simple and easy. But he was still

236

in no hurry, so he drew her down to the couch and sat beside her and poured the cognac for both of them.

It was now no longer comfortable on the couch, so Gaston switched the light out, and they moved over to the big four-poster bed.

"There," he whispered. "And take this beautiful robe off." He removed it for her and could feel another soft garment under it, her nightgown. There was still a very low light on the dressing table, and he could just see her form, stretched out on the bed. He didn't want her to take the nightgown off yet. He slid his hands over it and felt her body underneath it.

"Eva, you are beautiful! Why have we wasted so much time?"

The next morning, they were late coming down to breakfast. There was a note from Francoise. "Please enjoy your breakfast and excuse me for having had mine. I have to go the village on an errand but will be back about midday. Gaston, take Eva to the woods or the garden. Until then, enjoy yourselves. Francoise."

As Eva and Gaston started off for their walk, Gaston said, "Francoise will show you over the chateau and the chapel after lunch. Now we will go to the woods." They walked along the road and looked at the cows in the field and came at last to the woods where it was dark. The trees were fine, with long, straight trunks. Beyond them, as in a Botticelli painting, the light of the sky could be seen, and all around them on the ground was a carpet of bluebells.

"Well?" Gaston said as they paused to enjoy the sensation of being in the quiet dimness among the trees. "Well, mon amour?"

Eva suddenly remembered the vision she'd had in Undi's bathroom, of herself following her image through the woods—and she felt sure that these were the very same woods!

"Well, what, Gaston?" Eva smiled because she should have simply said, "Yes, yes, I am very happy. It's wonderful to have a lover, especially such a lover as you."

Gaston knew how she felt. When they walked back, he took her across to the walled garden. It, too, had suffered during the war but not badly. At one end, the wall had been broken and the top of it, where it was jagged and uneven, earth blown by the wind had filled the jagged holes, and now white daisies grew in it. There was a statue of a maiden facing the gate by which they entered, one of those gracefully curved maidens who always seem to be bending over a little to touch something. And in the center of all the flower-beds, there was what had once been a fountain. Now that, too, was full of flowers. Francoise was very fond of flowers and did a lot of gardening herself. A horse was looking at them through the gate. The scent of all the roses and the carnations and other flowers was so subtle, so delicious that Eva vowed never to use perfume from a bottle again. (But she did because the first thing Gaston did when they returned to Paris was buy some for her.)

"I intend to ask you to marry me, if you will," Gaston told her. "But I wanted, also, to have you as my mistress for a little while. Will you forgive me?"

Eva laughed and twined her arms around him. Since last night, she had developed a passion for kissing and couldn't stop. I, who had been aware of all that had taken place, knew that, for the first time, Eva was in love.

"Enough of that," Gaston protested, but he was delighted. He couldn't help putting his arms around her but said firmly, "Wait. Wait until tonight." He was trying to be firm, but there was also a delighted, helpless note in his voice. "My God! What have I started?" he asked, returning one of her kisses.

As they drove back to Paris on Sunday evening, they talked about Roland.

"If he doesn't want to study law or medicine, he might consider a trade as a sideline to his painting."

Eva considered this, and in her new frame of mind, she agreed. She also agreed to let Gaston pay for Roland's vacation. Accepting, without any shame, was part of the love she had for him.

"He can come back in time for our wedding. How do you like that idea?" Gaston asked her.

"I do like it. Oh, Gaston, shall we tell him now or wait a little?" Eva felt shy about telling her grown-up son that she had fallen in love.

"Let's have some time to ourselves. We'll write to him while he is away. You do think he would like to go, don't you, my dear?"

"I'm sure he will. He'll be very happy. You're so kind, Gaston. I adore you for it." She snuggled up to him and caressed him while he drove the car. She did it so seductively that he was afraid of having an accident and had to beg her to stop.

238

"I can't help myself, Gaston. I adore you so much."

"And I adore you too, madame. I will talk to Roland one afternoon after his class. Now behave yourself and let us reach Paris with all our bones intact."

And that was how and why Monsieur Moitessier and Roland came to be sitting on the terrace of the Coupole, having their talk.

There was something else that Gaston was curious about, but he didn't know whether Roland would tell him about it. "What happened to the group you were with?" he asked. "I never knew what it was all about. Do you still belong?"

Roland looked serious. "It exists, yes, but we have changed our policy a little." He looked at Gaston, wondering how much he knew. "It's a group some friends of mine formed, to protest the destruction of life on the planet. We had planned a dramatic form of protest . . ." He hesitated and then blurted out, "Self-immolation. Our leader . . ."

"My God," Gaston exclaimed, "were you involved in that affair? A fellow set fire to himself at the Trocadero. Were you in that, too?"

"I was there," Roland told him, "but it didn't happen. I mean, it was meant to happen, but something inexplicable happened instead. He disappeared."

He wanted to tell Gaston all about it, but he stopped, realizing that he wouldn't be believed. No one believed it, not even the people who had been there. So he and the others had agreed not to speak about it. Until the mystery was cleared up, they had decided there would be no more self-sacrifice. He was sorry now that he had said as much as he had.

But he needn't have worried because Gaston hadn't even heard that part of it. A story had gotten around about some fellow setting himself on fire, which no one could prove or say they actually saw. Gaston believed he had set fire to himself but not that he had disappeared. The mystery had not been solved. No one, not even those closest to Osiris knew what had happened to him—or to Ky and Sylvester. Isobel, too, had disappeared.

"What a horrible thing. Thank God, your mother doesn't realize you were involved in that."

"It's all right," Roland said. "Don't worry. I'm not going to set fire to myself. We've decided upon other ways to protest. Please don't say anything to my mother."

"I wouldn't dream of it. But you had better be careful, Roland. Don't go to such extreme measures. Did that fellow die? How terrible!"

"No, he didn't." Roland felt a certain bitterness. His feelings on the subject of war and pollution were just as strong as before. "You know, you have been speaking to me about security and the future. But how can anyone feel secure when we are all bent upon destroying the planet? How can there be any security when the overlords and the politicians and the warmongers and the industrialists are poisoning the earth? But we can't blame them alone. We're all guilty in one way or another. We don't blame any special group, but humanity itself. We seem bent on self-destruction anyway. So why not self-sacrifice? Don't think we are a political group because we're not. It's just that there's no security in the world, until we all change ourselves."

Gaston was just about to agree with Roland, when he remembered where some of his own money had come from. He was a very comfortable man, and his wealth had not all come from his own hardware business. About twenty years ago he had bought shares in a large concern that manufactured hardware. Later, this concern had gone on making small arms and then larger ones. Some of those arms had been sold to the arms dealers, who resold them throughout the Middle East, and Gaston could remember saying, "I hope to God they will never have to use them." Now, he had to admit that feelings of guilt gnawed away at him from time to time. At other times, he had his painting to think about. He couldn't confess all this to Roland, but he felt very uncomfortable and said, "Yes, I agree, we're all involved in one way or another. There's no denying it."

He asked himself whether Roland would accept his money if he knew where some of it had come from? But what could one do? He was an ordinary man, and he had no intention of giving up his security at this stage of his life.

Chapter 22

Luncheon with Georges

When Roland and Undi went out to dinner they usually went to a student restaurant, where they could have a reasonable meal for a few francs. But when Georges took her, they went to very fancy restaurants, indeed. This was not his regular way of life either, but with Undi at his side, Georges enjoyed going to restaurants he would never have gone to alone. Old restaurants where the waiters still bowed and tried to please and where the food was the best.

For this luncheon with her, Georges had chosen a very expensive place, and he felt excited. He believed the romance of the past still existed, and once Georges had made up his mind about something like that, it was not easy to destroy his illusions. In this way, I suppose, he was fortunate. I must say Undi enjoyed these luncheons and dinners with Georges. For both of them, it was a game. By now, they were good friends. Undi had cleverly managed to accomplish this without even realizing it. She liked him and she liked his attentions, as long as he didn't try to possess her. She denied having a love affair with Roland, but the Green Couch was not so easily deceived.

The headwaiter knew them. He himself led them to their seats.

"We've been here before, haven't we," Undi murmured, looking about at the other tables. She had a good view of the whole room. Georges could see only a part of it.

"Yes, this is the restaurant where dukes and barons used to bring beautiful actresses and the most famous courtesans—the most famous women in Paris. Do you like it, my princess?"

"I love it, your grace. But I'm tired of being a princess. I'd like to be one of those famous beauties of Paris, loaded down with diamond necklaces and heavily beaded gowns."

"Well, I do sometimes think of you as a famous beauty. But perhaps you'd like to be a duchess. I don't like to think of you as a courtesan. You can be a duchess, and I can be your humble groom to whom you've taken a fancy."

"I'm not sure, your grace, that a duchess would allow herself to be seen here, lunching with her groom. Wouldn't she sneak away to some wretched hotel for her miserable hour of love? No, I don't want to be a duchess. I'm an incognito 'famous beauty.'" She then took out of her handbag a cigarette holder, which she stretched out until it was about ten inches long. I imagine she learned about this kind of life from the Green Couch. That old piece of furniture thrived on memories of past grandeur. Undi looked about haughtily for a cigarette girl.

"You're smoking a lot," Georges observed, stepping out of character. "I didn't know you smoked."

"Oh yes, you did. You have often given me those gold-tipped Turkish cigarettes. You're not confusing me with that dolt, Suzanne, are you, your grace?"

"Never, my own Gigi." And to my surprise, Georges took a gold-rimmed monocle out of his breast pocket, screwed it into his eye socket, and looked around in a lordly fashion. A waiter came hurrying over, and Georges asked for the cigarette girl to be sent to their table. Then, while Undi played about with her long cigarette holder, he turned his attention to the ordering of the food. Squinting at Undi through the monocle, he asked whether she would like the oysters or the caviar.

"I never touch oysters," Undi replied with a shudder. It was true. Fish-Women were unable to eat seafood of any kind. It made them feel like cannibals. "And I can hardly bear the thought of caviar either. No, your grace, I'll have the pâté. At least that bears no resemblance to what it actually is. And I should like the artichoke."

"No oysters!" Georges could hardly believe it although he had been through all this a dozen times already. He looked stricken, disappointed, and incredulous. "Come, Gigi, my little one. You must eat something."

"And no vinegar, pray. I can't bear it, not even with artichoke. I'd like lemon. And, furthermore, if I am to have garlic, it must be the smallest smidgeon. Nothing is more vulgar than a strong odor of garlic, do you not agree, my great cabbage of a grand duke?"

"Ah, but I will have the oysters if you don't object too strongly, my little parsnip of a 'famous beauty.' Bring oysters and the pâte and the artichoke," he said, turning to the waiter. "And we would like champagne, the very best."

"I shall send the wine waiter, my lord. I mean, your grace."

"Please do." He turned to Undi. "I'm truly sorry, my dear, that you won't have the caviar. But, no doubt, you have your reasons. We won't quarrel over a few fish eggs, eh?" He looked up and squinted at the waiter. I marveled at the way he held the monocle in place. "Pâte de foie gras for her grace and the caviar for me. Oh, and the artichoke with lemon, not vinegar."

The waiter, bending forward, repeated it all very intelligently, as though it were a secret message he was going to carry in his head across the Swiss Alps to some other waiter in the pay of a foreign government. He waited for Georges to continue.

"And now, my precious, what next?"

"A steak Toulouse," Undi said haughtily. "That is the only way to have a steak, you know. You did know Henry, Count of Toulouse, didn't you, your grace? He would never have it any other way. Such a dear . . ."

"Indeed, no, I can't say I knew him. Heard of him, of course. So, a steak Toulouse it shall be." He looked at the waiter again. "Do you know what a steak Toulouse is, my good man?"

The waiter looked doubtful.

"Surely you know that!" Georges insisted sternly. The waiter had to admit he didn't know. Georges looked aghast. But it was clear that he didn't know either.

Undi, languidly eyeing her cigarette on the end of the holder, patiently explained. "You must take three pieces of steak, placing one on top of the other. Do you understand? You grill well and then serve the only piece worth eating, the one in the middle. Does he understand that, your grace?"

"But, of course. Certainly," the waiter gushed and then looked at Georges, who had tossed the menu aside impatiently. "Listen, my good fellow, can the chef make a bourride Bordelaise? Do you think he could do that?"

"But, naturally. Certainly," the waiter declared recklessly. "Of course."

"Do you know what a bourride Bordelaise is?' Georges asked suspiciously.

"But, of course!" But as both Georges and Undi regarded him with suspicion, he grew uneasy and finally confessed. "I will tell you the truth. I do not know. But I am not the chef, you understand. He will know."

"I am not so sure. Do you believe the chef will know? Are you convinced of that?"

The waiter shrugged. A long, expressive shrug, indeed, but it was hard to know what it expressed.

"Hmm. I believe he will *not* know," Georges murmured. 'Now, listen. I will tell you what a bourride Bordelaise is and how to prepare it. Are you listening?"

"Yes, your grace," the waiter said, looking around in a distracted way at his other tables.

"Take a large pan. Make a roux blond sauce and work into it some mixed herbs—parsley, watercress, fennel, minced lemon, bay, and thyme. Do not," he wagged his finger threateningly, "do not let him put in sliced lemon. It must be minced. Do you understand?"

"I understand, your Grace." The water shifted his weight and put it on his left foot instead of his right. "Minced, not sliced."

"Now, put in five pounds of ordinary deep sea fish, cut up, including the heads." Georges began to count them on his fingers. "Black conger, coal fish, whiting, pelouse, red mullet, dab, flounder, lephius, weever, gurnard, and hake. Have you got all that? Add salt, white pepper, saffron, cloves, and red cayenne pepper."

Undi inserted another mauve cigarette into the long holder and sat gazing at the smoke after she had lit it. She was trying not to listen. The very thought of eating fish made her feel awful. She was actually feeling a little bit depressed, and her gaiety was only half true. She knew she was about to deceive Georges, but she hardly realized that this was the cause of her depression.

"Cover with water and let boil until the flesh has come away," Georges was saying. "Meanwhile, you will have put in, cooked, and withdrawn a particularly fine fish, which you will have chosen for me to eat as a whole . . ."

"The Chosen Fish," Undi murmured. A picture came to her mind: The Lord of the Sea chose a particularly fine fish and it danced. A fine fish in scarlet veils did a belly dance for a monarch lying limply on his piled-up sponges, while a fish-attendant fanned him.

"Either a turbot or a sole or a brill. Personally, I prefer a haddock. Have you a haddock in the kitchen?"

The waiter rubbed the back of his left hand with his right hand. In shocked tones, he said, "Of course, your grace. Of course," as though the suggestion that they had no haddock was appalling. "Why not, your grace? Of course."

Yet he looked shifty, and Undi did not believe him. Well, one more haddock left alive in the sea. Good. There was little she could do about the fate of the other five pounds of ordinary sea fish—they were most likely all lying on ice in the kitchen anyway, all frozen stiff for weeks.

"Now, when the bouillon has boiled low, throw in the following sauce, which you will have prepared separately—oh, I do wish you could do this personally; can you not? No, I suppose you can't. Ah well. But the chef should have a young boy, an assistant. He should take a marble mortar . . ."

A dreamy expression had appeared on the waiter's face. "Alas, we have no marble mortars." He looked sadly and dreamily at Undi. "And no young boys. All we have are mixing machines."

"Well! I expected something like that. No matter. Tell them to take something resembling a marble mortar, for heaven's sake, and pound up five pounds of fresh garlic, salt, an egg yolk, and little by little, two or three teaspoons of oil. Tell him to use the pestle continuously until he has in the end a kind of mayonnaise. Now, do you understand all this? Speak, man, are you sure? You have written nothing down, nothing at all of what I've been saying to you. Will you remember all this when you go to repeat it to the chef? Or should I have him called in and tell it to him myself? Yes, I really think I should have the chef called in."

"No, no! Please don't. I assure you I will remember everything. A haddock. Certainly. A most remarkable fish. Excellent! A formidable fish indeed." He was about to fly off, but Georges called him back.

"No, wait. It's not finished. Almost but not quite. One more thing. Listen. Allow the bouillon to go on simmering for a good quarter of an hour—a *good* quarter, mind you. Then strain and pour it into a shallow dish on grilled croutons. Serve boiling hot. Bring it here to me with the haddock. The haddock should be lying in the middle and eaten like the beef in the pot-au-feu. Go!"

"Cer-tain-ly, your grace." And the waiter, released like an arrow from the bow, shot off toward the kitchen.

"I'm sorry for all that garlic, my dear duchess, but I assure you, you won't be able to tell. It disappears, you know, into the bouillon." But he looked worried. "I really don't believe that the chef will know how to prepare that dish. I think I should go into the kitchen myself and instruct him."

"I really wouldn't; really I wouldn't."

"No? Oh very well." He looked at her. "Have you received my last letter," he asked, "in which I laid bare my soul? It was thirty pages long."

"Yes, Georges. I received it. But what can I say to such a letter?"

"Cruel goddess!"

"Silence is the only answer to such a letter. But I must say, your grace, you write a beautiful French." She smiled sweetly. "Perhaps you should write your memoirs."

The wine waiter came now, and Georges chose the champagne. That took some time, but he didn't mind. He had all day and, besides, the dish he had ordered would take an hour or more, if it ever came at all. Undi, feeling anxious because she had to go to her room and pack, wondered whether they would ever leave the restaurant in time.

Looking round, she saw a group of young men at a nearby table. Georges couldn't see them because they were behind him. They were all elegant and chic young men who worked in fashion houses. One of them was Jules Mason. The young men all looked at her and at Georges. Undi pretended not to have noticed them. But she could hear what they were saying. Jules, who seemed to be the leader, or the oldest one of the group, said, "My dear, I told you you'd see interesting people here. They *do* still come here, you know. That's a count. I can't remember which one, but he's from one of the oldest families in France."

"I thought they all lost their heads in the Revolution."

"Not all, my dear. Not all."

"Who's the woman?"

"Don't tell me she's the countess? She doesn't look like one."

"Ah, no, but there are countesses and countesses. That's one of our models she's wearing." Undi was wearing the spring suit Georges had bought her.

"Divine hat. Also yours?"

"Of course. It's part of the ensemble. Looks well on her, doesn't it."

"I like the way she has her hair done."

The hat was a lightweight felt, dipping over one eye. Only one tendril of hair had escaped and spiraled down near her ear. The rest of her fair hair was tucked up under the hat. It made Undi look extremely youthful and sophisticated at the same time.

"Did you hear what they're going to eat? Toulouse Lautrec's darling mother used to have it prepared that way for him. Sweet woman, so they said."

Most of these young men spoke English. Three of them had been imported, as Jules put it, from England, to work as designers' assistants. One of them, who was very young—not more that eighteen and straight from the Royal College of Art in London—wore a glorious damask waistcoat. He sighed and murmured, 'I'd love to dress her. I can see her in black fringes and jet."

"Who, Toulouse Lautrec's mother?"

"No, silly. That girl. Now I know who she is. I've just recognized her. She's the nude dancer we saw the other night . . ."

"No, she's not. Far from it. I think she's Swedish. She's a therapist."

"Imagine him bringing his therapist here for luncheon!"

"Why not?"

"You said he was a count."

Undi was enjoying their conversation. It became more personal. They talked about each other. One of them, who was an assistant millinery designer and had been in Paris for only three weeks, was sporting a mink collar on his coat and, although it was getting warm now, he couldn't resist wearing it. He was also putting on very delicate airs. Jules couldn't help putting him in his place.

"Why, even I, who have been here for nine years, don't wear mink collars out of season. In fact, not even in winter. I haven't got one. Nor do I put on airs. After all, darling, it was I who got you the job."

Undi wasn't amused. She had been playing her part all through luncheon, to make up for what she was going to tell Georges because she knew it would make him unhappy. Now she wanted it to be over so that she could leave the restaurant. Georges noticed a change in Undi. She had lapsed into a troubled silence.

"What is it, my princess?"

"What?"

"Why are you so silent?"

"I've eaten too much. I feel silent." She looked at him. He knew something was wrong.

"Tell me. What is it?"

"I am going away for a little while. I would have told you before, but I only knew it myself last night."

"When? When are you going?'

"Tonight."

"Where are you going?"

"To the South of France."

"Ah." He looked relieved. "That's not very far. In fact, I have a villa there. Let me take you and you can use my villa. I promise I will let you stay, and I won't bother you."

"No, I can't accept that."

"Why? Am I a monster from whom you can't accept things?" He didn't add, "You have accepted clothes and jewelry and money." He didn't even think of those things.

"No, but . . ."

"Are you going with someone? Tell me."

"Yes. My friend."

"Which friend?"

"The one I've told you about."

"Who?"

"My girlfriend."

"I'll drive you both."

"No—thank you."

"Why not?"

"My friend has her own car. Her mother is going also."

"When are you leaving? What time?"

"This afternoon. I think I must go, Georges. What time is it? I mustn't be late." She looked at him. "Georges! Don't look like that. I won't be gone forever . . ."

"How long will you stay?"

"Oh, a couple of weeks. It's been a lovely luncheon. Don't look so sad. It's not sad. You should be pleased that I'm going for a vacation."

"I sense that you are concealing something."

"No, I'm not." Lying came so easily. "I'm not going out of your life. I don't want to lose you, really, I don't. Why do you always imagine that?"

"You hide yourself. You frustrate me on purpose! You are cruel." In his conception of her, she was alternately cruel and deceitful or kind and spiritual and noble. He never imagined her, though, as a young lady with a lover. He wouldn't let this enter his head at all. He only knew that she resisted him. He had never *wanted* to imagine *that*. He backed away from such an idea like a frightened horse. He only knew that she was not his lover.

Undi succeeded in calming Georges down, and he agreed to drive her straight back to the Rue Tilset so that she could get ready for the journey. It was after three o'clock.

He stopped before the gate, and she gave him one of the few embraces she had ever bestowed upon him. Feeling her arms around his neck, he imagined that this was the beginning of a new phase of their relationship. It was not until she had gone inside and he had driven away that he realized it had been her good-bye kiss.

Inside the court, Undi looked at the ugly walls. She was glad the time had come to leave them. "I'm sorry to leave you here," she said to the Cement Maiden. The poor maid was still without water, and her rounded breasts were dry and dusty.

"That's my fate . . . that's my fate. Cement, that's what I am, and what I will remain until I crumble away . . . crumble away . . . crumble away . . ."

This was sad. Undi didn't like to think about it. She crossed the court and waited for the iron lift to come down.

"And you," she asked the lift, "will you stay and crumble away?"

"I shall stay until the building crumbles. I cannot escape. Up and down, up and down. Never a change of direction. I'll go mad; mad— that's what will become of me." The poor iron lift moaned. "Iron won't crumble. It can only go mad."

"Oh, it's all too sad." Undi looked sympathetic as the lift carried her up to her floor.

The lift hiccuped and sobbed, "You can't help it, I know."

Inside the apartment, Undi went along the hall. She would pack and then say good-bye to Mademoiselle Raymonde. She fully expected that she would be gone before Monsieur Raymonde came home that evening. She didn't want to see him. It was true that he'd helped her to earn more money than she'd earned at the académie by sending her to a photographer he knew, but he had also wanted her to pose for him, and she didn't want to do that.

Mademoiselle Raymonde wasn't there. The apartment was silent and spooky, as it often was at that time of the day. As always, she had the uncomfortable sensation that the two people in the photographs were watching her, and she hurried past them, almost expecting them to come to life again. Inside her room. she undressed and put on her robe. The late night, the heavy lunch, her emotions—all combined to make her feel sleepy. So instead of packing, she lay down and fell asleep.

She was awakened by the sound of the doorbell. It was the special ring that she knew was Roland's, so she went along the hallway in her robe and let him in.

"Have you packed?" he asked. "We must be ready by five o'clock. Hurry, I want to get out of here before Monsieur Raymonde comes home."

"So do I."

Just as they were about to leave, the doorbell rang. It startled them both, and the best thing would have been to ignore it. But Undi started guiltily and ran out of the room and along the hallway in her silk gown; she had not yet put on her traveling clothes. When she reached the front door, she opened it and saw Georges on the landing. He was about to turn and walk down the stairs because he was unsure of himself and what he was doing. He wasn't exactly spying on Undi, but he had come back after they'd already said good-bye because he was suspicious. He

250

He had to sit down until his anger passed away.

tried to appear natural and at ease. In his hand was a package wrapped in gold paper.

'You should have candies for the journey. Here, I bought these." As he handed them to her, he tried to step into the hallway.

"No, not now. I'm sorry . . ." Undi stammered.

He dearly wanted to spend a few more minutes with her. She'd been so charming to him all through their luncheon, and this had given him the courage to come back.

"I can't see you now, Georges. I'm . . . just about to dress . . ."

"May I not come in for a moment?"

"No, not now." She looked back at the empty hallway.

"Is he home?" Georges whispered. He was almost afraid of encountering Monsieur Raymonde, although he didn't know why this should be so.

He looked awkward and embarrassed and at last said, "I hope you'll have a good journey. Take the candies. Your girlfriend will like them too." But he still tried to look past her into the hallway. He knew something was not right, and for a moment, he suspected Monsieur Raymonde. He wondered whether Undi's dislike for him—for she had said several times that she didn't like him—was a cover-up for God knows what!

The iron lift came up, and Undi succeeded in getting Georges to enter and go down to the courtyard where the concierge was watching for him. Then Undi went back to her room and quickly finished dressing. She and Roland would have liked to say good-bye to Mademoiselle Raymonde, but she hadn't come home.

"I might never see her again," Undi said, "because I'm never coming back."

When the lift came, they got in, and the lift rumbled downward. "I'll miss you—terribly," the lift whispered to Undi.

She felt such compassion for it that, as they were getting out, she turned back and said, in the tone of one who is addressing a butler, "That will be all. We won't need you any more tonight." She touched it lightly with her hand.

The lift uttered a peculiar sound and shot upwards. It went on to the top of the shaft, did not even pause, but passed right through the roof of the building.

Roland noticed nothing because he was already on his way out to see whether Helen and David were waiting in the street. He and Undi were going with them to the South of France.

Passing out into the courtyard, Undi went over to the Cement Maiden and whispered something to her. Then she went out to look for Roland. He was still waiting. Helen and David hadn't come yet. She stood with him for a few minutes and then returned to the court. In the few moments she had been absent, the concierge and her friend, Madame Bon-Bon, had come out to the courtyard and were standing there, amazed!

"Whoever heard of anyone stealing a lift!" the concierge marveled. "I simply cannot understand it. I went into my friend's apartment half an hour ago, and the lift was there. Now it is gone."

"Unbelievable," said Madame Bon-Bon, her red hair standing on end and her eyes wide with the mystery of it all.

The concierge said to Undi, "How did *you* come down?"

"Oh," Undi replied, "I walked. What else could I do?"

Just then, Roland came back and called her, so she went after him. As she crossed the courtyard, she heard a faint rumbling. She looked back and saw the Cement Maiden disintegrating. Something else to astound them! As she passed out of the courtyard, she heard a whisper, "A fragment of mist, a fragment of spray—I'm coming with you; I'm going away . . ." And she saw the faint fragment of mist. She felt glad. It was a comfort, somehow, to know that she had the power to release those two dear creatures. It lifted the depression she had suffered from all that afternoon.

Shortly after five o'clock, Monsieur Raymonde came home, and as soon as he entered the apartment, he walked straight along the hall and looked into Undi's room. It was empty, neat and tidy, except for a small towel on the bed. He picked it up, felt its dampness, and slowly lifted it to his nose and sniffed. There was a faintly recognizable odor still clinging to it. He didn't know what had made him do it, except that he was almost totally preoccupied with suspicions of Undi. He sensed Roland's presence in his home and it made him feel vicious. Undi had never led him on or provoked him, but the thought of her in her bright, little room had caused him to toss and turn in his bed at night.

While he stood there, the doorbell rang for the third time that afternoon, had he only known it, and in his vicious mood, he raced along the hallway thinking she must have come back. He opened the door violently and saw Georges, whose own suspicions had driven him back once more. He had to return to make sure she had not been deceiving him, yet he felt nervous and guilty for having doubted her.

Monsieur Raymonde knew Georges only as one of Undi's men friends—the one who had taken her out to luncheon. What the hell had been going on in his apartment while he was out trying to sell real estate?

"Oh," Georges said in alarm. "Er . . . is Mademoiselle Undi at home?" Coming face-to-face with Monsieur Raymonde embarrassed him at any time, but now it was worse.

"No, she is not, and thank God for it! She's a damned whore! A slut! You're better off without her! I'll kill them if they come back here!"

Georges staggered as if he'd been struck. He could say nothing in Undi's defense nor object to Monsieur Raymonde's language because he was staggering from the blow as if it had been physical. He had walked up the stairs. Now he turned and walked down again in a state of shock.

Monsieur Raymonde closed the door and went into his study, where he sat in the deep leather chair and slowly calmed down. After about twenty minutes, his hatred had evaporated. Even his frustration and humiliation subsided. All that was left was a sense of desolation. He looked at the photographs of his parents and then of his sister. The sight of his saintly sister calmed him. He realized what he had said to Monsieur Albertine and regretted it very much. He had given the poor man a shock, and he was sorry for that.

Georges went home and he, too, sat for a long time. *I'll kill them if they come back*, echoed repeatedly in his ears. He was dreadfully unhappy. Yet how could he blame Undi? He was much older than she, and he was impotent. Remembering how docile she had been that first night, he wondered whether she would have loved him if he'd succeeded in making love to her satisfactorily. None of these thoughts comforted him. At last, he got up and went to the cupboard where he took something out. It was an elongated, black box. Opening it, Georges took out his father's antique pistol. Sitting on the Green Couch, he held it in position and pulled the trigger.

Chapter 23

Black Ants

After her strange impulse that brought about the release of the imprisoned lift in the iron lift well and the sweet, sad cement maiden in the dried-up fountain, Undi suddenly transported herself and me as well in one of her no-time bubbles to the terrace of the palace. Seagull was perched on the balustrade on the Rock as usual, the sun was shining, the pink parakeets were flying overhead, and the palace itself was sparkling. But Undi didn't pause to enjoy any of this. She simply entered by way of one of the arches and began skimming along a corridor, her feet hardly touching the shimmering surfaces so that I, following her, had to do the same. I kept up with her because I was curious. Why, I asked myself, with Roland and Helen and David waiting for her outside on the Rue Tilset, had she suddenly taken off like this, to the Rock?

At the end of the corridor, we came to a pink marble staircase—a work of art by Marius, no doubt one of his Light images. Everything looked and felt radiant. The pink staircase, the walls that enclosed them, the blue ceiling above them decorated with golden grapes and little serpents at play were graceful and charming, but surprisingly, this delightful staircase was guarded at the bottom by a saber-toothed tiger, who had always frightened Undi. Such an alien creature! She had always passed him safely, and she did so again. When we reached the bottom, we skimmed along another corridor until we came to the next flight of stairs.

This was a very richly decorated part of the palace, and there were a number of these ornate staircases. Each was deeper and richer in color and penetrated more deeply into the heart of the Rock. Undi

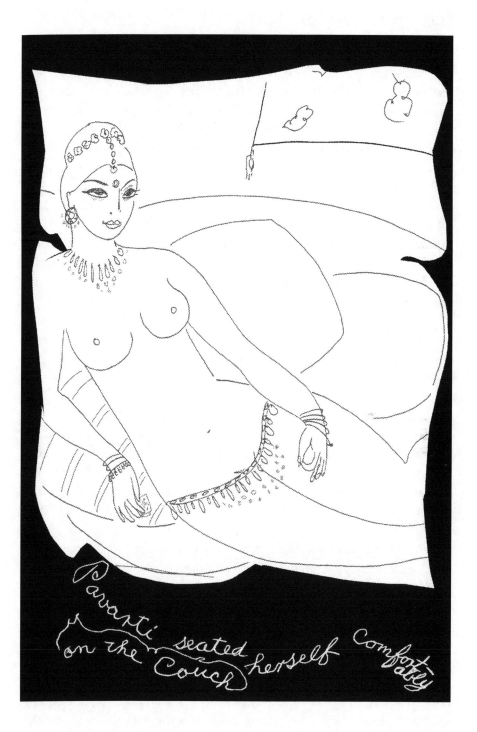

Parvati seated comfortably on the couch herself

257

then came to another staircase that had been made of bloodred, ruby light. It was a deep flight of steps filled with a sensuous, red, fiery glow. Near the last step stood a man wearing a stone mask. She had passed him before too, and although she was afraid of him, she always felt pity for him. But she didn't pause, going on along another corridor and another until she came to the last staircase. This was deep down and had been carved out of the substance of the Rock itself. Sculptural, simple, narrow, and deep, it was a blue green in color, and there were no decorations at all, except at the entrance where the stone carver was still at work carving mysterious signs and symbols. There was also the guardian at the foot of the stairs. He looked like a gargoyle with his tongue sticking out and his features distorted into a most terrifying grimace, which was calculated to put the fear of the Devil into his enemies.

Terrified, we hurried past. Then Undi slowed down, feeling along the walls of the dark passage into which we had descended.

Our hands were aware of the subtle swellings and hollows created by the sculptor's tools, and our bare feet (mine too, in my imagination) could sense the solid mass of the Rock beneath us. It was like being on the back of a great monster, the size of the world. The only illumination came from lamps set into the walls, but they were far apart. Undi went on, feeling her way until she came to an opening in the wall, but this was guarded by a curtain of hanging green snakes that swayed about as if a strong breeze blew from inside the chamber. When she stood before them, wanting to enter, they parted to allow her to pass through into what she believed was the very heart of the Rock. Of course, the green snakes didn't bother me when I followed her because they weren't aware of me.

Inside the chamber, which was like a cave, a soft green moss, very dark and velvety, covered the walls. The floor, too, was covered with this velvety growth, and she found it pleasant to walk on and not at all cold. On the contrary, it was almost warm. There was nothing at all in the cave except a deep, unexplored well, into which she had once dropped a pearl. She had come here because she had a feminine superstition about it. She believed it was related to a central part of her own being. The pearl and the reason for dropping it were a mystery to her, and she understood nothing about it. Neither did I. She could remember doing it—remembered lowering it on the end of a fine, silken cord, and she even remembered her spontaneous dance around the cave afterwards. She didn't dance now but just peered into the well, letting her fancy run on about the pearl. She lay down, and then the thread, so fine that she could hardly see it, was in her hand once again.

"What a pleasure it is, to do this," she said aloud almost as if she was talking to me. She held the thread between two fingers and watched the pearl go down into the darkness of the well. She lingered over it. The pearl was so light, yet she was able to feel its weight on the end of the thread, and her sensitive hand resisted its pull. She enjoyed the subtle sensation of letting her hand fall then lifting it again. It was like holding it in water and letting it go with the current and then resisting the force and feeling it in the palm of the hand or holding it against the wind and letting the wind blow it and then opposing the wind. It was a game. Some men, I knew, liked lifting heavy weights to achieve the same sensation, while some girls liked the weight of strong, big men bearing down on their fragile bodies. But this was only a pearl, and its delicate weight had taken possession of Undi's imagination. She felt that the subtlety of her feelings had never been finer. She was delighted by the way the fine thread hung straight with the weight of the pearl. When the thread was straight, everything was all right with the balance of the world, so said her imagination. Mine too. I was beginning to enjoy the game.

She knew that, if anything touched her, something would happen. If she heard a sound or even if she moved a little finger or if she inhaled an odor, the pearl would slip over the edge of this moment on which it was posed, and it would burst into some kind of flower—not necessarily a flower of beauty or of goodness. It could just as easily be a flower of poison, of evil, of destruction. And if this did not happen, the pearl would lift her, and she would float—not fly as she usually did nor swim, but float and become, once again, a fragment of spray and then disappear forever.

It still didn't happen! The sensation of waiting started to become unbearable. Although she had come to this deep chamber of her palace to be alone and gaze into the well, she began to wish she were not alone. A slight feeling of trouble and anxiety was coming over her, and she began to doubt that there was a pearl in the well, in herself, or anywhere. She began to feel things, rather than imagine them. Pictures started forming in her mind, of places and events she believed she had taken part in and of people she had never met yet whom she imagined she must have met at some time or another because of the clearness of these pictures. The pearl felt hard within her.

She even found herself living through situations and heard herself talking and arguing and saying how badly certain people had been behaving toward her and how badly she herself had behaved. Yet when it came to the point of what they had done or what she had done, she felt irritated and even violent because she believed answers were being deliberately hidden from her. She couldn't say against whom she was making these accusations or why. Then she tried to think and find reasons for her condition, but the reasons she found kept changing. The magic had gone from the chamber, and her flesh felt hot and itchy. She became anxious about her appearance, and she believed the scenes she had just passed through—with people behaving badly toward her and so on—had caused her eyes to water, the flesh around them to swell, and her brow to furrow. She longed desperately for a looking glass so that she could examine herself and make sure she looked all right. I could have told her she didn't.

Then, oh horrors! The black ants were crawling in and out of the well, and she saw that they had taken the place of the pearl on the thread. In her deep and secret passages, the ants would gnaw at her and destroy her. Already she could feel the sharp nips and the hot pains. They were crawling through her hair and into her eyes, and some of them were pinching the flesh under her arms.

Just then, Pavarti appeared, and Undi held back her groans of anguish. She tried to hide her condition from her goddess friend.

"Oh, Pavarti, how nice to see you."

But Pavarti replied as though to someone who was about to go on a journey. "Are you ready?"

Undi looked surprised. "Ready for what?"

"Don't you know?"

Undi tried to remember. "I think . . . I'm going on a vacation. To have a good time, to be happy . . ." But she'd almost said, "To be hurt, to be treated badly, to become frustrated and disappointed and disillusioned."

"You are going on a journey to undergo certain trials. Come along, dear Undi. It's time."

"Oh," Undi replied, as though she had suddenly realized. "Oh, those terrible trials. I forgot. Fancy! I was thinking about the pearl. It was so lovely. I was happy all alone down here, but then it changed into a black ant, and I have been in utter misery."

"You can think about the pearl later, but now you have to go through it. It won't be so easy, you know."

"Oh, I know," Undi said with a grimace. An ant nipped her again, but now she knew it wasn't a real ant and she was relieved. "Of course. Now I realize what's been happening. Somehow, the balance within me became disturbed and turned vicious. That's all. Oh, how thankful I am that it wasn't a real ant. I would hate to be consumed like that." She was no longer frightened, but she began to grumble because of the nuisance of it all. "It's not real, Pavarti. Let me go."

"You won't get out of it as easily as that," Pavarti told her. "You've started something, and you'll have to go through it before you can rediscover yourself."

Undi grumbled a bit more, but she got up. "I do think I should be allowed the pleasure of love without the pain. It is going to be about love, isn't it?"

"If it is love," Pavarti said. "That's a debatable question. There is no pain in love; don't you know that?" She looked unmoved. She had come simply as a friend, but she couldn't change things now. She saw no way out.

"Oh, all right. I'm ready," the victim sighed. She followed Pavarti and walked with her by way of the staircases back to the upper corridors, until they came to her dressing room. It was right next to the bathroom; she saw her handmaidens waiting.

Undi looked at these charming girls and resented them. She knew why they were there. They were waiting to dress her, pretending that they were sorry for her, while they were really enjoying her discomfort. They were fluttering, like a flock of pigeons, and they always did so every time they had to do this.

Oh well, I thought, it wasn't such a terrible thing. She would only be going through what thousands of others had gone through, and she would easily find some escape. They need not look so mournful, especially when they didn't mean it. She held her head high and allowed one of them to open the door for her and Pavarti. When they had entered the room, all the other handmaidens followed and the last one closed the door.

These were the same girls who had dressed Isis in those fragile draperies when she had been fragmented and unhappy. Then they were not much more than innocent water nymphs. Look at them now, fussing over her traveling outfit! And what names they had—Pauline, Moira, Liz, and Emily. Oh, and that one over there fingering her makeup was Geraldine. They didn't look like sea nymphs to me but, rather, like girls she had been to school with.

She must have heard me thinking. "That must be another memory," she was saying. Something miserable had happened to someone at school. At the same time, something rather intriguing had happened at school. What was she to believe?

Pavarti had gone to the couch, and now she was taking sunflower seeds out of a small, silver box. Languidly chewing on one of the seeds, she watched what the handmaidens were doing to Undi. They had brought sackcloth and ashes!

Undi looked at them uncomprehendingly for a moment and then exclaimed, "What's that?"

Liz explained that it was a costume for repentant sinners.

"Oh no! I'm not wearing that! Besides, I'm not a sinner. Take it away. At once!"

Liz was disappointed. She herself had been full of sad, sweet guilt lately. It sometimes made her weep.

"It's summer where I'm going," Undi said, "and I want a white dress and a pink sundress, a pair of jeans and a sun top, and a swimming suit—a bikini, don't forget—and some nice underwear and a, no, I won't really want a nightgown. Or shall I have one lovely one, just to walk around the room in? Yes, a silk nightgown, backless and transparent. And a pair of high-heeled shoes as well as yellow sandals."

The handmaidens had the satisfaction, at least, of deciding which outfit she would wear on the journey. "Everyone wears jeans now, but we think you should wear the white dress and the sandals and a pink shawl in case it gets cold. It would be nice."

"Oh, all right." Undi didn't seem to care very much. But then, suddenly, she seemed to realize something. "No, I think I should wear the jeans because we'll be going in a car with some Australian friends, Helen and David. So, I should wear jeans."

"She looks quite cheerful," Moira said. "You'd think she was going to have a wonderful time."

Pavarti looked up from the couch and said, "In a way, she is. She will be going through certain changes, and she'll sometimes feel unhappy. But there will be the good moments too. A lot depends on herself."

Emily, the youngest of the handmaidens, felt sorry for her mistress. "I think she looks tragic. I know if it were me, I'd feel like dying. I can't bear to be hurt."

Undi was beginning to feel bored. She'd forgotten the black ants for the moment and was looking forward to the journey. Why, what was all the fuss about? Everyone had a few problems; that was part of life. And anyway, it was all something that might happen in the future or had happened in the past. It wasn't happening right at this moment. At this moment, she was making preparations for the trip. But she felt uneasy, somehow. What could happen? She wished they would let her go and stop behaving as though this were some sort of tragedy. She felt like a victim. Her boredom gave way to fear again. Oh this was ridiculous. She would slap one of them in a minute!

Just as they were zipping up her jeans and draping the shawl over her shoulders, Eva and Isis came into the room. They walked towards Pavarti, who was still sitting on the couch, and Eva said, "Is she ready?"

"Almost," Pavarti replied. "Sit here until she's finished dressing. She's waiting for her sandals."

They sat, and Isis, wedged in a little between Pavarti and Eva, said sympathetically, "Poor, Undi. I hate to think of her being hurt." She didn't say "by Roland" because she remembered in time that he was Eva's son.

Undi paused in the act of smoothing out her T-shirt with the sequined heart on the front of it and cast a doubtful glance toward Isis.

Who says she's to be hurt by Roland? I wondered. *She's got an old Earth virus. That's what hurts.* No one heard me, of course. The ladies and all the handmaidens would have it that Undi was going to have to suffer and pay for something she'd done and wouldn't have had it any other way, even if they could have heard me.

Undi looked pleased now with her pretty feet comfortably fitted with yellow sandals that would have cost a fortune in the House of Gustav Roché. The handmaidens, wistful and sad though they were, were nevertheless pleased, too, with their handiwork. For Undi, the prospect of the journey had become a pleasing one. She blocked out the image of black ants and said almost gaily, "I'm ready; let us go."

She took Eva's arm and cast a glance at Pavarti, who rose from the couch and followed them. Isis was already at the doorway, waiting. As they passed through to the corridor, the handmaidens followed like bridesmaids.

The procession made its way to the terrace, where Undi paused and looked at the garden and the tips of the pines that grew further down the mountainside and then at the clear, blue sky. She sighed and said, "It's all so lovely. Why does one have to place it in danger?" She caught Isis's eye and felt moved to say in some surprise, "Isis! I feel as though we are changing places. You have grown so calm lately. I'm the disturbed one."

Everyone looked surprised, but only Isis seemed to understand what she was trying to say.

Undi's friends stood at the edge of the pines and watched her make her way down the mountainside. Emily could see her, slowly vanishing into the mist. She wanted to run after her, but Pavarti held her back.

"Can't I go with her? She looks lonely."

"No, she has to go on her own."

Chapter 24

Isis Enters the Dark Room

As soon as Undi had disappeared among the trees on the side of her mountain, the handmaidens flew back to the palace, where they tried on her gowns and helped themselves to her cosmetics. Only one, more thoughtful than the others, walked slowly with Eva and Isis and Pavarti, plaintively asking why people couldn't just get married and live happily ever after.

When they reached the palace, the handmaidens were rushing along the corridor toward the room of darkness. "Come along," they called out. "There's going to be a movie, an old-fashioned 'talkie' from the forties."

Eva said, "That room! It's full of surprises. Is there really going to be a movie?"

Neither Isis nor Pavarti could answer. But they looked in as they passed, and Eva saw that there was a light in the room and it was fitted with comfortable couches and a small square box like a television set. The maidens were sitting in easy chairs, giggling and licking sugar hearts and candy phallics. "Lovely, aren't they?"

"What's on?"

"Don't know." Lick, lick.

"*The Perils of Pauline*," Emily suggested.

"Don't be silly. That's an old serial from the twenties or thirties— probably a silent one too. We want a noisy one."

"*The Snake Pit*?" Moira wanted it to be *The Snake Pit*. She sometimes felt like a snake herself.

"No. I think it's going to be a cult film with weird things happening. I want to see a thing from outer space being born out of someone's stomach."

"You're all wrong. It's called *The Lovers*. I've seen it. You just wait! They actually make love. It's wonderful. It's French, with captions."

Their heads came together while Amanda described what they actually did in the love scene. "Well, you don't see all the details, but you can tell what's happening by the way her hand clutches the side of the bed. It's supposed to be a wonderful sensation."

"Oh, I'm tired of seeing big faces kissing each other. I'd like a movie about an American president."

Eva and Isis withdrew and continued to walk along the corridor. Pavarti was nowhere to be seen. They walked on until they came to the cloistered walk, and from there, they made their way to the enclosed garden on the other side of the palace. Here they sat and talked.

"Yes, I'm very happy. I used to think I enjoyed being alone. But now, I know I wasn't really living at all. It's wonderful to share everything with a man who cares about you." Eva looked radiant. Then she reminded herself to think of someone besides herself. "But what about you, Isis? You are all alone. Don't you feel lonely?"

"I'm not sure. I'm waiting. Something is going to happen, and I'm waiting for it. I don't believe Osiris is dead. I'll wait as long as I must."

"Don't wait too long, dear." Eva looked sweetly concerned. "Time passes, you know."

Isis smiled and then Eva remembered. "But, of course, you don't grow old, do you? I forgot. Will it never come to an end?"

"I thought it had," Isis told her. "I thought I had found my love and would be able to go back to where we came from, but it's not as simple as that. I'm still not ready. I feel there's something more I must do."

She suddenly changed the subject and said brightly, "Did I ever tell you about my spinning wheel, Eva?"

"No, but I've heard about it. Is it not unusual for women to spin these days?"

"Oh, lots of people do it. It was Undi who reminded me. I used to have a friend—Undi made me remember her when she suggested

I start to spin. She lived in Constantinople centuries ago. She was a courtesan who wanted to change her way of life."

"Naturally," murmured Eva, looking prim.

"Well, at that time and in that country, when a woman wanted to reform, or change her life and become a respected member of society, what do you think she did?"

"I don't know. What did she do?"

"To begin with, she changed her address. Then she bought a spinning wheel and set it up on a balcony where she sat spinning day after day. This was a sign, you see—a sort of public announcement that she wished to adopt a new way of life. If she stayed at the spinning wheel for six weeks, day after day, she was accepted, and her past was no longer held against her."

"Well, I think that's a wonderful idea! I wish they'd do it now. So many young people take the wrong path. They need a way back. What good ideas people used to think of. Was your friend able to forget her past?"

"Oh, yes. She changed a lot. She had been quite rich and had a fine house and prominent lovers, but her spirit was starved. That's why she did it. Something good happened to her too. A man who drove past her house every day noticed her. He was the emperor of Byzantine! Imagine that! Well, he fell in love with her and made her his empress, Theodora. I couldn't help thinking of her while I was spinning. Of course, my life is not as hers was. But all the suffering is the same, don't you agree? Undi must have been inspired when she told me to sit quietly and spin."

"Indeed," Eva agreed. "Isis," she said suddenly, "have you ever seen Marius making his pictures with Light?"

"Why do you ask? I've seen his pictures." How could she forget them? It was at the end of that weeklong spectacle of Light that Osiris had disappeared. "Marius! Where is he? Tell me about him, Eva" She felt sure that Marius knew what had become of Osiris.

"I thought you knew. I thought you would surely have seen him in the room of darkness. Did Undi never take you there?"

"Once, but we didn't see him. How *can* I see him? Tell me, Eva. Has he changed? What does he look like? Does he ride a golden chariot?" She believed that only through Marius would she find Osiris again.

"I've never seen a chariot. But you know what he looks like, Isis. He has strong, dark eyes, and he looked like a giant. He may have grown even more since then. It was dark, you know. I saw him in the darkness. Perhaps, Isis, if you enter the room when it's dark, you will see him too."

"Or perhaps he will see me. Eva, how could I find my way in the darkness?"

"Are you willing to risk it?" Eva asked. "The same thing doesn't happen to everyone. There may be danger."

Isis felt excited. She stood up and Eva stood with her. For some reason, they both wanted to hurry, but Eva held her back a little. "Don't hurry so. Don't you remember? They are in there, those handmaidens, looking at a movie. When you go in, you must go alone."

So they walked back slowly. As they turned into the corridor, they saw the maidens again, skipping and hopping like a flock of gazelles on their way to a small summerhouse in the garden. Eva stood outside the dark misty door of the dark room and said, "Is anyone there?"

No one answered. She said to Isis, "It's empty and it seems to be full of the darkness. Are you afraid? Do you want me to come in with you, dear?"

"I'm not sure. But I think I should go alone, don't you? I suddenly sense it's not quite as we thought. I may not see him. There's something quite unknown beyond this door, and I'm not entering in order to find someone, but to give up the last shreds that hold me . . ."

"Hold you to what, Isis?"

"To . . . everything. To all I know. All I am. It is frightening after all, Eva. Do you really believe I should?"

Eva felt impatient. "I don't understand you, Isis. A little while ago, you were eager to go. Now you're trying to find reasons not to. Why, when I entered this room, I didn't even think about it. Undi opened the door, and I walked in." She'd forgotten how the darkness had pressed down upon her and how her legs would hardly move.

"But a moment ago, you asked me whether I was willing to take the risk." Isis had forgotten her own immortality and was behaving like a superstitious girl.

"I don't know why I said that. There's no risk." Eva grew even more impatient and gave Isis a strong push. She passed right through the dark mist and Eva made the motion of closing a door. "There, now she's inside. What a fuss."

Yet as soon as she turned away, she was full of remorse. "What have I done? How do I know what will happen to her? Oh, dear. I should have let her decide for herself. It's not the same for everyone. She may be in great danger."

It was too late. She tried to move the mist away, but it had become solid, like ice. Placing her ear to what looked like a crack, she tried to listen. "Isis, are you all right?"

There was no answer from Isis, but she could hear the sound of wind. It was like a wind in the desert. Weird, lonely drawn-out wailing sounds, like spirits crying in the darkness, were trying to force their way into the corridor, pushing her away from the door.

So there was little she could do except pray that Isis would be all right. She had Gaston to return to. There was nothing she could do for Isis. Besides, she had to help Roland prepare for his journey. There was much to do. She took one last look at the ominous-looking mist that separated her from Isis and then left the palace.

Chapter 25

The Journey

As I was still with Undi when she stepped back from her time bubble to join Roland, I soon found myself traveling to the South of France in David and Helen's car. They had become friendly with Roland at Georges's party and invited him to join them and bring Undi.

He and Undi had seated themselves in the back seat, so I had settled myself just above Undi's left shoulder. I soon became aware that one of her troubles, which she was hardly aware of herself, was that she was disturbed by the friendship that had flowered between Roland and Isis after the disappearance of Osiris. There were also other Old Earth viruses at work (as Dr. Pandé would have said) so she wasn't as happy as she pretended to be.

By the time we reached our first stopping place, where they intended to spend the night, they all appeared to be in good spirits, and I watched with envy as they enjoyed a picnic supper and then entered the tent and sleeping bags and went to sleep. David and Helen used the tent, and Undi and Roland slept in sleeping bags.

Roland enjoyed sleeping in the open more than he thought he would. He had had doubts about it at the beginning of the trip because he hated getting up early in the morning, hated hard beds, and hated waking up with strangers. He didn't believe he would like any part of it, and although he should have been grateful for it, he felt pettishly irritated and had been almost mean in his refusal to admit to Undi that he was glad they did not have to spend money on the train fare.

The Australians were going to the South of France to pick up their yacht in Cannes and sail to Greece, but he and Undi had planned to go to a small village near Cannes and spend several weeks in the house his mother had told him about. They would get a large room with a small kitchen in the basement. Their room, his mother said, would not be in the basement but upstairs on the second floor, and there would be a clear view of the sea.

Now, on the first morning of the journey, Roland lay in his sleeping bag feeling quite cozy and comfortable. The grassy patch on which he lay was soft enough. Before going to sleep, he had looked up at the stars and marveled at their brightness as they twinkled and grew larger and smaller in their setting of deep, midnight blue sky. It was early now, and yet he felt refreshed and invigorated. He felt as if he were the only person here beside the river, and his eyes moved slowly, taking in the beauty of the heavy leaves and branches of the tree under which he lay. He seemed to have forgotten everything about his life and was concerned only with the shape of those leaves, so dark against the clear sky.

But raising himself on one arm at last, he was surprised to see Undi's sleeping face not far away. He looked at it for some time and felt a twinge of guilt for having forgotten her. Something made him look more closely, and it was as if he was seeing her for the first time. The clear light perhaps? It seemed to him there was nothing of the Undi he knew—or imagined he knew. The face he was looking at was still and calm, as calm as the morning air here by the stream. And it was as pale as the morning sky he had seen through the leaves. Her eyelids were like half moons with long lashes that rested on the palest of pale cheeks; only a faint pink of sunrise on them. The lips, delicately curved, were pale too and frightfully still. The fine nose made no effort to draw breath or to expel it. In fact, nothing moved. This, he thought, must be what people looked like when they were dead or when their spirits left them. He knew, of course, that she wasn't dead, but he thought there was something unusual about her.

David and Helen were still in their tent and showed no signs of stirring, and Roland rather wished they would because now he would have liked some company. He didn't lean over to wake Undi, however, but went on looking at the leaves of the trees around them. When he looked at Undi again, he was very surprised to see only her empty sleeping bag.

A wind sprang up, the leaves began to rustle, and everything seemed to wake up here and on the other side of the stream. Suddenly he remembered Osiris and all that had happened. He thought of Isis sitting alone at her spinning wheel, and he hoped she was all right, feeling he had abandoned her. He believed, as she did, that Osiris was alive, somewhere, but Isis had said that all they could do was wait, and he agreed with her. The effect of the shock of Osiris's disappearance had lessened, and Isis had encouraged him to accept Monsieur Moitessier's offer. So here he was, lying in a sleeping bag, under a tree beside a stream—something he would never have imagined for himself.

There was a commotion all over the place. Birds were chirping, and the water of the stream seemed to be rushing and making a rumpus. It was incredible. Then the tent flap was thrown back and David appeared, saying, "Jeez, what a morning!"

Roland wondered how Undi could have gotten out of her sleeping bag, unseen. It was uncanny. It was as if she had been able to see into his mind, had seen his thoughts and had simply gone away. But she couldn't have. She must be behind a tree, hiding herself and doing whatever she had to do.

David was down at the stream, standing in the water, splashing himself. Helen had crawled out of the tent, and she was blinking and yawning. She had on a man's T-shirt and a pair of briefs. She went to the river too, to have her wash, and when she came back, she said good morning and began to make coffee on the small portable stove. Roland felt obliged to get up also, although he would have been thankful to just lie there without moving or thinking.

Driving on again, they were at first very lively. Roland stopped worrying about Osiris and Isis and joined in, even shouting with David at two girls who drove past in a Volkswagen, while Undi and Helen had quite a lengthy flirtation with two good-looking men in a Mercedes, who slowed down and drove behind David's station wagon for a while. Undi had hardly spoken to Roland all morning, but she appeared to be cheerful.

Many of the cars speeding along had small skiffs and canoes and even small motorboats strapped to their roofs. The road was busy with cars and motorbikes, all speeding toward the South of France or Spain or Italy. Everything sparkled and there was a holiday spirit of youth and joy. At eleven o'clock, they stopped and had billy tea. Helen made it and explained that this was how the drovers and the Bushmen made it in the Australian bush. She boiled the water in the billy, an open can with a thin handle, and then threw the tea in, letting it simmer for a few seconds. The tea was strong and flavorful. It revived them; they had begun to feel sleepy. Roland began to enjoy himself and could not help comparing this outdoor life and fresh air with the cafés in Paris, where he and his friends inhaled smoke fumes and talked about art, politics, logic, love, and the terrible state of the world.

At last he gave up and went to sleep.

Undi looked out at the countryside. It had become mountainous. The grasses that grew at the side of the road were soft green, lime green, with pink earth showing through, and the short grass by the roadside had a velvety quality. She had more color in her face than when she had started the journey.

In no great hurry, they spent another night in the open, and the next morning drove on toward Marseilles and reached the port just as the fishermen were bringing in fish to be sold to people who were waiting for them on the wharves.

Here, Undi distinguished herself by paying good money for one of the fish and then throwing it back into the water. When Roland scolded her for the waste of money, she began to sob quite loudly. They had to hurry away with her, partly because of her sobs and partly because the fisherfolk—a man, two sons, and a wife—began to get excited and feel insulted.

After a delicious continental breakfast in a fisherman's café, they bought postcards and mailed them and were on the road again by ten-thirty, with Helen driving and David nodding off to sleep beside her. They were all sleepy, having started off that morning very early.

After about an hour's drive, they found themselves on a long, straight road. From there, they could see high mountains with snow on them, a long way off. The road was still straight, and they could see it running ahead of them for a very long way until it disappeared behind some hills. They could see something and thought it might be a cow lying on the road, but they were still too far away to be sure. They passed those hills, and it came into view again.

"But it's not the right color," Helen said, peering ahead. "They don't have green cows in France, do they?"

"Not unless it's gone green with age," David said.

They went into a slight hollow, just for a minute, and the object disappeared. But it was still there when they rose again. Roland said it was a bundle of green hay, and David said he'd changed his mind about it; it was a green hillock. But Undi already realized that it was the Green Couch, unlikely, as it seemed, for what would the Green Couch be doing on the road to the Cote d'Azure? There was only one answer—Georges must have passed this way, and quite recently!

The others were astonished. "What on earth is this thing?"

"It's a green couch, silly," Helen said to her husband.

"I know that, but what's it doing?"

"They probably leave them here for hitchhikers to rest on every five miles," Helen replied.

"But you don't understand," Roland said. "We know this couch. It comes from the académie where I paint. Most extraordinary. Incredible!"

Undi thought he sounded like Georges. She listened to the couch complaining.

"My God, what a bump! It's a wonder I'm still in one piece. Well, isn't anyone going to put me right-side up?" She was lying there with her legs in the air. "That idiotic man tied me to the roof of his car as if I were a canoe. All the way from Paris! It's a wonder I didn't slip off long before this. And now he probably hasn't even noticed. He might even have forgotten. He was speeding along at such a rate—looking for you, Undi, I'm sure. He kept on looking into all the vehicles we passed, and I know that's what he was doing." She paused and whispered to Undi, "I suppose you know he tried to kill himself in Paris?"

"Oh, poor Georges," Undi cried. "What happened?"

"He didn't succeed, or he wouldn't be here, would he? It was because of you, you ungrateful girl—something he found out about you. He tried to kill himself but he doesn't deserve sympathy. Monster! Imbecile! My God, you would have thought we were escaping from the Bosch or the Russians—rushing out of Paris like that with me strapped on top of his automobile. I'll tell you more about it later."

"Tell me now," Undi pleaded.

"He got his father's ridiculous old gun and didn't think to look and see whether there were bullets in it."

No one else could hear her, of course, for conversations with the Green Couch were always private. But Undi said to Roland and David, "Let's put her up the right way. She really doesn't like being upside down."

"I beg of you, Undi, take me along with you," the Green Couch said while they were doing it. "You can't leave me here."

"Of course; don't be afraid, darling. We'll put you inside the station wagon. Oh dear, poor Georges. I'm glad it didn't work," Undi turned to Roland. "Just imagine. Georges must be just ahead of us. I remember now, he once said he would take the couch to his villa in the South of France. Perhaps he passed us while we were having lunch."

"Albertine!" Roland exclaimed. "Yes, it must have been he." His old suspicion of Undi returned for a moment, but it passed quickly.

"Who is Albertine?" David asked. "And does he always travel with his furniture?"

They'd turned the couch right side up, and Helen and Undi sat on it. A car went by, and the driver shouted, "You're blocking the road!"

"He's a friend of Undi's," Roland was explaining to David and Helen. "He's an idiot! Imagine a man bringing a couch all the way to the South of France. Probably thinks he can paint it. Wants to paint a nude on a couch. You can paint nudes in Paris. Not here! Too many other things to paint."

"Gee, yes, it does seem a bit queer," David agreed. "Perhaps he intends to furnish his villa. Anyway, what are we going to do? Are we going to leave it here or what . . . ?"

"No, I entreat you, not in this wilderness. I'll be completely ruined," the Green Couch exclaimed. "What if it rains? The only liquid I've ever had spilt on me is champagne! Undi, I beg of you. Make them take me along. You can even send me back to that imbecile if you wish, but just don't leave me here . . . You wouldn't, of course, would you?"

"I told you not to worry," Undi whispered.

Helen said, "We could fit it in the back, David. It's a very good couch."

"She's an antique," Undi told her. "It's really quite remarkable." She wanted to tell Helen all about it, but there was no time for that now.

Roland and David were lifting the couch and trying to fit it into the back of the station wagon. Undi said she wanted to rest on the couch, so Roland sat in front with Helen and David. "Deluxe accommodation," David said, looking back at her.

"Now," Undi exclaimed when they resumed their journey, "tell me, how is Georges? Tell me what happened. Was it my fault? Oh, I'm so sorry. I've been unkind to him, I know."

"He went to the Rue Tilset, and whatever Monsieur Raymonde said must have upset him very much. It was rather exciting, a little bit like the old days you know. People died for love then much more than they do now. But what happened, you ask. He came in looking distraught and simply got out a pistol and turned it on himself."

"How dreadful! Was he hurt?"

"No, fortunately for my green velvet and satin upholstery, there was no mess. It made him feel foolish for a little while, but after a while he sat and stared up at his landscape paintings and suddenly jumped up and called his femme du ménage. When she came in, he asked her to pack some clothes for him. While she was doing that, he packed all his painting materials and carried them down to his car, and when he had all his suitcases and everything downstairs, he asked her to call Monsieur Guyot. I had no idea what he intended, I can tell you! Do you know what they did, child? They took hold of me, carried me downstairs and out to the car where they strapped me on top as though I were a canoe. I protested, of course, and I think he must have heard me for he said, 'Many people carry bigger boats than this on their cars, so I can carry a couch if I like.'"

"Oh dear, imagine!" Undi said. "I blame myself."

"Yes, imagine!" replied the Green Couch. "And as Georges was getting his car started, I heard Monsieur Guyot say to Madame Guyot, 'Do you think he has gone completely mad?' And Madame Guyot replied, 'He always has been, so why mention it now?'"

In spite of all this, the Green Couch still urged Undi to place herself under Georges's protection and warned her against setting up housekeeping with Roland.

"What you must do is telephone his villa and let him know I am safe," she cunningly suggested. "That will open up your relationship again."

"We'll see," Undi said. "In the meantime, you'll come with us to our room in Golfe Juan. You never know. Roland may want you to be his still life model—or he might paint you and me together."

Chapter 26

Golfe Juan

ownstairs in the basement of the villa were a number of small kitchens. One of these kitchens was theirs. The young woman who owned the house said so and showed Undi and Roland where everything was. They had breakfast down there, and afterward, they set out to walk to Vallauris. It was a town in the hills above Golfe Juan, and the walk was rather a long one. In this village, where Pablo Picasso had designed pottery and donated his work of sculpture in the small square to the town, they hoped to see some of his pots and vases and platters in the showroom where they were displayed.

They left the house and walked along the avenue, looking over stone walls at gardens and strange palms and cactus plants, which gave to the Cote d'Azure such an exotic appearance. Soon they turned right, and after walking along a track and passing a few isolated villas with larger and even more exotic gardens, they began to climb into the hills. Here were humbler houses, and people grew their own vegetables for themselves and the market. As they climbed upward, Roland saw a small house standing alone between trees. It was a simple structure with perhaps only two rooms, but it had a wonderful view of the sea.

"I would like to live here!" Roland exclaimed. "And here I would paint all day." He didn't say "we," and Undi felt hurt thinking he didn't want her to live there with him.

They stood and looked at the sea. There were small boats on the still, smooth surface. A long way out, on the horizon, a steamer was moving like a snail on a straight line, slowly, slowly, with the blue sky behind it. And the blue sky was like a giant bowl that curved from that horizon right around and above their heads. Above their heads, gray clouds were in the bowl, and they looked as if they were heavy with rain.

Walking on, however, they hoped to reach Vallauris before the rain came down. It held off, and they walked along the ridge of the hill. After a while, they were over the hill and on their way down a slope to the village. Trees grew closer together, and the road dipped slightly, and they could no longer see the sea.

Roland could see something else that interested him very much. He pointed out to Undi small areas of scenery and uttered the name of Cézanne. Making a window with his fingers, he looked through it and then showed her how he would select small portions of the landscape and make pictures of them. After doing this for a little while, it was easy to see the trees and the hollows and the rocks and the sky above as they appeared in the paintings of Cézanne.

The clouds had moved, and the sun shone. They walked on, and at last, they were on the road into Vallauris. The road curved and disappeared behind the first houses, and when they arrived, they saw that it ran on through the center of the village. There were shops on either side, and at the end of the road, there was a square overlooked by a large church.

In the main street, a number of shops sold pottery. There were all kinds of pots and platters, good and bad, beautiful and ugly. The large showroom where the pottery of Picasso was being displayed was about halfway along, between the entrance to the village and the church. But they walked to the square because, first of all, they wanted to see Picasso's famous murals, *War and Peace*, on permanent exhibition in a long, narrow building with a high, arched ceiling.

In the square, a statue of a man held a young animal in his arms. This was the statue Picasso had given to the town. It was a bronze statue and very strong. Children played around the base and tried to climb up the figure. One little boy had reached the arm and was swinging on it.

"Imbeciles," Roland said.

But Undi told him not to be angry with the children. "It's very strong and I don't think he'd mind. Better for children to play here than not."

Roland agreed that, after all, it was good for children to play close to a work of art and to feel themselves on familiar terms with it, so he stopped calling them names and stood before the statue examining it. A priest came out of the church and looked down at them. He seemed pleased as he looked away down the main street of the village.

They left the statue and went over to the corner of the square where there was a stone wall and a door. Behind the wall, large trees grew in a romantic garden. By standing on a seat outside the wall, they were able to see into the garden. The trees had very large leaves, like fans. Roland took one about twelve inches wide and gave it to Undi.

The door, which was at right angles to the garden wall, was also in a stone wall. They went into the War and Peace museum, a long, cold, stone building. In the first room, which was all of stone, there was nothing but a great stone bowl in the center of the floor, but beyond this room were the murals. The material on which they had been painted was fitted to the ceiling. and it followed the arch from the ceiling to the floor on both sides. Long benches stood before both pictures. This was all the room contained.

At first, they walked from one end of the room to the other, looking at the murals. At one end, two figures were peacefully occupied, one reading or writing and the other holding a bowl. In the center, a beautiful, winged horse and a nude woman were featured, and a child balanced something.

On the other side, black and sinister figures waged war upon a noble figure, who carried a shield. There was war and the shadows of war, showing destruction of beautiful and intellectual ideas and images.

Roland and Undi stayed in the strange, long, narrow room for about an hour, for the pictures entranced them so much that they were reluctant to leave them. To be there was like being in the company of brilliant people who made life rich and valuable.

But after some time, they grew very cold, and so they went away. They went along the main road and turned down a narrow passage until they came to the door of the Picasso studio-showroom. Here they entertained themselves looking at strange faces the artist had designed on great platters and jars and vases.

Coming from the building, they saw that the clouds had gathered again, so they decided to set out for Golfe Juan. They left the village and walked along the curved road and soon reached the long path that wound its way over the hills and down to the sea. While they were on this path, the rain came, and they got drenched. But they didn't mind very much for they were still under the spell of what they had seen. Roland felt greatly inspired. He spoke about the work of Cézanne and Picasso, and Undi knew that, as soon as they reached the villa, he would begin to paint.

A car came along, and Roland put up his hand. The man stopped and invited them to get in. They were driven back, almost to the gate of the villa. During the short drive, Roland told Undi to remain silent, and when they arrived and descended from the car, he thanked the man politely but would not let her speak. She smiled and behaved as he wanted her to, but she wondered why he didn't even want her to thank the man.

After luncheon, he took out his paints and brushes and a bottle of turpentine and spread them along the heavy, marble mantelpiece in their room. He had found a piece of wood and two tin mugs in a shed in the garden and had taken them, believing that they were not wanted. He had no easel, but he had a large sheet of cardboard and onto this he pinned his sheets of paper—for Roland painted on paper very quickly and only sometimes used a large canvas.

He was still feeling excited and stimulated and expected to do great things. He decided not to begin with Undi posing on the green couch but to work on a still life for which he didn't need a live model.

The still life he had arranged consisted of a bottle and a pot placed on a table near the window. There was a faded pink curtain at the window, and outside there were the lime green shutters and the strong green leaves of the tree. And there were the raindrops coming down so fast that they looked like straight lines against a gray sky. The bottle was emerald green, and the pot was turquoise. It was a good still life arrangement, but I could see that Roland was making a mistake. Great painters like Matisse had done it all before.

Roland was convinced that he would paint brilliantly. He set to work with a fabulous work of art in his mind, and he thought he would have no difficulty in reproducing that picture on his paper.

He worked with great concentration, and his hands got dirty. Sometimes his face got dirty too, and without thinking, he wiped his hands down the side of his velveteen trousers, leaving little, hard lumps of paint clinging to them, but he didn't mind about this. He ignored it.

After a while, he laid his sheet of cardboard on the floor because it would not stay propped up against the back of the chair, and he had to kneel before it. But he didn't get tired because he was so absorbed in what he was doing. He was intent upon getting his fabulous composition, not only of form but of color, onto his sheet of paper. He expected it to spring directly onto the paper from his inner vision by way of his hand.

Chapter 27

The Great Artist

It wasn't as easy as that. Roland covered sheet after sheet of paper with paint, working far into the night, while Undi waited patiently and then not so patiently for him to spend time with her. Even when he stopped painting, Roland didn't pay any attention to her because he was depressed and his mood was black. He began to look secretive, lying on his bed, saying nothing until Undi became quite concerned and worried about his health. To make her feel worse, it rained, and she didn't feel like going out for walks alone in bad weather, which lasted for five days.

On the sixth day, the rain stopped, the sun shone, the sky was blue, the sea sparkled, the air felt fresh, and Roland looked out and saw that life was good.

When Undi saw this, she said firmly, "Today we're going out. Put down your brushes and make yourself look cheerful, for it has been no great pleasure to live with you for the last five days. Come."

Roland looked surprised, but looking out at the sea and sky again, he did what she wanted. It was about two o'clock in the afternoon. By two thirty, they were walking along the coastal road in the direction of Cannes.

As they walked, they became more and more cheerful. They saw trees they like the shapes of and they saw villas that excited their imaginations. There was a little railway line on their left lined with palm trees, and at intervals were posts with clusters of lovely emerald-blue, glass bulbs—something to do with the train—which looked like glass flower trees. They agreed with each other that these would be splendid in a painting!

Occasionally, Undi would pick up a leaf and show it to him, or he would see some exotic plant and point it out to her. They would look together into a garden, straining to see over the stone wall the winding paths that led to the wooden verandas of exotic villas surrounded by tropical shrubs and palms.

Just before reaching Cannes, they turned away from the main road and began to climb the long, winding avenue that led to the top of a hill.

Undi was happier than she had been since they had left Paris. And as she grew happier, her lost confidence returned. Now that they were out in the sunshine, walking together and seeing things together, she felt at ease with Roland. She saw that his face, too, had become lighter, and he was young and sweet and gentle again.

It had taken a long time to walk this far. The sun was low, but it was still warm. They enjoyed walking along this winding avenue even more than they had enjoyed the road below the hill. Here there were very large villas with old stone walls overhung by thick trees. Sometimes, through a break in the trees, they could see right into the villas and even beyond them as far as the sea. Up here the afternoon was dreamy, still, and silent, except for the twittering of birds and the occasional bark of a dog.

"It is up here," she said to Roland, "that we will see the villa of the great artist who made the starry night for you and Eva when you were a baby. And he's the one who created pictures of Light over Paris."

"Is it true?" Roland asked. "I always thought it was a dream. I thought I saw him in a dream, in a burst of light."

"Oh, it was true. Look!"

When she said this, something happened. Roland saw a burst of light and then he saw a giant hand pinning a sheet of white paper to an easel. The hand then took a piece of colored chalk, and with the chalk, it made a curved line on the paper. A few more strokes were added, and it became a bird. Then the hand drew a branch under the bird's claws, and without lifting the chalk from the paper, it carried the line away until, in a twinkling, it had drawn a huge tree with rich, waxy leaves that mingled with the leaves of other trees. The lines ran to become sturdy trunks that sank into the earth covered with thick grass. Beyond these trees, the hand was at work drawing a house made

of Light. It became a stone villa, with a high, arched entrance and a lot of windows with opened shutters. Undi had introduced Roland to her enchanted world.

Flick, flick went the hand with the chalk, and doves were flying to and from the windows. Flick with the hand, and in the garden was a black and white hound, bounding from shrub to tree and to the front door under the high arch, there to scratch wickedly upon the carved wood. The hound had an intelligent and charming face.

Flick! Flick! Flick! And with each flick, a bird or a butterfly appeared, flying about in the garden. The giant hand enclosed the whole scene and drew a stone wall all around it with a large gate and a small one. Over the small gate, the magical hand of Great Artist made vine leaves, and under the vine leaves so that it was almost hidden, it wrote the name of the villa. Outside this gate, Roland and Undi stood like two children outside a circus tent or an enchanted garden.

As they stood there, the gate sprang open, and a young boy of about ten years, or perhaps twelve, stepped out. He was wearing a smart, red uniform, and he carried a drum and drumsticks.

"Is this where the great artist lives?" inquired Roland of the small boy.

"Yes," replied the boy. "It is."

"Then I would like to meet him, if you please."

"Ho . . . ha . . . would you indeed? But it's very difficult to penetrate the walls of this villa," the child replied and looked at them as if he expected to see some credentials.

"It would be easy," Undi said, half to herself, "to fly across the garden in the form of a bird and enter the studio of the great artist. He is probably at work on one of his compositions. The birds, see, are darting in and out, and so are the butterflies, with complete freedom. And I am sure that the great artist has quite forgotten himself in his work and doesn't frighten them at all. In fact, he is probably speaking to them, saying, 'Just a minute. I must mix some more blue' or 'How about that . . . that small area of pink?' without knowing whether he is speaking to them or to himself. It would be simple for us to fly into that room. He'd hardly notice us."

"And you're right about him speaking like that," the boy said. "He talks to anything that happens to be near him, but it's all good what he says, I can assure you of that."

288

Roland said again, "Look here. You see, it's like this. I have been working on a composition. It's a bottle and a pot—just an ordinary bottle and a common pot. But I can't seem to get anywhere with my composition and I thought, well . . . the advice of a great artist . . . you know . . . it might help."

"He has to be protected," the boy replied, shaking his head. "He would have no time to paint himself if he saw everyone who came to his door."

To this, Roland answered humbly, "Yes, I suppose so."

Then Undi spoke up again and said, "Perhaps the great artist needs a model. Tell him that the Undi is at his door."

Again the boy shook his head. "This month, he is painting only octopus and eels and other strange creatures of the sea, and I happen to know he has his models because I myself went with him to Antibes when the fishermen returned with their hauls. They gave us the odd creatures, who had been caught together with the fish."

"Oh, I didn't know he went in for such sport!" Undi cried, thinking of the fish whose life she had saved at Marseilles.

"Well, he does. We often have prawns and fish for supper here in the villa. Very good they are too."

Undi leaned against the wall and felt sick.

Roland and the child looked concerned, and they felt strong and masculine in the face of this exhibition of frail femininity. Roland whispered to the boy, "She cannot bear the thought of anyone eating fish."

The boy looked at her curiously and said, "That's a strange fad. I never heard of that before."

"It's nothing. I'm all right," Undi said, recovering. She turned to the boy, smiling sweetly. "Well, if you're sure we can't meet him . . . you *are* sure . . . I suppose you wouldn't go and tell him. It's important about the bottle and the pot."

"No. A thousand regrets, but he's working on something very big. I wouldn't like to be the one to disturb him now. You should hear him growl! I'm not even allowed near the studio when he's working."

"I can understand that!" Roland assured him. "I'm not fond of intruders when I'm painting either. We'll come back another day."

"That is up to you. Why, he might even call on you. You'd better give me your address, you know, just in case."

"But certainly!" Roland wrote the address on one of his little pieces of paper and gave it to the boy.

"Thank you," said the child, and stepping out onto the roadway, he added, "I must go now. Good-bye and good luck." And lifting his drumsticks into the air, he marched away as if he were about to start playing.

"Now, why do you imagine he plays a drum?" Undi said vaguely, trying to place the child. She remembered something about a boy named Raynard.

Roland shrugged, however, and said, as though he had quite forgotten about Undi not liking to eat fish and as though he had given up hope of meeting the great artist, "Let's have scallops for supper." The boy, speaking of the fishermen of Antibes had made him hungry for a good supper of fish.

Undi said dreamily, "Life is cruel. On the Island of Crete and on the other islands too, they beat the poor octopus to death to make them tender. The fishermen—they lifted their arms and then the tentacles flew in all directions before they came crashing down onto the rock, wet with the incoming tide. Once, I didn't mind these things; am I becoming soft? Now, I am so sensitive and fear not only my own pain but the pain of others too."

She brightened, however, as she thought of something else and smiled. "Everywhere on the island, Roland, you will find lovely paintings of them. They look so pretty and their curling tentacles have been used to make such lovely patterns on the vases, and you cannot help but love them—those strange creatures who are so often hated and despised except as dead meat. If you paint them, my love, make them look alive."

"Paint octopuses?" Roland mused. "Hmm . . . yes . . . perhaps. It's not a bad idea."

They looked again through a hole they found in the stone wall and saw Marius's spotted hound racing about in the garden. Brutis stopped before a bronze goat made of Light and barked, for he wanted the animal to play with him. The animal only gazed back at him with mysterious bronze eyes, so at last the hound flung himself down on the grass and chewed a bone and glared ferociously at the bronze goat every now and then, making ready to get up and tear off with the bone at the slightest sign of movement.

290

Undi and Roland found a place where they could see over the wall and some of the upper windows of the villa. And suddenly, there was Marius.

His head and shoulders appeared at the large, double window overlooking the garden. He looked fierce, as befitted a giant, and his strong, black, glittering eyes were examining some paint brushes he held in his hand. He growled and said, "Who's been touching *my* brushes?" The words rang out across the garden and over the wall to where they stood.

"No one, dearest," said a dark, handsome woman who appeared at the window and stood beside him. She placed her hand on his arm and said, "You did it yourself. Don't you remember?"

"Ah, yes, so I did!"

They both looked out and across the garden for a moment, and then they turned away.

"Who is she?" Undi wondered, feeling strangely jealous.

"It was he!" Roland exclaimed. "The man who made pictures with Light!" But just as soon as he said it, he forgot it again.

Even so, it was enough that he had seen the great artist. The sight of the giant inspired him greatly, and all the depression of the last few days was quite forgotten. They returned to the coastal road, and Roland was so excited his feet hardly touched the ground.

Chapter 28

Still Life

The bus traveled along the winding road between Cannes and Nice. Since it was still not the busy season, the road was quiet. A gentleness was all about, but at the same time, it was a gay, exotic gentleness because of the rich villas and the palm trees on one side of them and the little railroad and the palms with the sea beyond them on the other. The train came along like a toy, and the people in it looked out with smiles on their faces at the people in the bus. Before the people in the bus had time to respond, the toy train had passed and was speeding away in the direction of Nice. Perhaps it would go as far as Monte Carlo!

The sea was like a sheet of pink glass—pure, pure pink for that was the color of the sky now.

"Like the color of a shell," Roland thought and wondered how to capture this color. There was a trembling inside him when he saw that, second by second, the image was changing. He begged it to stay just a little longer, so delicate and pure, so that he would be able to understand it. The boats he could see a long way out were not really on the water, he discovered, but they were floating a few inches above it, and between them and the surface, there was a slim dark line!

Against the flat sheet of sea, which was hovering on the edge of mauve now, changing color in spite of his plea, the palm trees that stood out against the sky looked blue and olive green! There were two kinds—tall, slender ones with heavy fronds that made the long trunks bend into a graceful curve and short, thick ones like giant pineapples. They, too, were about to change color.

"No! Don't change . . ." But even as he said it, the change came, and he was filled with another ecstasy as sweet lavender covered the sea and sky. He begged *this* color to stay, and he trembled when he saw the palm trees turn green-black in that fraction of a second.

It was too much—this excitement of every second, this swift transition and giving up of one miraculous color in order to be swamped by another and with no time to linger on any.

"I'm greedy, greedy. I want it all." But as he said this, the darkness of evening began.

A great, soft, and thrilling blueness began to reveal itself, beyond a rich purple, and the palm trees at this moment reached their peak of utter mystery. Roland gave a sigh and accepted the final stillness of the blue night that was flowing across the sky toward them to cover and embrace them all.

He wondered what the great artist was making of all this. Was he looking out across the sea from his wide windows? Was he taking the colors and doing whatever he liked with them? He could see the giant hand taking them and spreading them with seeming carelessness onto a sheet of paper, and there they would remain for as long as the paper lasted. He would use them and there would be no voice within him to say, *Don't do this* or *Don't do that*. He would be free to do exactly what his mind and his heart told him to do. And his mind and his heart wanted the same thing, so there was no war between them.

Desire flooded through Roland again for the rich blissful colors he had just seen, but he was too excited, and he suddenly believed he understood what it would be like to be a deaf-mute and never be able to tell someone what loveliness you had seen. He looked at Undi and gave an excited laugh.

Then he thought of the great artist and longed for him with all his heart and loved him almost more than he had ever loved anything or anyone. He wanted to be close to him and to be his friend and drift in and out of him and be the hand that held the brush and be the arm and the shoulder and the wide chest that held within it the great heart. He wanted to be one with the whole body and even the feet that stood so firmly on the ground, a little apart, and he wanted to be the neck and the brown skin. He wanted even to be the air that filled those lungs. But most of all, he wanted to be the glittering eyes that saw as though they were seeing the world anew—fresh, surprising, fantastic, wonderful, miraculous! Those palm trees would flow into him and pass through the wonderful heart and mind, and when they next appeared, they would be palm trees such as had never been seen before; they would be art, and they would be marvelous and make you feel that at every moment the world was being reborn, just as that sky had been reborn every second with fresh pure color.

He thought about the nude he would paint, and he wondered, how would he paint it? He saw the soft lines and the shapes and the forms and the strong ones. He saw the expressions and the attitudes and the graceful form as a whole, lounging on the couch. He saw the soft hip or the distorted thigh and the classic throat and shoulder and the sweet rounded breast and the rounded arm and the stomach. And finally he saw the female form reduced to its ultimate simplicity or its uncompromising sternness. He saw the maiden carried off by the bull. Then he saw the sleeping nymph, and then the long, slender form or the simple, curving line again. The snake! The bird! The fish! The feline, and the other animals, and the snail, the dragonfly, the monkey, and the octopus, and the curling lines, and the straight, and yes! Even the smear of paint or the accidental splash of ink upon the paper! Even the great artist's splash of paint was a work of art!

With all these thoughts, time had ceased to exist, and they were at the end of their ride. Roland and Undi got down from the bus and walked along the avenue toward their villa.

Undi was in pain because Roland had forgotten she was with him. His closed lips and his dreamy eyes were not turned upon her. She begged this moment to pass, just as Roland on the bus had begged the sunset colors to remain.

Suddenly, her pain was gone too, and they were standing together before the gate of an old stone villa. It had a tower, and on the white walls of the tower there was a painted design of brilliant blue. It ran around the base of the tower and around the windows.

They talked to each other about it and discussed the blue design. The question was in both their minds and on their tongues. Was there a winding staircase in the tower? Now she was happy because they were together again.

Together, they thought it was a pity that the gate was locked. There was such an air of mystery! The mystery and the villa invited them to enter—to open the gate and creep across the garden that was filled with weeds and long grass. Even the path itself had disappeared beneath the thick growth, and here and there, great, old, blue jars stood half hidden by the greenery. They felt as if they had been invited to look into the jars and to pass onto the old stone steps leading to the carved door and to go through the doorway and enter the house itself and wander through the rooms. There they would see chairs draped with dust sheets and old paintings on the walls and photographs in silver frames on the small tables.

Up the wide staircase they would creep, past the bedrooms with their four-posters and their great old wardrobes and their rocking chairs and wooden chests. They'd move on to an attic, where they would discover old, white, plumed hats and pink taffeta dresses with yards and yards of pleated frilling, frayed down the front. Then they would reach the entrance to the tower, and they would begin the climb up the winding staircase and reach at last the room at the top of the tower, where they would find the old cane chair, the dead flower, and the yellowed love letter, with its pages of delicate handwriting.

The closed gate, the tall stern row of palm trees behind the high stone wall, and the grasses and the weeds themselves were also sentinels that held intruders away. Roland and Undi held hands and ran together across to the small shop where they bought their food every day.

When they had bought what they needed, Roland carried the groceries across to their house and pushed open the gate. In their garden was an island with shrubs and a tree growing on it. This was the tree that flapped its leaves against their window. The path divided and went on either side of this island, so Roland and Undi separated and took a path each—he to the right, and she to the left. They could not see each other because of the thick shrubs, which were quite high.

"This island should have a statue," she told herself and stepped onto it to pose as a white, marble nymph. Roland would come to look for her, and all he would find was a statue!

He didn't come, and she grew tired. She stepped down and went to look for him. He was doing the same thing on the other side, posing as a fawn, and she was sorry she had given in first, even though she was amused to see what a charming fawn he had become.

The moments of exultation were followed by greater moments of frustration. Roland's face grew dark. He grew silent. Now he lay upon

the bed staring at the window or turning his face away from Undi. Now he dreamed that the release he wanted existed somewhere else. It rained. They could not go out. It did not rain, but he would not go out, for he had to work and work. Time was passing. *I am getting older. I must paint. I must create the new art form!* His thoughts were all negative. He felt desperate.

I feel like lead. All my joy is gone. I do not even desire to work. What is life? Is it after all a vacuum? I hold my hand with the brush ready, in a vacuum. What happens? What are these lines I make upon the paper? Joyless. Meaningless. What has happened? I think I am dead and will never live again.

I turn to Undi. She sucks me in. Can I say this? Can I paint this? I lay with her, and for half a minute, some strange sensation overwhelms me. It is no pleasure—it only makes me less than I was. She waits, like a dark hole, to draw me in, not knowing that I will drown. I wish she would go away.

I dream of the clear, beautiful moments when life flowed through me, full of meaning. I write my thoughts, but I hide them. I must keep it all to myself, for what I say is ridiculous.

I came here. I was full of expectation. What an illusion! I am nothing. It frightens me. I will pass my life away as nothing, and one day, I will die, or there will be a terrible war and we'll all die. What for? Why do we live? I eat dust. I forget that this has happened before. I forget that there are the moments when I felt full of power.

Undi watched him. The room was littered with his papers. He was a mess. "He doesn't love me, so what am I doing here?"

One morning, she got out of bed and dressed herself, ready to go out. Roland watched from his pillow but said nothing. She could see that he was startled, so she softened toward him and went down to the kitchen instead. She prepared breakfast and went up to their room to tell him it was ready. He drank the coffee and went back to the room. It didn't help very much because he simply reorganized his painting materials and sat staring at the new still life arrangement he had made.

The next morning, she again dressed herself and went for a walk on the road that led to the sea. The railway line prevented her from going to the water's edge, so after a while she returned to the room. Roland was feverishly writing a letter. She said, "I saw that man who gave us a ride from Vallauris."

"Did you?" Roland muttered and went on writing.

"Yes. He asked me to go for a drive with him."

"But you didn't go, did you?"

"Who are you writing to?" Undi asked.

"Isis. I want to know whether there's any news of Osiris."

Undi thought the letter must be a long one, since he spent so much time over it. And several days later, when he received a reply, he read it and then put it in his pocket without sharing it with her.

Her discontent went on for too long. One morning, Undi rose early and got dressed without preparing breakfast. "Roland, I'm going for a walk," she said. "Don't work so hard. Good-bye."

He was still half asleep and hardly said anything. She walked down the stairs, out onto the porch, across the garden, around the island in the middle of it, and on through the gateway to the avenue outside. She walked on until she reached the village of Golfe Juan, where she sat on the terrace of the café and ordered coffee and a fresh, crispy croissant—crisp on the outside and soft and warm inside. It was comforting as well as delicious.

She sat for quite a long time then went on with her walk.

Chapter 29

Lost Illusions

"Undi! Here! Here, at last! How many times have I driven up and down this coast, hoping I'd see you. I've even walked along beaches. I never walk along beaches. You see, I'm destined to find you just when I'm not looking. I'd just about given up."

Opening the door of his car, he waited for her to get in. "Come, get in. Beside me. Where were you going? Why didn't you look me up? Ah, but, of course, you didn't know I was here, did you? Never mind. This is marvelous. Come, sit closer. Careful, not on those. Those are eggs. How is my princess? Let me look at you."

She had no intention of going back to Roland, so she was glad, after all, to see Georges. But when he began to look at her searchingly, she avoided his eyes. He could tell after a while that something was wrong with her. Her radiance was dimmed. Then he wondered if it was his own vision that was dim. He was reluctant to face the reality of what had happened in Paris. Yet, he was very glad he'd found her. He hastened to take her to one of the luxurious hotels where they were able to sit on the terrace and look at the sea.

"Are you thirsty? Would you like to have tea? Or would you prefer an aperitif?" As usual, he answered for her. "Yes, I'll order tea and cakes."

She let him do as he pleased because she didn't care. Summer visitors crowded the promenade and the beach. At the far end of the white terrace, a trio managed to make something playful and soothing out of an old musical, *The Desert Song*. Shafts of sunlight streaking between palm fronds created pleasing patterns of light and shade on the marble floor. A swift-footed waiter darting in and out soon came to their table. The luxury surrounding Undi made her dejection bearable.

To some, that dejection might have seemed out of proportion to what was, after all, a minor disappointment in love, or in sex itself, but to a Fish-Woman, it was horrible. She knew that, if she didn't go back to the sea and lose the memory of what had happened, her life forevermore would be ruled by the same fear and desire. *"Like a black ant forever gnawing away at my heart and my mind!"* Yet she was helpless and already afraid. She had committed the first two crimes against herself. She had not only walked away from Roland and done something foolish, but she'd been guilty of suspicion and petty jealousy of her dearest friend, Isis.

Georges asked her what she had been doing. If he had only known! If he could have seen his princess spying on Roland! For that was what it had amounted to. Yesterday, she had stolen away while he labored over his canvas and wandered away down to the village. There she'd met this man, the same man who had driven them from Vallauris that day. She didn't even like him very much, but she was frustrated and rebellious. *"I didn't even have the excuse that Isis used to have when she imagined she saw her beloved in every man she met."* She flushed when she remembered how they had gone to his hotel room and she had allowed him to make love to her, and after he had done so, she wished she hadn't and left as soon as she could. It was no wonder that Roland hadn't wanted her to speak to him! He must have known what kind of man he was.

She had wanted to go back to the room she shared with Roland and feel the comfort of their friendly relationship. But the thought of Isis had nagged at her. "He is probably glad I'm not there. He'll be able to write a long letter to Isis without having to hide it. Perhaps he'll ask her to come here so they can meet and he can tell her his thoughts."

The thought of Roland and Isis tormented her so much that she'd changed shape and made herself look like Isis. Only, in a fit of spite, she took the form not of her friend as she had been ever since the song of the nightingale had restored her beauty and given her peace, but of Isis as she was when she drank and used drugs and looked for Osiris in all the other men she met.

Although Isis always looked beautiful, even in her most wretched moments, her appearance changed when she was in distress. Undi succeeded very well in transforming herself. When she felt sure she had the power to go through with her ridiculous plan, she returned to the villa and sauntered up the stairs and into the room where Roland stood before his easel. Undi reflected bitterly that he hadn't even noticed she had gone, even though a few hours had passed.

Hearing her, Roland looked up. At first he thought it was Undi, but then he saw what he thought was Isis and was so overcome with surprise that he couldn't speak. But he noticed her disheveled appearance, and when he had time to collect himself, the thought crossed his mind that her appearance was caused by her grief over the disappearance of Osiris. But he was utterly confused and embarrassed when his visitor approached him and began to caress him. Had her intention been to find out how Roland felt about Isis, Undi did the worst thing she could have done, and she found out nothing at all. Roland had pushed her aside with gentleness and a compassion that made Undi even more jealous. He behaved like Osiris's loyal friend—sweet, kind, and concerned. Even when Undi went further and made Isis appear very seductive, he merely responded by offering her some of the brandy he and Undi kept on the mantelpiece.

Undi began to feel her power waning. Shape-changing is not something to play about with. Heliotropians use this power in order to understand other life forms and also to escape when danger threatens. Or they do it simply for fun. But they never shape-shifted for base or mean reasons. I was not surprised when Undi began to feel the power being drained from her. She'd been in the room for barely ten minutes when, suddenly, to Roland's further bewilderment, she jumped up and fled. Outside, on the avenue, she experienced a moment of terror, afraid she might turn into some mean, little animal. But she didn't. She could tell by touching herself that she was, at that moment, changing back to her own form.

Ashamed of her actions, she couldn't face going back to the villa, so she spent the night on the nearby beach. In the morning, she stood at the water's edge, looking at the sea. All she wanted was to turn into a fragment of spray and let the wind carry her to the Rock.

Then she'd heard a familiar voice. "Undi! I recognize you. Be careful. You won't find it. The Rock's vanished and so has your palace."

It was Seagull. "Sister Seagull! What's happened to the Rock? And my palace? Oh, I'm so glad to see you. But what has happened?"

"All gone. And you should be careful. The sea may not accept you back." Seagull then flew away without even saying good-bye.

Undi had returned to the main road that ran along beside the railroad track, and that was where Georges had seen her.

"You're not eating your pastry, Undi. My dear girl, what has happened? You're not yourself." Georges had known from the moment he saw her that she wasn't herself—not his princess. After all, he'd known it as he drove all the way from Paris, but he had hardly dared to admit it to himself. After his futile attempt to end his life with his father's old pistol, he had closed his mind and tried to deceive himself. It was more comfortable like that. Even now, he didn't want the truth. Yet he couldn't help asking.

To please him, she ate the pastry and tried to look bright and interested in him. "Georges, I have some good news for you. You'll be surprised."

Georges was indeed surprised. She hardly ever told him anything.

"What do you think we found on the road near Marseilles?"

"What you found . . ." Georges suddenly realized what she was going to tell him. For a moment his old, mad smile lit up his face. "Don't say it! The Green Couch!"

"Exactly. Imagine losing a couch and not realizing it."

"I can't believe it! Marvelous! Absolutely marvelous! I drove back, you know—retraced my footsteps. What am I saying? I *drove* back, looking everywhere. I thought someone had come along and picked it up, strapped it onto *their* car. I never imagined it was you. How is it possible we passed on the road without seeing each other?"

"I don't know." Now she regretted having told him. He would ask all sorts of questions, and he would even want to come with her to the villa and get his couch back. She was right. He did question her.

"Why don't you answer?" He was so insistent that she didn't know what to do or say. When he asked her why she didn't confide in him, she said she would.

"Do you really want me to confide in you? Do you really mean it?"

"How can you doubt it? Haven't I always been your friend? Undi, I want to know what is wrong." But something inside was saying, *Please don't tell me.*

Now Undi wanted to talk. *She'll talk and talk,* I said to myself, *and she'll say too much.* I wondered what would happen. It was clear to me that Georges was afraid he'd stop loving her, yet he went on insisting that she tell him everything. Even though he had suffered and had never gained any real satisfaction from her, she had the effect of a strong drink, and he imagined she'd brought joy into his life. So he didn't want to stop loving her.

It was too late to stop her anyway. She told him almost everything, only not what she had done last night. Just as well. That wasn't really his business.

"It wasn't true, Georges. I mean, I didn't come with a girl friend. I came with three other people. I'm sorry. I didn't want to hurt you." She looked at him and saw that he was already hurt, so she couldn't change that. But suddenly she was afraid of losing him. "I do care for you, Georges. Really I do. I'm fond of you . . ."

"I knew you weren't telling me the truth. Who were those people?"

She told him. "The one I came with is a student—a painter."

"A painter!" Georges groaned, realizing who it was. It was hard to believe. He'd forgotten about Roland.

"Yes. I've known him for some time. But I couldn't tell you. You're so . . . so . . ."

"So what?"

"You're possessive, Georges."

"I? Possessive? No such thing!" He looked a bit mean. "Are you in love with him?"

"I was," mumbled Undi. Then she burst out, "Oh, we were so happy in Paris. Now something's happened, and everything has changed. Perhaps it's my fault. It must be. I'm not the same as I was." She was crying—sniffing and choking on her words.

Georges started crying with her, only his tears were silent. He sat there with a woeful expression and watery eyes.

Looking up at him, she cried even more. "Oh, don't look like that, Georges. Anyway, I've left him. Perhaps I'd better go back to Paris."

"No," Georges exclaimed, so loudly that people turned to look at them.

It wasn't an unusual sight, to tell the truth. Couples sitting at tables on terraces often had words or flew into rages or wept. Sometimes it was the woman who looked injured, and sometimes it was the man. If they shouted at each other, the waiters looked worried and hoped they wouldn't break anything or, worse still, shoot each other. Sometimes it happened.

All Georges did was groan and say, "I can't bear this!"

What he couldn't bear was the thought of his princess being enslaved by an oafish boy who had no idea of her worth. He was jealous of the youth. Well, no, not exactly jealous. Roland's youth reminded him that, as a lover, he had not been much use to Undi. Realizing this humbled him. "Why go back to Paris? Let's go, Undi." He rose and she followed.

"Where are we going?" She, too, felt humble—willing to do whatever Georges suggested. She might have gone back to Roland had it not been for the foolish things she had done. She didn't want to face him until she'd forgotten about them.

"To my villa."

"Are you sure you want me? You asked me to confide in you and now you're sorry. I don't believe you can still love me after what I've told you."

"You're talking nonsense."

He sounded harsh. Undi looked at him with some alarm, suddenly wondering whether he was going to lock her up and make her pay for the way she'd hurt him

Chapter 30

Roland Abandoned

Roland was getting tired, but he went on standing before his easel, obsessed by the painting. Undi had murmured something about going for a walk. He had shrugged and gone on painting, trying to capture the last moments of the sunset and the deep blue-black of the palms as they'd been the night before when they walked back from the restaurant. It shouldn't have been such a dark painting because the sky had been deep pink, but his hand and his brush would not obey him, and now the canvas was so dark he had to put in a creamy moon where there had been no moon. The sea looked like a dark lake and not an ocean, and the palms did not have the power they'd had when he had looked at them, but they looked mysterious.

Looking at this picture he'd painted made him feel lonely and, at a slight sound from the garden, he went to the window. It surprised him to see how dark it was, but just the same, the streetlights were on, and he would have been able to see anyone who walked along the avenue. He looked at his watch. Nine o'clock. Only then did he wonder where Undi was. He was hungry. Neither of them had eaten, as was their custom, at seven, since yesterday.

It was then that he saw, or thought he saw, Isis coming into the room. He was puzzled and hardly knew what to do. Then, after her sudden and inexplicable departure, he was emotionally shaken. For a moment, he wondered whether Isis and Undi were playing some sort of trick on him. Were they together somewhere? he wondered. And if so, why didn't they come back? He could no longer go on painting without food, and after waiting for another fifteen minutes, he washed his hands, wrote a short note to say where he'd gone, and went out to the small restaurant they'd been to several times before. There he had a reasonably satisfying meal. He expected Undi to come to the restaurant, a little out of breath perhaps, and full of explanations. But she didn't come. The note was still there when he returned to the villa. The room felt cold and empty.

At first, he shrugged again and put a new canvas on the easel, after putting the dark picture on the mantelpiece where he could see it from time to time. Normally he didn't mind being alone while he worked, but now he felt unusually lonely. At half past eleven, he paused to wonder whether she had deliberately stayed away in order to make him pay more attention to her and told himself that if that were the case, she was to be disappointed. He didn't realize how anxious he was. I mean, at this stage of his life, Roland was passing through a time of desperation, and he couldn't afford to let someone else, especially a woman, take control of him. He had shown compassion toward Isis because she was not his responsibility, but he sensed that Undi might drown him in the sea of her desire if he were to let her do so.

Almost as soon as he said this to himself, he felt sorry. He realized he hadn't been very nice to her and was perhaps ruining her vacation—his own too, for that matter. After all, it was a gift, and he didn't have to worry about money. So what was he worried about? Roland was obsessed. He was thinking that it was a danger—two people living together. There was the danger of letting go and spending hours in bed, indulging in sex all the time. He couldn't let a woman and his own desire possess him like that. Each day spent without some creative effort and a great deal of work accomplished was a day wasted. It was different, he was telling himself, at the beginning of a love affair. Then the excitement itself was creative. But as he was thinking about this, he remembered her expression of disappointment and had to admit that, since coming here, he had not done much to make Undi happy.

This afternoon was probably the worst. After luncheon, he had gone straight to his easel while Undi rested on the bed, watching him. After a while, he'd felt disgusted with what he was doing. In spite of the wonderful images he had in his mind, his painting was a mess. He'd put down his brushes and went over to the other twin bed, ignoring Undi. He knew she was waiting and longing for him to come to her, but he wouldn't do that. It was her own fault if she allowed herself to become enslaved.

But, of course, he knew he'd been mean. He could not understand why this change in his feeling for her had taken place. Yes, he could. He was aware of the anxiety that sometimes took possession of him.

But what could have happened to her, he asked himself at eleven thirty. Should he do something? Like, go out and search for her? Or should he continue to paint until she returned? Intermingled with his growing concern for her was the puzzle of Isis. He didn't realize it, but he wanted Undi to be here so that he could tell her about Isis's strange behavior. He remembered that he'd almost fallen in love with Isis, but that feeling was gone now—not because of her visit but just because it had passed naturally. It made him think again of Osiris. He hadn't thought very much about him since they'd come here, but now he worried about Osiris too. He had a lot to think about. The mystery of Osiris's disappearance tormented him.

As his anxious thoughts flowed on, he went on painting. He'd arranged a still life of fruit and a bottle on the small round table and had started blocking them in on his canvas; he'd given up using the paper, and had hoped he'd have more success painting on canvas. Now he stared at it in amazement. Instead of the fruit and the bottle, he'd painted another dark night with deep, rich palm trees and another creamy moon! When his amazement has passed, he looked at it critically and did not feel too badly about it.

At twelve thirty, he began to feel sure Undi wasn't coming back—not tonight, at any rate. He looked into the old wardrobe to find out whether her clothes were missing, but she seemed to have taken nothing. Not that he could be sure of that because how was he to know what clothes she had or did not have? Looking into the drawer where she kept her handbag and their small store of money, he saw that most of the money was still there, but her bag was gone. He opened another box and saw the jewelry Georges had given her—not that he knew how she'd come by that jewelry. He did wonder a little bit, for he could see it was good jewelry. But he was glad she hadn't taken all the money. There was very little left in his pocket.

Of course, Roland told himself, it was still possible she'd come back. Perhaps she'd met some people and gone somewhere. By one o'clock, however, he felt certain she wouldn't come. *"I've hurt her, and she's gone!"* But Roland still couldn't believe she'd taken it all so seriously. Taken what seriously? Not exactly seriously. It was difficult for him to comprehend her fears and frustration, but he had to admit he'd been insensitive. He'd been untidy, selfish, and had hardly spoken to her for several days, except for the afternoon they'd spent together walking up a long avenue above the town.

He realized it was through her that he had seen the great artist and the wonderful works in his garden. A wave of tenderness passed through him, and he admitted to himself it was his own uncertainty and frustration that had been the cause of his behavior.

"I have to be honest with myself, however. I don't think I'll ever be madly in love with any woman—not madly enough to put her before my need to paint."

Yet he missed her now. He looked wistfully at the Green Couch, imagining Undi's delicate body curled up on the soft, mossy, green velvet. "Why didn't I start the nude when she was here to pose for me?"

"Because you're a fool," whispered the Green Couch.

"I can see it . . ."

"He can see it! Men are all the same," the old couch practically hissed at him, but he didn't hear her.

"I'd use light colors except for the couch—light pinks and blues. But they'd have to vibrate. Mauve and a lot of white. Deep shadows, but Undi's flesh should be golden with pink shadows. It'll be simple and monumental. I don't believe I'll even include the window shutters. She's on the couch in a space of her own. Or the sea. Yes, a couch floating on an ocean. Nothing else. It won't be necessary. All I'll want is the form on the couch . . ."

"Go to sleep, dear boy."

He didn't hear that either, but he went to sleep. The moonlight shone on the painting on the mantelpiece. The palm trees were as deep and mysterious as they had been that evening. It was probably the best painting Roland had ever done, and he didn't even recognize it as such.

Chapter 31

Within the Dark Painting

ot long after that, Undi glided into the room. She came through the open window, making no sound. Standing by the bed, she looked at him for a while and sighed. It seemed to her that he was sleeping soundly and hadn't missed her at all.

Then she went over to look at the painting. She saw it as she wished to see it. "Why, it's my lake on the Rock. The same rich color. The same indigo sky with stars and the same deep green water with the shores of the lake's blue-brown earth and mud. And the palms! How wonderful they look! Green black and blue black." The stars in the sky radiated light. She thought of Eva. And Pavarti too. "Imagine Roland understanding the spiritual colors of my friends." She wondered where Pavarti was now. She needed to talk to her. And Isis. She wanted Isis.

The stream of moonlight was interrupted by the moving shadow of the palm frond at the window. When it was still again, she let herself be carried on it into the heart of the picture. Seating herself on the shore of the lake, she saw Pavarti crawling about in the mud, shaped like a worm.

"Oh, Pavarti! What are you doing? You look primeval! Can you speak?"

"Of course." Pavarti changed shape and rose out of the slime in the form of the creamy lotus flower.

"What have you been doing in the mud?" Undi asked. She looked at the blue-brown slime, thinking how distasteful it was, not for crawling about in.

"You know what I've been doing. It's only wet mud. Sometimes I like to make love in the slime. We're in everything, Shiva and I. You know that. I found him just now in the form of a worm, and I joined him. It doesn't matter where I go; I always find my beloved."

"But a worm, Pavarti! Why?"

"But why not? A worm is wonderful. Surely you understand that with your knowledge of sea worms."

Undi looked as if she didn't understand.

"We dance. Even worms dance. They ripple and extend themselves and propel themselves forward, and they teach me to do the same. The dance of the worm is equal to the dance of the stars. Movement is movement, whether it be the highest or the lowest."

Now Pavarti was swaying about on the end of her long lotus stem. Her movement was sensuous. She looked so erotic that Undi looked down at her hands, away from her.

"Are you as licentious as they say? Or is it always Shiva?" Undi was thinking of the man she'd gone to bed with. She hadn't even liked him. It had given her little satisfaction.

Pavarti laughed. "I suppose it is. I find love in all things. It's the dance. It's the dance that I love."

"You look so beautiful, Pavarti." She couldn't help saying it, for Pavarti had closed her petals and emerged as her human self. She was as naked as she had been on the morning of the tea party, with only her belt of rubies and the jasmine flowers in her hair. Most of all, she resembled the Pavarti of the Elephanta Cave, as she had appeared to the sculptor of long ago when he had carved her image on the wall of the cave, leaning against the body of Shiva in an attitude of love.

"You know, don't you," Undi said, "that Isis has disappeared. She is lost somewhere in the darkness. We should be concerned about her!"

"I know. I witnessed her final disappearance. I was there."

"There? Where?"

"In the darkness. I was there in the shape of a fragment of moss on a stone. I knew exactly what happened. It was Death who passed near Isis."

"How awful! Did Isis die unfulfilled?" In her unhappy state of mind, Undi had feared death.

"No, not at all. Don't be so grief-stricken. It wasn't like that."

"She doesn't mean that death, but another." It was a familiar voice.

Undi looked up and saw that Isis herself was speaking as she approached across a patch of dry, sandy soil.

"Isis! What happened? You look reborn. I'm so relieved."

"I *am* reborn."

"Tell me. What happened?"

Isis answered, as many people do, with her own question.

"Why did you never take me into the dark room and leave me as you left Eva? Didn't you know what would happen?" Isis was smiling as though something amused her.

"I? Why? I suppose I never thought of it. I did take you, once. Why?"

"Eva took me—pushed me in and closed the door. It was awfully dark. I was afraid."

"Afraid of what? There's nothing to be afraid of in there. Did you see Marius? He's always making his pictures with Light. Don't you remember the time I took you? We missed him. Don't tell me you missed him again!"

"Yes, there was only darkness. You didn't tell me what an extraordinary room it is. Anything can happen there, Undi."

"Isis, please. Tell me what happened. You're right. Different things can happen to different people, but I've never believed there was any danger."

"That darkness! It began to fill up with howling wind, Undi. It came across a vast, empty space. Imagine a vast desert with howling spirits rising up from black sand dunes. I was there. I held up my arms so as not to bump into anything because I couldn't see. And I placed each foot carefully, feeling for every inch of ground because I was afraid of falling into some deep crevasse. The ground was rough and had small stones on it that stuck into my feet. The wind blew them into my face. And all the time, it was howling like an animal. It seemed to me that I was on the floor of some dried-up lake—some ancient, dried lake. I must have walked for miles. And then, after what seemed like hours, days—I don't know how many—with no light visible and nothing happening except the stones in my face and the endless walking, I began to feel as though I no longer existed."

"Oh, Isis!"

"I thought I had lost my identity and that frightened me and made me feel lonely. Then I almost lost my mind, and I felt as if I would scream and split into a hundred pieces. I imagined monsters following me, close behind and ready to catch hold of me. They shadowed me all the time. You saw, didn't you, Pavarti? But the fear had an odd effect. I suddenly understood fear and realized I'd been living with it for a long time."

"It must have been awful."

"It was. But since I didn't die of fright, I became angry and I despised the monsters."

"Did they go away?"

"No. I knew they weren't real, but it didn't make much difference. I was obliged to walk on, knowing they weren't real; yet they still followed me. This made me tremble. Then they suddenly went away, and I thought I'd feel better."

"Did you?"

"Not really. I felt horribly empty. I walked and walked, and everything was flat and dark, and in the end, I was empty and bored."

"Poor Isis! And all this was happening to you in my dark room?"

"Oh no. I think I was a long way from there. I was in a void. Then, all of a sudden, there was movement in the void. You can't imagine how I welcomed that. It was just another wind. Don't ask where it came from because I don't know. It became stronger and stronger, and as it did so, it blew enough of the darkness away for me to see something."

"What was it, Isis?"

"I could see a tiny, white form walking about on the dark, gray floor of a desert. I was excited because I thought I was not alone, but then I saw it was myself. It was a long way, but I could see what was happening. The wind was blowing against my little, white form, and I thought it would be blown away. But it stood firm. I remember thinking it had some secret strength I wasn't aware of in myself. The wind pierced my breast—the little white breast—and blew the spirit out of it. I saw that as if I were quite close. My spirit looked like thistledown. You know what thistledown is like, don't you? It floats on the breeze. But my poor little spirit was blown by the wind—wind so strong it was more like a gale. My lonely spirit went racing across the dunes—nothing but a little white spot. And it went farther and farther away from where I was watching it—far away down there on the black floor of the desert. And I, wherever I was, cried aloud because, without my spirit, I felt even emptier. Although the gale was very strong, I had enough strength to get into it, and I caught up with my spirit. As soon as that happened, the wind became gentler. My exhausted spirit and I lay down side by side and fell asleep. As I was drifting off, I remember I was too tired to try to get my spirit back inside. So we just lay there on a mossy bank feeling nothing and wanting nothing."

"It's true," Pavarti said to Undi. "I saw it all. Isis went to sleep. And there was a tiny light in the distance—far away. It was moving as though someone was carrying a lamp, searching on a dark night for a lost child or a lost animal. It came on and on, over small hills and across small, shadowy valleys, and although it moved from side to side, curving this way and that, it always turned toward us, as though whoever was holding the lamp had found the right path back to where Isis lay. It was as though she, in particular, was being searched for. Who else could it have been?"

"Was that when you were a fragment of moss, Pavarti?"

"Yes. I was so small it hardly mattered. But I could feel her stillness. The light came closer, and the whole expanse of the desert—more like a plain now—was gradually revealed. What a sight! For as far as one could see, all around the edge of the plain, were the fragments of Osiris! Broken fragments silhouetted against the sky like the ruins of noble, old buildings centuries after some great disaster has taken place. To me, they looked enormous, you understand. But I recognized them for what they were—the fourteen parts of Osiris that were scattered by the four winds long ago, over the ancient battlefield where they lay in complete disorder!"

"She always said there were fourteen parts. But who held the lamp, and where was the Death you spoke of?"

"It was Marius who held the Light. He, too, looked like a giant. He wasn't alone. With him was this Death, which is only another name for the One-Who-Must-Destroy-in-Order-to-Create. Over the wide plain they came, bringing the Light closer and closer. I wondered what form of destruction they were bringing in our direction. I wasn't afraid for myself for, anyway, I knew that Death is only change, but I was a little afraid for Isis. Had she been awake she might have tried to escape. Isn't that so, Isis? You might have been afraid to meet him face-to-face."

"I would, indeed. Tired as I was, I might have tried to run. And that would have spoiled everything because he wasn't there to kill me, only to destroy whatever was left of the demons of the past who lived inside me."

Isis had changed again. She had a new beauty, not the haggard beauty of the past and not the glamour of her days as a much sought after fashion model. It was a new serenity—a quality she had never had before. There was less mystery about her but more charm—the charm of a clear and beautiful intelligence. Even in Heliotrope, Isis had not possessed quite the same quality.

"Yes. It was fortunate for you that you slept when they reached you, Isis. You might never have reached that place again. It requires a long search. And having reached it, it would require great courage to stand and face the figure of Death, even though you may have longed for him. But you were asleep. Marius was with him, and Marius is a reassuring figure. You didn't even see him, but he made you sleep."

"It must have been he who carried the lamp," Undi murmured.

"Yes. He stood and shone the light on Isis, and while she slept, the destroyer dealt his blows and killed the last enemy within, as in other times they called out the devils in people. This destroyer was like a surgeon, probing and seeking and cutting and smiting, while Marius held the light. In fact, it was the light that woke her up."

Isis smiled. "I wasn't afraid any more. It was almost over. I remember seeing Marius—his eyes. They were kind, but they glittered. They seemed to stop the pain. It wasn't until I was fully awake that I saw the other figure. I wasn't afraid of him, although I knew at once what he was. But I couldn't stand up. I knew he'd finished the work of destruction, and I was aware of a different kind of emptiness, a vastness within me, which had a point of energy in it. He had taken everything except that."

"The destroyer cast aside his dark robe," Pavarti told Undi, "and put away his death-dealing instrument and revealed himself. He looked splendid and radiated so much light that Marius was able to extinguish the light in his lamp. Then the whole plain became as light as day, and Marius disappeared. As he did so, we saw the true shape of everything."

"The sun had risen," Isis went on, "and it was a glorious day. I felt very strong. I went from place to place, and wherever I went, all around the plain, I gathered in my arms a fragment of my beloved. As his body reformed itself into his true shape, it became alive with the flame of life. I realized what had happened. My search was at an end. I found a chariot of Light, like the one we had brought with us from Heliotrope, and when I had found the last fragment and Osiris was himself again, we entered the chariot. He took the reins and prepared to drive away. Marius watched us.

"As soon as we were above the ground, Osiris turned and looked at me and smiled. When he did, that point of light, or that energy I spoke of, grew larger and larger until it filled my empty heart with love. And his heart was full too. We shared the same love. I felt rich, and there was a sort of faint, bubbling amusement in me. Beside me, Osiris regained all his strength. We kept on driving. There were horses pulling us, and we came down onto a long strip of hard, sandy beach by a sea. The horses raced along on the hard sand, and the wind blew in our faces, and we both began to laugh with pleasure and joy—with the spray from the sea and the warm sunshine and everything . . ."

Undi thought this story was wonderful. She gazed at Isis and then at Pavarti and became conscious of warm sunshine and sea spray herself.

Just then, they all heard the sound of the nightingale. It soared up from some tree behind them, and the song was so brilliant that they all became silent. It was the same bird. As each note left its throat, it again became visible in the shape of a jewel. When the song ended, they saw it soaring upward in the shape of a necklace of gems until it entered a space that even they had never entered.

Undi said, "Ever since I came Back-from-Sea, I have imagined that everything in the universe starts with myself—somewhere within me. I've thought of myself as a center that can affect all things. But the birdsong—remember it, Isis? It's a creation that belongs neither to here nor to heaven or Earth, and it floats away with no care for anything. It is itself. I cannot find anything in it that affects my existence. Yet, I can never forget it. I'm tormented by the hope that, one day, its meaning will be revealed to me." She turned to Pavarti, but Pavarti was making her way across the lake in the shape of a flamingo.

When she looked a second time, it was only a swaying reed in the water. And there was no one beside her on the bank, for Isis had gone too. She looked up, half expecting to see Ki and Sylvester floating by with the two angels, but no, no one was there.

There was no point in talking about herself because no one was there to listen to her. She turned and retraced her steps until she stepped down from the painting and stood once again by Roland's bedside. After looking at him for a moment, she turned away, murmuring 'Good night, Roland. Good-bye."

He turned in his sleep but didn't wake.

Osiris and Isis reborn

Chapter 32

Dolphins to the Rescue

"We could place it here by the window. I'll set my easel up in this room. It wasn't where I intended to paint, but the couch will look well in here. I had begun to reconcile myself to painting the whole thing from memory. But now that you're here, Undi, I won't have to." He added silently, *I suppose that young idiot* will *let me take the couch.* Then, *He'll have to. It is mine, after all.* He looked at Undi. "Does that appeal to you, my dear?"

"Yes, Georges." She had noticed he no longer called her his princess. Now that he didn't do so, she rather wished he would. She would know then that he'd forgotten, and everything was as it had been. She was looking out of the long French window, enjoying the view in a glum sort of way. She could see a stone building standing on a cliff overlooking the bay. It was an old fortresslike building that had been transformed into a museum for some of the works of Picasso.

"It's a fine old building," Georges observed when he saw what she was looking at. "But in my opinion, it houses the wrong pictures." He didn't like Picasso. 'Does that young fool like modern art?"

Undi knew who he meant. She didn't want to talk about Roland. She wondered what Georges would say if she told him that Roland referred to him as 'that old idiot." "Yes, he does. He's a modern painter himself, trying to break away from the past."

"Ah, one of those." Georges made up his mind that should he and Roland ever meet, as he supposed they would when he went to Golfe Juan to get the couch, he would never agree with Roland on matters of art. In fact, he would have liked to dismiss Roland from his thoughts altogether, but he couldn't. Images of Roland and Undi together disturbed him constantly. He almost looked forward to going to the room Undi had shared with Roland, if only to see what it was like and perhaps banish some of those images.

"I should go and get the couch," he said to her. "Why waste time?"

"Not today," Undi pleaded. "It won't run away. Go tomorrow. Anyway," she added, "I won't come with you."

"No. Perhaps you're right. I'll go alone."

He had prepared a very charming room for her and, in fact, had done all he could to make her comfortable and happy. Telephoning his femme de ménage, a woman from the village, he had asked her to get new lace curtains for the French windows, and he himself had moved furniture and hung paintings he thought Undi would like. By dinnertime that evening, it was ready for her and looked attractive, with its four-poster bed, a bureau, round table and chair, and a long cane chaise lounge just outside on the terrace. She was charmed at first, but although she tried to hide it, she soon lapsed into a state of indifference.

They went out to dinner, and she thought of Roland. Had she been cruel to go without a word? Perhaps she had been, but she didn't believe she could ever go back, even to get her clothes. That didn't matter. Georges said he would buy some new ones for her. She felt uncomfortable with Georges now because she could tell that he, too, felt ill at ease, even though he did all he could for her and pretended that nothing was wrong.

Several days passed like this. Whenever Georges asked her for the address of the villa so that he could go and get the couch, she put him off and looked upset, and this made Georges even more ill at ease. On the afternoon of the third day, he had some business to attend to and asked her to go with him. She said she'd rather stay and rest on the terrace, so he went out and left her alone.

When he came back about an hour later, she was not there. He hoped she had not returned to Roland, yet he had believed her when she said she wasn't going back to him. So he waited, hoping she'd come back. When she did not, he went down to the village, thinking she might have gone shopping.

Traveling by bus, Undi had gone to the old house to see Marius. Walking up the hill where she and Roland had walked, her depression deepened. When she reached the large gate, half hidden by vines, she knocked and waited, but no one answered her. After waiting a few minutes, she went over the wall and up to the balcony where she'd last seen Marius, and finding the door open, she entered the house. Inside, she passed through the corridors and halls and looked into rooms. Marius was nowhere to be seen. She went down the stairs and at last came to the cave. There, she sat on the floor, just as we'd done that day when we left Heliotrope. She tried to Sing the ancient song. Nothing happened. This was not surprising. First of all, she needed all of us, for we all had to Sing together, and also she couldn't Sing. It wasn't in her. She didn't have the power. She hadn't really expected to. Sing, I mean. She'd just done it as a sort of gesture, which meant, I suppose, that she was ready to go home. But she wanted Marius. Every one of us wanted Marius. Somehow, without saying or doing anything, he had always been the leader.

Well, he wasn't there. The whole place was deserted, except for the mythological beasts and the Light sculptures in the garden and the woods. So Undi returned to Antibes where Georges had his villa. Only she didn't return to the villa. Instead, she wandered down to a rocky ledge behind the old museum. After sitting there for some time, she removed her clothing and entered the water. It was almost dark by now. Floating listlessly, she allowed herself to be carried out by the tide. It was not long before she discovered she was no longer at home in the water. Her memories persisted. But a strong wind blew up, and unfriendly waves tossed her about until she lost consciousness.

This time the fish who discovered her was the same old cod with bulging eyes and a pulled down mouth she had paid money for when they passed through Marseilles on their way south and had thrown back into the water. She'd seen him, flapping about frantically on the deck of a fishing boat, and had taken pity on him. Like his ancestor, he wanted to be sure before he tried to save her. He set off in search of the dolphins. "They will know what to do." He swam on for some time before he came upon the noble family.

When he found them they were having a great time, swooping about in the sea like birds in the air. Cutting through the surface every now and then, they took no notice of him. Lady Dolphin had a young one and was teaching him dolphin skills. She nudged him gently and showed him how to dive, how to swim upside down, and how to scratch his back and clean himself on rough surfaces. His father showed him how to tense his muscles and leap out of the water. He expressed his pleasure by opening his mouth and stretching it into a shape that resembled a human smile. They were all very active when the fish approached, and he couldn't get any of them to listen to him.

"You don't understand," the fish cried when they ignored him.

"We've no time to listen to speeches. Not just now, dear chap." The cod was given to speech making, and no one in the sea wanted to hear speeches.

Lord Dolphin slowed down, more out of politeness than anything else.

The fish spoke as quickly as he could, fearing the dolphin would swoop off again in another direction. "It's the Undi. She's drowning."

"Drowning, eh? Poor creature."

"But it's *the* Undi. She shouldn't be drowning. I know her."

Lord Dolphin paused and took notice.

"She's the one who saved me in Marseilles. We must save her."

"Are you sure?" Lord Dolphin paid attention now. "But she should be able to swim as well as you or I."

"She should, but she's not. She *is* drowning, I tell you."

Lady Dolphin was now at their side. She'd noticed her mate talking to the fish. "Whatever is the matter, dear?"

"He says that Undi—you know, from the Rock—is drifting about the sea in a helpless condition. Do you believe that's possible?"

"Oh. Well, it seems unlikely. But anything's possible. You say you've seen her, Fish?"

Just then, Sister Seagull landed on Lord Dolphin's back, full of news. "Undi's in trouble. She seems to make a habit of trying to drown herself. I just saw her. She can't go back to the Rock, you know. It's disappeared."

"We know that. It simply vanished one dark night."

Lady Dolphin made a decision. "Fish, lead the way. We'll do whatever we can."

They set off, but before long, the fish was left behind. He had given them the exact location, so they went on without him. Every few minutes, one of them would leap out of the water and look ahead.

On the way, they came upon a female whale and asked her to join in the search. She wasn't an enormous whale, but she was heavy with child. This didn't deter her. She cut through the water with them until they saw something in the distance. Lady Dolphin asked her to dive and come up with the Undi on her back.

"She's in human shape and mustn't be allowed to drown."

"She should be safe on *that* back," Lord Dolphin chuckled.

By this time, a lot of other fish had joined them. Anyone they encountered joined in. "What a terrible thing! She must have forgotten who she is. Why else would she do it?"

"Do what?"

"Swim. Humans go for swims. She must have thought she was human."

"But she's a spirit of the waves. She can't *not* swim."

Lady Dolphin looked up at Sister Seagull flying overhead. "Remember what I said when we last spoke about her. I said I hoped she would always remember who she was."

"I remember. There are times when a shape-changer can go too far. I saw her on a beach a few days ago, and I knew at once that's what had happened. She'd gone too far. I warned her."

A long stream of creatures of all shapes and sizes followed the dolphins.

Sister Seagull said that the Undi was safely up in the air on Whale's back. "She looks limp, but I think she's alive."

A swordfish skimmed through the water and up into the air. When he came down, he said, "She looks like a human jellyfish." A jellyfish took offense.

The whale lowered herself, and they could all see.

"If she had more legs and arms, I'd say she looks like a drowned octopus," remarked a flounder.

"Every time the water washes over her, her legs flap about like two of your tentacles," a dab said, turning to an octopus.

The octopus, a shy little creature, showed spirit and slapped the cheeky dab.

"Don't fight! This is serious," a butterfly fish said.

The cod caught up with them. He asked Whale to sink down a little farther so that he could examine the body.

Someone said he didn't have to; they all knew who she was.

Lord Dolphin told them he should be allowed the privilege. "He's the one who saw her first."

The fish then examined the body and proclaimed it to be the Undi.

The dolphin agreed. "It" the Undi, all right. And she's the one who saved your life in Marseilles? Then we must save her."

"You can save her, but what's the use? She'll go on doing the same thing over and over again."

"We could swim in and leave her close to the shore," suggested an intelligent seahorse.

"But if no one finds her, she'll be no better off. It's a terrible fate for an Undi to be trapped in a dead human body."

"Keep to the point," Lord Dolphin snapped, taking charge. "Now, we must consider carefully what is to be done."

"She can stay on my back," offered Whale. "I'll move in as close to the shore as possible. But if I have to leave suddenly, someone else will have to take her."

On Whale's back, Undi began to show signs of distress.

"I know what's wrong," Sister Seagull exclaimed. 'She needs water again. Take her down!" She'd realized that Undi was now at home neither in water nor in air. "She needs to go up and then down—to be immersed and then lifted out."

Whale sank low enough for the water to wash over Undi. She stopped thrashing about and grew calm again. But she was quite unconscious.

"Don't let her slide off," someone said.

"She's hovering between two worlds.", replied the swordfish.

"Really!"

"Form a circle around Whale," Lord Dolphin ordered. They did so. "Now if she slips off, one of you can catch her. And you, Whale, if you don't mind, just keep on going up and down."

"Can you manage, dear?" inquired Lady Dolphin solicitously.

"I believe so," good-tempered Whale replied. "Like this?" She did as she'd been asked, creating such a swell that a lot of them felt sick and she herself said, "If I continue to do this, I won't be able to answer for the consequences."

The fish scattered. A whale had never been known to regurgitate, but there was always a first time.

"Do you know what I think?" Lady Dolphin's son ventured to say.

"No, darling, what? Speak up." She and Lord Dolphin exchanged proud glances because their son was showing signs of intelligence.

"Um . . . er . . . well . . ."

"Come, child, speak. Say what you think. No one will laugh at you."

"Well, I think she's like someone who's . . . who's . . . well, halfway. She's going to be transformed into something else."

"How clever, darling! What an idea! There may be something in it. And while she hovers on the edge, she's most vulnerable? Well, what a unique situation!"

"It happens, you know," said the father dolphin.

"But that doesn't solve the immediate situation. If we leave her on the edge of some beach, the tide may carry her out again, and if we leave her on a rock, she may die like a fish out of water," Lady Dolphin told them.

"Oh, no! Horrible death!" cried Fish.

Dear, sweet Whale, who'd been going up and down more slowly, suddenly told them she had to leave. "I have to get to the spawning field as soon as possible It's a long way from here, and I think my time has come. I must go."

"Go along, dear. We'll manage." Lady Dolphin was already casting her eye around for someone to take Whale's place.

The Cod heard them. He knew the spawning field of the great whales. He'd passed over it once, and looking down, he had seen mothers suckling their monstrous young. The great eyes of the baby whales had roved vacantly from side to side as they clung with their mouths to the vast undersides of their mothers' bodies. There was something freakish about whales, he told himself—too big, and with such tiny, ethereal voices.

"Well, she'd better go on my back," Lord Dolphin said. "Gather 'round, chaps and catch her if she slips off."

Creatures gathered around him, not only the "chaps" as he called them but females too. They moved in that formation toward the Bay of Antibes.

But at the entrance to the bay, Lord Dolphin called a halt. Something unexpected was happening in the waters of the bay. They dared go no further. Even Cod stopped dead, for what he saw filled him with dread. The bay was full of fishing boats and small skiffs, full of men with lights, nets, harpoons, and fishing lines with enormous hooks.

"My God! Have you ever seen anything like that?" Each boat had a light to entice unwary fish into the nets and the harpoons. "Night fishing in Antibes! Keep clear if you want to stay alive."

They had expected to find the bay dark and silent. This was like a carnival—a carnival of death! The fish looked out across the water and saw the sinister forms of men. Standing up in their small craft, lit from below by the light of their lamps, they looked like monsters. The sight filled him with an almost superstitious horror. Yet it strengthened his resolve to be a hero and save the Undi.

Confusion had broken out among the smaller fish. The protective circle around Undi was broken. She slipped off Lord Dolphin's back. Turning about, Cod caught her by the hair, his mouth full of the stuff. One of the flying fish told them that, on the far side of the nets near the shore, there was a small craft with a huge man and a boy who had no weapons of any kind. Small fish who had escaped and slipped through the nets confirmed this.

"It's the Marius. He comes merely to observe. In fact, he saves whoever and whatever he can and takes them to his garden and keeps them in a large pool. Most of the time, he returns them to the water of the bay.

"I must get her to him," Cod cried. "I can do it. I've learned how to evade capture. I learned the worst way; you all know that. Give her to me."

Lord Dolphin took the Undi and handed her over to the Cod, and Cod again took her hair in his mouth. By this time, Undi looked almost transparent, but she was quite heavy, having so much water inside her. The fish had to exert all his strength. Lord Dolphin advised him to stay on the outskirts of the area where all the boaters were and then make a deep dive, coming up beside Marius's craft, if he could. It sounded easy.

Dragging Undi, Cod set off. It wasn't easy. Several times they were almost caught in the nets and he had to let go of Undi's hair, and then catch her again before she sank. He was also wounded slightly by one of the harpoons. Looking up, he saw one of the human monsters looking down incredulously, but he swam away before he and Undi

were caught. At last, he saw Marius's small craft. The time had come for the deep dive. He made it, pulling Undi up on the far side of the boat.

Marius, looking the other way, did not see them at first. Raynard, the young boy who was looking about at all that was going on, looked down when he heard Undi's attempts to breathe.

"Look, Master. Here's a very strange one. It's being towed by a fish. We've never had one like that before."

Marius looked. "What have we here? What are you doing with such an unlikely catch, fish?"

Cod had to let go of the yellow hair in order to answer him. Undi began to drift away.

"I know her!" the boy exclaimed. "She's the one who came to the gate asking to see you. She had a young man with her who wanted to learn from you. They left an address. But she was good-looking then."

"Yes, you're right. She doesn't look much good now, does she? I know her too." The fish had caught Undi and brought her back to the side of the boat. "Here, let me have her. Quickly." Marius stepped right out of the boat and water came up past his hips. When he took Undi in his arms, she hung limply, with water dripping from her dangling arms and legs and from the tips of her breasts. And a lot of it streamed from her hair.

"She's the Undi of the Rock, and I found her in this unhappy state, far out at sea," Cod explained. "I brought her to you because you'll know what to do with her. She's in some sort of halfway state and has to have alternate doses of air and water. Keep her above water for too long, and she'll suffocate; under the surface for too long, and she'll drown. Will you accept her?"

"Indeed. Trust me. And you, brave fish, you'd better watch yourself going back past the nets. Unless you'd rather come with me?"

"No, thank you. It's the last thing I want to do. But I trust you well enough to leave the Undi in your hands. Good-bye."

"As you wish," Marius replied. "I imagine you'll receive a hero's welcome when you get back. Take care."

The cod turned away, preparing to swim off. Far out near the entrance to the bay, there was a commotion. The young dolphin leaped into the air and saw Undi in the arms of Marius. They knew now that she was safe and the news was being passed around to those who'd just arrived on the scene. All the fish and other sea creatures surged forward, upsetting boats, dragging the nets into the path of swordfish, who made short work of tearing them apart and creating fear in the hearts of the fishermen. Dolphins, eels, octopus, jellyfish, sardines, a tribe of sea otters, codfish, dab, flounder, and an odd deep-sea walking fish, as well as a stingray, a manta ray, swordfish, and other such inhabitants of the sea churned up the surface of the water, confusing the fishermen. A Portuguese man-of-war hung around on the outskirts, wishing he could be of help. All the fish were surging around Marius's small craft.

The dolphins and the swordfish leaped high into the air, passing each other with perfect timing over the heads of Marius and his young assistant. Other dolphins and sea lions swam around, rising and falling, revealing their curved backs above the surface, and otters floated on their backs revealing their stomachs. Hundreds of smaller fish darted back and forth; colored butterfly fish and gorgeous black-and-white fish jumped like sparkling points of light, making the surface of the water look like a vast jewel-studded counterpane of rumpled satin. Translucent blue fish shone like moonstones, and octopus waved pearl-studded tentacles. Sister Seagull and a huge flock of seabirds, including a special breed with fine, red legs, fluttered about overhead, uttering shrill cries. They looked like excited spirits, appearing and disappearing as they did, in and out of the lights. The night was like a carnival of moving lights, as the fishermen's lamps swayed about, illuminating the astonishing scene. A giant swordfish was seen in perfect silhouette, as she sailed across the face of the moon. Farther out at the entrance to the bay, a multitude of great white whales spouted water ninety feet into the air, while even farther out, the sirens and sea spirits lifted their heads above the surface, and the sound of their unearthly songs could be heard across the bay.

When it was all over, the waters of Antibes became calm again, the fishermen rowed back to shore, and Cod swam back to Lord and Lady Dolphin and was proclaimed a hero.

Marius, with Undi in his arms, returned to his enormous limousine, which drove itself. The boy sat in front, while Marius sat in the back and supported Undi. And the inhabitants of Antibes were able to get some sleep.

At the door of the old stone house—a stone door that had been added to the huge eighteenth-century wing—Marius's femme de ménage greeted him with, "What? Something else to paint?" and looked askance at the limp form dangling from his arms.

"Yes," he replied. "Quickly, Madame Do-It, help me fill up the old bathtub."

They went upstairs to his enormous new atelier. But from an old atelier nearby, Marius dragged out an antique bathtub and, lifting it as easily as if he were indeed a giant, he carried it into the other large room. This bathtub had been standing idle for years, and into it, Marius had dropped odd things he didn't want to throw away. The tub had a face painted on one end of it and a tail at the other end, and its four legs had bull's feet on them. He did things like this from time to time to amuse himself and to "keep in touch," as he said, with the human things of life. The inside was blue, and the outside was an earth red, with black markings inspired by the bulls of Minos.

He and the boy pulled out old canvases, pieces of tin, figures carved out of wood, seashells, an old violin, a Roman toga, and a nineteenth-century newspaper; they pulled out a fragment of a bronze vase taken from the sea, together with the head of a plastic doll, the jawbone of a fox, an old cake tin containing lead droppings from a lead toy factory, and a once beloved sweatshirt he'd given up looking for.

"Put these in a safe place where I can find them and give my sweatshirt to Madame Do-It to be laundered," he said to the boy.

He found one last object and uttered a shriek of delight because it was one of his early drawings that he'd done on bark during his caveman days, or perhaps I should say, when he'd studied cave art. It was probably worth millions.

But there was no time for that now. Undi was gurgling and turning an unpleasant shade of turkey red. The tub was ready, and Raynard had dragged a long garden hose all the way up the stairs, so they lowered Undi into the bath and began to fill it halfway with water. Madame Do-It came with a packet of salt, and they poured some of that in too. Undi was soon floating with her face submerged. The boy was told to tilt her every now and then so that she could get some air. Being a boy of great ingenuity, he invented something on the spot, which took the job over for him and lifted Undi's head every five minutes.

"Master," he said, "here is the slip of paper with the address on it. The young man gave it to me."

"Ah yes, the young man. Give it to me." He took the slip of paper and put it in his pocket.

"Are you going to start work at once, monsieur?" asked Madame Do-It. "You'd better have something to eat first. If you don't, you'll close yourself up in here and you'll never eat." She looked at him severely. "You work and work and work . . ."

"And work and work. Yes, I do, don't I. And you fuss and fuss, trying to make me eat. But you're quite right. I need strength. And besides, your cooking is irresistible, you delectable old apple tart. Lead me to one of your great potato pies or your whatever it's going to be, and I and the boy will consume it." To Raynard, he added, "Will our jellyfish in the tub be all right?"

"Indubitably, master," replied the boy and followed Marius down to the kitchen.

They sat down to a nourishing vegetable casserole with lots of garlic and herbs and tomatoes, cabbage, and potatoes. As Marius ate, he gazed intently at a big, round cheese on the table. But what passed through his mind was not cheese. Images of another sort appeared to him in the vast landscape of his mind. Madame Do-It was well aware of this, but she didn't mind, as long as he ate what she gave him before suddenly jumping up and rushing upstairs not to be seen again for twenty-four hours or more. The boy too. She made sure he got enough to eat.

But today, Marius surprised her by tossing off his glass of wine and saying to the boy, "Do you have the bell, boy?"

"I certainly do, master."

"Then ring it. Call the lift," said Marius. Then he went back to his contemplation of the cheese.

"The lift!" repeated Madame Do-It.

The boy swallowed the last of his potato pie and went into the garden, where he beat a loud tattoo on his drum. That's what Marius had meant when he referred to a bell. Madame Do-It came out and stood on the doorstep. From under the wide portal, she looked up at the starry sky, this way and that.

After a while she said, "Here it comes," and the boy stopped making a racket with his drumsticks. A small object could be seen far away in the sky. As it floated toward them, it grew larger and larger and landed on the grass before them. The boy ran inside and told Marius it was there.

"Very well. I'm coming," Marius replied. He dabbed his mouth with a red, checked table napkin and went outside. The Iron Lift, who'd been in his service ever since its escape from the building on the Rue Tilset, had been transformed into a pleasure craft, and it spent most of its time awaiting orders from Marius. As soon as Marius had time, or when he had completed the enormous seascape he had in mind to paint, the Iron Lift would be dispatched to various locations to pick up people and transport them to Marius's sculpture garden for the grand garden fete he intended to give. That's what he had said.

But now he had a small job for the lift. He scribbled a note and attached it to the iron door. "Here's the address," he said, telling the lift where to go. "And don't forget to draw attention to the note." He slapped the lift kindly and sent it off. Then he and the boy went inside to finish the meal with some of Madame Do-It's famous pear tart.

Chapter 33

Georges and Roland

Georges saw the display of the sea creatures from his terrace. It didn't astonish him as much as it did the fishermen in the bay. Being farther away, he imagined it was some festive affair of the local people. In his distracted state of mind, he dismissed the phenomenon with the words *trained fish*. He'd once seen dolphins leaping out of the water in an aquarium. From where he stood, he hadn't seen Undi in the arms of Marius, but had he been able to, he might have been relieved, although very surprised, for her disappearance had caused him the greatest concern. He'd been searching the district for hours, driving back and forth along the coast in his car.

It had not entered his mind that she might have entered the water. Had he thought of such a thing, he would have imagined she'd tried to drown herself, whereas she'd only been trying to go back to the Rock. On the contrary, he imagined she had run away from him, and the thought that she might have run off without a word caused him pain. It also stimulated his imagination, just as Roland's imagination had been stimulated. Or, perhaps I should say, he became dizzy because of the illusions that started plaguing him. Standing on the terrace, watching the commotion in the bay, he was in one of his most bitter moods. Dark suspicions of Undi destroyed his ability to think. Doubts crept in through all his cracks like black smoke, and a voice hissed within him, *She took money from you. She lied. She made a fool of you. She cheated and despised you and thought you ugly while she pretended to like you.*

When he could no longer sustain those negative images of her, he made a complete turnabout and saw her as an innocent angel. He blamed himself, admitting to himself that she'd never made any promises; nor had she ever led him on. She hadn't done anything except be there with him sometimes. *I insisted on her taking the jewelry. In fact, even though I gave them all to her, she didn't take what she didn't want. She didn't tell lies—not until the day she was leaving Paris—because I never asked her if she was seeing someone else. She's always been kind to me.*

Then he remembered the long letters he'd written to her, pouring out his heart and his innermost thoughts. She'd never answered any one of them! He thought of the long discourses he'd had with himself and the sudden moments of illumination, which sprang from his— what should he call it?—his emotional excitement. Her silences had even stimulated him and had inspired those long streams of reasoning, which he considered to be creative thinking.

But was it? It didn't occur to Georges that all his mental activity produced only illusions. He saw Undi in one light, and then he saw her in another. He was afraid not to. He was afraid that if she weren't any of these things, she might be just a stupid, empty girl he'd been fantasizing about. And if that were so, he would be left in a barren, drab, empty world, deprived of the excitement and delight and pain of the lover. This played havoc with his feelings.

Pacing about on his terrace, he saw a night so full of wonderful beauty and mystery it made him pause. Then he began idolizing her again and thinking of her as a rare and fragile princess.

"Why don't you just say that you miss her?" I wanted to say. "You miss her, and you wish she were here, giving you her love. And if she's not and she doesn't give you her love, give way to your pain. Let your mind rest."

He couldn't hear me, of course, and now he started, as another thought, alarming this time, came from some corner of his busy mind. *Where is she? What could have happened?* Suppose she hadn't run away after all. Suppose she'd had an accident. Suppose she had—God forbid—killed herself!

My God! Imagine that! He now saw himself as the monster. *I'm thinking only of myself. She's been unhappy, and all I've thought of is myself. I've even been cold to her because of my jealousy. It's because I feel so wretchedly impotent.*

Unable to sit still, Georges paced up and down on the terrace. Genuine tenderness overcame him at last, as he thought of Undi when he had first seen her asleep on the model's stand—on the Green Couch.

The tenderness didn't last long. *She said she was coming to the South with a girlfriend, but it was a lie. Now she admits to having come with that young fool. A painter! That makes her behavior doubly treacherous. She knows I can't abide these so-called modern painters who know better than everyone else. She's suffered! She never suffered like that because of me. Oh no, I had to do all the suffering.*

It could have gone on forever! I didn't know why I was there, listening—if you could call it listening—to all this.

Suddenly, he wanted to meet Roland and see those paintings for himself. He knew now where Roland was. Earlier that day he'd actually seen Roland enter the garden of a villa in Golfe Juan, and he had taken particular note of the villa itself. But he was afraid to go, in case he should find Undi there in her young lover's arms.

He had stepped down from the terrace and, without realizing it, he had wandered down to the small, stone museum, where he was reminded of Picasso. This annoyed him. He turned and walked along the rocks behind the building. Still jealous, he again wondered whether Undi had returned to Roland. But he didn't really believe she would do that without telling him. So where was she?

He put his hand out to steady himself and found that he was grasping something soft and silky. At that moment, the moon shone brightly, and he could see what his hand held clearly. It was a woman's summer dress. On the same rock was a pair of white sandals. He knew them well, for he had bought them for Undi only the day before when they had gone shopping in Nice. Realization came at last!

It's true. She's thrown herself into the sea! What can I do? Undi, Undi! He looked down at the water. It revealed nothing.

Gathering up her clothes, he hurried back to the town. A taxi was standing at the corner, and he got in, directing the driver to Golfe Juan. Without knowing why, he was going directly to Roland. Perhaps he imagined Roland might swim out to sea looking for Undi. But I couldn't read anything in his mind, except this need to go to the villa and make contact with Roland.

When he got there, he rang the doorbell, and after a few minutes, a lady opened the door. This was Mademoiselle Grandjean who, with her sister, owned the villa. She looked at Georges curiously because he seemed to be agitated. But she pressed Roland's bell. He didn't know Roland's other name, so he had tried to describe him as a young painter with longish hair.

"At the top of the stairs," Mademoiselle Grandjean told him, so he entered and stood looking up, not quite sure now that he really wanted to go there or see Roland.

Yet he felt he had to. Who else would help him search for Undi?

Roland looked over the landing and recognized Georges. When Georges saw him, he hurried up and, catching hold of Roland's arm, he propelled him back into the room. It stank of marijuana. Roland had met a fellow sufferer, who'd just broken up with his girlfriend, and he'd sold Roland three of his precious joints. They were fairly strong. Roland had already smoked one.

Georges looked fearfully around, half expecting to see Undi. "She's not here? No, she's not. Then I fear something dreadful has happened." He saw the green couch and flopped down, crying, "Poor girl! Oh, my poor girl! My Princess! Oh, Undi!"

Roland, who hadn't shaved for days and hadn't eaten very much either, was bewildered. He'd done little else but paint and sleep and go to the window from time to time, half expecting Undi to come along the garden path, to return if only to get her things. The work he'd done lay about the room—on the spare bed, the chair, and on the mantelpiece. There was one, still wet, right underneath Georges at the moment, on the couch.

Roland had no fears for Undi's safety, imagining her to be enjoying herself with the playboy in the fast car. This imaginary person had assumed realistic proportions, and Roland even knew what he looked like—blond hair, white teeth, suntanned skin, with not a care in the world. An idiot, of course.

"What's happened?" he asked dreamily. "Have you seen her?"

"Look. Her clothes. She's done away with herself. I found these on a rock behind the museum at Antibes. She has drowned herself."

"But she can swim." Roland looked doubtful. "She always told me she could swim like a fish."

"Ah, but there's a difference between throwing oneself into the water without clothes and entering the water in order to swim. She didn't do that. She threw herself from the rock."

"Do you really think so? But I thought . . ."

"What did you think? The girl is gone, I tell you."

"I thought she was all right—having a good time. Is this really hers?" He looked at the dress, unable to connect it with Undi. He'd never seen it before.

"I bought it myself in Nice. What are we going to do?"

It shocked Roland to realize he'd been so far from the truth, imagining her in the company of the playboy with all the money, when she'd been with Georges all the time. He wasn't sure whether that was better or worse. He sat down took out the last two cigarettes, and offered one to Georges. Georges accepted, and they lit up and inhaled deeply.

"Did you call the police?" This was unreal, he told himself. Undi couldn't be drowned. She was a beautiful golden girl. Golden girls didn't drown themselves.

"No, fool that I am! I should have done that immediately. Oh, my God! Now it's too late!"

"Too late?" Roland was almost indignant. He was more likely to drown himself than Undi was. "I can't believe it."

"Nor I. But these are her clothes. This is her dress, and these are her shoes."

"She must have gone out for a moonlight swim. She'd do something like that. She may be climbing out of the water right now, looking for them."

"Do you think so? She'd have to walk home without them."

They paused for a moment, and then they both giggled.

"She wouldn't mind doing that," Roland said. "She doesn't care a bit about conventions."

They found this very amusing and sat there giggling even more loudly.

"Ah, yes. I remember the day I first met her. She was wearing nothing but a Chinese shawl or something like that. She carried it off as if it were the latest fashion. Remarkable girl."

"When was that?" Roland asked jealously.

"Ah, when. That is the question. It was supposedly when she first arrived in Paris. She'd just come from . . . where? I've never been able to find out."

"Neither have I!" Roland sat on his chair thinking of places Undi might have come from.

Georges wasn't paying much attention to Roland any more. He inhaled deeply, and he, too, sat there, puzzling over Undi. "She's elusive, that's true. But extremely intelligent. Understood everything I said. We had long, philosophical discussions. She absorbed everything. And elegant too! We created quite a stir when we appeared together in restaurants."

Then it was Roland's turn. "Women of her type are instinctive rather than clever. I found she acted according to her feelings. But she could afford to do that because she had good taste. She hardly ever did anything that offended."

Georges: "A goddess! A princess! Although it remains a mystery who her people were. It doesn't matter. I believe she came in answer to my call. It was a miracle, the way she came into my life."

Roland: "She opened up to me. Like a child in her simplicity. Too much so, I sometimes think. But she loved me. She showed that by all her actions. She sacrificed herself for me."

Georges: "She allowed me to enter the landscape of her soul. In this way, she never rejected me."

They went on talking and making all this up about Undi.

"When we were together, I found peace and strength. Afterward, I was able to paint. She calmed me."

"She excited me. I have been in a state of divine discontent."

"My little sister."

"My docile little sister."

They hadn't been listening to each other. Their cigarettes went out.

"And now, dear boy, I'll have to relieve you of this priceless green couch. I'm painting a reclining nude. I'll nee-dit." Georges was fumbling his speech.

"I'm about to paint one too. I was just about to prepare a new canvas." This wasn't true, but Roland thought it was. Roland had considered the project from time to time, but to tell the truth, the inspiration to paint Undi lying on the couch had not come to him. Now, suddenly, he imagined it was the only thing he wanted to do.

Georges had discovered he was sitting on a wet canvas. He realized he had spoilt one of Roland's paintings and was full of remorse with no thought for the seat of his trousers.

"I have an idea, my friend. You are here alone. Obviously you need more space. My villa is large enough for both of us. Let us take the couch now, together, and you will spend the rest of the summer with me. We'll be able to work together. Isn't that an excellent idea?"

"It certainly is. You mean to say you have enough space and I could have a studio all to myself?"

"A bedroom *and* a studio. And it opens onto a terrace. Come, let us go. I can't wait. Tomorrow you will come back and get the rest of your things. Now we'll take the couch. You take that end, and I will take the other. Careful now . . ."

"My goodness," said the Green Couch. "More excitement, two of them under one roof. Whatever will happen next?"

It was only when they set the couch down on the pavement that Georges remembered he didn't have his car with him. "What a nuisance. Never mind. Perhaps we'll find a taxi."

"Yes, a taxi. We must find a taxi." Roland looked about him. A thing that looked like a floating iron lift was hovering right beside him. "What is this?"

"Extraordinary!" Georges exclaimed. "There's a note attached. It's a taxi!"

"It's for me!" Roland took the note and read aloud. "This iron lift has come to transport you. Step in if you have the courage." He read it and reread it. "Transport me to where? And to what? Who cares? Let's go!"

Georges agreed with him. "Just what we need. It's a square flying saucer. Let's go. You're right."

"It's not really square. But perhaps you're right. Will it hold us all? I mean, will the couch fit into this not really square taxi." Roland said, collapsing into giggles.

They tried, and the couch went in sideways while they leaned against it. "Tell it where to go," Roland started to say.

But the lift rose into the air and sailed off.

"What a wonderful view of the coast," Georges remarked. "I'm not sure it's going in the right direction, but it doesn't matter, does it."

The flight was a smooth one, and they hovered for a while over the hillside before gliding down to the garden of the old stone house. The young boy greeted them with a roll of the drum, and Madame Do-It came out to watch them land. She stood in the doorway.

"Oh," she said, "you've brought your own couch. You needn't have bothered. We have plenty of chairs. But never mind. Bring it in, if you wish. He's waiting."

She led the way, and they followed, simpering and giggling and dragging the couch with them.

Chapter 34

Undi Reborn

arius had intended to show his new work to an intimate group, but now that Undi was in such a critical condition, he changed his plan. His plan now was to lead her out of the embryonic state she had settled into by means of his mastery over Light. With his ability to readjust instantly to any situation, he had a great idea for a new work of art he fully expected would awaken her from her coma.

Roland and Georges, still dragging the couch with them, were led up a wide staircase, along two corridors, into one of the ateliers and out the far side of it, through an archway, and along a dim passage where they could hear the sound of waves beating against rough stone and the cry of seabirds and a woman's voice singing a song no one had ever heard before. They then passed through a mist very much like the misty doorways sometimes to be encountered in the palace itself and at last into the new, secret atelier Marius had built especially for what he considered would be his greatest work.

On the way, Raynard and Madame Do-It had relieved them of the couch and removed it to the dark room, where Eva and Pavarti and one of Undi's handmaidens sat on it. Isis was there too, sitting on the high-backed chair in the room, and the rest of the handmaidens sat on cushions on the floor. I wondered where these odd pieces of furniture—if one could call them furniture—had come from. There was even a tall lampstand with a pink-shaded lamp casting a rosy glow over the room. It didn't look like the dark room at all, but I knew it was the same room. It was the kind of knowledge one has in a dream when one sees that something is the same, only different. The handmaidens were giggling and moving about as only the very young can. This was odd, I thought, when one considered how very old they actually were. They were behaving like teenagers waiting for one of their favorite movies to begin. Emily began handing the sweets around. It didn't strike me as odd—I mean, the dark room being here instead of in the palace on the Rock.

The hole was there, but it was a dark hole, floating in its own space. It was larger than it usually was. I supposed Marius wanted everyone to be able to see clearly.

Neither Shiva nor Osiris was there. Gaston Moitessier was not there, either. I was glad. I had resigned myself to Eva's happy love affair, but I didn't want to see them together. Not yet—not after what I'd seen in the bedroom in the chateau. If he had been here, they would have been sitting together on the couch holding hands or something like that. But she was alone, so I settled into a space just above her left shoulder, like the invisible spirit I was. Pavarti was on my other side.

Suddenly, the room became dark, and the hole filled up with Light. We could see Georges and Roland sitting on another couch very much like the Green Couch. I think it was made of Light, but of course, they didn't know that.

"Your son and Georges Albertine have become very friendly," remarked Daisy, one of the handmaidens. "I wonder how they'll feel when they come out of it?" She meant the effects of the cigarettes they'd smoked.

Eva didn't know what Daisy was talking about, but she thought she recognized Georges as the man who'd made such a fuss about pinning up the hem of the gray hostess gown.

Raynard came into view beating a rat-a-tat-tat on his drum. The hole opened, and everyone in the dark room could see the full picture, even as far as the walls of Marcus's new atelier. They were something like the walls of Undi's bathroom, creating their own moving Lights. Marius appeared as if he were stepping through the mist itself. He looked up and silenced the handmaidens with one fierce glance. His eyes glowed and then flashed, and the sweets disappeared. The busy little hands of the maidens became still and rested on their laps, and they became once again the graceful nymphs who had stripped the soiled garments from Isis and draped her in fragile veils of gossamer Light.

"I'd no idea Marius could look so fearsome," Eva said, moving closer to Pavarti in the dark.

"He expects everyone to be quiet. He needs to concentrate," replied Pavarti.

Then they saw Undi. She was no longer in the bathtub but lay curled up in her embryonic position in a rocky pool. She was pale and unnaturally still, and she was even more transparent than women are in Heliotrope when they sleep and their delicate bones and organs are partly visible. She was not asleep—not like that. It was a state she had retreated into, as though she had anticipated all the pain a woman can tolerate for love and had withdrawn from life. She did indeed look like a jellyfish, and it wasn't a very attractive sight. Georges and Roland could see her but made no move either toward her or to each other. They were quite in awe of Marius and their surroundings. Roland was excited because he was aware he was in the presence of a genius.

"Imagine the dawn," Marius said, "the first Light." He began a sort of dance with his arms and upper body, making wide circles. The atelier became darker, and the Light from the walls became entangled in Marius's slowly moving hands. It was a deep ethereal green Light, which became concentrated around Marius. Gradually, it broke up into a million tiny shapes, like the first forms of life, and drifted over to the rocky pool. The atelier itself appeared to be full of gently heaving green water, and Marius was still dancing slowly somewhere between the ceiling and the floor, except that the ceiling and the floor were no longer visible.

The tiny life forms settled around Undi in the rocky pool. She moved ever so slightly, and she, too, changed shape. She became like one of the plankton forms, and it was possible to see the queer, varied shapes of them because she changed shape constantly. At first, they had looked like tiny abstract shapes, but now the details of their features appeared, not only in Undi's form but in all of them as they, too, grew larger.

They inspired a feeling of terror because of their great mouths and jaws; their huge backs with enormous folds of jellylike skin; their scaly spines and lashing tails and long suckers; and all the features that made it possible for them to hold their own in the primordial soup where they probably lived on pieces of each other's worn-out tissues. They had become so large that one of them, with a great sucking hole of a mouth, appeared to force its way into the dark room, as if to suck up all of us sitting there, its brilliant light flooding the room. Then it disappeared. Marius was standing on his own two feet, but his atelier had undergone a change. The dome had gone, and the walls were lost in a darkness that had no borders; there was a dim light all around Marius and his immediate surroundings. Undi was now in the bathtub. Her head rose out of murky water, and her face, which had been a pale mask, shone with a pale green light around it like a halo.

What we had seen didn't make much sense. But we knew Marius and were well aware that he didn't do anything that made sense, not so that you could see, so we felt quite sure he would accomplish what he'd set out to do. Undi was already moving about in the green glow and appeared to be at home with the monstrous plankton.

Marius suddenly dove into space—not downward but in an upward arch. He seemed to be diving through thick, heavy water. It was like an underwater starry night, for in his wake, he left a shower of brilliant starfish. Following them, other primitive sea creatures, like alien space travelers, glided, pulsated, squirted, and propelled themselves about. They all sparkled in the murky darkness and spread so far that those on the outer edges faded in and out and, finally, away. Long sea snakes rose like growing, waving stems from holes in the ocean floor and then turned into sea plants, washed this way and that by ocean currents. Undi was back in the pool, herself again, if one could say that because she was still only a pinkish blob.

Marius looked at her critically and then threw his last starfish at her. As it touched her spongy form, she shuddered and then contracted and unfolded herself, stretching her limbs out to their full length. Marius laughed and then turned to Roland as if he had noticed him for the first time.

'You see. That's how it's done. You want to be a Light artist? Watch and learn."

Deep, mysterious, and hypnotic music came from the deep—long wails and flutelike squirts of sound and sudden clicks. Marius was moving about like the conductor of an orchestra, arms going up and down and out to the side, pointing his finger and pulling sound out of the shadows as he pulled Light when he was creating a picture. He did that now when the sound reached its crescendo, and tall undersea cliffs and rocks appeared, so high that they, too, disappeared into what had been the ceiling but was now a swirling mass of water. The walls of these underwater cliffs were encrusted with sharp, dangerous, and cruel forms of life and pitted with holes and burrows where shrimplike creatures and goofer fish spent their time cruising about and watching and waiting and darting in and out.

Undi rose from her rocky pool and darted with them. Lovely patterned butterfly fish swam in and out of the treacherous sea ferns and sea anemones, and Undi went with them. She became a flower of jelly with fluted edges and changed into a sea snake and then a seahorse and she swelled and shrank and appeared out of the gloom with long, poisonous threads trailing after her. And then she became a creature of the darkest hole, like a creature that has existed since the Dream Time, old and ugly. Her lips, perfect for straining matter into her mouth, were monstrous, and her tongue looked like a streamer of dead seaweed that lashed out into a soup of purple Light to wrap itself around some innocent creature swimming by. Then she was an even older monster from some Time-That-Never-Was, ancient, horned, and coated with sand, and with the weary, tragic, and lonely patience of one who, since Time-That-Has-Always-Been has failed to change its destiny—to change shape, to escape, to reach the Light above.

She was washed away by the heavy swell. In the rocky pool she lay panting, but her body was a good pink and it was firm. On the oval blob of a face, two half-moon shaped dark lines had appeared with eyelashes, wet, like stars that cast shadows on the rounded cheeks. The eyes were closed. It was still a sleeping face, but it was at least a face.

I noticed that the dark room was filling up. I saw the outline of Tiger Hound's head and the form of Osiris beside him. Other forms of other people had invaded the space, and in order to accommodate all of them, the walls rolled away. There was the murmur of all their voices, but that ceased as Marius flung a huge Portuguese man-of-war in our direction.

On and on he went, taking Undi through the evolving life of the sea—sea berries, ferns and sea trees and vines, even wrecked ships and huge sunset pink shells and brown and gold shells with shy creatures living in them. Undi herself prowled around on the ocean floor, nosing about among abandoned shells, looking for a way in to live and hide.

But the scene passed on like all the others, and she was back in her pool.

The head was raised and the hand extended. The delicate pink hand was edging its way around the rim of the pool, feeling the sharp edges of the rock and finding crevices to dig into. The head was turned, one eye was open, watching and absorbing the Light. It became a faint blush on the maidenly cheek. Above her head, a heavy, gentle manta ray with an olive green tail drifted by and was followed by a lumbering sea cow of light orange. She rose and followed in the form of a giant squid and changed into a shark, a swordfish, and a barracuda. We could see her gills, her scales, her horns and spikes, her beaks and hammernoses, and somehow we became aware of her organs of hearing, her heart and lungs, and her sex and organs of reproduction, and her ways of producing eggs. Marius was racing about like a demon from one end of the ocean to another, talking to himself, yelling at the Light, slapping it around, making it do what he wanted until at last he produced the whale.

At last, the creatures all passed out of sight and Undi sat up. Her arms came up like a dancer's arms. She looked all about and saw all that was going on.

Lightning flashed—rain, wind, mountains of water and foam, light and dark flashing by so quickly that she looked like a dancer in a disco. She rose out of the pool, diamond bright and silvery. Seals, sea otters, gulls, and albatross swooped about her and went their ways. And then the Sirens came.

In the dark room, there was a commotion as the handmaidens, one by one, leaped up from their cushions and turned into the spray they really were and dove through the hole and into the light of the rosy dawn all around Undi.

Marius at work in his magical studio

Chapter 35

Garden Feté

It was not the end. Night came and turned into day. The dark room, full of people, had opened up, and we were all in the garden. Then it was nighttime again with a wonderful moon rising over the towers of the old house. The night air was suddenly filled with the exotic scent of oriental lilies. The scent came in sudden gusts, as though the lilies opened themselves every now and then and let loose their very essence, which was caught by the sea breeze and wafted across the garden to all the guests.

The mythological beasts and the eight-foot tall, two-dimensional forms made of Light junk were mingling with dozens of people in carnival dress so that it was not easy to know who was who. There was music and magic lanterns, and hot air balloons appeared in the sky, waiting for passengers who wanted to see the scene from above. Others were moored to a small platform in a clearing.

Marius had sent out invitations days ago, asking everyone to come in carnival dress. They took this to mean they should come as themselves or what they always wanted to be or what they were in spite of themselves. Roland was already in costume. I asked myself whether this was another spiraling dream in which scenes change and spin and illogical things happen. But it wasn't. It was real. I regretted I couldn't have found a costume that would enable me to become visible, but no matter; I enjoyed being there, mingling with the guests.

Undi was nowhere to be seen. That was puzzling. We knew she had recovered fully because in our last view of her, she had appeared as her lovely self. Georges was confused, but he had managed to find a costume. It was a court dress that had belonged to his great-grandfather. It had been carefully packed away from dust and light for almost a hundred years. Although the trousers were baggy, the tailcoat was all right, and it looked nice on him.

Eva and Gaston were there too. I saw them stepping from the Iron Lift as the Mona Lisa and Leonardo da Vinci. That's not to say that Gaston fancied himself as the great master. He had merely worn this costume to please Eva. She did look a little bit like the famous beauty with the mysterious smile, and the noble costume suited her. Watching them, I couldn't help wondering what Eva would do when Gaston began to notice that she never grew older. *"I don't believe she'll be able to bring herself to leave him,"* I said to myself, wondering whether I was jealous. *"I wonder what she'll do. She's very much in love with him."*

At the moment, she was happy, and as the Mona Lisa, she was a great success. Gaston was delighted. He said he was afraid to leave her side for fear someone would steal her away. He need not have entertained such a thought, nor did he seriously, for they'd actually set a date for their wedding. The thought of matrimony, far from cooling their ardor, had increased it threefold. They strolled about, holding on to each other and looking into each other's eyes from time to time. It was clear to me that Eva was under a spell, and it made me wonder what would happen if we were to return to our rightful place in the stream of time and I were to find my body waiting for me in the small cave where we Sang the Time Tunnel. Would Eva and I ever be able to consummate our marriage and carry on as though this had never happened? It was a disturbing question, one I couldn't answer.

The scent of lilies was even stronger. Madame Rose and Monsieur Raferé with Mimi and Frou-Frou were the next ones to arrive. Mimi wore a blue ribbon, Frou-Frou, a mauve. Monsieur Raferé was dressed as a vendor of dreams. He carried a bag over his shoulder containing a collection of his wares. Madame Rose had simply worn her best black silk gown, but over it she wore a handsome black Spanish shawl embroidered with red roses, and rising from her well-poised head was a black and gold comb. It had been given to her by Georges Braque many years ago.

Upon seeing Eva and Gaston, she offered her congratulations. Word of the approaching wedding had gotten about. Monsieur Raferé added his good wishes. Eva told him she thought his costume and the character a stroke of genius.

"Thank you. I had thought of coming as a wizard with Mimi on my shoulder, but Frou-Frou would have been jealous. So here I am like this. I'm afraid I'm a little intoxicated by my own dreams. I hope I don't offend you?"

"Not at all." Eva smiled the inscrutable smile. They all turned and saw Monsieur Jacques, the secretary of the académie. He was wearing a clown suit and a false nose—an unnecessary adornment it seemed to me. I'd always thought his own looked false.

Monsieur Raferé thought so too. "I would dearly love to see him in a real nose. Wouldn't you, my Frou-Frou? And you too, my Mimi. We'd all love to see Monsieur Jacque in a real nose."

They were startled by a burst of sound. Students from the Beaux-Arts had somehow fixed themselves to a long rope ladder that hung from one of the hot air balloons, and they dangled above the guests, blowing on trumpets and horns. Dancers and actors who had taken part in Osiris's pop-drama were dancing about on the lawns. There was, by now, a large crowd of guests wandering through the grounds. At last, everyone was called to the tables laden with food and wine. Those who couldn't find seats at the long table took food from a buffet and sat at small tables or on the grass. Wine flowed freely, and there was more than enough for everyone.

Georges found himself seated next to Babs Widgery on one side, dressed as a Texas oil well, and on the other, Carrot dressed as Gainsborough's *Blue Boy*. Doreen, the girl who had painted the monstrous cabbage, sat opposite, dressed as a cabbage on a plate. The effect had been achieved by a circular skirt stiffened with wire. It spread out around her waist while her torso, encased in cabbage leaves, rose out of it. On her head, framing her rather pretty face, was a cabbage bonnet.

Most of the students from the académie were there dressed in costumes enhancing their own sense of themselves or what they would have liked to be. The old Russian was encased in a shabby old bearskin with the hat of a Russian boyar of the time of Ivan the Terrible jammed on his head. The bearskin was so moth-eaten that it was practically falling apart. It was also very dusty, causing people near him to sneeze. Next to him at the table was the young Swiss woman dressed as a fairy queen. She looked charming—much more so than when I'd seen her

in the atelier—in her silver crown and white tulle dress, with her hair frizzed and her blue eyes enhanced with blue eye shadow and lipstick on her lips. I thought her costume most successful because it made me aware of charms in her I'd not noticed before. When she smiled, it was as if a light had been turned on in her eyes and her mouth. Her white teeth sparkled.

One person's identity remained a mystery for the whole evening. He or she was dressed as an abstract painting. Whoever was concealed inside the abstract shape had two friends or attendants in masks who led it about, seated it, and lifted a flap and shoved food and drink though the hole, taking care not to let the face inside be seen. The attendants looked after it very well. Sometimes they took turns, one attending "the shape" while the other ate a little himself. I went into it and saw to my surprise that it was the mysterious neighbor who owned the art supply store.

"How kind those attendants are," Doreen said to Georges. "It's an abstract dormouse; you know, from *Alice in Wonderland*—a modern version."

I didn't think the proprietor of the art supplies store looked at all like a dormouse, but Georges was delighted. *Alice in Wonderland*, indeed! It was the first time he had ever been spoken to by a cabbage. He looked along to the end of the table and saw the banker's wife, whose portrait he had left unfinished in Paris. She was dressed as a movie actress of the silver screen who had starred with Rudolph Valentino in *The Sheik*. Beside her was that gloomy individual, her husband, dressed as the sheik himself. There was another sudden gust of breeze laden with lily scent and for a moment he felt just like Rudolph Valentino. I was glad for his sake. I'd had the impression his was a boring life.

Further along was Ethel from the life class, as Cleopatra, breastplates, snake, and all. And seated at one of the small tables, enjoying themselves in a modest way, were Monsieur and Madame Leguine from the Café des Grande Poissons, happy together as George Sand and Chopin. With them were Monsieur Maurice, the owner of the restaurant, as an American baseball player and old Monsieur Fouroux as the Wizard of Oz, who appeared to be fascinated by the elusive light forms standing about among the trees. From time to time, he made magic signs and gestures with his hands in their direction. Georges noticed this and whispered to Babs Widgery, "I wonder whether he expects them to come over and sit with him?"

""Oh, I wish they would," she replied. "I think they're too cute for words."

This made me look twice. I'd never have called Marius's Light images cute!

As I thought about this, I caught a glimpse of that enigma, Isobel. I had never been able to understand her. Who and what was she? Why had she helped Osiris in his attempt to set fire to himself? I had often wondered about her. On that occasion, she had behaved like a high priestess. I'd never seen her smile or act frivolously as young people do. There was always something heavy and foreboding about her. Here she was now in an extraordinary getup, all dripping with black and deep purple and gray transparent material and heavy copper or some such metal jewelry, her exotic eyes accentuated with even darker makeup edging them. I think she was meant to be the queen of the underworld or some such thing. Yet, in her hand she held a little Chinese fan with something written on it—a poem or a short fable. I went in closely and saw what it said. It was a fragment of a Chinese poem:. "That's where the little lady lives, all alone without a lover . . ." And there was the faint impression on the fan of a dragon crossing a stone bridge that spanned a stream. It was hard to understand some people!

But then I suddenly realized she was the same woman who'd looked out of the window of the Art Supply store on the day of the fire on the Rue de la Grande Chaumière! Why, I asked myself, had I never seen this before? The answer was, I suppose, that the woman leaning out of the window had a completely different appearance, and I wondered whether Isobel was a shape-changer. I was now convinced that the woman from the fire and Isobel were one and the same. It was very perplexing. I gave up and looked elsewhere.

Marius had appeared and was sitting at the head of the table. His entry onto the scene had excited everyone, and some were surprised by his costume. He wasn't at all what some of them had expected. The costume he wore was that of a simple Greek fisherman—blue cotton pants, a striped sweater, and a white flower over one ear. No one could get a sensible remark out of him. He wasn't interested in sense. All he wanted was people to enjoy themselves. "Enjoy, enjoy!"

Then he saw Monsieur Raymonde standing uncertainly on the landing site where the Iron Lift had deposited him and he called out, "Come. Come along, my friend. You're welcome. No one will eat you. There's enough food on the table already."

Monsieur Raymonde responded to Marius's kindness and came forward. He was wearing regular clothes and looked awkward because he had no costume.

"Wait, he has no costume. I'll get one for him," cried the fairy queen. She waved her wand, and from somewhere, she produced a saffron robe. This was thrown over his head, and a place was made for him at the table. He sat there, a new man—a monk from the snow-covered mountains of the Himalayas. They made him take his shoes off, but before they could be removed to a safe place, Brutis ran off with one of them and chewed it up. Marius roared at him as usual, and as usual, the dog took no notice of him.

"What a transformation," remarked Babs Widgery. "Why, some people have to meditate for years and eat mountains of brown rice in order to achieve what you have just accomplished within a matter of minutes. How d'you do it?"

Monsieur Raymonde merely nodded his head. I think he, too, was puzzled by the change he sensed in himself. He'd been sitting in his comfortable chair, leafing through one of his pornographic magazines and feeling reasonably satisfied now that he'd stopped feeling injured and humiliated, when he looked up and saw an iron lift very much like the one that had escaped from his own building, hovering outside the window, with a note attached inviting him to a garden fete. And here he was, enjoying himself as a Buddhist holy man, in a garden full of people, all being nice to him. What if the dog *had* eaten his shoe? It didn't matter. From now on, he'd be wearing sandals anyway.

Roland was sitting as close as he'd been able to Marius. He was still in awe of Marius, even more so because he had been accepted as a pupil. He was almost overwhelmed by this turn of events. He still wanted to see Undi. She'd changed. A surprising new character had emerged from Marius's mysterious new atelier. So far he'd caught only a single glance from her one day as she was turning a corner. Then he thought he had seen her mounting a staircase inside the house. He ran after her but she had disappeared through a tiny doorway halfway up the stairs. In his eyes, she'd become very desirable again. He had dressed himself as a Harlequin because he'd heard she was coming as a Columbine. But where was she? He had hoped to get close to her— perhaps sit near her at the table. But she hadn't even come down to the garden yet. He wondered why she took so long coming down from her room. She, like he, was staying in the rambling, old house, which had so many rooms, corridors, and staircases that it was possible to lose one's way, as in a maze. Or one could be dazzled by a blaze of light when he opened a mysterious door he'd never been aware of before.

As he sat there, he remembered Monsieur Raymonde's apartment and Undi's room where they had enjoyed their secret love—a guilty one, too, since Monsieur Raymonde had forbidden her to have visitors. Looking around, he was surprised to see the concierge and Madame Bon-Bon sitting together, enjoying themselves in their own way. They were dressed alike, as citizens of the French Republic, knitting and all, waiting for heads to roll on the guillotine, and did not seem to be aware that they were sitting on an old iron bedstead Marius had found and turned into a Chinese dragon with bits and pieces of old junk. They had no idea they looked odd. Madame Bon-Bon was looking up as if she was waiting for the lift to descend, and the Concierge was eating a chicken wing. Suddenly Madame Bon-Bon saw something else. She uttered an exclamation and pointed upward at two objects floating above the cliff side. Roland looked up to see what she was pointing to and then, as the objects came closer, he rose from his seat, calling excitedly, "David! Helen! Here! Come down here, near me!"

The young Australian couple was gliding on wind skis, which enabled the pair to soar in graceful movements over walls and treetops and even rooftops. Hearing his voice, Helen and David waved and began their descent. Looking radiantly healthy, they wore nothing but fig leaves they'd plucked from some thousand-year-old fig tree in Greece. There were no seats for them at the table, so the Green Couch was brought out from the house and they sat on her. Roland filled two plates from the buffet and brought them to his friends.

"Darlings, how lovely! But, please, don't drop any of that food on me. No greasy food, please." The Green Couch was the only one who wasn't in costume. But then, she didn't need one. No one else had thought of coming as a green velvet couch.

Nearby, several young men in Greek tunics sat on the grass in an adoring group around Jules Mason as Socrates. It was a pose, of course. They enjoyed pretending to be his disciples, and they were conscious of their attitudes and their bare legs and white sandals. What they felt for Jules was not always adoration. But they were all having a fine time, and they enjoyed this moment free of delicious little pinpricks of jealousy and bitchiness. And if they were to indulge themselves in the pleasure of adoring someone, it might as well be Jules, who was, after all, the oldest among them and wore Jean Cocteau's golden garland on his head—the one Jean Cocteau had worn when he had been honored recently in Paris. Jules had white leather thongs on his bare legs and was, after all, a very important person, so they sat around him and paid homage. Jules was not sitting on the grass but on a gilt stool of antique design dragged down from one of the attics of the old house. I was glad to see Jules. He had remarkable qualities I enjoyed.

He was enjoying the adulation of the young apprentices. Looking up, he spotted a charming lady in a summery floating sort of dress and a wide-brimmed hat with a wispy veil. He rose quickly to cross the lawn to where she stood, having just been brought down by the Iron Lift, so that he could be the first to greet her before anyone else came to whisk her away. He took her hand and said, "Mademoiselle Raymonde. Oh, my dear, what a divine costume. The Primavera in a hat? A saint? Or an angel? Come, my dear, and sit with us."

She, too, had an inscrutable smile. She followed him and graciously accepted the gilt stool to sit on. People could not resist Jules when he put his mind to winning them, even if he did have a motive for what he did and of whom he took notice. True, he was genuinely kind and appreciative, but he happened to be well aware that Mademoiselle Raymonde had just had an exhibition of her adorable little peep shows at a very fashionable gallery and was now the talk of Paris. She and her little boxes were "all the rage" and Jules loved people who were "all the rage." She could not, of course, be compared to Marius, who'd been hailed as the great modern genius, but she'd been accepted as a truly great primitive artist by all the critics and the fashionable people. What saved Jules from being a snob and an opportunist when he paid attention to people such as she was that he truly loved talent and enjoyed people enormously, and he was just as nice to a little nobody.

They all drank the wine and ate and laughed and talked and shouted and sang and enjoyed themselves. Even Madame Rose, affected by the scent of the lilies, flirted a little with a famous actor from the Comédie Française who was dressed as Moliere. Now and then a group of Osiris's inner circle, like Roco and Eddie Zimmerman, all inexplicably dressed as huntsmen of Sherwood Forest, asked each other the question, "What has happened to Osiris?"

"What's this I heard about him and Isis? Is it true she found his body on a beach?"

"What beach? I heard she found him, whole and unharmed, in a place called Watson's Bay in Sydney."

"That doesn't explain what happened. But thank God if it's true. I can't understand why he's never let us know what happened."

"Roland, what do you know? Has Undi told you anything? Will they be here tonight?"

Isobel was suddenly in their midst—no longer in her dreary draperies and weird jewelry as Queen of the Underworld, but as someone quite different. How many times a night was she to change her costume, I wondered. She was now someone very few people remembered any more—a British queen whose name was Boadicia. She'd suffered defeat by the Romans and had killed herself in AD 62 or thereabouts. I remembered her. I once saw her riding forth in her war chariot to do battle. Why should Isobel have changed from the Queen of the Underworld to the Queen of Ancient Briton in the course of one evening?

She sent out one of her silent messages. "Osiris will come. He will come in a golden chariot."

And while they all looked at each other in surprise, Eddie Zimmerman shouted and pointed to the sky. Isis and Osiris were flying in from the horizon, just as she'd said, in their golden chariot. No one knew whether Isobel had made a genuine pronouncement or whether she had already seen them and pretended to have psychic powers. I, too, silently and invisibly, joined in with the others as they called to Osiris and Isis to come down. They merely waved and drove on in their chariot until they were out of sight.

The young boy made a racket with his drumsticks and called out in a surprisingly loud and clear voice that there would now be some entertainment. A flying horse could be seen, gliding across the starlit sky.

"A flying horse! Is such a thing possible?" Georges exclaimed.

"Why not," Eva responded. "You've accepted stranger things, so why not a flying horse?"

"I?" Georges asked. "What have I accepted?"

"He is always like that. He believes something, and with the next breath, he doubts it." The speaker was Madame Guyot, his femme du ménage. She and her husband, Yves, were standing by the buffet, dressed as Turkish bath attendants in two of Georges's best bath towels.

The flying horse came closer. It was made of Light, and all around it was a wonderful green-blue glow. One of the young men clustered around Jules said it was the noble Pegasus of Homer's Greece.

'It can't be," another man said.

"If that's what he believes, let it be so. Henceforth, this horse shall be known as the Noble Pegasus," Marius cried, laughing at them. The white feathers of the great animal's wings could be clearly seen. Between them stood a female form, perfectly poised like a circus rider. Following the horse was a flock of nymphs dressed in fluttering draperies that appeared and disappeared in the flashes of Light, and behind them were the same two angels in their magic cloaks who often flew over Undi's palace. With them, holding their hands, were Ki and Sylvester. This was a surprise. We'd all thought they were dead. Isis and Osiris were back again in their chariot, and Tiger Hound and Pavarti followed them on the back of a great white heron.

"What a procession! A wonderful aerial display! Glorious!"

"Why, it's Undi on the horse's back," Eva said. "Don't you recognize her?" She turned to Gaston and told him it was her friend Undi with all her water spirits.

Gaston smiled indulgently and murmured, "Ah yes, our little runaway model. So that's what she is? A nymph? I knew she wasn't French, but I knew she was something special just the same."

The whole procession circled above their heads. Isis and Osiris and Tiger Hound and Pavarti glided down to join Marius at the table. The two angels with Ki and Sylvester continued on and turned into streaks of Light that danced about in the sky like the great northern lights that have always puzzled humankind, before gliding away toward the horizon. Tiger Hound and Pavarti and Isis and Osiris sat near each other, close to Marius. We were all coming together. Even Eva had excused herself and left Gaston to sit with them. I wondered whether this was the time. If Undi were to join us, would we steal away and go to the cave to Sing the Time Tunnel, leaving the guests to enjoy themselves as well as they could?

This was not to happen—not yet, at any rate. Eva returned to her place beside Gaston. And Undi had not yet arrived, but soon the winged horse, followed by the nymphs, settled onto the lawn, and Undi stepped down from his back, after which he rose into the air and flew away. The nymphs gathered around Undi, poised and ready for the dance. The music started—no one knew where such marvelous music came from—causing Undi to raise her arms and make the first step with her elegant raising of the leg. It was a most unusual ballet and a very beautiful one, and the guests were enchanted. As the music faded, so did the nymphs, leaving a gentle mist around Undi.

Watching Undi's skillful movements and the grace with which she danced, Georges felt sad. He remembered the night Isis had told him Undi was a nature spirit. It was what he himself had often called her and wanted her to be. But he had never truly believed it because his good, sensible, Swiss parents had made it very difficult for him to believe such things. Now, he wondered if it were true. He was in a state of confusion. What he saw was a lovely, young woman dancing on the lawn. And with her were pretty girls performing in their wispy costumes. Yet what he *had* seen was a flying horse with a nymph on its back. There *was* magic in it somewhere.

As he watched Undi dance, the realization that she never was and never would be his, shocked Georges, and when that passed he felt the pain of unrequited love. That was preferable to the emptiness that followed. Emptiness was indeed hard to bear.

Soon after that a gentle breeze blew up from the bay and played around Georges for awhile and then magically, passed on taking with it all the memories of his dream girl. He was confused, wondering what had happened to him. The sense of nothingness was uncomfortable. At a loss, he was about to rise from his seat at the table and would have wandered over to where the iron lift was waiting for passengers had fate not stopped him just at that moment. The Swiss girl in her fairy queen costume sat in the empty seat beside him.

"You are not leaving, are you? Don't go. The night's still young," she said.

She smiled so invitingly that Georges sat down again and allowed her to fuss over him so that he began to feel more like himself. He even smiled at her and she smiled back as though they had seen each other for the first time. She, who that day when Georges had abducted Undi, as they believed, from the Life Class in the Academie de la Grande Charmiere, had laughed out loud and exclaimed "What! Albertine, or whatever his name is. My God! How funny," now found him strangely attractive.

"That's the way life is here in Old Earth," I, Jason the Invisible said to myself. "You lose some and you win some. I couldn't help feeling a little jealous."

Gazing into the near future I could see Elvira, the Swiss girl, falling in love with Georges and he would respond with his love and they would be satisfied with each other. They'd even be happy. And I felt glad for his sake because I really liked Georges.

Chapter 36

Roland and Images of Light

When their dance was over, the nymphs moved off and were lost to view among the trees. It was late. The guests began to leave. The Iron Lift took two at a time and in a few minutes came back, ready for the next couple. Undi sat with Marius.

At last, Marius said to Roland, "You should go to bed, Roland. You have to get up early for your lesson. If you're late, you'll miss it." He was a stern taskmaster and did not consider a late night an excuse for tardiness. He knew by now that Roland, given a chance, was a late riser.

Roland was still hoping to have a word with Undi, but he obeyed reluctantly. Before leaving, he remembered to kiss his mother and shake hands with Gaston. Undi merely glanced at him, never moving away from Marius. He entered the house through a side doorway and managed to find his way to his bedroom.

"I'm so happy, Marius. You're going to make a Light artist out of him. Will he ever be as great as you are?" Eva, proud mother, said to Marius.

"I don't know about that," Marius replied with a grin. "But he's just about to find out what it takes." He looked at Undi sitting close to him. They both smiled. "He belongs to the future. Undi will lead him to the threshold."

Eva looked puzzled. She couldn't understand the relationship between Roland and Undi. "I thought it was over." She looked at Marius and back at Undi. It seemed to her that Undi and Marius were together at last.

Undi smiled at her and said, "It is over. Or, at least, it has changed. I've changed. But let's say I will lead him into a dance that will free his genius. You need not fear for him, Eva dear."

This was what she meant. For the next two weeks, Undi would spend hours every day practicing intricate dance steps and movements. From the window of the atelier where he worked endeavoring to master the secret of the Light, Roland would watch her as she executed spirals and waves of her body and arms down in the wide courtyard.

It was now three o'clock in the morning, and he had not slept. He began to yawn. Before he fell asleep, he made up his mind to arrange to have his short break earlier than usual during the day and go down to the court while she was at work exercising. If he were to be present, she would surely stop for a moment and speak to him. He admired the diligence with which she worked and saw now that this discipline had given her the skill and strength to stay poised so perfectly on the winged horse. Only as he was falling asleep did he remember with surprise that the winged horse had been made of the Light, and Undi must have held herself up there in the air by her own power. It was the last thing he was aware of before he went right off to dreamland.

The nap didn't last long. He was up at seven and in the atelier by seven thirty. Later that afternoon, he looked out the window and, seeing Undi, hurried down. He saw that she was working on a new exercise that lifted her into the air without anything to support her. At first he suspected some trick, but no, she turned so rapidly that the spiral movement carried her upward. When she saw him, she came down and said in a perfectly normal way, "Oh, hello, Roland. I'm learning to draw Light from its mysterious source and fly with it. This exercise is called Helio."

He made a move and she said sharply, "Don't come near me or you'll spoil it."

What she was doing was turning so fast in a spiraling movement that she turned into a white-hot cone made of the Light, or so it seemed. After a while, the cone detached itself from the ground and rose into the air. There, it went on turning for a minute or two and then slowed down so that Undi's form became visible again, her two feet pointing downward as though they were the point at which the earth's gravity entered and made contact, gently and subtly pulling her downward. Roland thought the exercise remarkable, but he was hurt by the offhand way she had told him to stay away from her.

She said, "That's the way it is." And he didn't know whether she meant that was the way she did the exercise or that was the way it was now between them.

Just the same, when he thought no one was watching him, he tried to do it himself, which was odd because he didn't know why he wanted to do it. He didn't want to be a dancer. Yet he felt it was important for him to do this, not only because it was to bring him closer to Undi but because he, too, wanted to find the mysterious Light source. Not that he was successful in rising into the air. What happened instead, although he didn't realize it, was that he grew an inch taller. Unable to speak to Undi alone (she still very cleverly avoided him), he wondered how he would ever reach her and ask how to achieve the elevation and become a cone of Light.

One day, he went down and concealed himself before she came to start her exercises, and he thought he had her. But like a slippery fish, she turned and was in the air before he had even crossed the courtyard. She pretended not to have noticed him.

This time, Undi did something different. She balanced on the ball of her foot, and extended her other leg and her arms to form an arabesque. Then she turned with her body in that horizontal position and became a disc of Light, which circled around above Raymond's head in ever-widening circles.

When he was alone later that day, he tried it himself but was still unable to rise. Yet this exercise had its effect; his arms grew longer and extended further out into space. But as yet, no Light came.

All this time, he imagined he was alone and unobserved. What he didn't know was that every time he went down to the courtyard on his own, Marius and Undi looked down on him from one of the upper-floor windows.

She grew even more elusive. And Marius left him alone more often. He had not actually had any personal instruction from Marius for about ten days, although Marius had given him plenty of work to do. He had to draw hundreds of circles and figure eights on a very wide board that was hanging from the ceiling. When the board was covered with his drawings, he had to rub them out and start again.

"Don't imagine I won't know," Marius had told him. "I'll be aware of everything you do."

So Roland worked hard making his sweeping circles and figure eights. The board was light and swayed about at his touch, but he learned how to touch it so sensitively that it hardly moved at all. All this time, he was unable to find Undi. They didn't even meet in the dining room, as his meals were served to him in the atelier. Madame Do-It sent Raynard up with them.

One day, he waited on a staircase that Marius used. Eventually Marius came down from his own secret atelier, and Roland said, "Master, where does Undi hide in this house?"

Marius smiled. "She doesn't hide. She comes and goes and does her exercises just as you and I do.'

"She's avoiding me. She was never like that before. She's changed.'"

"You'll find her. Don't worry. Why aren't you drawing and doing the lessons I set for you?"

"I've done five thousand circles and an equal number of figure eights. I haven't produced any Light yet."

"Do more and don't think about it. Just do it."

Roland went back to the atelier and gazed at the hanging board disconsolately. He looked up and saw that Marius was in the room with him. He was looking at the board, and although there were no markings on it because Roland had just rubbed them all out, Marius looked pleased.

"Your work is coming on. You are growing every day."

"Do you think so? For my part, I'm in despair."

"That's understandable. You are impatient. Doing the same exercises every day is not easy. You don't realize it, but you can see further than you could before, and your arm extends further into space." He waved his own hand, and a thin stream of Light extended from his finger, like a pencil. "Here, swing it."

Roland took the thin stream of Light and swept his arm around in a wide circle; there in space above his head was a bright, perfect circle. He was encouraged but still wanted Undi.

"You see?" Marius said. "It's a fine circle. It vibrates. Yes, you're coming on."

"But it's not only the work that bothers me. It's Undi. She flies away, and I can never catch her."

The same enigmatic expression Roland had noticed on other occasions passed over Marius's face. He looked like one of the oddly shaped figures in his garden, living in its own world. Then he smiled. "Yes, I've noticed that."

"I've developed a great longing for her."

"So you should."

"I think I'll go mad if I can't speak to her for a moment. Please, Marius—master—ask her to be kinder to me."

His teacher shrugged. "I'll try. But you know her. She does what she likes."

The next day, Roland was on the spot before Undi came into the courtyard. Upon seeing him, she stopped. On her face was the same enigmatic expression I'd seen on the face of Marius. I wondered what was going on.

"Undi, why are you avoiding me?"

"I? What do you want, Roland? Would you like to learn how to fly?"

She stood over him sternly while he did the exercises she gave him. He still couldn't rise. His feet seemed fastened to the ground. That, and his frustration over her, made him feel dejected. Nothing came out of him but a black mood.

"I'll kill myself. I'm no good, and I never will be."

Undi twirled away and disappeared, and Marius strolled across the court.

"What's that? Ridiculous! Why, only yesterday you created a circle of Light in the atelier. Come now, we've been through all this before. You know you always take a step forward . . ."

"And half a dozen backward. I'll never be able to catch her if I can't fly."

On the following afternoon, Undi came across the court with a docile expression on her face. "Marius says you're discouraged, Roland. That won't do. Come, let us do the exercise together."

This time, he caught her before she could escape, and, like a starving man, he tried to possess her. He found himself pinning a bright Light to the ground. He realized what she was doing. Like Europa of Grecian myth, she was changing shape rapidly while he held her tightly. She was no longer a white disc. The white disc had turned into another shape and another—each more odd, strange, and frightening than the previous one—and finally into flames. She was trying to frighten him into releasing her, testing his endurance and his courage. He made up his mind to hold on to her and endure whatever terrifying images he found in his arms, until she should become exhausted and resume her own shape and submit to him. But, although his test of strength and courage went on for a long time, she didn't weaken either. In the end, she slipped away from him in the form of a long, flowing thread, and in that form, she rose above his head and encircled the garden, forming the figures-of-eight he had spent many hours trying to draw.

After that, he practiced with even greater determination. She was there on the lawn every day, and the same thing always happened. The space above him was filled with her wondrous spirals and figures-of-eight and circles and longer and longer waving lines of Light.

The next day, she spiraled up and called to him. She extended her arm and leg and formed the arabesque and encircled the garden. As he stretched up, his feet left the ground, and he almost caught her. She was always a little bit ahead of him, and he was obliged to make even greater efforts and to draw upon more and more of his strength in order to do what she did so effortlessly.

Marius sometimes looked out from one of the balconies. Once, he shouted encouragement. To tell the truth, Roland was beginning to enjoy himself. The greatest part of the struggle was behind him. He no longer recognized Undi but instead recognized the Light in all the forms and shapes she assumed as she left the ground. She always flew a little ahead of him, and he followed with his feet a few inches from the ground.

One day, he found she had disappeared and he was skimming along on his own. She had taught him how to fly. As he flew, he left a trail of brilliant stars.

Chapter 37

Scent of the Lilies

Alone at last, Undi and Marius were sitting on the marble bench.

The moon was high in the sky. Looking down, to their surprise, they saw Marius's father with his friend, my father. They were sitting there on the Sea of Silver Beach, just as they'd been sitting when we last saw them.

"Marius, my boy," Leo said. "You'd better hurry back. It's almost the time of the Light."

"We're not sure that we can ever come back," Marius called out. "We had trouble getting here . . ." He didn't bother to explain about being carried on to the Stone Age or whatever it was, but his father already knew about it anyway.

"You didn't sing properly; that was the trouble. You sang the grace notes too slowly. You had too much to drink at Jason's wedding."

"By the way," my father added, "there's something I have to tell Jason. Is he there?"

"He's here, but he can't speak," Marius said.

I was surprised. How did Marius know I was there?

"He soon will, provided you sing properly. His body has been sitting cross-legged in a state of suspended animation ever since you all left. We left it, not wanting to do any damage." He called to me, "Jason, are you all right?"

"Father!" I shouted. "Yes, I am!"

"It's no use shouting. I can't hear you," my father, who could be irritating sometimes, responded. "But don't worry. I can tell you'll be back soon. I'm writing in Light now. The letters say so."

"I told him he'd never get the real meaning of the words unless he wrote in Light," Marius's father called out. "I had an awful job getting him to stop messing about in the sand. By the way, I'm glad you didn't mess with the ice during the Ice Age. It's started to melt very slowly here, and we're not going to drown after all."

They started fading away. My father just had time to shout out to us to sing the grace notes at the right tempo before they faded out altogether.

Then suddenly, they returned, this time with our mothers.

"What about you and our niece?" my mother said to Marius. "The one who wanted to find out about the Old Earth sea. You are getting married, aren't you? We're all looking forward to it."

"I'm not sure," Marius replied. "She says I'm her father figure."

"That's not true. You can't possibly be her father. My brother is her father. I'm her aunt. You'll find that out as soon as you get back. Make it soon."

"And listen, son," Marius's father called out, "did you find out anything about the Heliotropians who left here five hundred years ago? Five hundred and four, to be exact. You've been gone for four years. You'd better hurry back for the Light Festival. Tell Isis and Osiris. We need them. And we could celebrate your wedding during the festive season."

"Undi hasn't said yes yet," Marius said, answering all questions at once. "Yes, we've met them. There are some odd people here. Four years, you say? That's what I thought too. Isis and Osiris are ready for the festival. We'll begin Singing straight away. We're bringing those Heliotropians with us, at least some of them. They'll help with the singing. Let's hope we succeed. I'm glad Jason's body is all right. He'll be glad, too."

"One of them is a girl named Isobel," Undi said in answer to the question about the Heliotropians. "And there are two other darling people, a Madame Rose and her friend, Monsieur Raferé. They can talk to inanimate objects. And we're bringing a lovely green couch. She's my friend. I can't leave her behind."

"Yes, bring them with you. It's not their right time, but it won't hurt them to see what Heliotrope is like now. I'll be happy to look after them. I can't wait to see you. Good bye for now."

This time they faded out and didn't come back. When images of our parents had faded away from the beach Marius and Undi went to sit on the marble seat overlooking the sea. Undi had realized that she was in love with Marius. Undi confessed she'd been foolish and only hurt herself, but Marius said gallantly that he didn't know what she was talking about. Her affair with Roland is a thing of the past. They clung together talking and finding out about each other. He told her some of the things he'd done and people he'd met as he traveled the world searching for the genius that didn't exist.

"But he does exist," Undi said lovingly, "How could you not have known it was yourself all the time?" She lowered her head and looked contrite. "I should have known it as soon as I saw my lovely crystal palace. I'm so sorry I never once thanked you for it." Then she looked up and asked, "In all that time did you ever fall in loive with anyone else?"

"Of course not," Marius replied.

"But even if he had," I said to myself, "it's all in the past. Now he's completely hers."

They stayed like that, enthralled by the moonlight, the lapping sound of the water in the bay and, most of all, by the exotic scent of the lilies and their own sensuous emotions.

The rapture of love grew even stronger and more compelling. They could have gone into the privacy of a bedroom but here the magic of these moments kept them in the garden. Their delight in each other grew until they entered into a creative mode that made them forget their separateness. Somewhere in the garden a night owl uttered an unusual cry. They held each other and for a moment that they would never forget, they were united in the form of a single purple flame.

After a while Marius said, "Tomorrow we'll go home. Do you think you would like being married and living like that, you know, quietly and pleasantly with no excitement?"

Undi didn't answer for she was still in the state of bliss.

They kissed once more and Marius said it was time to go. He meant time for Undi to sleep but not for himself, because he had things to do.

Undi went into the house and the spaces opened up before her and closed behind her and led her so she didn't have to look for her room. They found it for her. As she lowered her head to the pillow, she felt or saw a book closing and she was asleep.

The scent of the Lilies drove Marius mad for Love

373

Chapter 38

A Most Unusual Way to Go Home

The next day Marius come back with Madame Rose, M. Rafere, Mimi, Frou-Frou and Isobel. I was was not surprised to see Madame Rose and M. Rafere; I had sometimes wondered whether they were Heliotropians, they being being able to speak to inanimate objects and all that. Isobel, on the other hand, was not not like any other Heliotropian I had ever known but she was accepted by the others, so I too accepted her, not that she knew it, or cared.

Undi, followed by Madame Do-it and the boy Raynard dragging the couch behind them, entered the room. Undi told everyone that the couch was coming with us. There was a feeling of restrained excitement in the room. The walls shuddered every now and then. The only person missing was my Eva. I knew she was happy with Gaston Moitessier, so I tried not to wish she was with us.

Marius told everyone I was there in the room with them. How did he know?

"He not missing," Marius said, "He just won't be able to sing without his body. He's a little bit sad about Eva, so don't say anything. Just let him be. I hope we'll find out what happened to him when we reach Heliotrope, if we ever do."

This caused a bit of a fuss with everyone looking around and trying to see me. It made me feel important until I caught a glimpse of another entity in the room, the figure of Fate in her appealing beach bikini and a big wide beach hat. She made me mad because I wanted to ask her what she had done to my body. But after one quick glance at me and a funny sort of smile she stepped into a time bubble that was all bent out of shape and disappeared.

Marius didn't notice that. He turned to everyone and said, "I'll be back soon. Don't leave this room." Then he went away.

We all waited. M. Rafere put down two dishes of cat food. Madame Rose and the green couch talked to each other in low tones about the old days in Paris. Isobel stood near a window with a cell phone in her hand, texting to someone in Lapland. The rest of our group waited, ready to jump to, should Marius rush in saying, "All right, everybody. Let's go."

But where and how? We soon found out what was to happen and it was hard to believe.

He had come back looking a little bit like Moses leading his people out of Egypt and said, "We can not sing the tunnel again because of all the mix up with Eva missing and all of you new people with your cats and green couches. The Ancient People wouldn't like it. So, we must all go into the old shelter next to the cave. From there we must walk quietly and calmly. No talking, laughing or asking questions. Walk along the corridor, stopping at every doorway. Enter whatever rooms or spaces you come to, walk around them and then leave. If you find yourself in any strange spaces or situations which you do not understand, remain cool. If you hear any strange voices in many different languages, don't show any signs of confusion. Unhurried walking is what's important here. Control your facial expressions. Don't look frightened. There is nothing to be afraid of, that is if you do as I say. You, Monsieur, keep control of the cats. They are not ordinary cats; they'll understand. Isobel, put that cell phone down on a side table. You are sure to pass one if you keep walking. And Madame, just pretent you're not a green couch. Wear a shawl or something and pretend you're human. Above all, don't make comments about any other pieces of furniture and, well, all of you, try to look, I don't know, noble or something."

We began to understand what was happening. The house itself was passing through the centuries and taking us home, almost as if it had become a many-spaced ship of the desert or a luxury train on one of the great train journeys from Golfe Juan to the future or just an omnipotent travel bus in the shape of a Mystery House full of tourists.

The journey must have started without our realizing it. We heard the billions of voices. We heard the crushing of the mountains, the fearful sound of the valleys' upheavals and the sad moans of the animals who were becoming extinct. We heard terrible explosions of bombs and volcanos and all kinds of human cries. And then, silence.

This was the silence of what had mistakenly been called No-time. It should really have been called Space-time, which was what it had been called in the twenty first century. It didn't make any difference what it was called. All it meant to us was that it was far from anything we could understand. Everyone, except for myself, went into a deep sleep. I didn't because I happened to get caught up in the mysterious dimensions that existed within the house. There I experienced something odd: millions of weird little things like atoms and string circles and things whirling about in space. They made me feel sleepy.

We were wakened by a sense of the elusive light forms opening a door. We all filed out into our own right time in the garden. The light forms wafted across the lawn to the edge of the trees. They stopped and formed a half circle around the body of a young man seated in crosslegged position. It didn't take me long to see whose body it was. I hastened across the lawn and slipped into it. The elusive light forms retreated into the depth of the trees. Nothing had changed. I was no longer Jason the Unbodied. They could see me!

We were just in time for our magical Light Festival. This is always a beautiful time for us. Isis and Osiris went to the top of the mountain. For ten days and nights the essence of their passion flowed down the slopes and enriched the lives of all Heliotropians.

In this blissful period Undi and Marius made their marriage vows to each other and then retreated into the tower of the Mystery House, which, in spite of what we had found out about it, was still an intriguing mystery. There they intended to make their home. Into the highest peak of the tower they invited all of us who had traveled together to Old Earth and there we had a little ceremony during which they placed the purple flame of their love on a high pedestal. Marius said this flame would be seen from anywhere in centuries past and centuries to come and Undi would watch it every day to make sure it never went out.

From far away in time and space the world's most famous playwrite gazed into the distance one evening from his casement window. Turning away to his writing desk he put plumed pen to paper and wrote these lines. "See how far that little candle throws its light. So shines a good deed in a naughty world."

In this case, the good deed, of course, was the purple flame of love.

Eileen Kramer grew up within sight and sound of the Australian bush. Her memories of childhood are of nature—the loud laughter of the kookaburras, tadpoles turning into frogs, the magical progress from stalk to leaf of fantastically patterned horned caterpillars, and the sight of glorious pink parrots flying in flocks against the blue skies. Holidays were spent either driving through the country or cruising in the *Astoria*, the family boat, along the coast of New South Wales, swimming in sheltered bays.

Given to dreaming too much, she was not a good pupil and left school as soon as possible (age fourteen) to go her own way. Her mother led her to the Sydney Public Library, where she chose the books she wanted to read. She was interested in biographies about people like Cleopatra and famous opera singers. At nineteen, she enrolled in the Sydney Conservatorium of Music. She studied theory of music, piano, and singing. After attending a performance of modern expressive dance by glamorous Viennese dancers of the Bodenwieser Dance Company, she enrolled in the Bodenwieser School and was eventually taken into Madame Bodenwieser's professional group.

As a dancer, she toured with the Bodenwieser Company throughout Australian coastal towns and cities, New Zealand, India, and South Africa and eventually gave her own dance concerts in London. As a child, she had made her dolls clothes; now as a dancer, she designed and made costumes for the dance company. In New York, she learned to make animated and dance films.

She became interested in writing and drew upon her childhood experiences, as well as her adult dancing life and her travels, for her subjects. She is now a member of the Trillium Performing Arts

Collective in Lewisburg, West Virginia, where she choreographs and performs in the expressive style of Bodenwieser.

Other books by Eileen Kramer include *Party for the Moon Man* (short stories), *Basic Shapes* (organic dress and costume design), *The Pilgrimage of Truth* (a screen play), and *Walkabout Dancer* (a memoir).